T0012748

The Immortals
of Meluha

Amish is a 1974-born, IIM (Kolkata)-educated banker-turned-author. The success of his debut book, The Immortals of Meluha (Book 1 of the Shiva Trilogy), encouraged him to give up his career in financial services to focus on writing. Besides being an author, he is also an Indian-government diplomat, a host for TV documentaries, and a film producer.

Amish is passionate about history, mythology and philosophy, finding beauty and meaning in all world religions. His books have sold more than 6 million copies and have been translated into over 20 languages. His Shiva Trilogy is the fastest selling and his Ram Chandra Series the second fastest selling book series in Indian publishing history. You can connect with Amish here:

- www.facebook.com/authoramish
- www.instagram.com/authoramish
- www.twitter.com/authoramish

Other Titles by Amish

SHIVA TRILOGY

The fastest-selling book series in the history of Indian publishing

The Secret of the Nagas (Book 2 of the Trilogy)

The Oath of the Vayuputras (Book 3 of the Trilogy)

RAM CHANDRA SERIES

The second fastest-selling book series in the history of Indian publishing

Ram – Scion of Ikshvaku (Book 1 of the Series)

Sita – Warrior of Mithila (Book 2 of the Series)

Raavan – Enemy of Aryavarta (Book 3 of the Series)

War of Lanka (Book 4 in the Series)

INDIC CHRONICLES

Legend of Suheldev

NON-FICTION

Immortal India: Young Country, Timeless Civilisation

Dharma: Decoding the Epics for a Meaningful Life

'{Amish's} writings have generated immense curiosity about India's rich past and culture.'

– Narendra Modi
(Honourable Prime Minister, India)

'{Amish's} writing introduces the youth to ancient value systems while pricking and satisfying their curiosity…'

– Sri Sri Ravi Shankar
(Spiritual Leader & Founder, Art of Living Foundation)

'{Amish's book is} riveting, absorbing and informative.'

– Amitabh Bachchan
(Actor & Living Legend)

'{Amish's writing is} a fine blend of history and myth…gripping and unputdownable.'

– BBC

'Thoughtful and deep, Amish, more than any author, represents the New India.'

– Vir Sanghvi
(Senior Journalist & Columnist)

'Amish's mythical imagination mines the past and taps into the possibilities of the future. His book series, archetypal and stirring, unfolds the deepest recesses of the soul as well as our collective consciousness.'

– Deepak Chopra
(World-renowned spiritual guru and bestselling author)

'{Amish is} one of the most original thinkers of his generation.'
— ***Arnab Goswami***
(Senior Journalist & MD, Republic TV)

'Amish has a fine eye for detail and a compelling narrative style.'
— ***Dr. Shashi Tharoor***
(Member of Parliament & Author)

'{Amish has} a deeply thoughtful mind with an unusual, original, and fascinating view of the past.'
— ***Shekhar Gupta***
(Senior Journalist & Columnist)

'To understand the New India, you need to read Amish.'
— ***Swapan Dasgupta***
(Member of Parliament & Senior Journalist)

'Through all of Amish's books flows a current of liberal progressive ideology: about gender, about caste, about discrimination of any kind… He is the only Indian bestselling writer with true philosophical depth – his books are all backed by tremendous research and deep thought.'
— ***Sandipan Deb***
(Senior Journalist & Editorial Director, Swarajya)

'Amish's influence goes beyond his books, his books go beyond literature, his literature is steeped in philosophy, which is anchored in bhakti, which powers his love for India.'
— ***Gautam Chikermane***
(Senior Journalist & Author)

'Amish is a literary phenomenon.'

— ***Anil Dharker***
(Senior Journalist & Author)

The Immortals of Meluha

Book 1
of the
Shiva Trilogy

Amish

HarperCollins *Publishers* India

www.authoramish.com

First published in 2010

This edition published in India by HarperCollins *Publishers* in 2022
4th Floor, Tower A, Building No. 10, Phase II, DLF Cyber City,
Gurugram, Haryana – 122002
www.harpercollins.co.in

2 4 6 8 10 9 7 5 3 1

Copyright © Amish Tripathi 2010, 2022

P-ISBN: 978-93-5629-052-5
E-ISBN: 978-93-5629-059-4

This is a work offiction and all characters and incidents described in this book are
the product of the author's imagination. Any resemblance to actual persons, living
or dead, is entirely coincidental.

Amish Tripathi asserts the moral right
to be identified as the author of this work.

All rights reserved. No part of this publication may be reproduced,
stored in a retrieval system, or transmitted, in any form or by any means, electronic,
mechanical, photocopying, recording or otherwise,
without the prior permission of the publishers.

Typeset in Garamond by Ram Das Lal

Printed and bound by CPI Group (UK) Ltd, Croydon CR0 4YY

This book is produced from independently certified FSC® paper to ensure
responsible forest management.

To Preeti & Neel...
You both are everything to me,
My words & their meaning,
My prayer & my blessing,
My moon & my sun,
My love & my life,
My soul mate & a part of my soul.

Om Namah Shivāya
The universe bows to Lord Shiva. I bow to Lord Shiva.

Contents

Acknowledgements

The acknowledgments written below were composed when the book was published in 2010. I must also acknowledge those that are publishing this edition of The Immortals of Meluha. The team at HarperCollins: Swati, Shabnam, Akriti, Gokul, Vikas, Rahul, and Udayan, led by the brilliant Ananth. Looking forward to this new journey with them.

***

They say that writing is a lonely profession. They lie. An outstanding group of people have come together to make this book possible. And I would like to thank them.

Preeti, my wife, a rare combination of beauty, brains and spirit who assisted and advised me through all aspects of this book.

My family: Usha, Vinay, Bhavna, Himanshu, Meeta, Anish, Donetta, Ashish, Shernaz, Smita, Anuj, Ruta. A cabal of supremely positive individuals who encouraged, pushed and supported me through the long years of this project.

My first publisher and agent, Anuj Bahri, for his absolute confidence in the Shiva Trilogy.

My present publishers Westland Ltd, led by Gautam Padmanabhan, for sharing a dream with me.

Sharvani Pandit and Gauri Dange, my editors, for making my rather pedestrian English vastly better and for improving the story flow.

Rashmi Pusalkar, Sagar Pusalkar and Vikram Bawa for the exceptional cover.

Atul Manjrekar, Abhijeet Powdwal, Rohan Dhuri and Amit Chitnis for the innovative trailer film, which has helped market the book at a whole new level. And Taufiq Qureshi, for the music of the trailer film.

Mohan Vijayan for his great work on press publicity.

Alok Kalra, Hrishikesh Sawant and Mandar Bhure for their effective advice on marketing and promotions.

Donetta Ditton and Mukul Mukherjee for the website.

You, the reader, for the leap of faith in picking up the book of a debut author.

And lastly, I believe that this story is a blessing to me from Lord Shiva. Humbled by this experience, I find myself a different man today, less cynical and more accepting of different world views. Hence, most importantly, I would like to bow to Lord Shiva, for blessing me so abundantly, far beyond what I deserve.

The Shiva Trilogy

Shiva! The Mahadev. The God of Gods. Destroyer of Evil. Passionate lover. Fierce warrior. Consummate dancer. Charismatic leader. All-powerful, yet incorruptible. A quick wit, accompanied by an equally quick and fearsome temper.

Over the centuries, no foreigner who came to our land – conqueror, merchant, scholar, ruler, traveller – believed that such a great man could possibly have existed in reality. They assumed that he must have been a mythical God, whose existence was possible only in the realms of human imagination. Unfortunately, this belief became our received wisdom.

But what if we are wrong? What if Lord Shiva was not a figment of a rich imagination, but a person of flesh and blood? Like you and me. A man who rose to become Godlike because of his karma. That is the premise of the Shiva Trilogy, which interprets the rich mythological heritage of ancient India, blending fiction with historical fact.

This work is therefore a tribute to Lord Shiva and the lesson that his life is to us. A lesson lost in the depths of time and ignorance. A lesson, that all of us can rise to be better people. A lesson, that there exists a potential God in every single human being. All we have to do is listen to ourselves.

The Immortals of Meluha is the first book in the trilogy that chronicles the journey of this extraordinary hero. Two more books are to follow: *The Secret of the Nagas* and *The Oath of the Vayuputras*.

List of Characters

Anandmayi: Ayodhyan princess, daughter of Emperor Dilipa.

Arishtanemi: Meluhan militia, protectors of Mount Mandar and the road to it.

Ayurvati: The chief of medicine at Meluha.

Bhadra, a.k.a Veerbhadra: A childhood friend and a confidant of Shiva. He is named Veerbhadra as he singlehandedly fought a tiger.

Bhagirath: Prince of Ayodhya, son of Emperor Dilipa.

Bharat: An ancient emperor of the Chandravanshi dynasty married to a Suryavanshi princess.

Brahaspati: Chief Meluhan scientist; belonged to the swan-tribe of Brahmins.

Brahma: A great scientist from the very ancient past.

Brahmanayak: Father of Daksha, previous emperor of Meluha.

Chenardhwaj: Governor of Kashmir, based at Srinagar.

Chitraangadh: Orientation executive of the immigrants' camp in Srinagar.

Daksha: Emperor of the Suryavanshi Empire of Meluha, married to Veerini and father of Sati.

Dilipa: Emperor of Swadweep, king of Ayodhya and chief of the Chandravanshis.

Drapaku: A resident of Kotdwaar in Meluha.

Jattaa: An official in Hariyupa.

Jhooleshwar: Governor of Karachapa in Meluha.

Kanakhala: The prime minister of Meluha, she is in charge of administrative, revenue and protocol matters.

Krittika: Close friend of, and attendant to Sati.

Manu: Founder of the Vedic way of life; born many millennia ago in Sangamtamil region.

Nandi: A captain in the Meluhan army.

Panini: Associate scientist of Brahaspati at Mount Mandar.

Parvateshwar: Head of Meluhan armed forces; in charge of army, navy, special forces and police.

Ram: The seventh Vishnu, who lived many centuries ago. He established the empire of Meluha.

Rudra: The earlier Mahadev, the Destroyer of Evil, who lived some millennia ago.

Sati: Daughter of King Daksha and Queen Veerini, the royal princess of Meluha.

Satyadhwaj: Grandfather of Parvateshwar.

Shiva: The chief of the Guna tribe. Hails from Tibet. Later called Neelkanth, the saviour of the land.

Tarak: A Karachapa resident.

The hooded Naga: A mysterious leader of the Nagas.

Veerini: Queen of Meluha, wife of Daksha and mother of Sati.

Vishwadyumna: A close associate of the hooded Naga figure.

Yakhya: Chief of the Pakrati tribe, opponent of the Gunas from Tibet.

CHAPTER 1

He Has Come!

1900 BC, Mansarovar Lake (At the foot of Mount Kailash, Tibet)

Shiva gazed at the orange sky. The clouds hovering above Mansarovar had just parted to reveal the setting sun. The brilliant giver of life was calling it a day once again. Shiva had seen just a few sunrises in his twenty-one years. But the sunset! He tried never to miss the sunset! On any other day, Shiva would have taken in the vista — the sun and the immense lake against the magnificent backdrop of the Himalayas stretching as far back as the eye could see. But not today.

He squatted and perched his lithe, muscular body on the narrow ledge extending over the lake. The numerous battle-scars on his skin gleamed in the shimmering reflected light of the waters. Shiva remembered well his carefree childhood days. He had perfected the art of throwing pebbles that bounced off the surface of the lake. He still held the record in his tribe for the highest number of bounces: seventeen.

On a normal day, Shiva would have smiled at the memory from a cheerful past that had been overwhelmed by the angst of the present. But today, he turned back towards his village without any hint of joy.

Bhadra was alert, guarding the main entrance. Shiva gestured with his eyes. Bhadra turned back to find his two back-up soldiers dozing against the fence. He cursed and kicked them hard.

Shiva turned back towards the lake.

God bless Bhadra! At least he takes some responsibility.

Shiva brought the chillum made of yak-bone to his lips and took in a deep drag. Any other day, the marijuana would have spread its munificence, dulling his troubled mind and letting him find some moments of solace. But not today.

He looked to his left, towards the edge of the lake where the soldiers of the strange foreign visitor were kept under guard. With the lake behind them and twenty of Shiva's own soldiers guarding them, it was impossible for them to mount any surprise attack.

They let themselves be disarmed so easily. They aren't like the blood-thirsty idiots in our land who are looking for any excuse to fight.

The foreigner's words came flooding back to Shiva. 'Come to our land. It lies beyond the great mountains. Others call it Meluha. I call it Heaven. It is the richest and most powerful empire in India. Indeed the richest and most powerful in the whole world. Our government has an offer for immigrants. You will be given fertile land and resources for farming. Today, your tribe, the Gunas, fight for survival in this rough, arid land. Meluha offers you a lifestyle beyond your wildest dreams. We ask for nothing in return. Just live in peace, pay your taxes and follow the laws of the land.'

Shiva mused that he would certainly not be a chief in this new land.

Would I really miss that so much?

His tribe would have to live by the laws of the foreigners. They would have to work every day for a living.

That's better than fighting every day just to stay alive!

Shiva took another puff from his chillum. As the smoke cleared, he turned to stare at the hut in the centre of his village, right next to his own, where the foreigner had been stationed. He had been told that he could sleep there in comfort. In fact, Shiva wanted to keep him hostage. Just in case.

We fight almost every month with the Pakratis just so that our village can exist next to the holy lake. They are getting stronger every year, forming new alliances with new tribes. We can beat the Pakratis, but not all the mountain tribes together! By moving to Meluha, we can escape this pointless violence and may be live a life of comfort. What could possibly be wrong with that? Why shouldn't we take this deal? It sounds so damn good!

Shiva took one last drag from the chillum before banging it on the rock, letting the ash slip out and rising quickly from his perch. Brushing a few specks of ash from his bare chest, he wiped his hands on his tiger skin skirt, rapidly striding towards his village. Bhadra and his back-up stood to attention as Shiva passed the gate. Shiva frowned and gestured for Bhadra to ease up.

Why does he keep forgetting that he has been my closest friend since childhood? My becoming the chief hasn't really changed anything. He doesn't need to be unnecessarily servile in front of others.

The huts in Shiva's village were luxurious compared to others in their land. A grown man could actually stand upright in them. The shelter could withstand the harsh mountain winds for nearly three years before surrendering to the elements. He flung the empty chillum into his hut as he strode to the hut where the visitor lay sleeping soundly.

Either he doesn't realise he is a hostage. Or he genuinely believes that good behaviour begets good behaviour.

Shiva remembered what his uncle, also his Guru, used to say. 'People do what their society rewards them for doing. If the society rewards trust, people will be trusting.'

Meluha must be a trusting society if it teaches even its soldiers to expect the best in strangers.

Shiva scratched his shaggy beard as he stared hard at the visitor.

He had said his name was Nandi.

The Meluhan's massive proportions appeared even more enormous as he sprawled on the floor in his stupor, his immense belly jiggling with every breath. Despite being obese, his skin was taut and toned. His child-like face looked even more innocent as he slept with his mouth half open.

Is this the man who will lead me to my destiny? Do I really have the destiny my uncle spoke of?

'Your destiny is much larger than these massive mountains. But to make it come true, you will have to cross these very same massive mountains.'

Do I deserve a good destiny? My people come first. Will they be happy in Meluha?

Shiva continued to stare at the sleeping Nandi. Then he heard the sound of a conch shell.

Pakratis!

'POSITIONS!' screamed Shiva, as he drew his sword.

Nandi was up in an instant, drawing a hidden sword from his fur coat that was kept to the side. They sprinted to the village gates. Following standard protocol, the women started rushing to the village centre, carrying their children along. The men ran the other way, swords drawn.

'Bhadra! Our soldiers at the lake!' shouted Shiva as he reached the entrance.

Bhadra relayed the orders and the Guna soldiers obeyed instantly. They were surprised to see the Meluhans draw weapons hidden in their coats and rush to the village. The Pakratis were upon them within moments.

It was a well-planned ambush by the Pakratis. Dusk was usually a time when the Guna soldiers took time to thank their Gods for a day without battle. The women did their chores by the lakeside. If there was a time of weakness for the formidable Gunas, a time when they weren't a fearsome martial clan, but just another mountain tribe trying to survive in a tough, hostile land, this was it.

But fate was against the Pakratis yet again. Thanks to the foreign presence, Shiva had ordered the Gunas to remain alert. Thus they were forewarned and the Pakratis lost the element of surprise. The presence of the Meluhans was also decisive, turning the tide of the short, brutal battle in favour of the Gunas. The Pakratis had to retreat.

Bloodied and scarred, Shiva surveyed the damage at the end of the battle. Two Guna soldiers had succumbed to their injuries. They would be honoured as clan heroes. But even worse, the warning had come too late for at least ten Guna women and children. Their mutilated bodies were found next to the lake. The losses were high.

Bastards! They kill women and children when they can't beat us!

A livid Shiva called the entire tribe to the centre of the village. His mind was made.

'This land is fit for barbarians! We have fought pointless battles with no end in sight. You know that my uncle tried to make peace, even offering access to the lake shore to the mountain tribes. But these scum mistook our desire for peace as weakness. We all know what followed!'

The Gunas, despite being used to the brutality of regular battle, were shell-shocked by the viciousness of the attack on the women and children.

'I keep no secrets from you. All of you are aware of the invitation of the foreigners,' continued Shiva, pointing to Nandi and the Meluhans. 'They fought shoulder-to-shoulder with us today. They have earned my trust. I want to go with them to Meluha. But this cannot be my decision alone.'

'You are our chief, Shiva,' said Bhadra. 'Your decision is our decision. That is the tradition.'

'Not this time,' said Shiva holding out his hand. 'This will change our lives completely. I believe the change will be for the better. Anything will be better than the pointlessness of the violence we face daily. I have told you what I want to do. But the choice to go or not is yours. Let the Gunas speak. This time, I follow you.'

The Gunas were clear about their tradition. This respect for the chief was not just based on convention, but also on Shiva's character. He had led the Gunas to their greatest military victories through his genius and sheer personal bravery.

They spoke in one voice. 'Your decision is our decision.'

— 𑀑𑀝𑀙𑀧𑀳 —

It had been five days since Shiva had uprooted his tribe.

The caravan had camped in a nook at the base of one of the great valleys dotting the route to Meluha. Shiva had organized the camp in three concentric circles. The yaks had been tied around the outermost circle, to act as an alarm in case of any intrusion. The men formed an intermediate ring of defenders to repulse any attack. And the women and children were in the innermost circle, just around the fire. The expendables first, defenders second and the most vulnerable in the inside.

Shiva was prepared for the worst. He believed that there would be an ambush. It was only a matter of time.

The Pakratis should have been delighted to have access to the prime lands, as well as free occupation of the lake front. But Shiva knew that Yakhya, the Pakrati chief, would not allow them to leave peacefully. Yakhya would like nothing better than to become a legend by claiming that he had defeated Shiva's Gunas and won the land for the Pakratis. It was precisely this weird tribal logic that Shiva detested. In an atmosphere like this, there was never any hope for peace.

Shiva relished the call of battle, revelled in its art. But he also knew that ultimately, the battles in his land were an exercise in futility.

He turned to an alert Nandi sitting some distance away. The twenty-five Meluhan soldiers were seated in an arc around a second camp circle.

Why did he pick the Gunas for his invitation to immigrate? Why not the Pakratis?

Shiva's thoughts were broken as he saw a shadow move in the distance. He stared hard, but everything was still. Sometimes the light played tricks in this part of the world. Shiva relaxed his stance.

And then he saw the shadow again.

'TO ARMS!' screamed Shiva.

The Gunas and Meluhans drew their weapons and took up battle positions as fifty Pakratis charged in. The stupidity of rushing in without any thought struck them hard as they encountered a wall of panicky animals. The yaks bucked and kicked uncontrollably, injuring many Pakratis before they could even begin their skirmish. A few slipped through. And weapons clashed.

A young Pakrati, obviously a novice, charged at Shiva, swinging wildly. Shiva stepped back, avoiding the strike. He brought his sword back up in a smooth arc, inflicting a superficial cut on the Pakrati's chest. The young warrior cursed and swung back, opening his flank. That was all that Shiva needed. He pushed his sword in brutally, cutting through the gut of his enemy. Almost instantly, he pulled the blade out, twisting it as he did, and left the Pakrati to a slow, painful death. Shiva turned around to find a Pakrati ready to strike a Guna. He jumped high and swung from the elevation slicing neatly through the Pakrati's sword arm, severing it.

Meanwhile Bhadra, as adept at the art of battle as Shiva, was fighting two Pakratis simultaneously, with a sword in each hand. His hump did not seem to impede his movements as he transferred his weight easily, striking the Pakrati on his left side at his throat. Leaving him to die slowly, he swung with his right hand, cutting across the face of the other soldier, gouging his eye out. As the soldier fell, Bhadra brought his left sword down brutally, ending the suffering quickly for this hapless enemy.

The battle at the Meluhan end of the camp was very different. They were exceptionally well-trained soldiers.

But they were not vicious. They were following rules, avoiding killing, as far as possible.

Outnumbered and led poorly, it was but a short while before the Pakratis were beaten. Almost half of them lay dead and the rest were on their knees, begging for mercy. One of them was Yakhya, his shoulder cut deep by Nandi, debilitating the movement of his sword arm.

Bhadra stood behind the Pakrati chief, his sword raised high, ready to strike. 'Shiva, quick and easy or slow and painful?'

'Sir!' intervened Nandi, before Shiva could speak.

Shiva turned towards the Meluhan.

'This is wrong! They are begging for mercy! Killing them is against the rules of war.'

'You don't know the Pakratis!' said Shiva. 'They are brutal. They will keep attacking us even if there is nothing to gain. This has to end. Once and for all.'

'It is already ending. You are not going to live here anymore. You will soon be in Meluha.'

Shiva stood silent.

Nandi continued, 'How you want to end this is up to you. More of the same or different?'

Bhadra looked at Shiva. Waiting.

'You can show the Pakratis that you are better,' said Nandi.

Shiva turned towards the horizon, seeing the massive mountains.

Destiny? Chance of a better life?

He turned back to Bhadra. 'Disarm them. Take all their provisions. Release them.'

Even if the Pakratis are mad enough to go back to their village, rearm and come back, we would be long gone.

A shocked Bhadra stared at Shiva. But immediately started implementing the order.

Nandi gazed at Shiva with hope. There was but one thought that reverberated through his mind. *'Shiva has the heart. He has the potential. Please, let it be him. I pray to you Lord Ram, let it be him.'*

Shiva walked back to the young soldier he had stabbed. He lay writhing on the ground, face contorted in pain, even as blood oozed slowly out of his guts. For the first time in his life, Shiva felt pity for a Pakrati. He drew out his sword and ended the young soldier's suffering.

— ⚶◐Ṯ⚶⊛ —

After marching continuously for four weeks, the caravan of invited immigrants crested the final mountain to reach the outskirts of Srinagar, the capital of the valley of Kashmir. Nandi had talked excitedly about the glories of his perfect land. Shiva had prepared himself to see some incredible sights, which he could not have imagined in his simple homeland. But nothing could have primed him for the sheer spectacle of what certainly was paradise. *Meluha.* The *land of pure life!*

The mighty Jhelum river, a roaring tigress in the mountains, slowed down to the rhythm of a languorous cow as she entered the valley. She caressed the heavenly land of Kashmir, meandering her way into the immense Dal Lake. Further down, she broke away from the lake, continuing her journey towards the sea.

The vast valley was covered by a lush green canvas of grass. On it was painted the masterpiece that was Kashmir. Rows upon rows of flowers arrayed all of God's colours, their brilliance broken only by the soaring Chinar trees, offering a majestic, yet warm Kashmiri welcome. The melodious singing of the birds calmed the exhausted ears of Shiva's tribe, accustomed only to the rude howling of icy mountain winds.

'If this is the border province, how perfect must the rest of the country be?' whispered Shiva in awe.

The Dal Lake was the site of an ancient army camp of the Meluhans. Upon the western banks of the lake, by the side of the Jhelum lay the frontier town that had grown beyond its simple encampments into the grand *Srinagar*. Literally, the '*respected city*'.

Srinagar had been raised upon a massive platform of almost a hundred hectares in size. The platform built of earth, towered almost five metres high. On top of the platform were the city walls, which were another twenty metres high and four metres thick. The simplicity and brilliance of building an entire city on a platform astounded the Gunas. It was a strong protection against enemies who would have to fight their way up a fort wall which was essentially solid ground. The platform served another vital purpose: it raised the ground level of the city, an extremely effective strategy against the recurrent floods in this land. Inside the fort walls, the city was divided into blocks by roads laid out in a neat grid pattern. It had specially constructed market areas, temples, gardens, meeting halls and everything else that would be required for sophisticated urban living. All the houses looked like simple multiple-storeyed block structures from the outside. The only way to differentiate a rich man's house from that of a poor man's, was that his block would be bigger.

In contrast to the extravagant natural landscape of

Kashmir, the city of Srinagar itself was painted only in restrained greys, blues and whites. The entire city was a picture of cleanliness, order and sobriety. Nearly twenty thousand souls called Srinagar their home. Now an additional two hundred had just arrived from Mount Kailash. And their leader felt a lightness of being he hadn't experienced since that terrible day, many years ago.

I have escaped. I can make a new beginning. I can forget.

— ⳨⦿ᚒ⳨⊕ —

The caravan travelled to the immigrant camp outside Srinagar. The camp had been built on a separate platform on the southern side of the city. Nandi led Shiva and his tribe to the Foreigners' Office, which was placed just outside the camp. Nandi requested Shiva to wait outside as he went into the office. He soon returned, accompanied by a young official. The official gave a practised smile and folded his hands in a formal Namaste. 'Welcome to Meluha. I am Chitraangadh. I will be your Orientation Executive. Think of me as your single point of contact for all issues whilst you are here. I believe your leader's name is Shiva. Will he step up please?'

Shiva took a step forward. 'I am Shiva.'

'Excellent,' said Chitraangadh. 'Would you be so kind as to follow me to the registration desk please? You will be registered as the caretaker of your tribe. Any communication that concerns them will go through you. Since you are the designated leader, the implementation of all directives within your tribe would be your responsibility.'

Nandi cut into Chitraangadh's officious speech to tell Shiva, 'Sir, if you will just excuse me, I will go to the immigrant camp quarters and arrange the temporary living arrangements for your tribe.'

Shiva noticed that Chitraangadh's ever-beaming face had lost its smile for a fraction of a second as Nandi interrupted his flow. But he recovered quickly and the smile returned to his face once again. Shiva turned and looked at Nandi.

'Of course, you may. You don't need to take my permission, Nandi,' said Shiva. 'But in return, you have to promise me something, my friend.'

'Of course, Sir,' replied Nandi bowing slightly.

'Call me Shiva. Not Sir,' grinned Shiva. 'I am your friend. Not your Chief.'

A surprised Nandi looked up, bowed again and said, 'Yes Sir. I mean, yes, Shiva.'

Shiva turned back to Chitraangadh, whose smile for some reason appeared more genuine now. He said, 'Well Shiva, if you will follow me to the registration desk, we will complete the formalities quickly.'

— ⚛ ◎ ⚇ ⚵ ⊕ —

The newly registered tribe reached the residential quarters in the immigration camp, to see Nandi waiting outside the main gates; he led them in. The roads of the camp were just like those of Srinagar. They were laid out in a neat north-south and east-west grid. The carefully paved footpaths contrasted sharply with the dirt tracks in Shiva's own land. He noticed something strange about the road though.

'Nandi, what are those differently coloured stones running through the centre of the road?' asked Shiva.

'They cover the underground drains, Shiva. The drains take out all the waste water of the camp. It ensures that the camp remains clean and hygienic.'

Shiva marvelled at the almost obsessively meticulous planning of the Meluhans.

The Gunas reached the large building that had been assigned to them. For the umpteenth time, they thanked the wisdom of their leader in deciding to come to Meluha. The three-storeyed building had comfortable, separate living quarters for each family. Each room had luxurious furniture including a highly polished copper plate on the wall in which they could see their reflection. The rooms had clean linen bed sheets, towels and even some clothes. Feeling the cloth, a bewildered Shiva asked, 'What is this material?'

Chitraangadh replied enthusiastically, 'It's cotton, Shiva. The plant is grown in our lands and fashioned into the cloth that you hold.'

There was a broad picture window on each wall to let in the light and the warmth of the sun. Notches on each wall supported a metal rod with a controlled flame on top for lighting. Each room had an attached bathroom with a sloping floor that enabled the water to flow naturally to a hole which drained it out. At the right end of each bathroom was a paved basin on the ground which culminated in a large hole. The purpose of this contraption was a mystery to the tribe. The side walls had some kind of device, which when turned, allowed water to flow through.

'Magic!' whispered Bhadra's mother.

Beside the main door of the building was an attached house. A doctor and her nurses walked out of the house to greet Shiva. The doctor, a petite, wheat-skinned woman was dressed in a simple white cloth tied around her waist and legs in a style the Meluhans called *dhoti*. A smaller white cloth was tied as a blouse around her chest while another cloth called an *angvastram* was draped over her shoulders. The centre of her forehead bore a white dot. Her head had been shaved clean except for a knotted tuft of hair at the back, called a *choti*. A loose string called a *janau* was tied from her left shoulder across her torso down to the right side.

Nandi was genuinely startled at seeing her. With a reverential Namaste, he said, 'Lady Ayurvati! I didn't expect a doctor of your stature here.'

Ayurvati looked at Nandi with a smile and a polite Namaste. 'I strongly believe in the field-work experience programme, Captain. My team follows it strictly. However, I am terribly sorry but I don't recognise you. Have we met before?'

'My name is Captain Nandi, my lady,' answered Nandi. 'We haven't met but who doesn't know you, the greatest doctor in the land?'

'Thank you, Captain Nandi,' said a visibly embarrassed Ayurvati. 'But I think you exaggerate. There are many far superior to me.' Turning quickly towards Shiva, Ayurvati continued, 'Welcome to Meluha. I am Ayurvati, your designated doctor. My nurses and I will be at your assistance for the time that you are in these quarters.'

Hearing no reaction from Shiva, Chitraangadh said in his most earnest voice, 'These are just temporary quarters, Shiva. The actual houses that will be allocated to your tribe will be much more comfortable. You have to stay here only for the period of the quarantine which will not last more than seven days.'

'Oh no, my friend! The quarters are more than comfortable. They are beyond anything that we could have imagined. What say *Mausi*?' grinned Shiva at Bhadra's mother, before turning back to Chitraangadh with a frown. 'But why the quarantine?'

Nandi cut in. 'Shiva, the quarantine is just a precaution. We don't have too many diseases in Meluha. Sometimes, immigrants may come in with new diseases. During this seven–day period, the doctors will observe and cure you of any such ailments.'

'And one of the guidelines that you have to follow in order to control diseases is to maintain strict hygiene standards,' said Ayurvati.

Shiva grimaced at Nandi and whispered, 'Hygiene standards?'

Nandi's forehead crinkled into an apologetic frown while his hands gently advised acquiescence. He mumbled, 'Please go along with it, Shiva. It is just one of those things that we *have* to do in Meluha. Lady Ayurvati is considered the best doctor in the land.'

'If you are free right now, I can give you your instructions,' said Ayurvati.

'I am free right now,' said Shiva with a straight face. 'But I may have to charge you later.'

Bhadra giggled softly, while Ayurvati stared at Shiva with a blank face, clearly not amused at the pun.

'I'm sure I don't understand what you're trying to say,' replied Ayurvati frostily. 'Without further ado let's begin with the ablutionary ritual.'

Ayurvati walked into the guest house, muttering under her breath, 'These uncouth immigrants…'

Shiva raised his eyebrows towards Bhadra, grinning impishly.

— ⸙ —

Late in the evening, after a hearty meal, all the Gunas were served a medicinal drink in their rooms.

'Yuck!' grimaced Bhadra, his face contorted. 'This tastes like yak's piss!'

'How do you know what yak's piss tastes like?' laughed Shiva, as he slapped his friend hard on the back. 'Now go to your room. I need to sleep.'

'Have you seen the beds? I think this is going to be the best sleep of my life!'

'I have seen the bed, dammit!' grinned Shiva. 'Now I want to experience it. Get out!'

Bhadra left Shiva's room, laughing loudly. He wasn't the only one excited by the unnaturally soft beds. Their entire tribe had rushed to their rooms for what they anticipated would be the most comfortable sleep of their lives. They were in for a surprise.

— ⸙ —

Shiva tossed and turned on his bed constantly. He was wearing an orange coloured dhoti. The tiger skin had been taken away to be washed — for hygiene reasons. His cotton angvastram was lying on a low chair by the wall. A half-lit chillum lay forlorn on the side-table.

This cursed bed is too soft. Impossible to sleep on!

Shiva yanked the bed sheet off the mattress, tossed it on the floor and lay down. This was a little better. Sleep was stealthily creeping in on him. But not as strongly as at home. He missed the rough cold floor of his own hut. He missed the shrill winds of Mount Kailash, which broke through the most determined efforts to ignore them. He missed the comforting stench of his tiger skin. No doubt, his current surroundings were excessively comfortable, but they were unfamiliar and alien.

As usual, it was his instincts which brought up the truth: *'It's not the room. It's you.'*

It was then that Shiva noticed that he was sweating. Despite the cool breeze, he was sweating profusely. The room appeared to be spinning lightly. He felt as if his body was being drawn out of itself. His frostbitten right toe felt as if it was on fire. His battle-scarred left knee seemed to be getting stretched. His tired and aching muscles felt as if a great hand was remoulding them. His shoulder bone, dislocated in days past and never completely healed, appeared to be ripping the muscles aside so as to re-engineer the joint. The muscles in turn seemed to be giving way to the bones to do their job.

Breathing was an effort. He opened his mouth to help his lungs along. But not enough air flowed in. Shiva concentrated with all his might, opened his mouth wide and sucked in as much air as he could. The curtains by the side of the window rustled as a kindly wind rushed in. With the sudden gush of air, Shiva's body relaxed just a bit. And then the battle began again. He focused and willed giant gasps of air into his hungry body.

Knock! Knock!

The light tapping on the door alerted Shiva. He was disoriented for a moment. Still breathing hard! His shoulder was twitching. The familiar pain was missing. He looked down at his knee. It didn't hurt anymore. The scar had vanished. Still gasping for breath! He looked down at his toe. Whole and complete now. He bent to check it. A cracking sound reverberated through the room as his toe made its first movement in years. Still breathing hard! There was also an unfamiliar tingling coldness in his neck. Very cold.

Knock! Knock! A little more insistent now.

A bewildered Shiva staggered to his feet, pulled the angvastram around his neck for warmth and opened the door. The darkness veiled his face, but Shiva could still recognise Bhadra. He whispered in a panic-stricken voice, 'Shiva, I'm sorry to disturb you so late. But my mother has suddenly developed a very high fever. What should I do?'

Shiva instinctively touched Bhadra's forehead. 'You too have a fever Bhadra. Go to your room. I will get the doctor.'

As Shiva raced down the corridor towards the steps he encountered many more doors opening with the now familiar message. 'Sudden fever! Help!'

Shiva sprinted down the steps to the attached building where the doctors were housed. He knocked hard on the door. Ayurvati opened it immediately, as if she was expecting him. Shiva spoke calmly. 'Ayurvati, almost my entire tribe has suddenly fallen ill. Please come fast, they need help.'

Ayurvati touched Shiva's forehead. 'You don't have a fever?'

Shiva shook his head. 'No.'

Ayurvati frowned, clearly surprised. She turned and ordered her nurses, 'Come on. It's begun. Let's go.'

As Ayurvati and her nurses rushed into the building,

Chitraangadh appeared out of nowhere. He asked Shiva, 'What happened?'

'I don't know. Practically everybody in my tribe suddenly fell ill.'

'You too are perspiring heavily.'

'Don't worry. I don't have fever. Look, I'm going back into the building. I want to see how my people are doing.'

Chitraangadh nodded, adding, 'I'll call Nandi.'

As Chitraangadh sped away in search of Nandi, Shiva ran into the building. He was surprised the moment he entered. All the torches in the building had been lit. The nurses were going from room to room, methodically administering medicines and advising the scared patients on what they should do. A scribe walked along with each nurse meticulously noting the details of each patient on a palm-leaf booklet. The Meluhans were clearly prepared for such an eventuality. Ayurvati stood at the end of the corridor, her hands on her hips. Like a general supervising her superbly trained and efficient troops. Shiva rushed up to her and asked, 'What about the second and third floor?'

Ayurvati answered without turning to him. 'Nurses have already reached every room in the building. I will go up to supervise once the situation on this floor has stabilised. We'll cover all the patients in the next half hour.'

'You people are incredibly efficient but I pray that everyone will be okay,' said a worried Shiva.

Ayurvati turned to look at Shiva. Her eyebrows were raised slightly and a hint of a smile hovered on her serious face. 'Don't worry. We're Meluhans. We are capable of handling any situation. Everybody will be fine.'

'Is there anything I can do to help?'

'Yes. Please go and bathe.'

'What?!'

'Please go have a bath. Right now,' said Ayurvati as she turned back to look at her team. 'Everybody, please remember that all children below the age of fifteen *must* be tonsured. Mastrak, please go up and start the secondary medicines. I'll be there in five minutes.'

'Yes, my lady,' said a young man as he hurried up the steps carrying a large cloth bag.

'You're still here?' asked Ayurvati as she noticed that Shiva hadn't left.

Shiva spoke softly, controlling his rising anger, 'What difference will my bathing make? My people are in trouble. I want to help.'

'I don't have the time or the patience to argue with you. You will go and bathe right now!' said Ayurvati, clearly *not* trying to control her rising temper.

Shiva glared at Ayurvati as he made a heroic effort to rein in the curses that wanted to leap out of his mouth. His clenched fists wanted to have an argument of their own with Ayurvati. But she was a woman.

Ayurvati too glared back at Shiva. She was used to being obeyed. She was a doctor. If she told a patient to do something, she expected it to be done without question. But in her long years of experience she had also seen a few patients like Shiva, especially from the nobility. Such patients had to be *reasoned* with. Not *instructed*. Yet, this was a simple immigrant. Not some nobleman!

Controlling herself with great effort, Ayurvati said, 'Shiva, you are perspiring. If you don't wash it off, it will kill you. Please trust me. You cannot be of any help to your tribe if you are dead.'

— ⵣ◎ⵘⵔ⊕ —

Chitraangadh banged loudly on the door. A bleary-eyed Nandi woke up cursing. He wrenched the door open and growled, 'This better be important!'

'Come quickly. Shiva's tribe has fallen ill.'

'Already? But this is only the first night!' exclaimed Nandi. Picking up his angvastram he said, 'Let's go!'

— ⵀⵔⵔⵟⵔ⊕ —

The bathroom seemed like a strange place for a bath. Shiva was used to splashing about in the chilly Mansarovar Lake for his bi-monthly ablutions. The bathroom felt strangely constricted. He turned the magical device on the wall to increase the flow of water. He used the strange cake-like substance that the Meluhans said was a soap to rub the body clean. Ayurvati had been very clear. The soap *had* to be used. He turned the water off and picked up the towel. As he rubbed himself vigorously, the mystifying development he had ignored in the past few hours came flooding back. His shoulder felt better than new. His surprised gaze fell to his knee. No pain, no scar. He then looked incredulously at his completely healed toe. And then he realised that it wasn't just the injured parts, but his entire body felt new, rejuvenated and stronger than ever. His neck, though, still felt intolerably cold.

What the devil is going on?

He stepped out of the bathroom and quickly wore a new dhoti. Again, Ayurvati's strict instructions were not to wear his old clothes which were infected by his toxic perspiration. As he was wrapping the angvastram around his neck for some warmth, there was a knock on the door.

It was Ayurvati. 'Shiva, can you open the door please? I just want to check whether you are all right.'

Shiva opened the door. Ayurvati stepped in and checked Shiva's temperature; it was normal. Ayurvati nodded slightly and said, 'You seem to be healthy. And your tribe is recovering quickly as well. The trouble has passed.'

Shiva smiled gratefully. 'Thanks to the skills and efficiency of your team. I am truly sorry for arguing with you earlier. It was unnecessary. I know you meant well.'

Ayurvati looked up from her palm-leaf booklet with a slight smile and a raised eyebrow. 'Being polite, are we?'

'I'm not all that rude, you know,' grinned Shiva. 'You people are just too supercilious!'

Ayurvati suddenly stopped listening as she stared at Shiva with a stunned look on her face. How had she not noticed it before? She had never believed in the legend. Was she going to be the first one to see it come true? Pointing weakly with her hands she mumbled, 'Why have you covered your neck?'

'It's very cold for some reason. Is it something to be worried about?' asked Shiva as he pulled the angvastram off.

A cry resounded loudly through the silent room as Ayurvati staggered back. Her hand covered her mouth in shock while the palm leaves scattered on the floor. Her knees were too weak to hold her up. She collapsed with her back against the wall, never once taking her eyes off Shiva. Tears broke through her proud eyes. She kept repeating, 'Om Brahmaye namah. Om Brahmaye namah.'

'What happened? Is it serious?' asked a worried Shiva.

'You have come! My Lord, you have come!'

Before a bewildered Shiva could respond to her strange

reaction, Nandi rushed in and noticed Ayurvati on the ground. Copious tears were flowing down her face.

'What happened, my lady?' asked a startled Nandi.

Ayurvati just pointed at Shiva's neck. Nandi looked up. The neck shone an eerie iridescent blue. With a cry that sounded like that of a long caged animal just released from captivity, Nandi collapsed on his knees. 'My Lord! You have come! The Neelkanth has come!'

The Captain bent low and brought his head down to touch the Neelkanth's feet reverentially. The object of his adoration however, stepped back, befuddled and perturbed.

'What the hell is going on here?' Shiva asked agitatedly.

Holding a hand to his freezing neck, he turned around to the polished copper plate and stared in stunned astonishment at the reflection of his *neel kanth;* his *blue throat.*

Chitraangadh, holding the door frame for support, sobbed like a child. 'We're saved! We're saved! He has come!'

CHAPTER 2

Land of Pure Life

Chenardhwaj, the governor of Kashmir, wanted to broadcast to the entire world that the Neelkanth had appeared in his capital city. Not in the other frontier towns like Takshashila, Karachapa or Lothal. *His* Srinagar! But the bird courier had arrived almost immediately from the Meluhan capital *Devagiri*, the *abode of the Gods*. The orders were crystal clear. The news of the arrival of the Neelkanth had to be kept secret until the emperor himself had seen Shiva. Chenardhwaj was ordered to send Shiva along with an escort to Devagiri. Most importantly, Shiva himself was not to be told about the legend. 'The emperor will advise the supposed Neelkanth in an appropriate manner,' were the exact words in the message.

Chenardhwaj had the privilege of informing Shiva about the journey. Shiva though, was not in the most amenable of moods. He was utterly perplexed by the sudden devotion of every Meluhan around him. Since he had been transferred to the gubernatorial residence where he lived in luxury, only the most important citizens of Srinagar had access to him.

'My Lord, we will be escorting you to Devagiri,

our capital. It is a few weeks' journey from here,' said Chenardhwaj as he struggled to bend his enormous and muscular frame lower than he ever had.

'I'm not going anywhere till somebody tells me what is going on! What the hell is this damned legend of the Neelkanth?' Shiva asked angrily.

'My Lord, please have faith in us. You will know the truth soon. The emperor himself will tell you when you reach Devagiri.'

'And what about my tribe?'

'They will be given lands right here in Kashmir, my Lord. All the resources that they need in order to lead a comfortable life will be provided for.'

'Are they being held hostage?'

'Oh no, my Lord,' said a visibly disturbed Chenardhwaj. 'They are *your* tribe, my Lord. If I had my way, they would live like nobility for the rest of their lives. But the laws cannot be broken, my Lord. Not even for you. We can only give them what had been promised. In the course of time my Lord, you can change the laws you deem necessary. Then we could certainly accommodate them anywhere.'

'Please, my Lord,' pleaded Nandi. 'Have faith in us. You cannot imagine how important you are to Meluha. We have been waiting for a very long time for you. We need your help.'

Please help me! Please!

The memory of another desperate plea from a distraught woman years ago returned to haunt Shiva as he was stunned into silence.

— 𓀀𓁸𓎤𓆃𓏢 —

'Your destiny is much larger than these massive mountains.'

Nonsense! I don't deserve any destiny. If these people knew of my guilt, they would stop this bullshit instantly!

'I don't know what to do, Bhadra.'

Shiva was sitting in the royal gardens on the banks of the Dal Lake while his friend sat by his side, carefully filling some marijuana into a chillum. As Bhadra used the lit stick to bring the chillum to life, Shiva said impatiently, 'That's a cue for you to speak, you fool.'

'No. That's actually a cue for me to hand you the chillum, Shiva.'

'Why will you not council me?' asked Shiva in anguish. 'We are still the same friends who never made a move without consulting each other!'

Bhadra smiled. 'No we are not. You are the Chief now. The tribe lives and dies by your decisions. It cannot be corrupted by any other person's influence. We are not like the Pakratis, where the Chief has to listen to whoever is the loudmouth in their counsel. Only the chief's wisdom is supreme amongst the Gunas. That is our tradition.'

Shiva raised his eyes in exasperation. 'Some traditions are meant to be broken!'

Bhadra stayed silent. Stretching his hand, Shiva grabbed the chillum from Bhadra. He took one deep puff, letting the marijuana spread its munificence into his body.

'I've heard just one line about the legend of the Neelkanth,' said Bhadra. 'Apparently Meluha is in deep trouble and only the Neelkanth can save them.'

'But I can't seem to see any trouble out here. Everything seems perfect. If they want to see real trouble we should take them to our land!'

Bhadra laughed slightly. 'But what is it about the blue throat that makes them believe you can save them?'

'Damned if I know! They are so much more advanced than us. And yet they worship me like I am some God. Just because of this blessed blue throat.'

'I think their medicines are magical though. Have you noticed that the hump on my back has reduced a little bit?'

'Yes it has! Their doctors are seriously gifted.'

'You know their doctors are called Brahmins?'

'Like Ayurvati?' asked Shiva, passing the chillum back to Bhadra.

'Yes. But the Brahmins don't just cure people. They are also teachers, lawyers, priests, basically any intellectual profession.'

'Talented people,' sniffed Shiva.

'That's not all,' said Bhadra, in between a long inhalation. 'They have a concept of specialisation. So in addition to the Brahmins, they have a group called Kshatriyas, who are the warriors and rulers. Even the women can be Kshatriyas!'

'Really? They allow women into their army?'

'Well, apparently there aren't too many female Kshatriyas. But yes, they are allowed into the army.'

'No wonder they are in trouble!'

The friends laughed loudly at the strange ways of the Meluhans. Bhadra took another puff from the chillum before continuing his story. 'And then they have Vaishyas, who are craftsmen, traders and business people and finally the Shudras who are the farmers and workers. And one caste cannot do another caste's job.'

'Hang on,' said Shiva. 'That means that since you

are a warrior, you would not be allowed to trade at the marketplace?'

'Yes.'

'Bloody stupid! How would you get me my marijuana? After all that is the only thing you are useful for!'

Shiva leaned back to avoid the playful blow from Bhadra. 'All right, all right. Take it easy!' he laughed. Stretching out, he grabbed the chillum from Bhadra and took another deep drag.

We're talking about everything except what we should be talking about.

Shiva became serious once again. 'But seriously, strange as they are, what should I do?'

'What are you thinking of doing?'

Shiva looked away, as if contemplating the roses in the far corner of the garden. 'I don't want to run away once again.'

'What?' asked Bhadra, not hearing Shiva's tormented whisper clearly.

'I said,' repeated Shiva loudly, 'I can't bear the guilt of running away once again.'

'That wasn't your fault...'

'YES IT WAS!'

Bhadra fell silent. There was nothing that could be said. Covering his eyes, Shiva sighed once again. 'Yes, it was...'

Bhadra put his hand on his friend's shoulder, pressing it gently, letting the terrible moment pass. Shiva turned his face. 'I'm asking for advice, my friend. What should I do? If they need my help, I can't turn away from them. At the same time, how can I leave our tribe all by themselves out here? What should I do?'

Bhadra continued to hold Shiva's shoulder. He breathed

deeply. He could think of an answer. It may have been the correct answer for Shiva, *his friend*. But was it the correct answer for Shiva, *the leader*?

'You have to find that wisdom within yourself, Shiva. That is the tradition.'

'O the hell with you!'

Shiva threw the chillum back at Bhadra and stormed away.

— ༀ૦ૐℑↂ⊗ —

It was only a few days later that a minor caravan consisting of Shiva, Nandi and three soldiers was scheduled to leave Srinagar. The small party would ensure that they moved quickly through the realm and reached Devagiri as soon as possible. Governor Chenardhwaj was anxious for Shiva to be recognised quickly by the empire as the true Neelkanth. He wanted to go down in history as the governor who had found the Lord.

Shiva had been made 'presentable' for the emperor. His hair had been oiled and smoothened. Lines of expensive clothes, attractive ear-rings, necklaces and other jewellery were used to adorn his muscular frame. His fair face had been scrubbed clean with special *Ayurvedic* herbs to remove years of dead skin and decay. A cravat had been fashioned of cotton to cover his glowing blue throat. Beads, cleverly darned onto the fabric, gave it the appearance of the traditional necklace that Meluhan men sported during times of ritual. The cravat felt warm around his still cold throat.

'I will be back soon,' said Shiva as he hugged Bhadra's mother. He was amazed to see that the old lady's limp was a little less noticeable.

Their medicines are truly magical.

As a morose Bhadra looked at him, Shiva whispered, 'Take care of the tribe. You are in charge till I come back.'

Bhadra stepped back, startled. 'Shiva you don't have to do that just because I am your friend.'

'I have to do it, you fool. And the reason why I have to do it is that you are more capable than I am.'

Bhadra stepped up and embraced Shiva, lest his friend notice the tears in his eyes. 'No Shiva, I am not. Not even in my dreams.'

'Shut up! Listen to me carefully,' said Shiva as Bhadra smiled sadly. 'I don't think the Gunas are at any risk here. At least not to the same extent as we were at Mount Kailash. But even so, if you feel you need help, ask Ayurvati. I observed her when the tribe was ill. She showed tremendous commitment towards saving us all. She is trustworthy.'

Bhadra nodded, hugged Shiva once again and left the room.

— 𝕏⊚Ʊ⼇⊕ —

Ayurvati knocked politely on the door. 'May I come in, my Lord?'

This was the first time that she had come into his presence since that fateful moment seven days back. It seemed like a lifetime to her. Though she appeared to be her confident self again, there was a slightly different look about her. She had the appearance of someone who had been touched by the divine.

'Come in Ayurvati. And please, none of this "Lord"

business. I am still the same uncouth immigrant you met a few days back.'

'I am sorry about that comment, my Lord. It was wrong of me to say that and I am willing to accept any punishment that you may deem fit.'

'What's wrong with you? Why should I punish you for speaking the truth? Why should this bloody blue throat change anything?'

'You will discover the reason soon enough, my Lord,' whispered Ayurvati with her head bowed. 'We have waited for centuries for you.'

'Centuries?! In the name of the holy lake, why? What can I do that any amongst you smart people can't?'

'The emperor will tell you, my Lord. Suffice it to say that after all that I have heard from your tribe, if there is one person worthy of being the Neelkanth, it is you.'

'Speaking of my tribe, I have told them that if they need any help, they can turn to you. I hope that is all right.'

'It would be my honour to provide any assistance to them, my Lord.'

Saying this, she bent down to touch Shiva's feet in the traditional Indian form of showing respect. Shiva had resigned himself to accepting this gesture from most Meluhans but immediately stepped back as Ayurvati bent down.

'What the hell are you doing, Ayurvati?' asked a horrified Shiva. 'You are a doctor, a giver of life. Don't embarrass me by touching my feet.'

Ayurvati looked up at Shiva, her eyes shining with admiration and devotion. This was certainly a man worthy of being the Neelkanth.

— ᛏ◍ᛃᚁ⊕ —

Nandi entered Shiva's room carrying a saffron cloth with the word 'Ram' stamped across every inch of it. He requested Shiva to wrap it around his shoulders. As Shiva complied, Nandi muttered a quick short prayer for a safe journey to Devagiri.

'Our horses wait outside, my Lord. We can leave when you are ready,' said Nandi.

'Nandi,' said an exasperated Shiva. 'How many times must I tell you? My name is Shiva. I am your friend, not your Lord'

'Oh no, my Lord,' gasped Nandi. 'You are the Neelkanth. You *are* the Lord. How can I take your name?'

Shiva rolled his eyes, shook his head slightly and turned towards the door. 'I give up! Can we leave now?'

'Of course, my Lord.'

They stepped outside to see three mounted soldiers waiting patiently, while tethered close to them were three more horses. One each for Shiva and Nandi, while the third was assigned for carrying their provisions. The well-organised Meluhan Empire had rest houses and provision stores spread across all major travel routes. As long as there were enough provisions for one day, a traveller carrying Meluhan coins could comfortably keep buying fresh provisions that would last a journey of months.

Nandi's horse had been tethered next to a small platform. The platform had steps leading up to it from the other side. Clearly, this was convenient infrastructure for obese riders who found it a little cumbersome to climb onto a horse. Shiva looked at Nandi's enormous form, then at his unfortunate horse and then back at Nandi.

'Aren't there any laws in Meluha against cruelty to animals?' asked Shiva with the most sincere of expressions.

'Oh yes, my Lord. Very strict laws. In Meluha ALL life is precious. In fact there are strict guidelines as to when and how animals can be slaughtered and...'

Suddenly Nandi stopped speaking. Shiva's joke had finally breached Nandi's slow wit. They both burst out laughing as Shiva slapped Nandi hard on his back.

— ⋏◎∪⭧⊕ —

Shiva's entourage followed the course of the Jhelum which had resumed its thunderous roar as it crashed down the lower Himalayas. Once on the magnificent flat plains, the turbulent river calmed down again and flowed smoothly on. Smooth enough for the group to board one of the many public transport barges and sail quickly down to the town of Brihateshpuram.

From there on, they went eastwards down a well marked road through Punjab, the heart of the empire's northern reaches. *Punjab* literally meant the *land of the five rivers*. The land of the Indus, Jhelum, Chenab, Ravi and Beas. The four eastern rivers aspired to grasp the grand Indus, which flowed farthest to the west. They succeeded spectacularly, after convoluted journeys through the rich plains of Punjab. The Indus itself found comfort and succour in the enormous, all embracing ocean. The mystery of the ocean's final destination though was yet to be unravelled.

'What is Ram?' enquired Shiva as he looked down at the word covering every inch of his saffron cloth.

The three accompanying soldiers rode at a polite distance behind Shiva and Nandi. Far enough not to overhear any conversation but close enough to move in quickly at the first sign of trouble. It was a part of their standard Meluhan service rules.

'Lord Ram was the emperor who established our way of life, my Lord,' replied Nandi. 'He lived around one thousand two hundred years ago. He created our systems, our rules, our ideologies, everything. His reign is known simply as '*Ram Rajya*' or '*the rule of Ram*'. The term 'Ram Rajya' is considered the gold standard in how an empire must be administered, in order to create a perfect life for all its citizens. Meluha is still governed in accordance with his principles. Jai Shri Ram.'

'He must have been quite a man! For he truly created a paradise right here on earth.'

Shiva did not lie when he said this. He truly believed that if there was a paradise somewhere, it couldn't have been very different from Meluha. This was a land of abundance, of almost ethereal perfection! It was an empire ruled by clearly codified and just laws, to which every Meluhan was subordinated, including the emperor. The country supported a population of nearly eight million, which without exception seemed well fed, healthy and wealthy. The average intellect was exceptionally high. They were a slightly serious people, but unfailingly polite and civil. It seemed to be a flawless society where everyone was aware of his role and played it perfectly. They were conscious, nay obsessive, about their duties. The simple truth hit Shiva: if the entire society was conscious of its duties, nobody would need to fight for their individual rights. Since *everybody's rights* would be automatically taken care of through *someone else's duties*. Lord Ram was a genius!

Shiva too repeated Nandi's cry, signifying *Glory to Lord Ram*. '*Jai Shri Ram*.'

— ༗⊙𐤒Ⴑ⊕ —

Having left their horses at the government authorised crossing-house, they crossed the river Ravi, close to *Hariyupa*, or the *City of Hari*. Shiva lingered for sometime as he admired Hariyupa from a slight distance, while his soldiers waited just beyond his shadow, having mounted their freshly allocated horses from the crossing-house on the other side of the Ravi. Hariyupa was a much larger city than Srinagar and seemed grand from the outside. Shiva considered exploring the magnificent city but that would have meant a delay in the trip to Devagiri. Next to Hariyupa, Shiva saw a construction project being executed. A new platform was being erected as Hariyupa had grown too populous to accommodate everyone on its existing platform.

How the hell do they raise these magnificent platforms?

Shiva made a mental note to visit the construction site on his return journey. At a distance, Jattaa, the Captain of the river crossing house, was talking to Nandi as he climbed the platform to mount his fresh horse.

'Avoid the road via Jratakgiri,' advised Jattaa. 'They suffered a terrorist attack last night. All the Brahmins were killed and the village temple was destroyed. The terrorists escaped as usual before any backup soldiers could arrive.'

'When in Lord Agni's name will we fight back? We should attack their country!' snarled a visibly angry Nandi.

'I swear by Lord Indra, if I ever find one of these Chandravanshi terrorists, I will cut his body into minute pieces and feed it to the dogs,' growled Jattaa, clenching his fists tight.

'Jattaa! We are followers of the Suryavanshis. We cannot even think of barbaric warfare such as that!' said Nandi.

'Do the terrorists follow the rules of war when they attack us? Don't they kill unarmed men?'

'That does not mean that we can act in the same way, Captain. We are Meluhans!' said Nandi shaking his head.

Jattaa did not counter Nandi. He was distracted by Shiva who was still waiting at a distance. 'Is he with you?' he asked.

'Yes.'

'He doesn't wear a caste amulet. Is he a new immigrant?'

'Yes.' replied Nandi, growing uncomfortable with the questions about Shiva.

'And you're going to Devagiri?' asked an increasingly suspicious Jattaa, looking harder towards Shiva's throat. 'I've heard some rumours coming from Srinagar…'

Nandi interrupted Jattaa suddenly. 'Thank you for your help, Captain Jattaa.'

Before Jattaa could act on his suspicions, Nandi quickly climbed the platform, mounted his horse and rode towards Shiva. Reaching quickly, he said, 'We should leave, my Lord.'

Shiva wasn't listening. He was perplexed once again as he saw the proud Captain Jattaa on his knees. Jattaa was looking directly at Shiva with his hands folded in a respectful Namaste. He appeared to be mumbling something very quickly. Shiva couldn't be sure from that distance, but it seemed as if the Captain was crying. He shook his head and whispered, 'Why?'

'We should go, my Lord,' repeated Nandi, a little louder.

Shiva turned to him, nodded and kicked his horse into action.

— ⚲◉Ʊᛩ⊕ —

Shiva looked towards his left as he rode upon the straight road, observing Nandi goading his valiant horse along. He turned around and was not surprised to see his three bodyguard soldiers riding at exactly the same distance as before. Not too close, and yet, not too far. His glance also took in Nandi's jewellery which he suspected were not merely ornamental. He wore two amulets on his thick right arm. The first one had some symbolic lines which Shiva could not fathom. The second one appeared to have an animal etching. Probably a bull. One of his gold chains had a pendant shaped like a perfectly circular sun with rays streaming outwards. The other pendant was a brown, elliptical seed-like object with small serrations all over it.

'Can you tell me the significance of your jewellery or is that also a state secret?' teased Shiva.

'Of course I can, my Lord,' replied Nandi earnestly. He pointed at the first amulet that had been tied around his massive arm with a silky gold thread. 'This is the amulet which represents my caste. The lines drawn on it symbolise the shoulders of the *Parmatma, the almighty.* This means that I am a Kshatriya.'

'I am sure there are clearly codified guidelines for representing the other castes as well.'

'Right you are, my Lord. You are exceptionally intelligent.'

'No, I am not. You people are just exceptionally predictable.'

Nandi smiled as Shiva continued. 'So what are they?'

'What are what, my Lord?'

'The symbols for the Brahmins, Vaishyas and Shudras.'

'Well, if the lines are drawn to represent the head of the Parmatma, it would mean the wearer is a Brahmin. The symbol for a Vaishya would be the lines forming a symbol of the thighs of the Parmatma. And the feet of the Parmatma on the amulet would make the wearer a Shudra.'

'Interesting,' said Shiva with a slight frown. 'I imagine most Shudras are not too pleased about their placement.'

Nandi was quite surprised by Shiva's comments. He couldn't understand why a Shudra would have a problem with this long ordained symbol. But he kept quiet for fear of disagreeing with his Lord.

'And the other amulet?' asked Shiva.

'This second amulet depicts my chosen-tribe. Each chosen-tribe takes on jobs which fit its profile. Every Meluhan, in consultation with his parents, applies for a chosen-tribe when he turns twenty-five years old. Brahmins choose from birds, while Kshatriyas apply for animals. Flowers are allocated to Vaishyas while Shudras must choose from amongst fish. The Allocation Board allocates the chosen-tribe on the basis of a rigorous examination process. You must qualify for a chosen-tribe that represents both your ambitions and skills. Choose a tribe that is too mighty and you will embarrass yourself throughout your life if your achievements don't measure up to the standards of that tribe. Choose a tribe too lowly and you will not be doing justice to your own talents. My chosen-tribe is a bull. That is the animal that this amulet represents.'

'And if I am not being rude, what does a bull mean in your rank of Kshatriya chosen-tribes?'

'Well, it's not as high as a lion, tiger or an elephant. But it's not a rat or a pig either!'

'Well, as far as I am concerned, the bull can beat any lion or elephant,' smiled Shiva. 'And what about the pendants on your chain?'

'The brown seed is a representation of the last Mahadev, Lord Rudra. It symbolises the protection and regeneration of life. Even divine weapons cannot destroy the life it protects.'

'And the Sun?'

'My Lord, the sun represents the fact that I am a follower of the *Suryavanshi* kings — the kings who are *the descendants of the Sun.*'

'What? The Sun came down and some queen...' teased an incredulous Shiva.

'Of course not, my Lord,' laughed Nandi. 'All it means is that we follow the solar calendar. So you could say that we are the followers of the "path of the sun". In practical terms it denotes that we are strong and steadfast. We honour our word and keep our promises even at the cost of our lives. We never break the law. We deal honourably even with those who are dishonourable. Like the Sun, we never take from anyone but always give to others. We sear our duties into our consciousness so that we may never forget them. Being a Suryavanshi means that we must always strive to be honest, brave and above all, loyal to the truth.'

'A tall order! I assume that Lord Ram was a Suryavanshi king?'

'Yes, of course,' replied Nandi, his chest puffed up with pride. 'He was *the* Suryavanshi king. Jai Shri Ram.'

'Jai Shri Ram,' repeated Shiva.

— 🏹⊙Ü♀⊕ —

Nandi and Shiva crossed the river Beas on a boat. Their soldiers waited for the following craft. The Beas was the last river to be crossed after which the straight road stretched towards Devagiri. Unseasonal rain the previous night had made the crossing-house Captain consider cancelling the day's crossings across the river. However the weather had been relatively calm since the morning, allowing the Captain to keep the service operational. Shiva and Nandi shared the boat with two other passengers as well as the boatman who rowed them across. They had traded in their existing horses at the crossing-house for fresh horses on the other side.

They were a short distance from the opposite bank when a sudden burst of torrential rain came down from the heavens. The winds took on a sudden ferocity. The boatman made a valiant effort to row quickly across, but the boat tossed violently as it surrendered to the elements. Nandi stretched towards Shiva in order to tell him to stay low for safety. But he did not do it gently enough. His considerable weight caused the boat to list dangerously, and he fell overboard.

The boatman tried to steady the boat with his oars so he could save the other passengers. Even as he did so, he had the presence of mind to pull out his conch and blow an emergency call to the crossing-house on the other side. The other two passengers should have jumped overboard to save Nandi but his massive build made them hesitate. They knew that if they tried to save him, they would most likely drown.

Shiva felt no such hesitation as he quickly tossed aside his angvastram, pulled off his shoes and dived into the turbulent river. Shiva swam with powerful strokes and quickly reached a rapidly drowning Nandi. He had to use all of his considerable strength to pull Nandi to the surface. In spite of being buoyed by the water, Nandi weighed significantly more than what any normal man would. It was fortunate that Shiva felt stronger than ever since the first night at the Srinagar immigration camp. Shiva positioned himself behind Nandi and wrapped one arm around his chest. He used his other arm to swim towards the bank. Nandi's weight made it very exhausting work, but Shiva was able to tow the Meluhan Captain to the shore, just as the emergency staff from the crossing-house came rapidly towards them. Shiva helped them drag Nandi's limp body on to the land. He was unconscious.

The emergency staff then began a strange procedure. One of them started pressing Nandi's chest in a quick rhythmic motion to the count of five. Just as he would stop, another emergency staff would cover Nandi's lips with his own and breathe hard into his mouth. After which, they would repeat the procedure all over again. Shiva did not understand what was going on but trusted both the expertise as well as the commitment of the Meluhan medical personnel.

After several anxious moments, Nandi suddenly coughed up a considerable amount of water and woke up with a start. At first he was disoriented but he quickly regained his wits and turned abruptly towards Shiva, screeching, 'My Lord, why did you jump in after me? Your life is too precious. You must never risk it for me!'

A surprised Shiva supported Nandi's back and whispered calmly, 'You need to relax, my friend.'

Agreeing with Shiva, the medical staff quickly placed Nandi on a stretcher and carried him into the rest house abutting the crossing-house. The other boat passengers were observing Shiva with increasing curiosity. They knew that the fat man was a relatively senior Suryavanshi soldier, judging by his amulets. Yet he called this fair, caste-unmarked man 'his Lord'. Strange. However, all that mattered was that the soldier was safe. They dispersed as Shiva followed the medical staff into the rest house.

CHAPTER 3

She Enters His Life

Nandi lay semi-conscious for several hours as the medicines administered by the doctors worked on his body. Shiva sat by his side, repeatedly changing the wet cloth on his burning forehead to control the fever. Nandi kept babbling incoherently as he tossed and turned in his sleep, making Shiva's task that much more difficult.

'I've been searching... long...so long... a hundred years... never thought I.... find Neelkanth... Jai Shri Ram...'

Shiva ignored Nandi's babble as he tried to keep the fever down. But his ears had caught on to something.

He's been searching for a hundred years?!

Shiva frowned.

The fever's affecting his bloody brain! He doesn't look a day older than twenty years!

'I've been searching for a hundred years...,' continued the oblivious Nandi. '...I found... Neelkanth...'

Shiva stopped for a moment and stared hard at Nandi. Then shaking his head dismissively, he continued his ministrations.

— 𑀓𑀁𑀝𑀢𑀓𑀁 —

Shiva had been walking on a paved, signposted road along the River Beas for the better part of an hour. He had left the rest house to explore the area by himself, much against a rapidly recovering Nandi's advice. Nandi was out of danger, but they had been advised to wait for a few days nevertheless, so that the Captain could be strong enough to travel. There was not much for Shiva to do at the rest house and he had begun to feel restless. The three soldiers had tried to shadow Shiva, but he had angrily dismissed them. 'Will you please stop trying to stick to me like leeches?'

The rhythmic hymns sung by the gentle waters of the Beas soothed Shiva. A cool tender breeze teased his thick lock of hair. He rested his hand on the hilt of his scabbard as his mind swirled with persistent questions.

Is Nandi really more than a hundred years old? But that's impossible! And what the hell do these crazy Meluhans need me for anyway? And why in the name of the holy lake is my bloody throat still feeling so cold?

Lost in his thoughts, Shiva did not realise that he had strayed off the road into a clearing, where, staring him in the face was the most beautiful building he had ever seen. It was built entirely of white and pink marble. An imposing flight of stairs led up to the top of a high platform, which had been adorned by pillars around its entire circumference. The ornate roof was topped by a giant triangular spire, like a giant 'Namaste' to the Gods. Elaborate sculptures were carved upon every available space on the structure.

Shiva had been in Meluha for many days now and all the buildings he had seen so far were functional and efficient. However, this particular one was oddly flamboyant. At the entrance, a signpost announced, 'Temple of Lord Brahma'. The Meluhans appeared to reserve their creativity for religious places.

There was a small crowd of hawkers around the courtyard in the clearing. Some were selling flowers, others were selling food. Still others were selling assorted items required for a *puja*. There was a stall where worshippers could leave their footwear as they went up to the temple. Shiva left his shoes there and walked up the steps. As he entered the main temple he found himself staring at the designs and sculptures, mesmerized by the sheer magnificence of the architecture.

'What are you doing here?'

Shiva turned around to find a Pandit staring at him quizzically. His wizened face sported a flowing white beard matched in length by his silvery mane. Wearing a saffron dhoti and angvastram, he had the calm, gentle look of a man who had already attained *nirvana*, but had chosen to remain on earth to fulfil some heavenly duties. Shiva realised that the Pandit was the first truly old person that he had seen in Meluha.

'I am sorry. Am I not allowed in here?' asked Shiva politely.

'Of course you are allowed in here. Everyone is allowed into the house of the Gods.'

Shiva smiled. However, before he could respond the Pandit questioned him once again, 'But you don't believe in these Gods, do you?'

Shiva's smile disappeared as quickly as it had appeared.

How the hell does he know?

The Pandit answered the question posed by Shiva's eyes. 'Everyone who enters this place of worship has eyes only for the idol of Lord Brahma. Almost nobody notices the brilliance of the architects who built this lovely temple. You, however, have eyes only for the work of the architects. You have not yet cast even a glance upon the idol.'

Shiva grinned apologetically. 'You guessed right. I don't believe in symbolic Gods. I believe that God exists all around us. In the flow of the river, in the rustle of the trees, in the whisper of the winds. He speaks to us all the time. All we need to do is listen. However, I apologise if I have caused some offence by not being respectful towards your God.'

'You don't need to apologise, my friend,' smiled the Pandit. 'There is no "your God" or "my God". All Godliness comes from the same source. It's just the manifestations that are different. But I have a feeling that one day you will find a temple worth walking into purely for prayer and not its beauty.'

'Really? Which temple might that be?'

'You will find it when you are ready, my friend.'

Why do these Meluhans always talk in bizarre riddles?

Shiva nodded politely, his expression suggesting an appreciation for the Pandit's words that he did not truly feel. He thought it wise to flee the temple before he outlived his welcome.

'I should be getting back to my rest house now, Pandit*ji*. But I eagerly look forward to finding the temple of my destiny. It was a pleasure meeting you,' said Shiva, as he bent down to touch the Pandit's feet.

Placing his hand on Shiva's head, the Pandit said gently, *Jai Guru Vishwamitra. Jai Guru Vashishtha.'*

Shiva rose, turned and walked down the steps. Looking at Shiva walking away from him, clearly out of earshot, the Pandit whispered with an admiring smile, for he had recognised his *fellow traveller in karma.* 'The pleasure was all mine, my *karmasaathi.*'

Shiva reached the shoe stall, put on his shoes and offered a coin for the service. The shoe-keeper politely declined. 'Thank you Sir, but this is a service provided by the government of Meluha. There is no charge for it.'

Shiva smiled. 'Of course! You people have a system for everything. Thank you.'

The shoe-keeper smiled back. 'We are only doing our duty, Sir.'

Shiva walked back to the temple steps. As he sat down, he breathed in deeply and let the tranquil atmosphere suffuse him with its serenity. And then it happened. The moment that every unrealised heart craves for. The unforgettable instant that a soul, clinging on to the purest memory of its previous life, longs for. The moment which, in spite of a conspiracy of the Gods, only a few lucky men experience. The moment when *she* enters *his* life.

She rode in on a chariot, guiding the horses expertly into the courtyard, while a lady companion by her side held on to the railings. Although her black hair was tied in an understated bun, a few irreverent strands danced a spellbinding *kathak* in the wind. Her piercingly magnetic, blue eyes and bronzed skin were an invitation for jealousy from the Goddesses. Her body, though covered demurely in a long angvastram, still ignited Shiva's imagination into sensing the lovely curves which lay beneath. Her flawless face was a picture of concentration as she manoeuvred the chariot skilfully into its parking place. She dismounted the chariot with an air of confidence. It was a calm confidence which had not covered the ugly distance towards arrogance.

Her walk was dignified. Stately enough to let a beholder know that she was detached, but not cold. Shiva stared at her like a parched piece of earth mesmerised by a passing rain cloud.

Have mercy on me!

'My lady, I still feel that it's not wise to wander so far from the rest of your entourage,' said her companion.

She answered. 'Krittika, just because others don't know the law, doesn't mean that we can ignore it. Lord Ram clearly stated that once a year, a pious woman has to visit Lord Brahma. I will not break that law, no matter how inconvenient it is to the bodyguards!'

The lady noticed Shiva staring at her as she passed by. Her delicate eyebrows arched into a surprised look and then an annoyed frown. Shiva made a valiant attempt to tear his glance away, but realised that his eyes were no longer in his control. She continued walking up, followed by Krittika.

She turned around at the top of the temple steps, to see the caste unmarked immigrant at a distance, still staring at her unabashedly. Before turning and walking into the main temple, she muttered to Krittika, 'These uncouth immigrants! As if we'll find our saviour from amongst these barbarians!'

It was only when she was out of sight that Shiva could breathe again. As he desperately tried to gather his wits, his overwhelmed and helpless mind took one obvious decision — there was no way he was leaving the temple before getting another look at her. He sat down on the steps once again. As his breathing and heartbeat returned to normal, he finally began to notice the surroundings that had been consecrated by her recent presence. He stared once again at the road on the left from where she had turned in. She had ridden past the cucumber seller standing near the banyan tree.

Incidentally, why is the cucumber seller not trying to hawk his wares? He just seems to be staring at the temple. Anyway, it is not any of my business.

He followed the path that her chariot had taken as it had swerved to its left, around the fountain at the centre of the courtyard. It had then taken a sharp right turn past the shepherd standing at the entrance of the garden.

But where were this shepherd's sheep?

Shiva continued to look down the path that the chariot had taken to the parking lot. Next to the chariot stood another man who had just walked into the temple complex, but had inexplicably not entered the temple itself. He turned to the shepherd and appeared to nod slightly. Before Shiva could piece together the information from his observation, he felt her presence once again. He turned immediately to see her walking down the steps, with Krittika silently behind. On still finding this rude, caste-unmarked, obviously foreign man staring at her, she walked up to him and asked in a firm but polite voice, 'Excuse me, is there a problem?'

'No. No. There's no problem. But I feel that I've seen you somewhere before,' replied a flustered Shiva.

The lady was not sure how to respond to this. It was obviously a lie but the voice was sincere. Before she could react, Krittika cut in rudely. 'Is that the best line you can come up with?'

As Shiva was about to retort, he was alerted by a quick movement from the cucumber seller. Shiva turned to see him pulling out a sword as he tossed his shawl aside. The shepherd and the man next to the chariot also stood poised in traditional fighter positions with their swords drawn. In a flash Shiva drew his sword and stretched out his left hand protectively, to pull the object of his fascination behind him. She however deftly side-stepped his protective hand, reached into the folds of her angvastram and drew out her own sword. Surprised, Shiva flashed her a quick, admiring smile. Her eyes flashed right back, acknowledging the unexpected yet providential partnership.

She whispered under her breath to Krittika, 'Run back into the temple. Stay there till this is over.'

Krittika protested. 'But my lady…'

'NOW!' she ordered.

Krittika turned and ran up the temple steps. Shiva and the lady stood back to back in a standard defensive-partner position, covering all the directions of any possible attack. The three attackers charged in. Two more jumped in from behind the trees. Shiva raised his sword defensively just as the shepherd came up close. Feigning a sideward movement to draw the shepherd into an aggressive attack, Shiva dropped his sword low. He hoped to tempt him to move in for a kill wound and in response, he would have quickly raised his sword and dug it deep into the shepherd's heart.

The shepherd, however, moved unexpectedly. Instead of taking advantage of Shiva's opening, he tried to strike Shiva's shoulder. Shiva quickly raised his right arm and swung viciously, inflicting a deep wound across the shepherd's torso. As the shepherd fell back, another attacker moved in from the right. He swung from a distance. Not too smart a move, as it would merely have inflicted a surface nick. Shiva stepped back to avoid the swing and brought his sword down in a smooth action to dig deep into the attacker's thigh. Screaming in agony, this attacker too fell back. As yet another attacker joined in from the left, Shiva began to realise that this was indeed a very strange assault.

The attackers seemed to know what they were doing. They seemed like accomplished warriors. But they also seemed to be in a bizarre dance of avoidance. They did not appear to want to kill but merely injure. It was due to their circumspection that they were being beaten back easily. Shiva parried another attack from the left and pushed his sword viciously into the man's shoulder. The man screamed in pain as Shiva pushed him off the blade with his left hand. Slowly, but surely, the attackers were being worn out. They were suffering too many injuries to seriously carry on the assault for long.

Suddenly a giant of a man ran in from behind the trees carrying swords in both hands. The man was cloaked in a black hooded robe from head to toe while his face was hidden behind a mask. The only visible parts of his body were his large impassive almond-shaped eyes and strong fleshy hands. He charged upon Shiva and the lady as he barked an order to his men. He was too large to battle with agility. But his slow pace was compensated by his unusually skilled arms. Shiva perceived from the corner of his eye that the other attackers were picking up the injured and withdrawing. The hooded figure was performing a brilliant rearguard action as his men retreated.

Shiva realised that the man's hood would impair his peripheral vision. Here was a weakness that could be exploited. Moving to the left, Shiva swung ferociously, hoping to peg him back so that the lady could finish the job from the other side. But his opponent was up to the challenge. As he stepped slightly back, he deflected Shiva's swing with a deft move of his right hand. Shiva noticed a leather band on the hooded figure's right wrist. It had a sharp symbol on it. Shiva swung his sword back but the hooded figure moved aside effortlessly. He pushed back a brutal flanking attack from the lady with his left hand. He was keeping just enough distance from Shiva and the lady to defend himself while at the same time keeping them engaged in combat.

All of a sudden the hooded figure disengaged from the battle and stepped back. Even as he retreated, his swords continued to point menacingly at Shiva and the lady. His men had disappeared into the trees. On reaching a safe distance, he turned around and ran after his men. Shiva considered chasing him but almost immediately decided against it. He might just rush into an ambush.

Shiva turned to the lady warrior and inquired, 'Are you alright?'

'Yes I am,' she nodded before asking with a sombre expression. 'Are you injured?'

'Nothing serious. I'll survive!' he grinned.

In the meantime, Krittika came running down the temple steps and asked breathlessly, 'My lady. Are you alright?'

'Yes I am,' she answered. 'Thanks to this foreigner here.'

Krittika turned to Shiva and said, 'Thank you very much. You have helped a very important woman.'

Shiva did not seem to be listening though. He continued to stare at Krittika's mistress as if he were possessed. Krittika struggled to conceal a smile.

The noble woman averted her eyes in embarrassment,

but said politely, 'I am sorry, but I am quite sure that we have not met earlier.'

'No it's not that,' said a smiling Shiva. 'It's just that in our society, women don't fight. You don't weild your sword too badly for a woman.'

O hell! That came out all wrong.

'Excuse me?' she said, a slightly belligerent tone creeping into her voice, clearly upset about the *for-a-woman* remark. 'You don't fight too badly either for a barbarian.'

'Not too badly?! I'm an exceptional sword fighter! Do you want to try me?'

O bloody hell! What am I saying? I'm not going to impress her like this!

Her expression resumed its detached, supercilious look once again. 'I have no interest in duelling with you, foreigner.'

'No. No. Don't get me wrong. I don't want to duel with you. I just wanted to tell you that I am quite good at sword-fighting. I am good at other things as well. And it came out all wrong. I rather like the fact that you fought for yourself. You are a very good swordsman. I mean a swordswoman. In fact, you are quite a woman…,' bumbled Shiva, losing the filter of judgement, exactly at the time when he needed it the most.

Krittika, with her head bowed, smiled at the increasingly appealing exchange.

Her mistress, on the other hand, wanted to chastise the foreigner for his highly inappropriate words. But he had saved her life. She was bound by the Meluhan code of conduct. 'Thank you for your help, foreigner. I owe you my life and you will not find me ungrateful. If you ever need my help, do call on me.'

'Can I call on you even if I don't need your help?'

Shit! What am I saying?!

She glared at the caste-unmarked foreigner who clearly did not know his place. With superhuman effort, she controlled herself, nodded politely and said, 'Namaste.'

With that, the aristocratic woman turned around to leave. Krittika continued to stare at Shiva with admiring eyes. However, on seeing her mistress leaving, she too turned around hurriedly and followed.

'At least tell me your name,' said Shiva, walking to keep pace with her.

She turned around, staring even more gravely at Shiva.

'Look, how will I find you if I need your help?' asked Shiva sincerely.

Momentarily disarmed, she remained silent. The request seemed reasonable. She turned towards Krittika and nodded.

'You can find us at Devagiri,' answered Krittika. 'Ask anyone in the city for Lady Sati.'

'Sati...,' said Shiva, letting the ethereal name roll over his tongue. 'My name is Shiva.'

'Namaste, Shiva. And I promise you, I will honour my word if you ever need my help,' said Sati as she turned and climbed into her chariot, followed by Krittika.

Expertly turning the chariot, Sati urged her horses into a smooth trot. Without a backward look she sped away from the temple. Shiva kept staring at the fast disappearing profile of the chariot. Once it was gone, he continued to stare at the dust with intense jealousy. It had been fortunate enough to have touched her.

I think I'm going to like this country.

For the first time in the journey, Shiva actually looked

forward to reaching the capital city of the Meluhans. He smiled and started towards the rest house.

Have to get to Devagiri quickly.

CHAPTER 4

Abode of the Gods

'What! Who attacked you?' cried a concerned Nandi as he rushed towards Shiva and examined his wounds.

'Relax Nandi,' replied Shiva. 'You are in worse shape than I am after your adventure in the water. It's just a few superficial cuts. Nothing serious. The doctors have already dressed the wounds. I am alright.'

'I am sorry, my Lord. It's entirely my fault. I should never have left you alone. It will never happen again. Please forgive me, my Lord.'

Pushing Nandi gently back on to the bed, Shiva said, 'There's nothing to forgive, my friend. How can this be your fault? Please calm down. Getting excited will not do your health any good.'

Once Nandi had calmed down a bit, Shiva continued, 'In any case, I don't think they were trying to kill us. It was very strange.'

'Us?'

'Yes, there were two women involved.'

'But who could these attackers be?' asked Nandi. Then a disturbing thought dawned on Nandi. 'Did the attackers wear a pendant with a crescent moon on it?'

Shiva frowned. 'No. But there was this one strange man. The best swordsman among them. He was covered from head to toe in a hooded robe, his face hidden by a mask, the kind I've seen you people wear at that *colour festival*. What is it called?'

'*Holi*, my Lord?'

'Yes, the *holi* kind of mask. In any case, you could only see his eyes and his hands. His only distinguishing feature was a leather bracelet with a strange symbol on it.'

'What symbol, my Lord?'

Picking up a palm-leaf booklet and the thin charcoal writing-stick from the side table, Shiva drew the symbol.

Nandi frowned. 'That is an ancient symbol that some people used for the word Aum. But who would want to use this symbol now?'

'Aum?' asked Shiva.

'My Lord, Aum is the holiest word in our religion. It is considered the primeval sound of nature. The hymn of the universe. It was so holy that for many millennia, most people would not insult it by putting it down in written form.'

'Then how did this symbol come about?'

'It was devised by Lord Bharat, a great ruler who had

conquered practically all of India many thousands of years ago. A rare *Chandravanshi* who was worth respecting, he had even married a *Suryavanshi* princess with the aim of ending our perpetual war.'

'Who are the *Chandravanshis*?' asked Shiva.

'Think of them as the very antithesis of us, my Lord. They are the followers of the kings who are *the descendants of the moon*.'

'And they follow the lunar calendar?'

'Yes, my Lord. They are a crooked, untrustworthy and lazy people with no rules, morals or honour. They are cowards who never attack like principled Kshatriyas. Even their kings are corrupt and selfish. The Chandravanshis are a blot on humanity!'

'But what does the Aum symbol have to do with this?'

'Well, King Bharat created this symbol of unity between the Suryavanshis and the Chandravanshis. The top half in white represents the Chandravanshis.

The bottom half in red represents the Suryavanshis.

The amalgam of these is the emergent common path represented in orange.

The crescent moon to the right of the symbol was the pre-existing Chandravanshi symbol.

And the sun above it was the pre-existing Suryavanshi symbol.

In order to signify that this was a pact blessed by the Gods, Lord Bharat mandated the representation of this symbol as the holy word Aum.'

'And then what happened?'

'As expected, the pact died along with the good king. Once the influence of Lord Bharat was removed, the Chandravanshis were soon up to their old tricks and the war began once again. The symbol was forgotten. And the word Aum reverted to its original form of pure sound without a written representation.'

'But the symbol on the bracelet of this hooded man was not coloured. It was all black. And the parts of the symbol didn't look like lines to me. They looked like a drawing of three serpents.'

'Naga!' exclaimed a shocked Nandi, before mumbling a soft prayer and touching his Rudra pendant for protection.

'Now who the bloody hell are the Nagas?' asked Shiva.

'They are cursed people, my Lord,' gasped Nandi. 'They are born with hideous deformities because of the sins of their previous births. Deformities like extra hands or horribly misshapen faces. But they have tremendous strength and skills. The Naga name alone strikes terror in any citizen's heart. They are not even allowed to live in the Sapt Sindhu.'

'The Sapt Sindhu?'

'Our land, my Lord, the land of the seven rivers. The land of the Indus, Saraswati, Yamuna, Ganga, Sarayu, Brahmaputra and Narmada. This is where Lord Manu mandated that all of us, Suryavanshis and Chandravanshis, live.'

Shiva nodded as Nandi continued. 'The city of the Nagas exists to the south of the Narmada, beyond the border of our lands. In fact, it is bad luck to even speak of them, my Lord!'

'But why would a Naga attack me? Or any Meluhan for that matter?'

Cursing under his breath, Nandi said, 'Because of the Chandravanshis! What levels have these two-faced people sunk to? Using the demon Nagas in their attacks! In their hatred for us, they don't even realise how many sins they are inviting upon their own souls!'

Shiva frowned. During the attack, it hadn't appeared as if the Naga was being used by the small platoon of soldiers. In fact, it looked like the Naga was the leader.

— ⋏◉Ⴎ⇡⊕ —

It took another week for them to reach Devagiri. The capital city of the Meluhans stood on the west bank of the Saraswati, which emerged at the confluence of the Sutlej and Yamuna rivers. Sadly, though, her majestic flow and mighty girth had now ebbed. But even in her reduced state, she was still massive and awe-inspiring. Unlike many of the tempestuous rivers of the Punjab though, the Saraswati was achingly calm. The river seemed to sense that her days were drawing to an end. Yet, she did not fight aggressively to thrust her way through and survive. Instead, she unselfishly gave her all to those who came to seek her treasures.

The soaring Devagiri though, was in complete contrast to the mellow Saraswati. Like all Meluhan cities, Devagiri too was built on giant platforms, an effective protection against floods as well as enemies. However, Devagiri differed from other Meluhan cities in its sheer size. The city sprawled atop three giant platforms, each of them spreading over three hundred and fifty hectares, significantly larger than the other cities. The platforms were nearly eight metres high and were bastioned by giant blocks of cut stone interspaced with baked bricks. Two of the platforms, named *Tamra* and *Rajat*, literally, *bronze* and *silver*, were for the common man, whereas the platform named *Svarna* or *gold* was the royal citadel. The platforms were connected to each other by tall bridges, made of stones and baked bricks, which rose above the flood plains below.

Along the periphery of each enormous platform were towering city walls, with giant spikes facing outwards. There were turrets at regular intervals along the city walls from where approaching enemies could be repelled. This spectacle was beyond anything that Shiva had ever seen. In his mind, the construction of a city like this must truly be man's greatest achievement.

Shiva's entourage rode up towards the drawbridge across the field of spikes to the Tamra platform. The drawbridge had been reinforced with metal bars at the bottom and had roughened baked bricks laid out on top so that horses and chariots would not slip. There was something about the bricks he had seen across the empire that had intrigued Shiva. Turning to Nandi he asked, 'Are these bricks made by some standard process?'

'Yes my Lord,' replied a surprised Nandi. 'All the bricks in Meluha are made in accordance with specifications and guidelines given by the Chief Architect of the empire. But how did you guess?'

'They are all of exactly the same dimension.'

Nandi beamed with pride at both his empire's efficiency as well as his Lord's power of observation. The platform rose at the end of the drawbridge, with a road spiralling up to the summit in one gentle turn, facilitating the passage of horses and chariots. In addition, there was a broad flight of stairs leading straight up the incline for pedestrians. The city walls and the platform extended steeply onto the sides around this slope, making it a valley of death for any enemy foolish enough to attack the platform from this direction.

The city gates were made of a metal that Shiva had never seen before. Nandi clarified that they were made of iron, a new metal that had just been discovered. It was the strongest of all the metals but very expensive. The ore required to make it was not easily available. At the platform entry, on top of the city gates, was etched the symbol of the Suryavanshis — a bright red circular sun with its rays blazing out in all directions. Below it was the motto that they lived by '*Satya. Dharma. Maan*': *Truth. Duty. Honour.*

Even this initial introduction to the city had left Shiva awestruck. However, what he witnessed at the top of the platform, within the city gates, was truly breathtaking both in its efficiency and simplicity. The city was divided into a grid of square blocks by the paved streets. There were footpaths on the side for pedestrians, lanes marked on the street for traffic in different directions, and of course, there were covered drains running through the centre. All the buildings were constructed as standard two storied block structures made of baked bricks. On top were wooden extensions for increasing the height of the building, if required. Nandi clarified to Shiva that the layout of the buildings differed internally depending on their individual requirements. All windows and doors were built into the side walls of buildings, never facing the main road.

The blank walls that faced the main roads bore striking black etchings depicting the different legends of the Suryavanshis, while the walls themselves were painted in the sober colours of grey, light blue, light green or white. The most common background colour though, appeared to be blue. The holiest colour for the Meluhans was blue, denoting the sky. Green, representing nature, happened to be placed just after blue in the colour spectrum. Meluhans liked to divine a grand design in every natural phenomenon and thought it wondrous that blue was placed just before green in the colour spectrum. Just as the sky happened to be above the earth.

The most recurring illustrations on the walls were about the great emperor, Lord Ram. His victories over his enemies, his subjugation of the wicked Chandravanshis, incidents depicting his statesmanship and wisdom, had all been lovingly recreated. Lord Ram was deeply revered, and many Meluhans worshipped him like a God. They referred to him as *Vishnu*, an ancient title for the greatest of the Gods meaning *protector of the world and propagator of good*.

As Shiva learned from Nandi, the city was divided into many districts consisting of four to eight blocks. Each district had its own markets, commercial and residential areas, temples and entertainment centres. Manufacturing or any other polluting activity was conducted in separate quarters away from the districts. The efficiency and smoothness with which Devagiri functioned belied the fact that it was the most populous city in the entire empire. The census conducted two years back had pegged the population of the city at two hundred thousand.

Nandi led Shiva and the three soldiers to one of the city's numerous guest houses, built for the many tourists that frequented Devagiri, for both business and leisure. Having duly handed over their exhausted horses to the care of the stable boy, they strode in to register themselves. Shiva took in the guest house with a familiar eye, similar to so many he had seen throughout their journey. There was a central courtyard with the building built around it. The rooms were comfortably furnished and spacious.

'My Lord, it's almost dinner time,' said Nandi. 'I will speak with the housekeeper and get some food organised. We should eat early and get enough sleep since our appointment with the Emperor has been fixed at the beginning of the second prahar tomorrow.'

'Sounds like a good idea.'

'Also, if it is all right with you, shall I dismiss the soldiers and send them back to Srinagar?'

'That also sounds like a good idea,' said a smiling Shiva. 'Why Nandi, you are almost like a fount of brilliant ideas!'

Nandi laughed along with Shiva, always happy to be the harbinger of a smile on his Lord's face. 'I'll just be back, my Lord.'

Shiva lay down on his bed and was quickly lost in the thoughts that really mattered to him.

I'll finish the meeting with the Emperor as soon as it is humanly possible, give him whatever the bloody hell he wants and then scour the city for Sati.

Shiva had considered asking Nandi about the whereabouts of Sati but had eventually decided against it. He was painfully aware that he had made a less than spectacular impression on her at their first meeting. If she hadn't made it easy for him to find her, it only meant that she wasn't terribly stirred by him. He didn't want to compound his mistake by speaking casually about her with others.

He smiled as the memory of her face came flooding back to him. He replayed the magical moments when he had seen her fighting. Not the most romantic of sights for most men of his tribe. But for Shiva, it was divine. He sighed recalling her soft, delicate body, which had suddenly developed brutal, killer qualities upon being attacked. The curves that had so captivated him swung smoothly as she transferred her weight to swing her sword. The soberly tied hair had swayed sensuously with each movement of the sword arm. He breathed deeply.

What a woman!

— ⵏⵉⵊⵙⵉⵝ⊕ —

Early next morning Shiva and Nandi crossed the bridge between the Tamra and Svarna platforms to reach the royal citadel. The bridge, another marvel of Meluhan engineering, was flanked on the sides by a thick wall. Holes punched into the walls enabled defenders to shoot arrows or pour hot oil on enemies. The bridge was bisected by a massive gate, a final protection in the likelihood of the other platform being lost to an enemy.

Shiva was completely taken by surprise when they crossed over to the Svarna platform, not by the grandeur of the royal area but by the lack of it. He was shocked that there was no opulence. Despite ruling over such a massive and wealthy empire, the nobility lived in a conspicuously simple manner. The structure of the royal citadel was almost exactly like the other platforms. There were no special concessions made for the aristocrats. The same block structures that dominated all of Meluha were to be found in the royal citadel as well. The only magnificent structure was to the far right and sported the sign 'Great Public Bath'. The Bath also had a glorious temple to Lord Indra built on the left-hand side. The temple was built of wood and it stood on a raised foundation of baked bricks, its cupola plated with solid gold! It seemed that special architecture was reserved only for structures built for the Gods or ones that were for the common good.

Probably just like how Lord Ram would have wanted.

The only concession to the emperor, however, was that his standard block structure was larger than the others. Significantly larger.

— 人◎ᔑ♌⊕ —

Shiva and Nandi entered the royal private office to find Emperor Daksha sitting on a simple throne at the far end of the modestly furnished room, flanked by a man and a woman.

Daksha greeted Shiva with a formal Namaste and said, 'I hope your journey was comfortable.'

He looked too young to be an emperor of such a large country. Though he was marginally shorter than Shiva, they differed in their musculature. While the strapping Shiva was powerfully built, Daksha's body indicated that it had not been strained by too much exercise. It wasn't that he was obese either, just average. The same could be said about his wheat-complexioned face. Average sized, dark eyes flanked a straight nose. He wore his hair long like most Meluhan men and women. The head bore a majestic crown with the sun symbol of the Suryavanshis manifested in the centre through sparkling gem stones. His clothes consisted of an elegantly draped dhoti and an angvastram placed over his right shoulder. A large amount of functional jewellery, including two amulets on his right arm, complemented Daksha's average appearance. His only distinguishing feature was his smile — which spread its innocent conviction all the way to his eyes. Emperor Daksha looked like a man who wore his royalty lightly.

'Yes it was, your highness,' replied Shiva. 'The infrastructure in your empire is wonderful. You are an extraordinary emperor.'

'Thank you. But I only deserve reflected credit. The work is done by my people,'

'You are too modest, your Highness.'

Smiling politely, Daksha asked, 'May I introduce my most important aides?' Without waiting for an answer, he pointed to the woman on his left, 'This is my prime minister, Kanakhala. She takes care of the administrative, revenue and protocol matters.'

Kanakhala did a formal Namaste to Shiva. Her head was shaved except for a tuft of smooth hair at the back which had been tied into a knot. She had a string called the janau tied across from her left shoulder down to the right side of her torso. Though young-looking like most Meluhans, the flab on her torso between the white blouse and dhoti didn't escape Shiva's keen eye. She had a dark and incredibly smooth complexion and like all her countrymen, wore jewellery that was restrained and conservative. Shiva noticed that the second amulet on Kanakhala's arm showed a pigeon. Not a very high chosen-tribe amongst the Brahmins. Shiva bent low and did a formal Namaste in reply.

Pointing to his right, Daksha said, 'And this is my chief of the armed forces, General Parvateshwar. He looks after the army, navy, special forces, police etc.'

Parvateshwar looked like a man that Shiva would think twice about taking on in a battle. He was taller than Shiva and had an immensely muscular physique that dominated the space around him. His curly long hair had been combed back severely and fell from under his crown in a disciplined array. His smooth, swarthy skin was marked by the proud signs of long years in battle. His body was hairless, in a rare departure from the normally hirsute Kshatriya men who considered body hair a sign of machismo. As if to make up for this deficiency, Parvateshwar maintained a thick and long moustache which curled upwards at the edges. His eyes reflected his uncompromisingly strong and righteous character. The second amulet on his arm showed Parvateshwar as a tiger, a very high chosen-tribe amongst the Kshatriyas. He nodded curtly at Shiva. No Namaste. No elaborate bow of his proud head. Shiva, however, smiled warmly and greeted Parvateshwar with a formal Namaste.

'Please wait outside, Captain,' advised Parvateshwar, looking at Nandi.

Before Nandi could respond, however, Shiva cut in. 'My apologies. But is it alright if Nandi stays here with me? He has been my constant companion since I left my homeland and has become a dear and trusted friend.'

'Of course he may,' replied Daksha.

'Your Highness, it is not appropriate for a Captain to be witness to this discussion,' said Parvateshwar. 'In any case, his service rules clearly state that he can only escort a guest into the emperor's presence and not stay there while a matter of state is discussed.'

'Oh relax Parvateshwar. You take your service rules too seriously sometimes.' Turning to Shiva, Daksha continued, 'If it is alright with you, may we see your neck now?'

Nandi slid behind Shiva to untie the cravat. Seeing the beads darned on the cravat to convey the impression that the throat was covered for religious reasons, Daksha smiled and whispered, 'Good idea.'

Even as the cravat came off, both Daksha and Kanakhala moved in close to inspect Shiva's throat. Parvateshwar did not step forward but strained his neck slightly in order to get a better look. Daksha and Kanakhala were clearly stunned by what they saw.

Daksha reached out and lightly touched Shiva's throat in awe, 'The colour emerges from within. There is no dye. It is real.'

Daksha and Kanakhala glanced at each other, tears glistening in their astounded eyes. Kanakhala folded her hands into a Namaste and began mumbling a chant under her breath. Daksha looked up at Shiva's face, trying desperately to suppress the ecstasy that coursed through his insides. With a controlled smile, the Emperor of Meluha said, 'I hope we have not done anything to cause you any discomfort since your arrival in Meluha.'

Despite Daksha's controlled reaction, Shiva could see that both the emperor as well as his prime minister were taken aback by his blue throat.

Just how important is this bloody blue throat for the Meluhans?

'Umm, none at all your Highness,' replied Shiva as he tied the cravat back around his neck. 'In fact, my tribe and I have been delighted by the hospitality that we have received here.'

'I'm happy about that,' smiled Daksha, bowing his head politely. 'You may want to rest a bit and we could talk in greater detail tomorrow. Would you like to shift your residence to the royal citadel? It is rumoured that the quarters here are a little more comfortable.'

'That is a very kind offer, your Highness.'

Daksha turned to Nandi and asked, 'Captain, what did you say your name was?'

'My name is Nandi, your Highness.'

'You too are welcome to stay here. Make sure that you take good care of our honoured guest. Kanakhala, please make all the arrangements.'

'Yes, your Highness.'

Kanakhala gestured towards one of her aides, who escorted Shiva and Nandi out of the royal office.

As Shiva exited the room, Daksha went down on his haunches with great ceremony and touched his head to the ground on which Shiva had just stood. He mumbled a soft prayer and then stood up to look at Kanakhala with tears in his eyes. Kanakhala's eyes, however, betrayed impatience and a touch of anger.

'I don't understand, your Highness,' glared Kanakhala. 'The blue mark was genuine. Why did you not tell him?'

'What did you expect me to do?' cried a surprised Daksha. 'This is his second day in Devagiri. You want me to just accost him and tell him that he is the Neelkanth, our saviour? That he is destined to solve all our problems?'

'Well, if he has a blue throat, then he is the Neelkanth, isn't he? And if he is the Neelkanth, then he is our saviour. He has to accept his destiny.'

An exasperated Parvateshwar interjected. 'I can't believe that we are talking like this. We are Meluhans! We are the Suryavanshis! We have created the greatest civilisation ever known to man. Are we to believe that an unskilled, uneducated barbarian is to be our saviour? Just because he has a blue throat?'

'That is what the legend says Parvateshwar,' countered Kanakhala.

Daksha interrupted both his ministers. 'Parvateshwar, I believe in the legend. My people believe in the legend. The

Neelkanth has chosen my reign to make his appearance. He will transform all of India in line with the ideals of Meluha — a land of truth, duty and honour. His leadership can help us end the Chandravanshi crisis once and for all. All the agonies they now inflict upon us will be over — from the terrorist attacks to the shortage of Somras to the killing of the Saraswati.'

'Then why delay telling him, your Highness?' asked Kanakhala. 'The more days we waste, the weaker becomes the resolve of our people. You are aware of the terrorist attack just a few days back in a village not far from Hariyupa. As our response becomes weak, our enemies become bolder, your Highness. We must inform the Lord quickly and announce his arrival to our people. It will give us the strength to fight our cruel enemies.'

'I will tell him. But I am trying to be more farsighted than you. So far our empire has only faced the morale-sapping influence of fraudulent Neelkanths. Imagine the consequences if people were to discover that the true Neelkanth has arrived but refuses to stand by us. First we must be sure that he is willing to accept his destiny. Only then will we announce his arrival to our people. And I think that the best way to convince him is to share the whole truth with him. Once he sees the unfairness of the attacks we face, he will fight with us to destroy evil. If that takes time, so be it. We have waited for centuries for the Neelkanth. A few more weeks will not destroy us.'

CHAPTER 5

Tribe of Brahma

Shiva was walking in the verdant gardens of the royal guest house. His belongings were being moved into the royal guest house by Nandi along with an efficient aide of Kanakhala. Shiva sat down on a comfortable bench overlooking a bed of red and white roses. The cool breeze in the open gardens brought a smile to his face. It was early afternoon and the garden was deserted. Shiva's thoughts kept going back to the conversation he had had with the Emperor in the morning. Despite Daksha's controlled reaction, Shiva could understand that his blue throat was of great significance to the Meluhans, even to the Emperor. It meant that the legend of the Neelkanth, whatever it was, was not restricted to some small sect in Kashmir. If the Emperor himself took it so seriously, all of Meluha must need the help of the Neelkanth.

But what the bloody hell do they want help for? They are so much more advanced than we are!

His thoughts were interrupted by the sounds of a *dhol*, a percussion instrument, and some *ghungroos*, which were anklets worn by dancers. Someone seemed to be practising in the garden. A hedge separated the dance pavilion from the rest of the garden. Shiva, himself a passionate dancer, would normally have stepped in to move to the rhythm of the beat, but his mind was preoccupied. Some words floated in from the group that was dancing.

'No my lady, you must let yourself go,' said a distinguished male voice. 'It's not a chore that you have to do. Enjoy the dance. You are trying too hard to remember all the steps rather than letting the emotion of the dance flow through you.'

Then a lady's voice interjected. 'My lady, Guru*ji* is right. You are dancing correctly, but not enjoying it. The concentration shows on your face. You have to relax a bit.'

'Let me get the steps right. Then I can learn to enjoy them.'

The last voice made Shiva's hair stand up on end. It was her. It was Sati. He quickly got up and followed the sound of the voices. Coming up from behind the hedge, he saw Sati dancing on a small platform. She had her hands raised rigidly to her sides as she enacted the various movements of the dance. She danced in keeping with the steps, first to the left and then to the right. She moved her shapely hips to the side and placed her hands precisely on her waist, to convey the mood of the dance. He was mesmerised once again.

However, he did notice that though Sati's steps were right, the Guru*ji* had a point. She was moving in a mechanical manner; the uninhibited surrender that is characteristic of a natural dancer was absent. The varying emotions of bliss and anger in the story being told were missing in her movements. Also, unlike a proficient dancer, Sati wasn't using the entire platform. Her steps were small, which kept her movements restricted to the centre.

The dance teacher sat facing her and playing on a dhol to give Sati her beats. Her companion Krittika sat to the right. It was the dance teacher who noticed Shiva first and immediately stood up. Sati and Krittika turned around as well and were clearly astonished to find Shiva standing in front of them. Unlike Sati, Krittika could not control her surprise and blurted out, 'Shiva?'

Sati, in her characteristic composed and restrained manner, asked sincerely, 'Is everything alright, Shiva? Do you need my help?'

How have you been? I've missed you. Don't you ever smile?

Shiva continued to stare at Sati, the words running through his mind, not on his lips. A smiling Krittika looked at Sati for her reaction. An even more serious Sati repeated, very politely, 'Can I help you with something, Shiva?'

'No, no, I don't need any help,' replied Shiva as reality seemed to enter his consciousness once again. 'I just happened to be in the area and I heard your dancing. I mean your conversation. Your dance steps were not loud enough to be heard. You were dancing very accurately. Actually, technically it was all…'

Krittika interjected. 'You know a bit about dancing, do you?'

'Oh, not much. Just a little,' said Shiva to Krittika with a smile, before turning rapidly back to Sati. 'My apologies Sati, but Guru*ji* is right. You were being far too methodical. As they say in the land that I come from, the *mudras* and the *kriyas* were all technically correct. But the *bhav* or emotion was missing. And a dance without bhav is like a body without a soul. When the emotions of the dancer participate, she would not even need to remember the steps. The steps come to you. The bhav is something that you cannot learn. It comes to you if you can create the space in your heart for it.'

Sati listened patiently to Shiva without saying a word. Her eyebrows were raised slightly as the barbarian spoke. How could he know more than a Suryavanshi about dancing? But she reminded herself that he had saved her life. She was duty bound to honour him.

Krittika, however, took offence at this caste-unmarked foreigner pretending that he knew more about dancing than her mistress. She glowered at Shiva. 'You dare to think that you know more than one of the best dancers in the realm?'

Shiva gathered that he may have caused some offence. He turned to Sati in all seriousness. 'I am terribly sorry. I didn't mean to insult you in any way. Sometimes I just keep talking without realising what I am saying.'

'No, no', replied Sati. 'You did not insult me. Perhaps you are right. I don't feel the essence of the dance as much as I should. But I am sure that with Guru*ji*'s guidance, I will pick it up in due course.'

Seizing his chance to impress Sati, Shiva said, 'If it is alright with you, may I perform the dance? I am sure that I am not as technically correct as you. But perhaps, there may be something in the sentiment that will guide me through the correct steps.'

That was well put! She can't say no!

Sati looked surprised. This was unexpected. 'Umm, okay,' she managed to say.

A delighted Shiva immediately moved to the centre of the stage. He took off the angvastram covering his upper body and tossed it aside. Krittika's anger at the perceived insult to her mistress was quickly forgotten as she beheld Shiva's rippling physique. Sati, though, began to wonder how Shiva would bend such a muscular body into the contortions that were required of this dance. Flexibility was usually sacrificed by a human body at the altar of strength.

Playing lightly on his dhol, the Gilu*ji* asked Shiva, 'What beat are you comfortable with, young man?'

Shiva folded his hands into a Namaste, bent low and said, 'Guru*ji*, could you just give me a minute please? I need to prepare for the dance.'

Dancing was something Shiva was as accomplished in as in warfare. Facing east, he closed his eyes and bowed his head slightly. Then he went down on his knees and reverentially touched the ground with his head. Standing up, he turned his right foot outwards. Then he raised his left leg off the floor in a graceful arching movement till the foot was above knee height, as he bent his right knee slightly to balance himself. His left foot bisected the angle between his right foot and his face. A calm breeze provided relief to the silence that enveloped the audience. Enraptured, the Guru*ji*, Sati and Krittika gazed at Shiva with amazement. They did not understand what he was doing but could feel the energy that Shiva's stance was emanating.

Shiva raised both his arms in an elegant circular movement to the sides to bring them in line with his shoulder. His right hand was holding an imaginary *dumru*, a small, handheld percussion instrument. His left hand was open with its palm facing upward, almost like it was receiving some divine energy. He held this pose for some time; his glowing face indicated that Shiva was withdrawing into his inner world. His right hand then moved effortlessly forward, almost as if it had a mind of its own. Its palm was now open and facing the audience. Somehow, the posture seemed to convey a feeling of protectiveness to a very surprised Sati. Almost languidly, his left arm glided at shoulder height and came to rest with the palm facing downwards and pointing at the left foot. Shiva held this pose for some time.

And then began the dance.

Sati stared in wonder at Shiva. He was performing the same steps as her. Yet it looked like a completely different dance. His lyrical hand movements graced the mystical motion of his body.

How could a body this muscular also be so flexible? The Guru*ji* tried helplessly to get his dhol to give Shiva the beats. But clearly that wasn't necessary. As it was Shiva's feet which were leading the beat for the dhol!

The dance conveyed the various emotions of a woman. In the beginning it conveyed her feelings of joy and lust as she cavorted with her husband. The next emotion was anger and pain at the treacherous killing of her mate. Despite his rough masculine body, Shiva managed to convey the tender yet strong emotions of a grieving woman.

Shiva's eyes were open. But the audience realised that he was oblivious to them. Shiva was in his own world. He did not dance for the audience. He did not dance for appreciation. He did not dance for the music. He danced only for himself. In fact, it almost seemed like his dance was guided by a celestial force. Sati realised that Shiva was right. He had opened himself and the dance had come to him.

After what seemed like an eternity the dance came to an end, with Shiva's eyes firmly shut. He held the final pose for a long time as the glow slowly left him. It was almost as if he was returning to this world. Shiva gradually opened his eyes to find Sati, Krittika and the Guru*ji* gaping at him wonder-struck.

The Guru*ji* was the first to find his voice. 'Who are you?'

'I am Shiva.'

'No, no. Not the body. I meant who are *you*?'

Shiva crooked his eyes together in a frown and repeated, 'I am Shiva.'

'Guru*ji*, may I ask a question?' asked Sati.

'Of course you may.'

Turning to Shiva, Sati asked, 'What was that you did before the dance? Was it some kind of preparatory step?'

'Yes. It's called the *Nataraj* pose. The pose of *the Lord of dance*.'

'The Nataraj pose? What does it do?'

'It aligned my energy to the universal energy so that the dance emerges on its own.'

'I don't understand.'

'Well, it's like this: amongst our people, we believe that everything in the world is a carrier of *shakti* or *energy*. The plants, animals, objects, our bodies, everything carries and transmits energy. But the biggest carrier of energy that we are physically in touch with is Mother Earth herself — the ground that we walk on.'

'What does that have to do with your dance?'

'You need energy for everything that you do. You have to source the energy from around you. It comes from people, from objects, from Mother Earth herself. You have to ask for it respectfully.'

'And your Nataraj pose helps you to access any energy that you want?' asked the Guru*ji*.

'It depends on what I want the energy for. The Nataraj pose helps me to ask respectfully for energy for a dance that wants to come to me. If I wanted the energy for a thought to come to me, I would have to sit cross-legged and meditate.'

'It seems that the energy favours you, young man,' said the Guru*ji*. 'You are the *Nataraj, the Lord of dance.*'

'Oh no!' exclaimed Shiva. 'I am just a medium for the boundless Nataraj energy. Anyone can be the medium.'

'Well, then you are a particularly efficient medium, young man,' said the Guru*ji*. Turning to Sati, he said, 'You don't need me if you have a friend like him, my child. If you want to be taught by Shiva, it would be my honour to excuse myself.'

Shiva looked at Sati expectantly. This had gone much better than he expected.

Say yes, dammit!

Sati however seemed to withdraw into herself. Shiva was startled to see the first signs of vulnerability in this woman. She bowed her head, an act which did not suit her proud bearing and whispered softly, 'I mean no disrespect to anyone, but perhaps I do not have the skills to receive training of this level.'

'But you do have the skill,' argued Shiva. 'You have the bearing. You have the heart. You can very easily reach that level.'

Sati looked up at Shiva, her eyes showing just the slightest hint of dampness. The profound sadness they conveyed took Shiva aback.

What the hell is going on?

'I am very far from any level, Shiva,' mumbled Sati.

As she said that, Sati found the strength to control herself again. The politely proud manner returned to her face. The mask was back. 'It is time for my puja. With your permission Guru*ji*, I must leave.' She turned towards Shiva. 'It was a pleasure meeting you again Shiva.'

Before Shiva could respond, Sati turned quickly and left, followed by Krittika.

The Guru*ji* continued to stare at a flummoxed Shiva. At length, he bent low with a formal Namaste towards Shiva and said, 'It has been my life's honour to see you dance.'

Then he too turned and left. Shiva was left wondering about the inscrutable ways of the Meluhans.

— ⋏◐ᕟ⩑⊕ —

Late in the morning the next day Shiva and Nandi entered the private royal office to find Daksha, Parvateshwar and Kanakhala waiting for them. A surprised Shiva said, 'I am sorry your Highness. I thought we were to meet four hours into the second prahar. I hope I haven't kept you waiting.'

Daksha, who had stood up with a formal Namaste, bowed low and said, 'No, my Lord. You don't need to apologise. We came in early so that we wouldn't keep you waiting. It was our honour to wait for you.'

Parvateshwar rolled his eyes at the extreme subservience that his emperor, the ruler of the greatest civilisation ever established, showed towards this barbarian. Shiva, controlling his extreme surprise at being referred to as the 'Lord' by the emperor, bowed low towards Daksha with a Namaste and sat down.

'My Lord, before I start telling you about the legend of

the Neelkanth, do you have any questions that you would like to ask?' enquired Daksha.

The most obvious question came to Shiva's mind.

Why in the holy lake's name is my blessed blue throat so important?

But his instincts told him that though this appeared to be the most obvious question, it could not be answered unless he understood more about the society of Meluha itself.

'It may sound like an unusual question your Highness,' said Shiva. 'But may I ask you what your age is?'

Daksha looked at Kanakhala with surprise. Then turning back towards Shiva with an amazed smile, he said, 'You are exceptionally intelligent my Lord. You have asked the most pertinent question first.' Crinkling his face into a conspiratorial grin, Daksha continued, 'Last month I turned one hundred and eighty four.'

Shiva was stunned. Daksha did not look a day older than thirty years. In fact nobody in Meluha looked old. Except for the Pandit that Shiva had met at the Brahma temple.

So Nandi is more than a hundred years old.

'How can this be, your Highness?' asked a flabbergasted Shiva. 'What sorcery makes this possible?'

'There is no sorcery at all my Lord,' explained Daksha. 'What makes this possible is the brilliance of our scientists who make a potion called the *Somras*, the *drink of the Gods*. Taking the Somras at defined times not only postpones our death considerably, but it also allows us to live our entire lives as if we are in the prime of our youth — mentally and physically.'

'But what is the Somras? Where does it come from? Who invented it?'

'So many questions my Lord,' smiled Daksha. 'But I will try my best to answer them one by one. The Somras was invented many thousands of years ago by one of the greatest Indian scientists that ever lived. His name was Lord Brahma.'

'I think there is a temple dedicated to him that I visited on my way to Devagiri. At a place named Meru?'

'Yes my Lord. That is where he is said to have lived and worked. Lord Brahma was a prolific inventor. But he never kept any of the benefits of his inventions to himself. He was always interested in ensuring that his inventions were used for the good of mankind. He realised early on that a potion as powerful as the Somras could be misused by evil men. So he implemented an elaborate system of controls on its use.'

'What kind of controls?'

'He did not give the Somras freely to everyone,' continued Daksha. 'After conducting a rigorous country-wide survey, he chose a select group of adolescent boys of impeccable character — one from each of the seven regions of ancient India. He chose young boys so that they would live with him at his *gurukul* and he could mould their character into becoming selfless helpers of society. The Somras medicine was administered only to these boys. Since these boys were practically given an additional life due to the Somras, they came to be known as the *dwija* or *twice born*. The power of the Somras combined with the tutelage of Lord Brahma, along with their other inventions, resulted in this select group achieving a reverential status never seen before. They honed their minds to achieve almost superhuman intelligence. The ancient Indian title for men of knowledge was *Rishi*.

Since Lord Brahma's chosen men were seven in number, they came to be known as the *Saptrishi*.'

'And these Saptrishis used their skills for the good of society.'

'Yes my Lord. Lord Brahma instituted strict rules of conduct for the Saptrishis. They were not allowed to rule or to practice any trade — essentially anything that would have accrued personal gain. They had to use their skills to perform the task of priests, teachers, doctors, amongst other intellectual professions where they could use their powers to help society. They were not allowed to charge anything for their services and had to live on alms and donations from others.'

'Tough service rules,' joked Shiva with a slight wink at Parvateshwar.

Parvateshwar did not respond but Daksha, Kanakhala and Nandi guffawed loudly. Shiva took a quick look at the prahar lamp by the window. It was almost the third prahar. The time that Sati would probably come out to dance.

'But they followed their code of conduct strictly my Lord,' continued Daksha. 'Over time, as their responsibilities grew, the Saptrishis selected many more people to join their tribe. Their followers swore by the same code that the Saptrishis lived by and were also administered the Somras. They devoted their lives to the pursuit of knowledge and for the wellbeing of society without asking for any material gain in return. It is for this reason that society accorded these people almost devotional respect. Over the ages the Saptrishis and their followers came to be known as the *Tribe of Brahma* or simply, the *Brahmins*.'

'But as with all good systems over long periods of time, some people stopped following the Brahmin code, right?'

'Absolutely, my Lord,' answered Daksha, regretfully shaking his head at the familiar human frailty. 'As many millennia went by, some of the Brahmins forgot the strict code that Lord Brahma had enforced and the Saptrishis had propagated. They started misusing the awesome powers that the Somras gave them. Some Brahmins started using their influence over a large number of people to conquer kingdoms and start ruling. Some Brahmins misused other inventions of the Saptrishis as well as Lord Brahma and accumulated fabulous wealth for themselves.'

'And some of the Brahmins,' interjected Kanakhala with a particular sense of horror, 'even rebelled against the Saptrishi Uttradhikaris.'

'Saptrishi Uttradhikaris?' inquired Shiva.

'They were the *successors to the Saptrishis* my Lord,' clarified Kanakhala. 'When any of the Saptrishis knew that he was coming to the end of his mortal life, he would appoint a man from his gurukul as his successor. This successor was treated for all practical purposes like the Saptrishi himself.'

'So rebelling against the Saptrishi Uttradhikaris was like rebelling against the Saptrishis themselves?'

'Yes, my Lord,' answered Kanakhala. 'And the most worrying part of this corruption was that it was being led by the higher chosen-tribe Brahmins like the eagles, peacocks and the swans. In fact, due to their higher status, these chosen-tribes were actually not even allowed to work under the Kshatriyas and Vaishyas, lest they get enticed by the lure of the material world. Yet they succumbed to the temptations of evil before anyone else.'

'And chosen-tribes like yours, the pigeons, remained loyal to the old code despite working for the Kshatriyas?' asked Shiva.

'Yes, my Lord,' replied Kanakhala, her chest puffed up with pride.

The town bell sounded out the beginning of the third prahar. All the people in the room, including Shiva, said a quick short prayer welcoming the new time chapter. Shiva had learnt some of the ways of the Meluhans. A Shudra came in, reset the prahar lamp precisely and left as quietly as he came. Shiva reminded himself that anytime now Sati would start her dance lessons in the garden.

'So what revolution caused the change your Highness?' asked Shiva turning to Daksha. 'You, Parvateshwar and Nandi are Kshatriyas and yet you clearly have taken the Somras. In fact I have seen people of all four castes in your empire look youthful and healthy. This means that the Somras is now given to everybody. This change must have obviously happened due to a revolution, right?'

'Yes, my Lord. And the revolution was known as Lord Ram. The greatest emperor that ever lived! Jai Shri Ram!'

'Jai Shri Ram!' repeated everyone in the room.

'His ideas and leadership transformed the society of Meluha dramatically,' continued Daksha. 'In fact, the course of history itself was radically altered. But before I continue with Lord Ram's tale, may I make a suggestion?'

'Of course, your Highness.'

'It is into the third prahar now. Should we move to the dining room and have some lunch before continuing with this story?'

'I think it is an excellent idea to have lunch your Highness,' said Shiva. 'But may I be excused for some time? There is another pressing engagement that I have. Could we perhaps continue our conversation tomorrow if that is alright with you?'

Kanakhala's face fell immediately while Parvateshwar's was covered with a contemptuous grin. Daksha, however, kept a smiling face. 'Of course we could meet tomorrow my Lord. Will the beginning of the second hour of the second prahar be all right with you?'

'Absolutely, your Highness. My apologies for this inconvenience.'

'Not at all my Lord,' said an ever smiling Daksha. 'Can one of my chariots take you to your destination?'

'That's very kind of you, your Highness. But I will go there by myself. My apologies once again.'

Bidding a Namaste to everyone in the room, Shiva and Nandi walked out quickly. Kanakhala looked accusingly at Daksha. The emperor just nodded his head, gesturing with his hands for calm. 'It's all right. We are meeting tomorrow, aren't we?'

'My Lord, we are running out of time,' said Kanakhala. 'The Neelkanth needs to accept his responsibilities immediately!'

'Give him time, Kanakhala. We have waited for so long. A few days is not going to cause a collapse!'

Parvateshwar got up suddenly, bowed low towards Daksha and said, 'With your permission your Highness, may I be excused? There are more practical matters that need my attention as compared to educating a barbarian.'

'You will speak of him with respect Parvateshwar,' growled Kanakhala. 'He is the Neelkanth!'

'I will speak of him with respect only when he has earned it through some real achievements,' snarled Parvateshwar. 'I respect only achievements, nothing else. That is the fundamental rule of Lord Ram. Only your karma is important. Not your birth. Not your sex. And certainly not the colour of your throat. Our entire society is based on merit. Or have you forgotten that?'

'Enough!' exclaimed Daksha. 'I respect the Neelkanth. That means everybody will respect him!'

CHAPTER 6

Vikarma, the Carriers
of Bad Fate

Nandi waited at a distance in the garden as he had been asked to, while Shiva stepped behind the hedge that separated the dance arena from the garden. The silent dance stage had already convinced Nandi that his Lord would not find anybody there. However, Shiva was filled with hope and waited expectantly for Sati. After having waited for the larger part of an hour, Shiva realised that there would be no dance practice today. Deeply disappointed, he walked silently back to Nandi.

'Is there somebody I can help you find, my Lord?' asked an earnest Nandi.

'No Nandi. Forget it.'

Trying to change the topic, Nandi said, 'My Lord, you must be hungry. Should we go back to the guest house and eat?'

'No, I'd like to see a little more of the city,' said Shiva, hoping that fate would be kind to him and he would run into Sati in the town. 'Shall we go to one of the restaurants on the Rajat platform?'

'That would be wonderful!' smiled Nandi who hated the simple Brahmin-influenced vegetarian food served at the royal guest house. He missed the spicy meats that were served in rough Kshatriya restaurants.

— ⅄◉Ⴎ⅄⊕ —

'Yes, what is it Parvateshwar?' asked Daksha.

'My Lord, I am sorry about the sudden meeting. But I've just received some disturbing news which I must share with you in private.'

'Well, what is it?'

'Shiva is already causing trouble.'

'What have you got against the Neelkanth?' Groaned Daksha, rolling his eyes in disapproval. 'Why can't you believe that the Neelkanth has come to save us?'

'This has nothing to do with my views on Shiva, my Lord. If you will please listen to what I have to say. Chenardhwaj saw Shiva in the gardens yesterday.'

'Chenardhwaj is here already?'

'Yes your Highness. His review with you has been fixed for the day after tomorrow.'

'Anyway, so what did Chenardhwaj see?'

'He is also sickeningly taken in by the Neelkanth. So I think we can safely assume that he doesn't have any prejudice.'

'All right, I believe you. So what did he see the Neelkanth do?'

'He saw Shiva dancing in the gardens,' answered Parvateshwar.

'So? Is there a law banning dance that I am not aware of?'

'Please let me continue, your Highness. He was dancing while Sati watched in rapt attention.'

His interest suddenly aroused, Daksha leaned forward to ask, 'And?'

'Sati behaved correctly and left the moment Shiva tried to get too familiar. But Chenardhwaj heard Shiva whisper something when Sati left.'

'Well, what did he whisper?'

'He whispered — *Holy Lake, help me get her. I will not ask for anything else from you ever again!*'

Daksha appeared delighted. 'You mean the Neelkanth may actually be in love with my daughter?'

'Your Highness, you cannot forget the laws of the land,' exclaimed a horrified Parvateshwar. 'You know that Sati cannot marry.'

'If the Neelkanth decides to marry Sati, no law on earth can stop him.'

'My Lord, forgive me but the rule of law is the very foundation of our civilisation. That's what makes us who we are. Better than the Chandravanshis and the Nagas. Not even Lord Ram was above the law. Then how can this barbarian be considered so important?'

'Don't you want Sati to be happy?' asked Daksha. 'She's also called Parvati for a reason — it's because she is your Goddaughter. Don't you want her to find joy once again?'

'I love Sati like the daughter I never had, your Highness,' said Parvateshwar, with a rare display of emotion in his eyes. 'I would do anything for her. Except break the law.'

'That is the difference between you and me. For Sati's sake, I would not mind breaking any law. She is my daughter. My flesh and blood. She has suffered enough already. If I can find some way to make her happy, I will do it. No matter what the consequences!'

— 𐎹◎᚛⼻⊕ —

Shiva and Nandi tethered their horses in the parking lot next to the main Rajat platform market. Moving forward, Nandi guided Shiva towards one of his favourite restaurants. The inviting aroma of freshly cooked meat brought forth a nostalgic hunger in Nandi that had not been satisfied in the past two days at the royal guest house. The owner however stopped Shiva at the entry.

'What's the matter, brother?' asked Nandi.

'I am deeply sorry brothers. But I too am undergoing religious vows at this time,' said the restaurant owner politely, pointing to the beads around his throat. 'And you know that one of the vows is that I cannot serve meat to fellow religious vow keepers.'

Nandi blurted out in surprise, 'But who has taken religious…'

He was stopped by Shiva who signalled downwards with his eyes at the bead covered cravat around his throat. Nandi nodded and followed Shiva out of the restaurant.

'This is the time of the year for religious vows, my Lord,' explained Nandi. 'Why don't you wait on the side? There are some good restaurants on the street at the right. I will go and see if I can find a restaurant owner who has not taken his vows.'

Shiva nodded his ascent. As Nandi hurried off, Shiva looked around the street. It was a busy market area with restaurants and shops spread out evenly. But despite the large number of people and the buzz of commerce, the street was not noisy. None of the shopkeepers stepped out to scream and advertise their wares. The customers spoke softly and in an unfailingly polite manner, even if they were bargaining.

These well-mannered idiots would not be able to conduct any business in our boisterous mountain market!

Shiva, lost in his observation of the strange practices of the Meluhans, did not hear the announcement of the town crier till he was almost right behind him.

'Procession of vikarma women. Please move!'

A surprised Shiva turned to find a tall Meluhan Kshatriya looking down at him. 'Would you care to move aside, sir? A procession of vikarma women will soon pass this way for their prayers.'

The crier's tone and demeanour was unquestionably courteous. But Shiva was under no illusions. The crier was not *asking* Shiva to move. He was *telling* him. Shiva stepped back to let the procession pass as Nandi touched him gently on his arm.

'I have found a good restaurant, my Lord,' said an ecstatic Nandi. 'It serves my favourite dishes. And the kitchen is open for yet another hour. A lot of food to stuff ourselves with!'

Shiva laughed out loud. 'It's a wonder that just one restaurant can actually make enough food to satisfy your hunger!'

Nandi laughed along good naturedly as Shiva patted his friend on the back.

As they turned and walked into the lane, Shiva asked, 'Who are vikarma women?'

'Vikarma people, my Lord,' said Nandi sighing deeply,

'are people who have been punished in this birth for the sins of their previous birth. Hence they have to live this life out with dignity and tolerate their present sufferings with grace. This is the only way they can wipe their karma clean of the sins of their previous births. Vikarma men have their own order of penance and women have their own order.'

'There was a procession of vikarma women on the road we just left. Is their puja a part of the order?' asked Shiva.

'Yes, my Lord. There are many rules that the vikarma women have to follow. They have to pray for forgiveness every month to Lord Agni, the purifying Fire God, through a specifically mandated puja. They are not allowed to marry since they may contaminate others with their bad fate. They are not allowed to touch any person who is not related to them or is not part of their daily life. There are many other conditions as well that I am not completely aware of. If you are interested, we could meet up with a Pandit at the Agni temple later and he could tell you all about vikarma people.'

'No, I am not interested in meeting the Pandit right now,' said Shiva with a smile. 'He might just bore me with some very confusing and abstruse philosophies! But tell me one thing. Who decides that the vikarma people had committed sins in their previous birth?'

'Their own karma, my Lord,' said Nandi, his eyes suggesting the obvious. 'For example if a woman gives birth to a still born child, why would she be punished thus unless she had committed some terrible sin in her previous birth? Or if a man suddenly contracts an incurable disease and gets paralysed, why would it happen to him unless the universe was penalising him for the sins of his previous life?'

'That sounds pretty ridiculous to me. A woman could have given birth to a still born child simply because she did not take proper care while she was pregnant. Or it could just be a disease. How can anyone say that she is being punished for the sins of her previous birth?'

Nandi, shocked by Shiva's statements, struggled to find words to respond. He was a Meluhan and deeply believed in the concept of karma being carried over many births. He mumbled softly, 'It's the law, my Lord…'

'Well, to be honest, it sounds like a rather unfair law to me.'

Nandi's crestfallen face showed that he was profoundly disappointed that Shiva did not understand such a fundamental concept of Meluha. But he also kept his own counsel for fear of opposing what Shiva said. After all, Shiva was his Lord.

Seeing a dejected Nandi, Shiva patted him gently on the back. 'Nandi, that was just my opinion. If the law works for your people, I am sure there must be some logic to it. Your society might be a little strange at times, but it has some of the most honest and decent people I have ever met.'

As a smile returned almost instantly to Nandi's face, his whole being was stricken by his immediate problem. His debilitating hunger! He entered the restaurant like a man on a mission, with Shiva chuckling softly behind.

A short distance away on the main road, the procession of vikarma women walked silently on. They were all draped in long angvastrams which were dyed in the holy blue colour. Their heads were bowed low in penitence, their *puja thalis* or *prayer plates* full of offerings to Lord Agni. The normally quiet market street became almost deathly silent as the pitiful women lumbered by. At the centre of the procession, unseen by Shiva, with her head bowed low, draped in a blue angvastram that covered her from head to toe, her face a picture of resigned dignity, trudged the forlorn figure of Sati.

— ⵊⵔⵓⵔⵓ⊕ —

'So where were we, my Lord?' said Daksha, as Shiva and Nandi settled down in his private office the next morning.

'We were about to discuss the changes that Lord Ram brought about, your Highness. And how he defeated the rebellion of the renegade Brahmins,' answered Shiva.

'That's right,' said Daksha. 'Lord Ram did defeat the renegade Brahmins. But in his view, the core problem ran deeper. It wasn't just a matter of some Brahmins not following the code. There was a conflict between a person's natural karma and what society forced him to do.'

'I don't understand your Highness.'

'Let me explain. Do you know what was the essential problem with the renegade Brahmins? Some of them wanted to be Kshatriyas and rule. Some of them wanted to be Vaishyas, make money and live a life of luxury. However, their birth confined them to being Brahmins.'

'But I thought that Lord Brahma had decreed that people became Brahmins through a competitive examination process,' said Shiva.

'That is true my Lord. But over time this process of selection lost its fairness. Children of Brahmins became Brahmins. Children of Kshatriyas became Kshatriyas and so on. The formal system of selection soon ceased to exist. A father would ensure that his children got all the resources and support needed to grow up and become a member of his own caste. So the caste system became rigid.'

'Did that also mean that there could have been a person talented enough to be a Brahmin but if he was born to Shudra parents, he would not get the opportunity to become a Brahmin?' asked Shiva.

'Yes Shiva,' said Parvateshwar, speaking for the first time to Shiva. He noticed that Parvateshwar did not fawn all over him and call him Lord. 'In Lord Ram's view, any society that conducted itself on any principle besides merit could not be stable. He believed that a person's caste should be determined *only by that person's karma*. Not his birth. Not his sex. No other consideration should interfere.'

'That is nice in theory, Parvateshwar,' argued Shiva. 'But how do you ensure it in practice? If a child is born in a Brahmin family, he would get the upbringing and resources which would be different from that of a child born in a Shudra family. So this child would grow up to be a Brahmin even if he was less talented than the Shudra boy. Isn't this unfair to the child born in the Shudra family? Where is the "merit" in this system?'

'That was the genius of Lord Ram, Shiva,' smiled Parvateshwar. 'He was of course a brave General, a brilliant administrator and a fair judge. But his greatest legacy is the system he created to ensure that a person's karma is determined only by his abilities, nothing else. That system is what has made Meluha what it is — the greatest nation in history.'

'You can't underestimate the role that Somras has played, Parvateshwar,' said Daksha. 'Lord Ram's greatest act was to provide the Somras to everyone. The elixir is what makes Meluhans the smartest people in the universe! The Somras is what has given us the ability to create this remarkable and near perfect society.'

'Begging your pardon, your Highness,' said Shiva before turning back to Parvateshwar. 'But what was the system that Lord Ram set up?'

'The system is simple,' said Parvateshwar. 'As we agreed, the best society is the one where a person's caste is decided purely by his abilities and karma. Not by any other factor. Lord Ram created a practical system that ensured this. All children that are born in Meluha are compulsorily adopted by the empire. In order to ensure that this is done methodically, a great hospital city called Maika was built deep in the south, just north of the Narmada river. All pregnant women have to travel there for their delivery. Only pregnant women are allowed into the city. Nobody else.'

'Nobody else? What about her husband, her parents?' asked Shiva.

'No, there are no exceptions to this rule except for one. This exception was voted in around three hundred years ago. Husbands and parents of women of noble families were allowed to enter,' answered Parvateshwar, his expression clearly showing that he violently disagreed with this corruption of Lord Ram's system.

'Then who takes care of the pregnant woman in Maika?'

'The hospital staff. They are extremely well trained,' continued Parvateshwar. 'Once the child is born, he or she is kept in Maika for a few weeks while the mother travels back to her own city.'

'Without her child?' asked a clearly surprised Shiva.

'Yes,' replied Parvateshwar, with a slight frown as if this

was the most obvious thing in the world. 'The child is then put into the Meluha Gurukul, a massive school created by the empire close to Maika. Every single child receives the benefit of the same education system. They grow up with all the resources of the empire available to them.'

'Do they maintain records of the parents and their children?'

'Of course they do. But the records are kept in utmost secrecy and are available only with the record-keeper of Maika.'

'That would mean that neither in the Gurukul nor in the rest of the empire, would anybody know who the child's birth parents are,' reasoned Shiva, as he worked out the implications of what he was hearing. 'So every child, regardless of whether he is born to a Brahmin or a Shudra, would get exactly the same treatment at the Gurukul?'

'Yes,' smiled Parvateshwar. He was clearly proud of the system. 'As the children enter the age of adolescence, they are all given the Somras. Thus every child has exactly the same opportunity to succeed. At the age of fifteen, when they have reached adulthood, all the children take a comprehensive examination. The results of this examination decide which varna or caste the child will be allocated to — Brahmin, Kshatriya, Vaishya or Shudra.'

Kanakhala cut in. 'And then the children are given one more year's caste-specific training. They wear their varna colour bands — white for Brahmins, red for Kshatriyas, green for Vaishyas and black for Shudras — and retreat to the respective caste schools to complete their education.'

'So that's why your caste system is called the varna system,' said Shiva. '*Varna* means *colour*, right?'

'Yes my Lord,' smiled Kanakhala. 'You are very observant.'

With a withering look at Kanakhala, Parvateshwar added sarcastically, 'Yes, that was a very difficult conclusion to draw.'

Ignoring the barb, Shiva asked, 'So what happens after that?'

'When the children turn sixteen, they are allocated to applicant parents from their caste. For example, if some Brahmin parents have applied to adopt a child, one randomly chosen student from Maika, who has won the Brahmin caste in the examination, is allotted to them. Then the child grows up with these adopted parents as their own child.'

'And society is perfect,' marvelled Shiva, as the simple brilliance of the system enveloped his mind. 'Each person is given a position in society based only on his own abilities. The efficiency and fairness of this system is astounding!'

'Over time my Lord,' interjected Daksha, 'we found the percentage of higher castes actually going up in the population. Which means that everybody in the world has the ability to excel. All it takes is for a child to be given a fair chance to succeed.'

'Then the lower castes must have loved Lord Ram for this?' asked Shiva. 'He gave them an actual chance to succeed.'

'Yes they did love him,' answered Parvateshwar. 'They were his most loyal followers. Jai Shri Ram!'

'But I guess not too many mothers would have been happy with this. I can't imagine a woman willingly giving up her child as soon as he is born with no chance of meeting him ever again.'

'But it's for the larger good,' said Parvateshwar, scowling at the seemingly stupid question. 'And in any case, every mother who wants an offspring can apply for one and be allocated a child who suits her position and dreams. Nothing can be worse for a mother than having a child who does not measure up to her expectations.'

Shiva frowned at Parvateshwar's explanation, but let the argument pass. 'I can also imagine that many of the upper castes like the Brahmins would have been unhappy with Lord Ram. After all, they lost their stranglehold on power.'

'Yes,' added Daksha. 'Many upper castes did oppose Lord Ram's reforms. Not just Brahmins, but even Kshatriyas and Vaishyas. Lord Ram fought a great battle to defeat them. Those from among the vanquished who survived are the Chandravanshis we see today.'

'So your differences go that far back?'

'Yes,' said Daksha. 'The Chandravanshis are corrupt and disgusting people. No morals. No ethics. They are the source of all our problems. Some of us believe that Lord Ram was too kind. He should have completely destroyed them. But he forgave them and let them live. In fact, we have to face the mortification of seeing the Chandravanshis rule over Lord Ram's birthplace — Ayodhya!'

Before Shiva could react to this information, the bell of the new prahar was rung. Everyone said a quick prayer to welcome the subsequent time chapter. Shiva immediately looked towards the window. A look of expectancy appeared on his face.

Daksha smiled as he observed Shiva's expression. 'We could break for lunch now, my Lord. But if you have another engagement you would like to attend, we could continue tomorrow.'

Parvateshwar glared at Daksha disapprovingly. He knew exactly what the emperor was trying to do.

'That would be nice, your Highness,' smiled Shiva. 'Is my face such a giveaway?'

'Yes it is my Lord. But that is a gift you have. Nothing is prized more than honesty in Meluha. Why don't you leave for your engagement and we could convene here again tomorrow morning?'

Thanking Daksha profusely, Shiva left the room with Nandi in tow.

— 人◎∪♀⊛ —

Shiva approached the hedge with excitement and trepidation. Scarce had he heard the beat of the dhol emanating from the direction of the garden, he despatched Nandi to the guest house for lunch. He wanted to be alone. He let out a deep sigh of ecstasy as he crept up behind the hedge to find Sati practising under the watchful eye of the Guru*ji* and Krittika.

'So good to see you again, Shiva,' said the Guru*ji* as he stood up with a formal Namaste.

'The pleasure is all mine, Guru*ji*,' said Shiva, as he bent down to touch the Guru*ji*'s feet as a sign of respect.

Sati stood silently at a distance with her gaze on the floor. Krittika said enthusiastically, 'I just couldn't get your dance out of my mind!'

Shiva blushed at the compliment. 'Oh it wasn't all that good.'

'Now you're fishing for compliments,' teased Krittika.

'I was wondering if we could start off where we left the last time,' said Shiva, turning towards Sati. 'I don't think I have to be your teacher or anything like that. I just wanted to see you dance.'

Sati felt her strange discomfort returning once again. What was it about Shiva that made her feel that she was breaking the law when she spoke to him? She was allowed to talk to men as long as she kept a respectable distance. Why should she feel guilty?

'I will try my best,' said Sati formally. 'It would be enriching to hear your views on how I can improve myself. I really do respect you for your dancing skills.'

Respect?! Why respect? Why not love?!

Shiva smiled politely. He knew instinctively that saying anything at this point of time would spoil the moment.

Sati took a deep breath, girded her angvastram around her waist and committed herself to the Nataraj pose. Shiva smiled as he felt Mother Earth project her *shakti*, her *energy*, into Sati.

Energised by the earth she stood upon, Sati began her dance. And she had really improved. The emotions seemed to course through her. She had always been technically good, but the passion elevated her dance to the next level. Shiva felt a dreamy sense of unreality overcome him again. Sati maintained a magnetic hold over him as she moved her lithe body with the dance steps. For some moments, Shiva imagined that he was the man that Sati was longing for in her dance. When she finally came to a stop, the audience spontaneously applauded.

'That was the best I have ever seen you dance,' said the Guru*ji* with pride.

'Thank you Guru*ji*,' said Sati as she bowed. Then she looked expectantly at Shiva.

'It was fantastic,' exclaimed Shiva. 'Absolutely fabulous. Didn't I tell you that you had it in you?'

'I thought that I didn't get it exactly right at the moment of attack,' said Sati critically.

'You're being too hard on yourself,' consoled Shiva. 'That was just a slight error. It happened only because you missed out on holding one angle at your elbow. That made your next move a little odd.' Rising swiftly to his feet, Shiva continued, 'See, I'll show you.'

He walked quickly towards Sati and touched her elbow to move it to the correct angle. Sati immediately recoiled in horror as there was a gasp from the Guru*ji* as well as Krittika. Shiva instantly realised that something terrible had happened.

'I am sorry,' said Shiva, with a look of sincere regret. 'I was just trying to show you where your elbow should be.'

Sati continued to stare at Shiva, stunned into immobility.

The Guru*ji* was the first to recover his wits and realise that Shiva must undergo *the purification ceremony*. 'Go to your Pandit, Shiva. Tell him you need a *shudhikaran*. Go before the day is over.'

'What? What is a shudhikaran? Why would I need it?'

'Please go for a shudhikaran, Shiva,' said Sati, as tears broke through her proud eyes. 'I would never be able to forgive myself if something were to happen to you.'

'Nothing will happen to me! Look, I am really sorry if I have broken some rule by touching you. I will not do it again. Let's not make a big deal of this.'

'IT IS A BIG DEAL!' shouted Sati.

The violence of Sati's reaction threw Shiva off balance. *Why the hell is this simple thing being blown completely out of proportion?*

Krittika came up close to Sati while being careful not to touch her, and whispered, 'We should go back home, my lady.'

'No. No. Please stay,' pleaded Shiva. 'I won't touch you. I promise.'

With a look of hopeless despair, Sati turned to leave, followed by Krittika and Guru*ji*. At the edge of the hedge, she turned around and beseeched Shiva once again, 'Please go for your shudhikaran before nightfall. Please.'

At the look of uncomprehending mutiny on Shiva's face, the Guru*ji* advised, 'Listen to her, Shiva. She speaks for your own good.'

$$- \text{入} \odot \text{Ⴎ} \text{�} \oplus -$$

'What bloody nonsense!' yelled Shiva as his disturbed thoughts finally broke through his desperate efforts at silent acceptance. He was lying in his bedroom at the royal guest house. He had not undergone the shudhikaran. He had not even bothered to find out what the ceremony was.

Why would I need to be purified for touching Sati? I want to spend all my remaining years touching her in every possible way. Am I going to keep on undergoing a shudhikaran every day? Ridiculous!

Just then a troubling thought entered Shiva's mind.

Is it because of me? Am I not allowed to touch her because I am caste-unmarked? An inferior barbarian?

'No. That can't be true,' whispered Shiva to himself. 'Sati doesn't think like that. She is a good woman.'

But what if it's true? Maybe if she knows that I am the Neelkanth…

CHAPTER 7

Lord Ram's Unfinished Task

'You seem to be a little distracted this morning, my Lord. Are you alright?' asked a concerned Daksha.

'Hmm?' said Shiva as he looked up. 'I'm sorry your Highness. I was a little distracted.'

Daksha looked at Kanakhala with a concerned expression. He had seen a similar look of despair on Sati's face at dinner the previous night. But she had refused to say anything.

'Do you want to meet later?' asked Daksha.

'Of course not, your Highness. It's alright. My apologies. Please continue,' said Shiva.

'Well,' continued a concerned Daksha, 'we were talking about the changes that Lord Ram brought about in society.'

'Yes,' said Shiva, shaking his head slightly to get the disturbing image of Sati's last plea out of his mind.

'The Maika system worked fantastically well. Our society boomed. Ours was always one of the wealthiest lands on earth. But in the last one thousand two hundred years we have shot dramatically ahead of everyone else. Meluha has become the richest and most powerful country in the world by far. Our citizens lead ideal lives. There is no crime. People do what they are suited for and not what an unfair social order would compel them to do. We don't force or fight unprovoked wars with any other country. In fact, ours has become a perfect society.'

'Yes, your Highness,' agreed Shiva, slowly getting into the conversation. 'I don't believe that perfection can ever be achieved. It is more of a journey than a destination. But your society is certainly a near perfect society.'

'Why do you think we are not perfect?' argued Parvateshwar aggressively.

'Do you think it is perfect Parvateshwar?' asked Shiva politely. 'Is everything in Meluha exactly the way Lord Ram would have mandated?'

Parvateshwar fell silent. He knew the obvious, even if he didn't like the answer.

'The Lord is right Parvateshwar,' said Daksha. 'There are always things to improve.'

'Having said that, your Highness,' spoke Shiva, 'your society is wonderful. Things do seem very well ordered. What doesn't make sense to me then, is why you and your people are so concerned about the future. What is the problem? Why is a Neelkanth required? I don't see anything that is so obviously wrong that disaster would be just a breath away. This is not like my homeland where there are so many problems that you wouldn't know where to begin!'

'My Lord, a Neelkanth is needed because we are faced with challenges that we cannot confront. We keep to ourselves and let other countries lead their lives. We trade with other societies but we never interfere with them. We don't allow uninvited foreigners into Meluha beyond the frontier towns. So we think it's only fair that other societies leave us alone to lead our lives the way we want to.'

'And presumably they don't, your Highness?'

'No they don't.'

'Why?'

'One simple word, my Lord,' replied Daksha. 'Jealousy. They hate our superior ways. Our efficient family system is an eyesore to them. The fact that we take care of everyone in our country makes them unhappy because they can't take care of themselves. They lead sorry lives. And rather than improving themselves, they want to pull us down to their level.'

'I can understand. My tribe used to face a lot of jealousy in Mount Kailash since we had control over the shore of the Mansarovar Lake and hence the best land in the region. But sometimes I wonder if we could have avoided bloodshed if we had shared our good fortune more willingly.'

'But we do share our good fortune with those who wish to, my Lord. And yet, jealousy blinds our enemies. The Chandravanshis realised that it was the Somras that guaranteed our superiority. Funnily enough, even they have the knowledge of the Somras. But they have not learnt to mass produce it like we do and hence haven't reaped all its benefits.'

'Sorry to interrupt, your Highness, but where is the Somras produced?'

'It is produced at a secret location called Mount Mandar. The Somras powder is manufactured there and then distributed throughout the Meluhan empire. At select temples specially trained Brahmins prepare the solution with water and other ingredients and then administer it to the population.'

'Alright,' said Shiva.

'The Chandravanshis could not become as powerful as us since they did not have enough Somras. Eaten up with jealousy, they devised a devious plan to destroy the Somras and hence us. One of the key ingredients in the Somras is the waters of the Saraswati. Water from any other source does not work.'

'Really? Why?'

'We don't know my Lord. The scientists can't explain it. But only the waters of the Saraswati will do. That is why, the Chandravanshis tried to kill the Saraswati to harm us.'

'Kill the river?' asked Shiva incredulously.

'Yes my Lord!' said Daksha, as his childlike eyes flared with indignation at the Chandravanshi perfidy. 'The Saraswati is formed by the confluence of two mighty rivers up north — the Sutlej and the Yamuna. In an earlier era the course of the Sutlej and the Yamuna was considered neutral territory, from which both the Chandravanshis as well as the Suryavanshis drew water for the Somras.'

'But how did they try to kill the Saraswati your Highness?'

'They diverted the course of the Yamuna so that instead of flowing south, it started flowing east to meet their main river, Ganga.'

'You can do that?' asked Shiva in amazement. 'Change the course of a river?'

'Yes, of course you can,' answered Parvateshwar.

'We were livid,' interjected Daksha. 'But we still gave them an opportunity to make amends for their duplicity.'

'And?'

'What can you expect from the Chandravanshis, my Lord?' said Daksha in disgust. 'They denied any knowledge of this. They claimed that the river made such a dramatic change in its course all by itself, due to some minor earthquake. And even worse, they claimed that since the river had changed course of its own accord, we Meluhans would simply have to accept what was essentially God's will!'

'We of course refused to do that,' said Parvateshwar. 'Under the leadership of King Brahmanayak, his Highness' father, we attacked Swadweep.'

'The land of the Chandravanshis?' asked Shiva.

'Yes Shiva,' said Parvateshwar. 'And it was a resounding victory. The Chandravanshi army was routed. King Brahmanayak magnanimously let them keep their lands and even their system of governance. We didn't even demand any war reparations or a yearly tribute. The only term of the surrender treaty was the return of the Yamuna. We restored the Yamuna to her original course which eventually met with the Saraswati.'

'Did you fight in that war, Parvateshwar?'

'Yes,' said Parvateshwar, his chest swollen with pride. 'I was a mere soldier then. But I did fight in that war.'

Turning to Daksha, Shiva asked, 'Then what is the problem now, your Highness? Your enemy was comprehensively defeated. Then why is the Saraswati still dying?'

'We believe that the Chandravanshis are up to something once again. We don't understand it as yet. After their defeat, the area between our two countries was converted into a no-man's land and the jungle has reclaimed it. This includes the early course of the Yamuna as well. We have stuck to our part of the agreement and have never disturbed that region. It appears that they haven't honoured their end of the bargain.'

'Are you sure about that your Highness? Has the

area been checked? Has this been discussed with the Chandravanshis' representative in your empire?'

'Are you trying to say that we are lying?' countered Parvateshwar. 'True Suryavanshis don't lie!'

'Parvateshwar!' scolded Daksha angrily. 'The Lord was not implying any such thing.'

'Listen to me, Parvateshwar,' said Shiva politely. 'If I have learnt one thing from the pointless battles of my land, it is that wars should be the last resort. If there is an alternative available what is the harm in saving some young soldier's life? Surely, a mother would bless us for it.'

'Let's not fight! Wonderful! What a great saviour we have!' Parvateshwar muttered under his breath.

'You have something to say Parvateshwar?' barked Kanakhala. 'I have told you before. You will not insult the Neelkanth in my presence!'

'I don't take orders from you,' growled Parvateshwar.

'Enough!' ordered Daksha. Turning to Shiva, he continued, 'I am sorry my Lord. You are right. We shouldn't just declare war without being sure. That is why I have avoided a war until now. But just look at the facts. The flow of the Saraswati has been gradually waning for the last half century.'

'And the last few years have been horrible,' said Kanakhala as she controlled her tears at the thought of the slow death of the river most Meluhans regarded as a mother. 'The Saraswati doesn't even reach the sea now and ends in an inland delta just south of Rajasthan.'

'And the Somras cannot be made without water from the Saraswati,' continued Daksha. 'The Chandravanshis are aware of this and that is why they are trying to kill her.'

'What does the Swadweep representative have to say about it? Has he been questioned?'

'We have no diplomatic relations with Swadweep, my Lord,' said Daksha.

'Really? I thought having representatives of other countries was one of your innovative systems. It gives you an opportunity to understand them and maybe avoid jumping into a war. I had heard of a diplomatic mission from Mesopotamia coming in two days ago. Then why not have this with Swadweep as well?'

'You don't know them, my Lord. They are untrustworthy people. No follower of the Suryavanshi way of life will sully his soul by even speaking to a Chandravanshi willingly.'

Shiva frowned but didn't say anything.

'You don't know the levels they have sunk to my Lord. Over the last few years they have even started using the cursed Nagas in their terrorist attacks on us!' said Kanakhala, with a disgusted look.

'Terrorist attacks?'

'Yes, my Lord,' said Daksha. 'Their defeat kept them quiet for many decades. And because of our overwhelming victory in the previous war, they now believe that they cannot overpower us in an open confrontation. So they have resorted to a form of assault that only repulsive people like them can be capable of. Terrorist attacks.'

'I don't understand. What exactly do they do?'

'They send small bands of assassins who launch surprise attacks on non-military but public places. Their idea is to attack non-combatants — the Brahmins, Vaishyas or Shudras. They try to devastate places like temples, public baths — areas that might not have soldiers who can fight back — but whose destruction will wreck the empire's morale and spread terror.'

'That's disgusting! Even the Pakratis in my land, a bunch of complete barbarians, would not do that,' said Shiva.

'Yes,' said Parvateshwar. 'These Chandravanshis don't fight like men. They fight like cowards!'

'Then why don't you attack their country? Finish this once and for all.'

'We would like to my Lord,' said Daksha. 'But I am not sure we can defeat them.'

Shiva observed Parvateshwar seething silently at the insult to his army, before turning towards Daksha. 'Why, your Highness? You have a well trained and efficient force. I am sure your army can defeat them.'

'Two reasons, my Lord. Firstly, we are outnumbered. We were outnumbered even a hundred years back. But not by a very significant margin. Today, we estimate that they have a population of more than eighty million as compared to our eight million. They can put up a much larger army against ours — their sheer numbers will cancel out our technological superiority.'

'But why should your population be less? You have people who live beyond the age of two hundred years! Your population should be higher.'

'Sociological causes, my Lord,' said Daksha. 'Our country is rich. Children are a matter of choice, and not a duty. Parents adopt children from the Maika system in small numbers, may be one or two, so that they can devote more attention to their upbringing. Fewer mothers are giving birth at Maika as well. In Swadweep the children of the poor are often treated as mere bonded labour meant only to supplement the family income. Resultantly, the whole country, though deprived, has a large population.'

'And the second reason for avoiding war?'

'The second reason is something that is under our control. We fight in accordance with "rules of war", with norms and ethics. The Chandravanshis do no such thing. And I fear this is a weakness in us that our ruthless enemies can exploit.'

'Rules of war?' asked Shiva.

'Yes. For example, we will not attack an unarmed man. A better-armed person like a cavalry man will not attack a lesser-armed person like a spear wielding foot-soldier. A swordsman will never attack a person below his waist because that is unethical. The Chandravanshis don't care for such niceties. They will attack whoever and however they find expedient to ensure victory.'

'Begging your pardon, your Highness,' said Parvateshwar. 'But that difference is what makes us who we are. Like Lord Ram had said, a person's character is not tested in good times. It is only in bad times that a person shows how steadfast he is to his dharma.'

'But Parvateshwar,' sighed Daksha. 'We are not under attack by people who are as ethical and decent as we are. Our way of life is under assault. If we don't fight back in any which way we can, we will lose.'

'My apologies once again, your Highness,' said Parvateshwar. 'I have never said that we should not fight back. I am eager to attack. I have been asking repeatedly for permission to declare war on the Chandravanshis. But if we fight without our rules, our codes, our ethics, then "our way of life" is as good as destroyed. And the Chandravanshis would have won without even fighting us!'

The conversation came to a halt with the ringing of the prahar town bell, as everyone said a quick prayer. Shiva turned towards the window, wondering if Sati would be dancing today.

Daksha turned to Shiva expectantly. 'Do you need to leave my Lord?'

'No, your Highness,' said Shiva, hiding the pain and confusion he felt inside. 'I don't believe I am expected anywhere at this point in time.'

Daksha's smile disappeared along with his hopes, on hearing this. Shiva continued, 'If it is alright with you, your Highness, may we continue our conversation? Perhaps we can delay our lunch a little.'

'Of course we may, my Lord,' smiled Daksha, pulling himself together.

'I have got the story so far, your Highness. Whereas I can understand your reasons for not wanting to attack right now, I can also see that you clearly have a plan, in which my blue throat has some strange role to play.'

'Yes, we do have a plan, my Lord. I feel that as an emperor, my giving in unthinkingly to the righteous anger of some of our people will not solve our problem. I believe that the people of Swadweep themselves are not evil. It is their Chandravanshi rulers and their way of life that has made them evil. The only way forward for us is to save the Swadweepans themselves.'

'Save the Swadweepans?' asked Shiva, genuinely surprised.

'Yes, my Lord. Save them from the evil philosophy that infects their soul. Save them from their treacherous rulers. Save them from their sorry, meaningless existence. And we can do this by giving them the benefits of the superior

Suryavanshi way of life. Once they become like us, there will be no reason to fight. We will live like brothers. This is the unfinished task of my father, King Brahmanayak. In fact, it is the unfinished task of Lord Ram.'

'That is a big task to take on, your Highness,' said Shiva. 'It is sweeping in its kindness and reason. But it is a very big task. You will need soldiers to defeat their army and missionaries to bring them to your side. It is not going to be easy.'

'I agree. There are many in my empire who have concerns about even attacking Swadweep, and I am putting forth a much bigger challenge to them, of reforming Swadweep. That is why I did not want to launch this without the Neelkanth, my Lord.'

Shiva remembered his uncle's words, spoken many years ago, in what was almost another life. *Your destiny lies beyond the mountains. Whether you fulfil it or run away once again, is up to you.*

As Daksha resumed speaking, Shiva refocused his attention on him.

'The problems that we are facing were prophesied, my Lord,' continued Daksha. 'Lord Ram had himself said that any philosophy, no matter how perfect, works only for a finite period. That is the law of nature and cannot be avoided. But what the legends also tell us is that when the problems become insurmountable for ordinary men, the Neelkanth will appear. And that he will destroy the evil Chandravanshis and restore the forces of good. My Lord, you are the Neelkanth. You can save us. You can complete the unfinished task of Lord Ram. You must lead us and help us defeat the Chandravanshis. You must rally the Swadweepans to the side of good. Otherwise I fear that this beautiful country that we have, the near perfect society of Meluha, will be destroyed by endless wars. Will you help us my Lord? Will you lead us?'

Shiva was confused. 'But I don't understand, your Highness. What exactly would I do?'

'I don't know, my Lord. We only know our goal and that you will be our leader. The path we take is up to you.'

They want me to destroy the entire way of life of eighty million people all by myself! Are they mad?

Shiva spoke carefully. 'I empathise with your people and their hardships, your Highness. But to be quite honest, I don't really understand how one man can make a difference.'

'If that man is you my Lord,' said Daksha, his moist eyes opened wide in devotion and faith, 'he can change the entire universe.'

'I am not so sure about that, your Highness,' said Shiva with a weak smile. 'What difference will I make? I am no miracle worker. I cannot snap my fingers and cause bolts of lightning to descend upon the Chandravanshis.'

'It is your presence itself that will make the difference, my Lord. I invite you to travel through the empire. See the effect your blue throat has on the people. Once my people believe that they can do it, they will be able to do it!'

'You are the Neelkanth, my Lord,' added Kanakhala. 'The people have faith in the bearer of the blue throat. They will have faith in you. Will you help us, my Lord?'

Will you run away once again?

'But how do you know that my blue throat makes me the genuine Neelkanth?' asked Shiva. 'For all you know, there may be many Meluhans with a blue throat waiting to be discovered!'

'No, my Lord,' said Daksha. 'It cannot be a Meluhan. The legend says that the Neelkanth will be a foreigner. He cannot be from the Sapt-Sindhu. And that his throat will turn blue when he drinks the Somras.'

Shiva did not answer. He looked stunned as truth suddenly dawned upon him.

Srinagar. The first night. Somras. That's how my body got repaired. That's why I'm feeling stronger than ever.

Daksha and Kanakhala looked at Shiva breathlessly, waiting for his decision. Praying for his *right* decision.

But why only me? All the Gunas were given the Somras. Was my uncle right? Do I really have a prophesied destiny?

Parvateshwar stared at Shiva with narrowed eyes.

I don't deserve a prophetic destiny. But maybe this is my chance to redeem myself.

But first...

Shiva asked with controlled politeness, 'Your Highness, before I answer, may I ask you a question?'

'Of course, my Lord.'

'Do you agree that honesty is required to make any friendship work? Even if it means deeply offending your friend with the truth?'

'Yes, of course,' replied Daksha, wondering where Shiva was going with this.

'Complete honesty is not just the bedrock of an individual relationship, but of any stable society,' interjected Parvateshwar.

'I couldn't agree more,' said Shiva. 'And yet, Meluha wasn't honest with me.'

Nobody said anything.

Shiva continued in a courteous, but firm tone. 'When my tribe was invited to Meluha, we were under the impression that you needed immigrants to build a work force. And I was happy to escape my benighted land. But now I realise that you were systematically searching for the Neelkanth.'

Turning to Nandi, Shiva said, 'We weren't told that a medicine called the Somras would be administered to us as soon as we entered. We weren't told that the medicine would have such effects.'

Nandi looked down with guilty eyes. His Lord had the right to be angry with him.

Turning to Daksha, Shiva continued, 'Your Highness, you know that the Somras was probably administered to me on my first night in Kashmir, without my knowledge.'

'I am truly sorry for that act of perfidy My Lord,' replied Daksha with folded hands and downcast eyes. 'It's something that I will always be ashamed of. But the stakes were too high for us. And the Somras has considerable positive effects on one's body. It causes no harm.'

'I know. I am not exactly upset about having to live a long and healthy life,' said Shiva wryly. 'Do you know that my tribe was also probably given the Somras that night? And they fell seriously ill, perhaps because of the Somras.'

'They were under no risk my Lord,' said Kanakhala apologetically. 'Some people are predisposed towards certain diseases. When the Somras enters the body, it triggers the immediate occurrence of these diseases, which when cured, never recur. Hence, the body remains healthy till death. Your tribe is actually much healthier now.'

'No doubt they are,' said Shiva. 'That is not the point. Both my tribe and I are the better for it. Yet I hardly expected such deceit in the land of Lord Ram. You should have told us the complete truth at Mount Kailash. Then you should have let *us* make an informed choice rather than *you* making it for us. We probably would still have come to Meluha anyway but then it would have been *our* choice.'

'Please forgive us the deception, my Lord,' said Daksha, with guilty regret. 'It is not our way to do something like this. We pride ourselves on our honesty. But we had no choice. We are truly sorry, my Lord. Your people are well taken care of. They are healthier than ever. They will live long, productive lives.'

Parvateshwar finally broke his silence, speaking about what had always been in his heart ever since the search had begun many decades ago. 'Shiva, we are truly sorry about what has been done. You have every right to be angry. Lying is not our way. I think what was done is appalling and Lord Ram would never have condoned this. Deception is the instrument of the weak and even extenuating circumstances can provide no excuse. I am deeply sorry.'

Shiva raised his eyebrow a bit.

Parvateshwar is the only one apologising instead of making excuses. He is a true follower of the great king Ram.

Shiva smiled.

Daksha let out an audible sigh of relief.

Shiva turned towards Daksha. 'Let us put this in the past, your Highness. Like I said, there are some things about your nation that could be improved. No doubt about that. But it is amongst the best societies that I have seen. And it *is* worth fighting for. But I have a few conditions.'

'Of course, my Lord,' said Daksha, eager to please.

'At this point of time, I am not saying that I can perform the tasks that you expect of me nor am I saying that I cannot do it. All I am saying is that I will try my best. But to begin with, I want to spend some more time understanding your society before I can be sure of how I can help. I am assuming that from now on nothing will be hidden from me nor will I be misled.'

'Of course, my Lord.'

'Secondly, you still need immigrants to expand your population. But you should not mislead them. I think that you should tell them the entire truth about Meluha and let them make an informed decision on whether they want to come here. Or you don't invite them at all. Is that fair?'

'Of course it is, my Lord,' said Daksha. Nodding briefly towards Kanakhala, he committed, 'We will implement that immediately.'

'Furthermore, it is clear to me that I am not going back to Kashmir. Can my tribe, the Gunas, be brought to Devagiri? I would like them to be with me.'

'Of course, my Lord,' said Daksha with a quick look at Kanakhala. 'Instructions will be sent today itself to bring them to Devagiri.'

'Also, I would like to visit the location where you manufacture the Somras. I would like to understand this drink of the Gods. Something tells me that it is important to do so.'

'Of course you may, my Lord,' said Daksha, his face finally breaking into a nervous smile. 'Kanakhala will take you there tomorrow itself. I too will be there along with my family for a scheduled puja at the temple of Lord Brahma. Perhaps we could meet.'

'That would be nice,' said Shiva smiling. Then taking a deep breath he added, 'And lastly, I guess that you would like to announce the arrival of the Neelkanth to your people.'

Daksha and Kanakhala nodded hesitantly.

'I would like to request that you don't do that for now.'

Daksha and Kanakhala's face fell immediately. Nandi's eyes were glued to the floor. He had stopped listening to the conversation. The enormity of his prevarication was tearing him apart.

'Your Highness, I have a terrible feeling that when people know I am the Neelkanth, every action and word of mine will be over-interpreted and over-analysed,' explained Shiva. 'I am afraid that I don't know enough about your society or my task to be able to handle that at this point of time.'

'I understand my Lord,' said Daksha, willing a half-smile back on his face. 'You have my word. Only my immediate staff, my family and the people you yourself allow will know of the Neelkanth's arrival. Nobody else.'

'Thank you, your Highness. But I will say it again: I am a simple tribal man who just happened to acquire a blue throat because of some exotic medicine. Honestly, I still don't know what one man like me can do in the face of the odds that you face.'

'And I'll say it again my Lord,' said Daksha, with a child-like smile. 'If that man is you, he can change the entire universe!'

CHAPTER 8

Drink of the Gods

Shiva strode towards the royal guest house with a leaden-footed Nandi close behind, head bowed in self-recrimination. 'I wish to dine alone,' said Shiva over his shoulder. All Nandi could muster was, 'I am so sorry, my Lord.'

Shiva turned around to gaze at Nandi.

'You are right, my Lord. We were so lost in our own troubles and the search for the Neelkanth that we didn't realise the unfairness of our actions on immigrants. I misled you my Lord. I lied to you.'

Shiva didn't say anything. He continued to stare intensely into Nandi's eyes.

'I am so sorry my Lord. I have failed you. I will accept whatever punishment you give me.'

Shiva's lips broke into a very faint smile. He patted Nandi lightly on his shoulders, signalling he had forgiven him. But his eyes delivered a clear message. 'Never lie to me again, my friend.'

Nandi nodded and whispered, 'Never, my Lord. I am so sorry.'

'Forget it Nandi,' said Shiva, his smile a little broader now. 'It's in the past.'

They turned and continued walking. Suddenly Shiva shook his head and chuckled slightly. 'Strange people!'

'What is it, my Lord?' asked Nandi.

'Nothing really. I was just wondering at some of the interesting things about your society.'

'Interesting, my Lord?' asked Nandi, feeling a little more confident now that Shiva was speaking to him again.

'Well, some people in your country think that the mere existence of my blue throat can help you achieve impossible tasks. Some people actually think that my name has suddenly become so holy that they can't even speak it.'

Nandi smiled slightly.

'On the other hand,' continued Shiva, 'some people clearly think that I am not required. In fact, they even think that my touching them is so polluting that I need to get a shudhikaran done!'

'Shudhikaran? Why would you need that my Lord?' asked Nandi, a little concerned.

Shiva weighed his words carefully. 'Well, I touched someone. And I was told that I would need to undergo a shudhikaran.'

'What? Who did you touch my Lord? Was it a vikarma person?' asked a troubled Nandi. 'Only the touch of a vikarma person would mean that you would need to get a shudhikaran.'

Shiva's face abruptly changed colour. A veil lifted from his eyes. He suddenly understood the significance of the events of the previous day. Her hasty withdrawal at being touched. The shocked reactions from the Guru*ji* and Krittika.

'Go back to the guest house, Nandi. I will see you there,' said Shiva, as he turned towards the guest house garden.

'My Lord, what happened?' asked Nandi, trying to keep pace with Shiva. 'Did you get the shudhikaran done or not?'

'Go to the guest house Nandi,' said Shiva walking rapidly away. 'I will see you there.'

— ᛃ◉ᚢᚦ⊕ —

Shiva waited for the larger part of an hour. But it was in vain, for Sati did not make an appearance. He sat on the bench by himself, cursing the moment when that terrible thought had entered his mind.

How could I have even thought that Sati would find my touch polluting? I am such a bloody idiot!

He replayed the moments of that fateful encounter in his mind and analysed every facet of it.

'I would never be able to forgive myself if something were to happen to you.'

What did she mean by that? Does she have feelings for me? Or is she just an honourable woman who can't bear to be the cause of someone else's misfortune? And why should she think of herself as inferior? This entire concept of the vikarma is so damned ridiculous!

Realising that she wasn't going to come, Shiva got up. He kicked the bench hard, getting a painful reminder that his once numb toe had got its sensation back. Cursing out loud, he started walking back to the guest house. As he passed the stage, he noticed that there was something lying on the dance floor. He bent down and picked it up. It was her bead bracelet. He had seen it on her right hand. The string did not seem broken.

Had she purposely dropped it here?

He smelt it. It had the fragrance of the holy lake on a

sun-kissed evening. He brought it delicately to his lips and kissed it gently. Smiling, he dropped the bracelet into the pouch tied around his waist. He would come back from Mount Mandar and meet her. He *had* to meet her. He would pursue her to the end of the world if required. He would fight the entire human race to have her. His journey in this life was incomplete without her. His heart knew it. His soul knew it.

— ⋏◎ᶌ⨄⊕ —

'How much farther, Madam Prime Minister?' asked Nandi, behaving like an excited child.

A visit to the mythical Mount Mandar, the hub where the drink of the Gods was manufactured, was a rare honour for any Meluhan. Most Suryavanshis considered Mount Mandar the soul of their empire. As long as it was safe, so was the Somras.

'It's only been an hour since we left Devagiri, Captain,' said Kanakhala smiling. 'It's a day's journey to Mount Mandar.'

'Actually the blinds on the carriage windows prevent me from judging the angle of the sun and hence the passage of time. That's the reason why I was asking.'

'The prahar lamp is right behind you, Captain. The blinds have been drawn for your own protection.'

Shiva smiled at Kanakhala. He could understand that the blinds were not for *their* protection, but for the safety of Mount Mandar. To keep its location secret. Very few people knew of its exact location. An elite team of soldiers called the Arishtanemi protected the road to Mount Mandar and the travellers on it. Apart from the scientists of Mount Mandar, the Arishtanemi soldiers or any other person authorised by the Emperor, nobody else was allowed to go to the mountain or to even know its location. If the Chandravanshi terrorists attacked Mount Mandar, all would be lost for Meluha.

'Who would we be meeting there, Kanakhala?' asked Shiva.

'My Lord, we would be meeting Brahaspati. He is the Chief Scientist of the empire. He leads the team of scientists who manufacture the Somras for the entire country. Of course, they also conduct research in many other fields. A bird courier has already been sent to him informing him of your arrival. We will be meeting him tomorrow morning.'

Shiva nodded slightly, smiled at Kanakhala, and said, 'Thank you.'

As Nandi looked at the prahar lamp again, Shiva went back to his book. It was an interesting manuscript about the terrible war that was fought many thousands of years ago, between the *Devas* — the *Gods*, and the *Asuras* — the *demons*. An eternal struggle between opposites: good and evil. The Devas, with the help of Lord Rudra, the *Mahadev*, the *God of Gods*, had destroyed the Asuras and established righteousness in the world again.

— ⟨ 🕉 ⟩ —

'I hope you slept well, my Lord,' said Kanakhala as she welcomed Shiva and Nandi into the chamber outside Brahaspati's office.

It was the beginning of the last hour of the first prahar. Days began early at Mount Mandar.

'Yes, I did,' said Shiva. 'Though I could hear a strange rhythmic sound all through the night.'

Kanakhala smiled but did not offer any explanation. She bowed her head and opened the door to let Shiva into Brahaspati's office. Shiva walked in followed by Kanakhala and Nandi. There were various strange instruments spread throughout Brahaspati's large office, neatly organised on tables of different heights. Palm leaf notes were placed alongside each of the instruments where some experiments had clearly been conducted. The room was in muted blue. A large picture window in the corner afforded a breathtaking view of the dense forest at the foot of the mountain. Many simple, low seats had been arranged together in a square in the centre of the room. It was a frugal room, in line with a culture that celebrated simplicity over ostentation at every turn.

Brahaspati was standing in the middle of the room, his hands folded in a Namaste. Of medium height, much shorter than Shiva, his wheat-coloured skin, deep set eyes and well-manicured beard gave Brahaspati a distinguished appearance. Serene of expression and shaven of head, his choti bespoke of Brahmanical learning. His body was slightly overweight. His broad shoulders and barrel chest would have been markedly pronounced if they had been exercised a bit, but Brahaspati's body was a vehicle for his intellect and not the temple that it is to a warrior or Kshatriya. He wore a typical white cotton dhoti and an angvastram draped loosely over his shoulders. He wore a janau tied from his left shoulder down to the right side of his hips.

'How are you Kanakhala?' asked Brahaspati. 'It has been a long time.'

'Yes it has, Brahaspati,' said Kanakhala, greeting Brahaspati with a Namaste and a low bow.

Shiva noticed that the second amulet on Brahaspati's arm showed him as a swan. A very select chosen-tribe among Brahmins.

'This is Lord Shiva,' said Kanakhala, pointing towards Shiva.

'Just Shiva will do, thank you,' smiled Shiva, with a polite Namaste towards Brahaspati.

'Alright then. Just Shiva it is. And, who might you be?' asked Brahaspati, turning towards Nandi.

'This is Captain Nandi,' answered Kanakhala. 'Lord Shiva's aide.'

'A pleasure to meet you, Captain,' said Brahaspati, before turning back to Shiva. 'I don't mean to sound rude Shiva. But would it be possible for me to see your throat?'

Shiva nodded. As he took off his cravat, Brahaspati came forward to examine the throat. His smile disappeared as he saw Shiva's throat radiating a bright blue hue. Brahaspati was speechless for a few moments. Slowly gathering his wits, he turned towards Kanakhala. 'This is not a fraud. The colour comes from the inside. How is this possible? This means that...'

'Yes,' said Kanakhala softly, with a happiness that seemed to emanate from deep inside. 'It means the Neelkanth has come. Our saviour has come.'

'Well, I don't know about that,' said an embarrassed Shiva, retying the cravat around his throat. 'But I will certainly try my best to help your wonderful country. It is for this reason that I have come to you. Something tells me that it is important for me to know how the Somras works.'

Brahaspati still seemed to be in a daze. He continued to watch Shiva but his attention seemed elsewhere. It appeared as if he was working out the implications of the true Neelkanth's arrival.

'Brahaspati...' said Kanakhala, as she tried to call the chief scientist back into the here and now.

'Huh!'

'Can you tell me how the Somras works, Brahaspati?' asked Shiva again.

'Of course,' said Brahaspati, as his eyes refocused on the people in front of him. Noticing Nandi he asked, 'Is it alright to speak in front of the Captain?'

'Nandi has been my friend through my sojourn in Meluha,' said Shiva. 'I hope it is alright if he stays here.'

Nandi felt touched that his Lord still trusted him so openly. He swore once again, on pain of death, to never lie to his Lord.

'Whatever you say, Shiva,' said Brahaspati, smiling warmly.

Shiva noticed that Brahaspati was not submissive or excessively deferential on discovering that he *was* the Neelkanth. Just like Parvateshwar, Brahaspati called Shiva by his name and not 'My Lord'. However, Shiva felt that while Parvateshwar's attitude was driven by a distrustful surliness, Brahaspati's was driven perhaps by an assured affability.

'Thank you,' smiled Shiva. 'So, how does the Somras work?'

— 人◎Ʊ⚘⊕ —

The royal procession moved slowly on the road to

Mount Mandar. A pilot guard of one hundred and sixty cavalrymen rode in front of the five royal carriages in columns of four abreast. A rearguard of another one hundred and sixty rode behind the royal carriages, in a similar formation. A side guard of forty each marched along the left and right flanks. Each carriage also had ten soldiers and five serving maids seated on the side supports. The soldiers were the legendary Arishtanemi, the most feared militia in all of India.

The five carriages were made of solid wood, with no windows or apertures, except for upward pointed slits at the top for ventilation. There was a grill in front, behind the rider, that allowed in light and air. This could be shut instantly in case of an attack. All the carriages were of exactly the same dimension and appearance, making it impossible to know which carriage carried the royal family. If a person had *divyadrishti*, *divine vision*, to look beyond what human eyes could see, he would observe that the first, third and fourth carriages were empty. The second carried the royal family — Daksha, his wife Veerini and his daughter Sati. The last carriage carried Parvateshwar and some of his key brigadiers.

'Father, I still don't understand why you insist on taking me along to pujas. I am not even allowed to attend the main ceremony,' said Sati.

'I have said this to you many times,' smiled Daksha, as he patted Sati's hand fondly. 'No puja of mine is complete unless I have seen your face. I don't care about the damned law.'

'Father!' whispered Sati with an embarrassed smile and a slight, reproachful shake of her head. She knew it was wrong of her father to insult the law.

Sati's mother, Veerini, looked at Daksha with an awkward smile. Then taking a quick look at Sati, she returned to her book.

At a short distance from the royal procession, hidden by the dense forest, a small band of fifty soldiers moved along silently. The soldiers wore light leather armour on their torso and had their dhotis tied in military style to ensure ease of movement. Each of them carried two swords, a long knife and a hardshield made of metal and leather which was tied loosely around the back. Their shoes had grooves that could hold three small knives. Two men walked at the head of the band. One of them, a handsome young man with a battle scar embellishing his face, wore a dark brown turban which signified that he was the Captain. His leather armour had been tied a little loose and a gold chain and pendant had slipped out carelessly. The pendant had a beautiful, white representation of a horizontal crescent moon, the Chandravanshi symbol.

Next to him walked a giant of a man covered in a long robe from head to toe. A hood stitched onto the robe was pulled up over his head while his face was covered with a black mask. Very little of him was visible except for his strong fleshy hands and his expressionless, almond-shaped eyes. A leather bracelet was tied to his right wrist with the serpent Aum symbol embroidered onto it. Without turning to the Captain, the hooded figure said, 'Vishwadyumna, your mark is visible. Put it in and tighten your armour.'

An embarrassed Vishwadyumna immediately pushed the chain inside and pulled the two strings on the side of his shoulder to tighten the breastplate.

'My Lord, begging your pardon,' said Vishwadyumna. 'But perhaps we could move ahead and confirm that this is the route to Mount Mandar. Once we know that, we'll be sure that our informant was correct. I am sure that we can come back to kidnap her later. We are dangerously outnumbered in any case. We can't do anything right now.'

The hooded figure replied calmly, 'Vishwadyumna, have I ordered an attack? Where does the question of us being outnumbered come in? And we are moving in the direction of Mount Mandar. A few hours delay will not bring the heavens down. For now, we follow.'

Vishwadyumna swallowed hard. There was nothing he hated more than opposing his lord's views. After all, it was his lord who had found the rare Suryavanshi sympathetic to their cause. This breakthrough would make it possible for them to rip out and destroy the very heart of Meluha. He spoke softly, 'But my Lord, you know the Queen doesn't like delays. There is unrest brewing amongst the men fueled by a feeling that perhaps the focus is being lost.'

The hooded figure turned sharply. His body seemed to convey anger but his voice was composed. 'I am not losing focus. If you want to leave, please go. You will get your money. I will do this alone if I have to.'

Shocked to see the rare display of emotion in his leader, Vishwadyumna retracted immediately. 'No, my Lord. That is not what I was trying to imply. I am sorry. I will stay with you till you release me. You are right. A few hours will make no difference keeping in mind that we have waited for centuries.'

The platoon continued tracking the royal caravan silently.

— ✴ⵔ☋⩚⊕ —

'At a conceptual level, how the Somras works is ridiculously simple,' said Brahaspati. 'The almost impossible task was to convert the concept into reality. That was the genius of Lord Brahma. Jai Shri Brahma!'

'Jai Shri Brahma,' repeated Shiva, Kanakhala and Nandi.

'Before understanding how the medicine slows down the ageing process dramatically, we have to understand what keeps us alive,' said Brahaspati. 'There is a fundamental thing that none of us can live without.'

Shiva stared at Brahaspati, waiting for him to expound.

'And that fundamental thing is energy,' explained Brahaspati. 'When we walk, talk, think, in fact when we do anything that can be called being alive, we use energy.'

'We have a similar concept amongst our people,' said Shiva. 'Except, we call it Shakti.'

'Shakti?' asked a surprised Brahaspati. 'Interesting. That word has not been used to describe energy for many centuries. It was a term employed by the Pandyas, the ancestors of all the people of India. Do you know where your tribe has come from? Their lineage?'

'I am not really sure but there is an old woman in my tribe who claims to know everything about our history. Perhaps we should ask her when she comes to Devagiri.'

'Perhaps we should!' smiled Brahaspati. 'In any case, getting back to the subject, we know that nothing can be done by our body without energy. Now where does this energy come from?'

'From the food that we eat?' suggested Nandi, timidly. He was finally developing the confidence to speak in front of such important people.

'Absolutely right. The food that we eat stores energy, which we can then expend. That's also why we feel weak when we don't eat. However, you don't get energy merely by eating. Something inside the body has to draw the energy so that we can put it to good use.'

'Absolutely,' agreed Shiva.

'The conversion of food into energy is performed by the air we breathe,' continued Brahaspati. 'The air has various gases in it. One of these gases is called oxygen, which reacts with our food and releases energy. If we don't get oxygen, our body would be starved of energy and we would die.'

'But this is the process that keeps us alive,' said Shiva. 'What does the medicine have to do with it? The medicine has to work on that which causes us to grow old, become weak and die.'

Brahaspati smiled. 'What I've told you does have something to do with how we age. Because as it appears, nature has a sense of humour. The thing that keeps us alive is also what causes us to age and eventually die. When oxygen reacts with our food in order to release energy, it also releases free radicals called oxidants. These oxidants are toxic. When you leave any fruit out and it becomes rancid, this is because it has been "oxidised" or the oxidants have reacted with it to make it rot. A similar "oxidising process" causes metals to corrode. It happens especially with the new metal we have discovered — iron. The same thing happens to our body when we breathe in oxygen. The oxygen helps convert the food we eat into energy. But it also causes the release of oxidants into our body which start reacting inside us. We rust from the inside and hence age and eventually die.'

'By the holy God Agni!' exclaimed Nandi. 'The thing that gives us life is also what slowly kills us?'

'Yes,' said Brahaspati. 'Think about it. The body tries to store everything that you need from the outside world in order to survive. It stores enough food to survive for a few days without it. It stocks up on water so that a few days of thirst will not kill you. It seems logical, right? If your body needs something, it keeps some of it as backup for possible shortages.'

'Absolutely,' agreed Shiva.

'On the other hand, the body does not store enough oxygen, the most crucial component of staying alive, to last for more than just a few minutes. It doesn't make any sense at all. The only explanation is that the body realises that despite being an elixir, oxygen is also a poison. Hence it is dangerous to store.'

'So, what did Lord Brahma do?' asked Shiva.

'After a lot of research, Lord Brahma invented the Somras, which when consumed, reacts with the oxidants, absorbs them and then expels them from the body as sweat or urine. Because of the Somras, there are no oxidants left in the body.'

'Is that why the perspiration released from the body is poisonous the first time a person drinks the Somras?'

'Yes. Your sweat is particularly dangerous the first time you drink the Somras. Having said that, remember, sweat and urine released from the body even after a person has drunk the Somras for years remains toxic. So you have to eject it from the body and make sure that it does not affect anyone else.'

'So, that's why the Meluhans are so obsessed with hygiene.'

'Yes. That's why all Meluhans are taught about two things from a young age — water and hygiene. Water is the cleanest absorber of the effluents that the Somras generates and excretes as toxins. Meluhans are taught to drink gallons of water. And everything that can be washed, should be washed! The Meluhans bathe at least twice a day. All ablutions are done in specific rooms and underground drains then safely carry the waste out of the city.'

'Strict hygiene standards!' smiled Shiva, as he remembered his first day in Kashmir and Ayurvati's strong words. 'How is the Somras manufactured?'

'Manufacturing the Somras is not without its fair share of difficulties. It requires various ingredients that are not easily available. For example, the Sanjeevani tree. The empire has giant plantations to produce these trees. The manufacturing procedure also generates a lot of heat. So we have to use a lot of water during the processing to keep the mixture stable. Also, the crushed branches of the Sanjeevani tree have to be churned with the waters of the Saraswati river before processing begins. Water from other sources doesn't work.'

'Is that the strange noise I keep hearing: the churners?'

'That's exactly what it is. We have giant churning machines in a massive cavern at the base of this mountain. The Saraswati waters are led in here through a complex system of canals. The water is collected in an enormous pool in the cavern which we affectionately call *Sagar*.'

'*Sagar*? An *ocean*? Is that what you call a pool of water?' asked a surprised Shiva, for he had heard legends about the massive, never-ending expanse of water called Sagar.

'It is a bit of a hyperbole,' admitted Brahaspati with a smile. 'But if you did see the size of the pool, you would realise that we are not that off the mark!'

'Well I would certainly like to see the entire facility. It

was too late by the time we got in last night so I haven't seen much of the mountain as yet.'

'I will take you around after lunch,' said Brahaspati.

Shiva grinned in reply. He was about to say something, but checked himself in time, looking at both Kanakhala and Nandi.

Brahaspati noticed the hesitation. He felt Shiva might want to ask him something, but not in front of Nandi and Kanakhala. Brahaspati turned to them and said, 'I think Shiva wants to ask me something. May I request you to wait outside?'

It was a measure of the respect that Brahaspati commanded, that Kanakhala immediately rose to leave the room after a formal Namaste, followed by Nandi. Brahaspati turned to Shiva with a smile. 'Why don't you ask the question you really came to ask?'

CHAPTER 9

Love and its Consequences

'I didn't want to question you in front of them. Their faith is overwhelming,' explained Shiva with a wry grin. He was beginning to like Brahaspati. He enjoyed being around a man who treated him like an equal.

Brahaspati nodded. 'I understand, my friend. What do you want to ask?'

'Why me?' asked Shiva. 'Why did the Somras have this strange effect on me? I might have a blue throat, but I don't know how I am going to become the saviour of the Suryavanshis. The Emperor tells me that I am supposed to be the one who will complete Lord Ram's unfinished work and destroy the Chandravanshis.'

'He told you that?' asked Brahaspati, his eyes wide with surprise. 'The Emperor can be a little tiresome at times. But suffice it to say that what he told you is not completely correct. The legend doesn't exactly say that the Neelkanth will save the Suryavanshis. The legend says two things. First, that the Neelkanth will *not be* from the Sapt-Sindhu. And second, the Neelkanth will be the "destroyer of evil". The Meluhans believe that this implies that the Neelkanth will destroy the Chandravanshis, since they are obviously evil. But destroying the Chandravanshis doesn't mean that the Suryavanshis will be saved! There are many other problems, besides the Chandravanshis, that we need to solve.'

'What kind of problems? Like the Nagas?'

Brahaspati seemed to hesitate for a moment. He replied carefully. 'There are many problems. We are working hard to solve them. But coming back to your question, why did the Somras have this effect on you?'

'Yes, why did it? Why did my throat turn blue? Leave alone stopping the degeneration of my body, the Somras actually repaired a dislocated shoulder and a frostbitten toe.'

'It repaired an injury?' asked an incredulous Brahaspati. 'That's impossible! It is just supposed to prevent diseases and ageing, not repair injuries.'

'Well, it did in my case.'

Brahaspati thought for a bit. 'We will have to do experiments to come up with a definitive answer. For now though, I can think of only one explanation. I have been told that you come from the high lands beyond the Himalayas, right?'

Shiva nodded.

'The air gets thinner as you go higher up the mountains,' continued Brahaspati. 'There is less oxygen in thinner air. That means your body was used to surviving with less oxygen and resultantly was less harmed by the oxidants. Therefore the anti-oxidants in the Somras may have had a stronger effect on you.'

'That could be one of the reasons,' agreed Shiva. 'But if that was the case, then the necks of all my tribesmen should also have turned cold and blue. Why just me?'

'A good point,' conceded Brahaspati. 'But tell me one thing. Did your tribe also experience an improvement in their pre–existing conditions?'

'Actually, yes they did.'

'So maybe the diluted air you all lived in did have some role to play. But since your entire tribe did not develop blue throats, it is obvious that the "thinner air" theory may be a partial explanation. We can always do some more research. I am sure there is a scientific explanation for the blue throat.'

Shiva's piercing look revealed that he had read the intent behind Brihaspati's last statement. 'You don't believe in the legend of the Neelkanth, do you?'

Brahaspati smiled at Shiva awkwardly. He was beginning to like Shiva and did not want to say anything to insult him. But he wasn't going to lie either. 'I believe in science. It provides a solution and a rationale for everything. And if there is anything that appears like a miracle, the only explanation is that a scientific reason for it has not been discovered as yet.'

'Then why do the people of Meluha not turn to science for solving their problems?'

'I am not sure,' said Brahaspati thoughtfully. 'Perhaps it is because science is a capable but cold-hearted master. Unlike a Neelkanth, it will not solve your problems for you. It will only provide you with the tools that you may need to fight your own battles. Most people find it easier to wait for the arrival of the Messiah rather than act to solve their own problems.'

'So what do you think is the role that the Neelkanth has to play in Meluha?'

Brahaspati looked at Shiva sympathetically. 'I would

like to think that true Suryavanshis should fight their own demons rather than put pressure on someone else and expect him to solve their problems. A true Suryavanshi's *duty* is to push himself to the limit of his abilities and strength. The coming of the Neelkanth should only redouble a Suryavanshi's efforts, since it is obvious that the time for the destruction of evil is near.'

Shiva nodded.

'Are you concerned that it may be too much of a strain for you to take up a responsibility that you don't really want, because of the pressure of faith?' asked Brahaspati.

'No, that is not my concern,' replied Shiva. 'This is a wonderful country and I certainly want to do all I can to help. But what if your people depend on me to protect them and I can't? Right now, I can't say that I can do all that is expected of me. So how can I give my word?'

Brahaspati smiled. According to his rule book, any man who took his own word so seriously was deserving of respect.

'You appear to be a good man, Shiva. You will probably face a lot of pressure in the coming days. Be careful, my friend. Because of the blue throat and the blind faith it generates, your decisions will have ramifications for the entire land. Remember, whether a man is a legend or not is decided by history, not fortune-tellers.'

Shiva smiled, glad to have finally found a man who understood his predicament. And more importantly, was willing to at least *offer* some advice.

— ⋀◍⎁⋔⊕ —

It was late in the evening. Having spent a thoroughly

enjoyable afternoon on a detailed tour of Mount Mandar with Brahaspati, Shiva lay on his bed, reading a book. A spent chillum lay on the side table.

A few aspects of the story he was reading, 'The Righteous War against the Asuras', troubled him. The Asuras were demons and were expected to behave like demons who had a pathological hatred for the Devas. They routinely attacked Deva cities, trying to force them to accept the Asura way of life. This was not a surprise to Shiva. What he hadn't expected though were the unusually unethical means the Devas sometimes adopted in the pursuit of victory. Lord Rudra, though personally a great man, seemed to ignore the indiscretions of the Devas in the interest of the larger good.

Shiva heard a commotion outside the Guest House. He looked out of his first floor balcony and noticed that the royal caravan had just arrived. The Arishtanemi soldiers quickly lined up for the traditional salute. Some people appeared to be disembarking from the far side of the second carriage. Even though they appeared to be the royal family, Shiva noted the absence of servitude and pageantry on the part of the Arishtanemi. Shiva suspected that this could be due to the usual Meluhan obsession with perceived equality.

However, Shiva's equality theory was challenged when he looked at the fifth carriage from which Parvateshwar alighted. Here, the Arishtanemi seemed to be in a tizzy. The senior Captain rushed in front of Parvateshwar and executed a Meluhan military salute — a quick click of the heels, the body rigid in attention and the right hand, balled into a fist, brought rapidly and violently to his left chest. The salute was followed by a deep bow of respect to the commander of the army. The soldiers at the back repeated their Captain's greeting. Parvateshwar formally saluted in return, accompanied with a slight bow of his head. He started towards his soldiers, inspecting them, while the Captain politely fell two steps behind.

Shiva had a feeling that the admiration reserved for Parvateshwar was not because of the post he held. It was for the man himself. For all his surliness, Parvateshwar had the reputation of a brave warrior, a soldier's General respected as a man who was true to his word. Shiva could see the strength of that repute in the eyes of each Arishtanemi who bent low on receiving the attention of his General.

A little while later, Shiva heard a soft knock on his door. He did not need to guess who waited on the other side. Sighing softly, he opened the door.

Daksha's fixed smile disappeared and he started a little as the unfamiliar odour of marijuana assaulted his senses. Kanakhala, standing to the Emperor's right, appeared equally perplexed.

'What is that stench?' Daksha asked Brahaspati, who stood to the left. 'Perhaps you should change the Lord's room. How can you subject him to this discomfort?'

'I have a feeling that Shiva is comfortable with this aroma, your Highness,' said Brahaspati.

'It is a smell that travels with me, your Highness,' said Shiva. 'I like it.'

Daksha was baffled. His face did nothing to hide his revulsion. But he quickly recovered his composure. After all, the Lord was happy with the malodour. 'I'm sorry to disturb you, my Lord,' said Daksha, his smile back in place. 'I just thought I would inform you that my family and I have reached the guest house.'

'It's very kind of you to inform me, your Highness,' said Shiva with a formal Namaste.

'My family and I were hoping for the honour of having breakfast with you tomorrow morning, my Lord.'

'The honour would be mine, your Highness.'

'Excellent. Excellent,' beamed Daksha as he moved on to the question that dominated his mind. 'What do you think of the Somras, my Lord? Isn't it really the drink of the Gods?'

'Yes your Highness. It does appear to be a miraculous drink.'

'It is the basis of our civilisation,' continued Daksha. 'Once you have taken a tour of our land, you will see the goodness of our way of life. I am sure you will find it in your heart to do something to save it.'

'Your Highness, I already think highly of your country. It truly is great and treats its citizens well. I wouldn't doubt that it is a way of life that is worth protecting. However, what I am not sure about is what I can do. Yours is such an advanced civilisation and I am just a simple tribal man.'

'Faith is a very potent weapon, my Lord,' said Daksha, his hands joined in supplication. 'All that is needed is for you to have as much faith in yourself as we have in you. I am sure that if you spend a few more days in our country and see the effect that your presence has on our people, you will realise what you can do.'

Shiva gave up arguing against Daksha's childlike belief.

Brahaspati winked at Shiva before coming to his rescue. 'Your Highness, Shiva looks tired to me. It has been a long day. Maybe he should retire and we could meet tomorrow?'

Daksha smiled, 'Perhaps you are right, Brahaspati. My

apologies for troubling you, my Lord. We will see you at breakfast. Have a good night.'

'Good night,' wished Shiva in return.

— ⚲◉ᘮ⚸⊕ —

Sati waited quietly at the table as Daksha glanced nervously at the prahar lamp. To the left were Kanakhala, Brahaspati and Parvateshwar. To his right was an empty chair. For the 'Neelkanth', thought Sati. Next to the empty chair sat Sati and to her right was her mother, Veerini. Daksha had agonised deeply over the seating to get it exactly right.

Sati looked over the arrangements. A formal table and chairs for breakfast rather than the preferred low table and floor cushions that Meluhans normally sat upon to eat. The beloved banana leaf had been replaced by gold plates. The taste enhancing *kulhads,* or *mud cups*, had been replaced by refined silver glasses. She thought that her father was really pulling out all stops for this breakfast meeting. She had seen him pin his hopes on too many so-called Neelkanths earlier. Miracle men who had turned out to be frauds. She hoped that her father would not have to face disillusionment once again.

The crier announced Shiva and Nandi. As Daksha rose with a reverential Namaste to receive the Lord, Parvateshwar rolled his eyes at the servile behaviour of his Emperor. At the same instant, Sati bent down to pick up a glass that she had accidentally knocked over.

'My Lord,' said Daksha pointing to the people standing around the table. 'Kanakhala, Brahaspati and Parvateshwar, you already know. At the far right is my wife, Queen Veerini.'

Shiva smiled politely as he returned Veerini's Namaste with a formal Namaste and a low bow.

'And next to her,' said Daksha with a broad smile as Sati came up holding the glass she had retrieved, 'is my daughter, Princess Sati.'

The breath went out of Shiva as he looked at his life staring back at him. His heart beat a frantic rhythm. He could swear that he had got a whiff of his favourite fragrance in the world: the aroma of the holy lake at sunset. As before, he was mesmerized.

There was an uncomfortable silence in the room. Except for the noise made by the unfortunate glass which fell from Sati's hand again. The clang of the rolling glass distracted Sati slightly from her fixed gaze. With superhuman effort, she managed to control the look of shock on her face. She was breathing heavily, as if she had just danced a duet with Shiva. What she did not know was that her soul was doing exactly that.

Daksha gazed at the dumbstruck couple with glee. He had the look of a director who had just seen his play being perfectly executed. Nandi, standing right behind Shiva, could see Sati's expression. Suddenly everything became clear to him. The dance practices, the vikarma touch, the shudhikaran and his Lord's anguish. While some part of him was afraid, another reconciled to it quickly. If his Lord wanted this, he would support it in every way possible. Brahaspati stared blankly at the couple, deep in thought about the implications of this unexpected situation. Parvateshwar looked at the goings on with barely concealed repugnance. What was happening was wrong, immoral and worst of all, illegal.

'My Lord,' said Daksha pointing towards the empty seat at his right. 'Please take your seat and we shall begin.'

Shiva did not react. He had not heard Daksha's words. He was in a world where the only sound was the harmonious melody of Sati's heavy breathing. A tune he could blissfully dance to for his next seven lives.

'My Lord,' repeated Daksha, a little louder.

A distracted Shiva finally looked at Daksha, as if from another world.

'Please take your seat, my Lord,' said Daksha.

'Yes of course, your Highness,' said Shiva averting his eyes in embarrassment.

As Shiva sat down, the food was brought in. It was a simple delicacy that the Meluhans loved for breakfast. Rice and some cereals were fermented and ground into a thick batter. Small portions of this batter were then wrapped in banana leaves and steamed into cylindrical roundels. It was served while still draped in the banana leaf, along with some spicy lentils for taste. The dish was called an idli.

'You're the Neelkanth?' a still shocked Sati whispered softly to Shiva, as she had willed some calmness into her breathing.

'Apparently so,' replied Shiva with a playful grin. 'Impressed?'

Sati answered that question with a raised disdainful brow. The mask was back. 'Why would I be impressed?'

What?!

'My Lord,' said Daksha.

'Yes, your Highness,' said Shiva, turning towards Daksha.

'I was thinking,' said Daksha. 'Our puja should be over by this evening. However, I have to stay here for two more days for some reviews with Brahaspati. There is no point in Veerini and Sati getting thoroughly bored out here in the meantime.'

'Thank you, your Highness,' said Brahaspati with a sly grin. 'Your vote of confidence in the interest that the royal family has in Mount Mandar is most reassuring.'

The entire table burst out laughing. So did Daksha, exhibiting a sporting spirit.

'You know what I mean Brahaspati!' said Daksha, shaking his head. Turning back to Shiva, he continued, 'From what I am led to believe, my Lord, you were planning to leave for Devagiri tomorrow morning. I think it may be a good idea for Veerini and Sati to accompany you. The rest of us can catch up with you two days later.'

Sati looked up in alarm. She wasn't sure why, but something told her that she shouldn't agree to this plan. Another part of her said that she had no reason to be scared. In all the eighty-five years that she had spent as a vikarma, she had never broken the law. She had the self-control to know what was right, and what wasn't.

Shiva though had no such compunctions. With very obvious delight, he said, 'I think that is a very good idea, your Highness. Nandi and I could travel with both her Highnesses back to Devagiri.'

'It's settled then,' said a visibly content Daksha. Turning to Parvateshwar, he said, 'Parvateshwar, please ensure that the Arishtanemi escort are broken up into two groups for the return journey.'

'My Lord, I don't think that is wise,' said Parvateshwar. 'A large part of the Arishtanemi are still in Devagiri preparing for the material transfer. Also, the standing contingent in Mount Mandar cannot be reduced under any circumstances. We may not have enough soldiers for two caravans. Perhaps, we could all travel together day after tomorrow.'

'I am sure there won't be a problem,' said Daksha. 'And don't you always say that each Arishtanemi is equal to fifty enemy soldiers? It's settled. The Lord Neelkanth, Veerini and Sati will leave tomorrow morning. Please make all the arrangements.'

Parvateshwar went unhappily back to his thoughts as Shiva and Sati started whispering to each other again.

'You did go for a shudhikaran, didn't you?' asked Sati seriously.

'Yes,' said Shiva. He wasn't lying. He had gone for a purification ceremony on his last night at Devagiri. He didn't believe he needed it. However, he knew that Sati would ask him the next time they met. And he didn't want to lie to her.

'Though I think the idea of doing a shudhikaran is completely absurd,' whispered Shiva. 'In fact, the entire concept of the vikarma is ridiculous. I think it is one of the few things in Meluha that is not fair and should be changed.'

Sati looked up suddenly at Shiva, her face devoid of any expression. Shiva stared hard into her eyes, trying to gauge some of the thoughts running through her mind. But he hit a blank wall.

— 人◎ᚒ4⊕ —

It was the beginning of the second prahar the next day when Shiva, Veerini, Sati and Nandi departed for Devagiri along with a hundred Arishtanemi. Daksha, Parvateshwar and Kanakhala stood outside the guest house to see them off. Brahaspati had been detained by some scheduled experiments.

The entourage had to sit in the same carriage as there were guidelines that a minimum of four carriages had to be kept aside for any caravan that carried the Emperor. Since the royal procession had come in five carriages, that left only one carriage for this caravan. Parvateshwar was deeply unhappy about the unorthodox way in which members of the royal family were travelling without any dummy carriages, but his objections had been overruled by Daksha.

Sitting on one of the comfortable sofas inside the carriage, Sati noticed that Shiva was wearing his cravat again. 'Why do you cover your throat all the time?'

'I am uncomfortable with all the attention that comes along with anyone seeing the blue throat,' replied Shiva.

'But you will have to get used to it. The blue throat is not going to disappear.'

'True,' answered Shiva with a smile. 'But till I get used to it, the cravat is my shield.'

As the caravan left, Parvateshwar and Kanakhala came up to Daksha.

'Why do you have so much faith in that man, my Lord?' asked Parvateshwar of Daksha. 'He has done nothing to deserve respect. How can he lead us to victory when he has not even been trained for it? The entire concept of the Neelkanth goes against our rules. In Meluha a person is supposed to be given a task only if he is found capable of it and is trained by the system.'

'We are in a state of war, Parvateshwar,' replied Daksha. 'An undeclared one, but a state of war all the same. We face a terrorist attack every other week. These cowardly Chandravanshis don't even attack from the front so that we can fight them. And our army is too small to attack their territory openly. Our "rules" are not working. We need a miracle. And the first rule of serendipity is that miracles come when we forget rational laws and have faith. I have faith in the Neelkanth. And so do my people.'

'But Shiva has no faith in himself. How can you force him to be our saviour when he himself doesn't want to be one?'

'Sati will change that.'

'My Lord, you are going to use your own daughter as bait?' asked a horrified Parvateshwar. 'And do you really want a saviour who decides to help us just because of his lust?!'

'IT IS NOT LUST!'

Parvateshwar and Kanakhala kept quiet, shocked by Daksha's reaction.

'What kind of a father do you think I am?' asked Daksha. 'You think I will use my daughter so? She just may find comfort and happiness with the Lord. She has suffered enough already. I want her to be happy. And if in doing so, I help my country as well, what is the harm?'

Parvateshwar was about to say something, but thought the better of it.

'We need to destroy the Chandravanshi ideology,' continued Daksha. 'And the only way we can do that is if we can give the benefits of our lifestyle to the people of Swadweep. The common Swadweepans will be grateful for this, but their Chandravanshi rulers will try everything within their power to stop us. They may be able to resist us, but try as they might, they cannot stop a people led by the Neelkanth. And if Sati is with the Neelkanth, there is no way he would refuse to lead us against the Chandravanshis.'

'But your Highness, do you really think the Lord would come to our side just because he is in love with your daughter?' asked Kanakhala.

'You have missed the point. The Lord does not need to be convinced to be on our side,' said Daksha. 'He already is. We are a great civilisation. Maybe not perfect, but great all the same. One has to be blind to not see that. What the Neelkanth needs is motivation and the belief in himself to lead us. That belief in himself will emerge when he gets closer to Sati.'

'And how is that going to happen, your Highness?' asked Parvateshwar, frowning slightly.

'Do you know what is the most powerful force in a man's life?' asked Daksha.

Kanakhala and Parvateshwar looked at Daksha nonplussed.

'It is his intense desire to impress the person he loves the most,' expounded Daksha. 'Look at me. I have always loved my father. My desire to impress him is what is driving me even today. Even after his death, I still want to make him proud of me. It is driving me to my destiny as the King who will re-establish the pure Suryavanshi way of life across India. And when the Neelkanth develops a deep desire to make Sati proud of him, he will rise to fulfil his destiny.'

Parvateshwar frowned, not quite agreeing with the logic, but keeping quiet all the same.

'But what if Sati seeks something different?' asked Kanakhala. 'Like a husband who spends all his time with her.'

'I know my daughter,' replied Daksha confidently. 'I know what it takes to impress her.'

'That's an interesting point of view, my Lord,' smiled Kanakhala. 'Just out of curiosity, what do you think is the most powerful force in a woman's life?'

Daksha laughed out loud. 'Why do you ask? Don't you know?'

'Well the most powerful force in my life is the desire to get out of the house before my mother-in-law wakes up!'

Both Daksha and Kanakhala guffawed loudly.

Parvateshwar didn't seem to find it funny. 'I am sorry but that is no way to speak about your mother-in-law.'

'Oh relax, Parvateshwar,' said Kanakhala. 'You take everything too seriously.'

'I think,' said Daksha smiling, 'the most powerful force in a woman's life is the need to be appreciated, loved and cherished for what she is.'

Kanakhala smiled and nodded. Her emperor truly understood human emotions.

CHAPTER 10

The Hooded Figure Returns

As the caravan emerged from the carefully chiselled passage leading out of the depths of Mount Mandar, Veerini requested that the carriage be stopped for a minute. Veerini, Sati, Shiva and Nandi went down on their knees and offered a short prayer to the mountain for its continued benefaction. Watching over them on high alert was the Arishtanemi Bhabravya, a strapping man of sixty years with an intimidating moustache and beard.

After a short while, Bhabravya came up to Veerini and said with barely concealed impatience: 'Your Highness, perhaps it's time to get back into the carriage.'

Veerini looked at the Captain and got up with a quick nod. Sati, Shiva and Nandi followed.

— ⅄⊚Ʊ⅄⊕ —

'It's her,' said Vishwadyumna putting down the scope and turning towards his Lord.

The platoon was at a safe distance, concealed from the caravan. The dense and impenetrable foliage was an effective shield.

'Yes', said the hooded figure and let his eyes linger on Shiva's muscular body. Even without using the scope he was in no doubt that this was the same man who had fought him at the Brahma temple some weeks ago. 'Who is that man?'

'I don't know my Lord.'

'Keep your eye on him. He was the one who foiled the last attack.'

Vishwadyumna wanted to say that the previous attempt failed because it was unplanned. The presence of the caste-unmarked man had little role to play. Vishwadyumna could not understand the recent irrational decisions of his Lord. It was unlike him. Perhaps it was the closeness of the ultimate objective that was clouding his judgement. Vishwadyumna was, however, wise enough to keep his thoughts to himself. 'Perhaps we could track them for around an hour before we attack, my Lord. It will be a safe distance from the Arishtanemi back-up. We can get this over and done with quickly and report back to the Queen that the informer was correct.'

'No, we'll wait for a few hours more till they are at least a half day's distance away from Mount Mandar. Their new carriages have systems that can send an emergency signal immediately. We need to ensure that our task is over before their back-up arrives.'

'Yes, my Lord,' said Vishwadyumna, happy to see that his Lord's famed tactical brilliance had not diminished.

'And, remember, I want it done quickly,' added the hooded figure. 'The more time we take, the more people get hurt.'

'Yes, my Lord.'

— ꜰⵁⵜⵁ⊕ —

It was the beginning of the third prahar when the caravan stopped at the half-way clearing for lunch. The forest had been cut back to a distance that made a surprise attack impossible. The Queen's maids quickly unpacked the food and began heating it in the centre of the clearing. The royal party and Shiva were sitting closer to the head of the caravan, in the same direction as Devagiri. Bhabravya stood on the higher ground in the rear, keeping an eagle eye on the surroundings. Apart from the royal party, half the Arishtanemi soldiers had also sat down to eat while the others kept watch.

Shiva was about to take a second helping of rice when he heard the crack of a twig down the road. Stopping mid-way, he listened intently for another sound. There was none. His instincts told him this was a predator, who on realising that he had made a mistake, was now keeping still. Shiva looked over at Sati to see if she had heard the sound. She too was staring intently down the road. There was a soft crunch as the foot on the broken twig eased its pressure slightly. It would have been missed by most, except for a focussed listener.

Shiva immediately put his plate down, pulled out his sword and fixed his shield on his back. Bhabravya saw Shiva across the caravan and drew his sword as well, giving quick, silent signals to his men to do the same. The Arishtanemi were battle ready in a matter of seconds. Their swords unsheathed, Sati and Nandi too assumed traditional fighter positions.

Sati whispered to Veerini without turning, 'Mother, please sit in the carriage and lock it from within. Take the maids inside with you. But get them to disconnect the horses from the carriage first. We are not retreating and we don't want the enemy kidnapping you either.'

'Come with me Sati,' pleaded Veerini as her maids rushed to pull out the holds on the carriage.

'No, I'm staying here. Please hurry. We may not have much time.'

Veerini rushed into the carriage followed by the maids who quickly locked it from the inside.

At a distance, Bhabravya whispered to his aide. 'I know their tactics. I have seen these cowards on the southern border. They will send an advance suicide party, pretend to retreat and draw us into a stronghold. I don't care about the losses. We will chase those bastards and destroy every single one of them. They have run into the Arishtanemi. They will pay for this mistake.'

Shiva, meanwhile, turned to Sati and whispered carefully, 'I think they must be aiming for a high profile target. Nothing would be more significant than the royal family. Do you think that you too should wait in the carriage?'

Sati's eyes darted up towards Shiva in surprise. A pained look crossed her face before being replaced by a defiant glare. 'I am going to fight…'

What's wrong with her?! What I said is completely logical. Make the main objective of the enemy difficult and they will lose the will to fight.

Shiva pushed these thoughts out of his mind so he could focus on the road. The rest of the caravan strained every nerve to listen intently for any movement from the enemy. They were prepared for the ambush. It was the enemy's turn to make the first move. Just as they were beginning to think that it may have been a false alarm, the sound of a conch shell reverberated from down the road — from the direction of Mount Mandar. Shiva turned around but did not move. Whoever was making the noise was moving rapidly towards them.

Shiva could not recognise the cacophonic sound. However, the Arishtanemi from the southern border knew exactly what it was. It was the sound of a *Nagadhvani* conch. It was blown to announce the launch of a Naga attack!

Though impatient to fight, Bhabravya did not forget the standard operating procedures. He gestured towards an aide, who rushed to the carriage and pulled out a red box fixed at the bottom. Kicking it open, the aide pressed a button on the side. A tubular chimney-like structure extended straight up from the box for nearly twenty-five feet. The chimney ensured that the smoke signal was not lost in the dense forest and could be seen by the scouts at both Devagiri and Mount Mandar. The soldier picked up a branch from the fire and pushed it into the last of the four slots on the right side of the box. Red smoke fumed out of the chimney, signifying the presence of the highest level of danger. Help was six hours away. Four, if the back-up rode hard. Bhabravya did not intend the battle to last that long. He intended to kill each of the Nagas and the Chandravanshis long before that.

The attack began from the side of the road leading to Mount Mandar. A small band of ten Chandravanshi soldiers charged at the Arishtanemi. One soldier was holding the Naga conch shell and blowing hard. Another amongst them had covered his entire face and head with a cloth, except for small slits for his eyes. The Naga himself!

Shiva did not move. He could see the battle raging at the far end of the caravan. There were only ten Chandravanshis. The Arishtanemi did not need any support. He signalled to Sati and Nandi to stay where they were. Sati agreed as she too expected this attack to be a ruse.

The battle was short and fierce. The Chandravanshi soldiers fought viciously but were outnumbered. As Bhabravya expected, they turned in no time and retreated fast.

'After them,' yelled Bhabravya. 'Kill them all.'

The Arishtanemi dashed behind their Captain in pursuit of the retreating Chandravanshis. Most of them did not hear Shiva cry out loud. 'No! Stay here. Don't chase them.'

By the time some of the Arishtanemi heard Shiva's order, a majority had already left, chasing the Chandravanshis. Shiva was left in the clearing with Sati, Nandi and just twenty-five soldiers. Shiva turned back towards the side of the road leading to Devagiri — the direction from which the original sound of the cracking twig had come.

He turned again to look at the remaining Arishtanemi. Pointing towards his back, he spoke with a voice that was both steady and calm, 'This is where the actual attack will come from. Get into a tight formation in fours, facing that direction. Keep the princess in the middle. We will have to hold them back for about five or ten minutes. The other Arishtanemi will return when they realise that there are no Chandravanshis to fight in that direction.'

The Arishtanemi looked at Shiva and nodded. They were battle-hardened men. They liked nothing more than a clear-headed and calm leader who knew exactly what he was doing. They quickly got into the formation ordered by Shiva and waited.

Then the real attack began. Forty Chandravanshi soldiers led by a hooded figure emerged from the trees, walking slowly towards the Suryavanshi caravan. The outnumbered Arishtanemi remained stationary, waiting for their enemy to come to them.

'Surrender the princess to us and we will leave,' said the hooded figure. 'We want no unnecessary bloodshed.'

The same joker from the Brahma temple. He's got a strange costume, but he fights well.

'We don't want any bloodshed either,' said Shiva. 'Leave quietly and we promise not to kill you.'

'You're the one who's looking at death in the face, barbarian,' said the hooded figure, conveying anger through his posture rather than his voice, which remained eerily composed.

Shiva noticed the brown-turbaned officer look impatiently at the hooded figure. He clearly wanted to attack and get this over and done with.

Dissension in the ranks?

'The only face I'm looking at is a stupid festival mask. And it's soon going to be shoved down your pathetic little throat! Also tell that brainless lieutenant of yours that he shouldn't give battle plans away.'

The hooded figure remained calm. Not turning to look at Vishwadyumna.

Damn! This man is good.

'This is the last warning, barbarian,' repeated the hooded figure. 'Hand her over right now.'

Sati suddenly turned towards the carriage as she realised something, shouting, 'Mother! The new emergency conch shell close to the front grill. Blow it now!'

A loud plea for help emitted from the carriage. Bhabravya and his men had been summoned. The hooded figure cursed as he realised his advantage had been taken away. He had very little time to complete his operation. The other Suryavanshis would be back soon. 'Charge!'

The Arishtanemi stayed in position.

'Steady,' said Shiva. 'Wait for them. All you have to do is buy time. Keep the princess safe. Our friends will be back soon.'

As the Chandravanshis came closer, Sati suddenly broke through the cordon and attacked the hooded figure. Sati's surprise attack slowed the charge of the Chandravanshis. The Arishtanemi had no choice. They charged at the Chandravanshis like vicious tigers.

Shiva moved quickly to protect the right flank of Sati as an advancing Vishwadyumna got dangerously close to her. Vishwadyumna swung his sword to force Shiva out of his way. However, the speed of Shiva's advance left Vishwadyumna unbalanced. Shiva easily parried the blow and pushed Vishwadyumna back with his shield. Nandi meanwhile moved rapidly to the left of Sati to block the Chandravanshis trying to charge down that side.

In the meantime, Sati was attacking the hooded figure with fierce blows. He, on the other hand, seemed intent upon simply defending himself and was not striking back. He wanted her alive and unharmed.

Shiva cut Vishwadyumna savagely across the shoulder that had been exposed when he was pushed back. Grimacing, Vishwadyumna brought his shield up to fend off another attack from Shiva. In tandem, his sword arm thrust at Shiva's torso. Shiva quickly pulled his shield in to protect himself. But not quickly enough. Vishwadyumna was able to slash Shiva's chest. Stepping back and jumping to his right, Shiva brought his sword swiftly down in a brutal jab. While Vishwadyumna promptly brought his shield up to block the attack, Shiva's unorthodox move unsettled him. He staggered back realising that Shiva was an excellent swordsman. It was going to be a long and hard duel.

Nandi had already brought down one Chandravanshi soldier who had broken a law of combat that prohibited attacking below the waist, and cut Nandi's thigh. Bleeding profusely, Nandi was ferociously battling another soldier who had attacked him from the left. The Chandravanshi brought his shield down hard on Nandi's injured leg, making him stagger and fall. The Chandravanshi thought he had his man. Raising his sword high with both his hands, he was about to bring it down to finish the job but he suddenly arched forward, as if a brutal force had pounded him from the back. As he fell, Nandi saw a knife buried deep in the Chandravanshi's back. Looking up, he saw Shiva's left arm continue down in a smooth arc from the release of the dagger. With his right hand, Shiva brought his sword up to block a vicious cut from Vishwadyumna. As Nandi stumbled back to his feet, Shiva reached behind to pull his shield in front again.

The hooded figure knew that time was running out. The other Arishtanemi would be back soon. He tried to move behind Sati, to club her on the back of the head and knock her unconscious but she was too quick. She moved swiftly to the left to face her enemy again. Taking a knife out of her angvastram folds with her left hand, she slashed outwards to cut deep across the hooded figure's immense stomach. The knife sliced through the robe but its effect was broken by the armour.

And then with a resounding roar, Bhabravya and the other Arishtanemi rushed back to fight alongside their mates. Seeing themselves vastly outnumbered, the hooded figure had no choice. He ordered his soldiers to retreat. Shiva stopped Bhabravya from chasing the Chandravanshis once again.

'Let them go, brave Bhabravya,' said Shiva. 'We will have

other opportunities to get them. Right now the primary objective is to protect the royal family.'

Bhabravya looked at Shiva with admiration for the way this foreigner fought, and not the blue throat of which he was unaware. He nodded politely. 'It makes sense, foreigner.'

Bhabravya quickly formed the Arishtanemi soldiers into a tight perimeter and pulled the wounded within. Dead bodies were not touched. At least three Arishtanemi had lost their lives while nine Chandravanshi bodies lay in the clearing. The last one had taken his own life since he was too wounded to escape. Better to meet one's maker than to fall into enemy hands alive and reveal secrets. Bhabravya ordered his soldiers to stay low and keep their shields in front for protection against any arrows. And thus they waited till the rescue party arrived.

— 𑀓𑀽𑀼𑀖𑀰 —

'My God,' cried an anxious Daksha as he hugged Sati tight.

The rescue party of five hundred soldiers had reached by the fourth hour of the second prahar. Daksha, Brahaspati and Kanakhala had accompanied the caravan despite Parvateshwar's warnings of the risks. Releasing Sati from his grip, Daksha whispered as a small tear escaped his eyes, 'You are not injured, are you?'

'I am alright father,' said Sati self-consciously. 'Just a few cuts. Nothing serious.'

'She fought very bravely,' said Veerini, as she beamed with pride.

'I think that is a mother's bias,' said Sati, as her serious expression was restored. Turning towards Shiva, she continued, 'It was Shiva who saved the day, father. He figured out the real plan of the Chandravanshis and rallied everyone at the crucial moment. It was because of him that we beat them back.'

'Oh, I think she's too generous,' said Shiva.

She's impressed. Finally!!

'She isn't being generous at all, my Lord,' said a visibly grateful Daksha. 'You have begun your magic already. We have actually beaten back a terrorist attack. You don't know how significant this is for us!'

'But it wasn't a terrorist attack, your Highness' said Shiva. 'It was an attempt to kidnap the princess.'

'Kidnap?' asked Daksha.

'That hooded man certainly wanted her alive and unharmed.'

'What hooded man?!' cried Daksha, alarmed.

'That was the Naga, your Highness,' said Shiva, surprised at Daksha's hysterical response. 'I have seen that man fight. He is an excellent warrior. A little slow in his movements, but excellent all the same. But while fighting Sati he was trying his best not to hurt her.'

The colour drained completely from Daksha's face. Veerini glared at her husband with a strange mixture of fear and anger. The expressions on their faces made Shiva feel uncomfortable, as if he was intruding on a private family moment.

'Father?' asked a worried Sati. 'Are you alright?'

Hearing no response from Daksha, Shiva turned to Sati and said, 'Perhaps it's best if you speak to your family alone. If you don't mind, I will go check if Nandi and the other soldiers are alright.'

— ⟨symbols⟩ —

Parvateshwar was walking amongst his men, checking on the injured and ensuring that they received medical help. Bhabravya walked two steps behind. The General came up to the Chandravanshi who had been killed by Shiva while protecting Nandi. He roared in horror, 'This man has been stabbed in the back!'

'Yes, my Lord,' said Bhabravya with his head bowed.

'Who did this? Who broke the sacred rules of combat?'

'I think it was the foreigner, my Lord. But I heard that he was trying to protect Captain Nandi who had been attacked by this Chandravanshi. And the Chandravanshi himself was not following the combat rules having attacked Nandi below the waist.'

Parvateshwar turned with a withering look at Bhabravya, causing him to cower in fear. 'Rules are rules,' he growled. 'They are meant to be followed even if your enemy ignores them.'

'Yes, my Lord.'

'Go make sure that the dead get proper cremations. Including the Chandravanshis.'

'My Lord?' asked a surprised Bhabravya. 'But they are terrorists.'

'*They* may be terrorists,' snarled Parvateshwar. 'But *we* are Suryavanshis. We are the followers of Lord Ram. There are civilities that we maintain even with our enemies. The Chandravanshis will get proper cremations. Is that clear?'

'Yes, my Lord.'

— ⋀◎ᙍ𝄁⊕ —

'Why do you call the foreigner "Your Lord"?' asked an injured Arishtanemi lying next to Nandi.

Shiva had just departed after spending half an hour with Nandi and the other injured soldiers. If one had a look at the injured at this point, it would be impossible to believe that they had fought a battle just a few hours earlier. They were talking jovially with each other. Some were ribbing their mates about how they had fallen for the red-herring towards the beginning of the battle. In the Kshatriya way, to laugh in the face of death was the ultimate mark of a man.

'Because he *is* my Lord,' answered Nandi simply.

'But he is a foreigner. A caste-unmarked foreigner,' said the Arishtanemi. 'He is a brave warrior, no doubt. But there are so many brave warriors in Meluha. What makes him so special? And why does he spend so much time with the royal family?'

'I can't answer that, my friend. You will know when the time is right.'

The Arishtanemi looked at Nandi quizzically. Then shook his head and smiled. He was a soldier. He concerned himself only with the here and now. Larger questions did not dwell for too long in his mind. 'In any case, I think the time *is* right to tell you that you are a brave man, my friend. I saw you fight despite your injury. You don't know the meaning of the word surrender. I would be proud to have you as my *bhraata*.'

That was a big statement from the Arishtanemi. The bhraata system that was prevalent in the Meluhan army assigned a mate of equal rank to each soldier up to the rank of captain. The two *bhraatas* would be like *brothers* who would always fight together and look out for each other. They would willingly fight the world for each other, would never love the same woman and would always tell each other the truth, no matter how bitter.

The Arishtanemi were elite soldiers of the empire. An Arishtanemi offered to be a bhraata only to his own kind. Nandi knew that he could never really be the Arishtanemi's bhraata. He had to stay with the Lord. But the honour of being offered the brotherhood of an Arishtanemi was enough to bring tears to Nandi's eyes.

'Don't get teary on me now,' chortled the Arishtanemi, wrinkling his nose in amusement.

Nandi burst out in laughter as he slapped the Arishtanemi on his arm.

'What is your name, my friend?' asked Nandi.

'Kaustav,' replied the Arishtanemi. 'Someday we shall battle the main Chandravanshi army together, my friend. And by the grace of Lord Ram, we will kill all those bastards!'

'By Lord Agni, we will!'

— ⏀ —

'It was interesting how you got into the Naga's mind,' said Brahaspati as he watched Shiva getting the gash on his torso cleaned and dressed.

Shiva had insisted that his injuries receive medical attention only after every other soldier's wounds had been tended.

'Well, I can't really explain it,' said Shiva. 'How the Naga would think just seemed so obvious to me.'

'Well, I can explain it!'

'Really? What?'

'The explanation is that you are the omnipotent "N", whose name cannot be spoken!' said Brahaspati, opening his eyes wide and conjuring his hands up like an ancient magician.

They burst out laughing, causing Shiva to bend backwards. The military doctor gave Shiva a stern look, at which he immediately quietened down and let him finish tending to the wound. Having applied the Ayurvedic paste and covered it with the medicinal neem leaf, the doctor bandaged the wound with a cotton cloth.

'You will need to change that every second day, foreigner,' said the doctor pointing at the bandage. 'The royal doctor in Devagiri will be able to do it for you. And don't let this area get wet for a week. Also, avoid the Somras during this period since you will not be able to bathe.'

'Oh he doesn't need the Somras,' joked Brahaspati. 'It's already done all the damage it can on him.'

Shiva and Brahaspati collapsed into helpless laughter again as the doctor walked away, shaking his head in exasperation.

'But seriously,' said Brahaspati calming down. 'Why would they attack you? You have not harmed anybody.'

'I don't think the attack was on me. I think it was for Sati.'

'Sati! Why Sati? That's even more bizarre.'

'It probably wasn't specifically for Sati,' said Shiva. 'I think the target was the royal family. The primary target was probably the Emperor. Since he wasn't there, they went for the secondary target, Sati. I think the aim was to kidnap a royal and use that person as leverage.'

Brahaspati did not respond. He seemed worried. Clasping his hands together and bringing them close to his face, he looked into the distance, deep in thought. Shiva reached into his pouch and pulled out his chillum, before carefully filling it with some dried marijuana. Brahaspati turned to look at his friend, unhappy with what he was doing.

'I've never told you this before Shiva and I probably shouldn't as, well... since you are a free man,' said Brahaspati. 'But I consider you my friend. And it is my duty to tell you the truth. I have seen some Egyptian merchants in Karachapa with this marijuana habit. It's not good for you.'

'You're wrong, my friend,' said Shiva, grinning broadly. 'This is actually the best habit in the world.'

'You probably don't know, Shiva. This has many harmful side effects. And worst of all, it even harms your memory, causing untold damage to your ability to draw on past knowledge.'

Shiva's face suddenly became uncharacteristically serious. He gazed back at Brahaspati with a melancholic smile. 'That is exactly why it is good, my friend. No idiot who smokes this is scared of forgetting.'

Shiva lit up his chillum, took a deep drag and continued, 'They are scared of *not* forgetting.'

Brahaspati stared sharply at Shiva, wondering what terrible past could have prompted his friend to get addicted to the weed.

CHAPTER 11

Neelkanth Unveiled

The next morning the royal caravan resumed its journey to Devagiri after spending the night at a temporary camp in the clearing. It wasn't safe to travel at night under the circumstances. The wounded, including Nandi, were lying in the first three carriages and the fifth one. The royal family and Shiva travelled in the fourth. All the soldiers who had fought in the previous day's battle were given the privilege of riding on horses in relative comfort. Brahaspati and Kanakhala walked along with the rest of the troops, in mourning for the three slain Arishtanemi. Parvateshwar, Bhabravya and two other soldiers bore a make-shift wooden palanquin that carried three urns containing the ashes of the martyrs. The urns would be given to their families for a ceremonial submersion in the Saraswati. Shiva, Sati and Nandi too wanted to walk but the doctor insisted they were in no condition to do so.

Parvateshwar walked with pride at the bravery of his soldiers. *His boys*, as he called them, had shown they were made of a metal forged in Lord Indra's own furnace. He cursed himself for not being there to fight with them. He castigated himself for not being there to protect his Goddaughter, *his* Sati, when she was in danger. He prayed for the day when he would finally get a chance to destroy the cowardly Chandravanshis. He also silently pledged that he would anonymously donate his salary for the next six months to the families of the slain soldiers.

'I didn't think he would fall to these levels!' exclaimed Daksha in disgust.

Shiva and Sati, comfortably asleep in the carriage, were woken up by Daksha's outburst. Veerini looked up from the book that she was reading, narrowing her eyes to concentrate on her husband.

'Who, your Highness?' asked Shiva groggily.

'Dilipa! That blight on humanity!' said Daksha, barely concealing his loathing.

Veerini continued to stare hard at her husband. She slowly reached out, pulled Sati's hand in hers, brought it close to her lips and kissed it gently. Then she put her other hand protectively on top of Sati's hand. Sati looked at her mother warmly with a hint of a smile and rested her tired head on Veerini's shoulders.

'Who is Dilipa, your Highness?' asked Shiva.

'He is the Emperor of Swadweep,' answered Daksha. 'Everyone knows that Sati is the apple of my eye. And they were possibly trying to kidnap her in order to force my hand!'

Shiva gazed at Daksha with sympathy. He could understand the outrage of the Emperor at the latest Chandravanshi treachery.

'And to reduce yourself to a level where you use a Naga for this nefarious plan,' said a furious Daksha. 'This shows what the Chandravanshis are capable of!'

'I don't know if the Naga was being used, your Highness,'

said Shiva softly. 'It appeared as though he was the leader.'

Daksha however was too lost in his righteous anger to even explore Shiva's insinuation. 'The Naga may have been the leader of this particular platoon, my Lord, but he would almost certainly be under the overall command of the Chandravanshis. No Naga can be a leader. They are cursed people born with horrific deformities and diseases in this birth as a punishment for terrible crimes that they have committed in their previous birth. The Nagas are embarrassed to even show their face to anyone. But they have tremendous power and skills. Their presence strikes terror in the heart of all Meluhans, and most Swadweepans as well. The Chandravanshis have sunk low enough to even consort with those deformed demons. They hate us so much that they have become blind to the sins they are bringing upon their own souls by interacting with the Nagas.'

Shiva, Sati and Veerini continued to hear Daksha's ranting in silence.

Turning towards Shiva, Daksha continued, 'Do you see the kind of vermin we are up against, my Lord? They have no code, no honour. And they outnumber us ten to one. We need your help my Lord. It's not just my people, but my family as well. We are in danger.'

'Your Highness, I will do all that I can to help you,' said Shiva. 'But I am not a General. I cannot lead an army against the Chandravanshis. I am just a simple tribal leader. What difference can one man make?'

'At least let me announce your presence to the court and the people, my Lord,' urged Daksha. 'Just spend a few weeks travelling through the empire. Your presence will raise the morale of the people. Look at the difference you made yesterday. We actually foiled a terrorist attack because of you, because of your presence of mind. Please, let me announce your arrival. That is all I ask.'

Shiva looked at Daksha's earnest face with trepidation. He could feel Sati's and Veerini's eyes on him. Especially Sati's.

What am I getting myself into?

'All right,' said Shiva in resignation.

Daksha rose and embraced Shiva in a tight grip of gratitude.

'Thank you, my Lord!' exclaimed Daksha, even as Shiva released himself from the warm hug with a sharp intake of air. 'I will announce your presence at the court tomorrow itself. Then you can leave for a tour of the empire in another three weeks. I will personally make all the arrangements. You will have a full brigade travelling with you for security. Parvateshwar and Sati will accompany you as well.'

'No!' protested Veerini in a harsh tone that Sati had never heard her mother use. 'Sati is not going anywhere. I am not going to allow you to put our daughter's life in danger. She is staying with me in Devagiri.'

'Veerini, don't be silly,' said Daksha calmly. 'You really think that something would happen to Sati if the Lord Neelkanth was around? She is safest when she is with the Lord.'

'She is not going. And that is final!' glared Veerini in a firm voice, clutching Sati's hand tightly.

Daksha turned towards Shiva, ignoring Veerini. 'Don't worry, my Lord. I will have all the arrangements made. Parvateshwar and Sati will also travel with you. You will just have to restrain Sati sometimes.'

Shiva frowned. So did Sati.

Daksha smiled genially. 'My darling daughter has the tendency to be a little too brave at times. Like this one time, when she was just a child, she had jumped in all by herself, with nothing but her short sword, to save an old woman being attacked by a pack of wild dogs. She nearly got herself killed for her pains. It was one of the worst days of my life. I think it is the same impulsiveness which worries Veerini as well.'

Shiva looked at Sati. There was no expression on her face.

'That's why,' continued Daksha, 'I am suggesting that you keep her restrained. Then there should be no problem.'

Shiva glanced again at Sati. He felt a surge of admiration coupled with the boundless love he felt for her.

She did what I couldn't do.

— ⵣ🌙ⵑⵑ⊕ —

The next morning, Shiva found himself seated next to Daksha in the Meluhan royal court. The magnificence of the court left him wonderstruck. Since this was a public building, the usual Meluhan reticence had been bypassed. It was built next to the Great Public Bath. While the platform had been constructed of the standard kiln-bricks, the structure itself, including the floor, was made of teak wood. Brawny wooden pillars had been laid into set grooves on the platform. The pillars had been extravagantly sculpted with celestial figures like *apsaras, devas* and *rishis* — *celestial nymphs, Gods* and *sages* — amongst others. An ornately carved wooden roof that had been inlaid with gold and silver designs crowned the top of the pillars. Pennants of the holy blue colour and royal red colour hung from the ceiling. Each niche on the walls had paintings depicting the life of Lord Ram. But Shiva had little time to admire the glorious architecture of the court. Daksha's expectations would be apparent in his speech and were causing him considerable discomfort.

'As many of you may have heard,' announced Daksha, 'there was another terrorist attack yesterday. The Chandravanshis tried to harm the royal family on the road from Mount Mandar to Devagiri.'

Murmurs of dismay filled the court. The question troubling everyone was how the Chandravanshis had discovered the route to Mount Mandar. Shiva meanwhile kept reminding himself that this wasn't a terrorist attack. It was just a kidnap attempt.

'The Chandravanshis had planned their attack with great deception,' said Daksha, drowning out the murmurs with his booming voice.

The talented architects of the court had designed the structure in such a manner that any voice emanating from the royal platform resonated across the entire hall. 'But we beat them back. For the first time in decades, we beat back a cowardly terrorist attack.'

An exultant roar went up in the court at this announcement. They had beaten back open military assaults from the Chandravanshis before. But until today, the Meluhans had found no answer to the dreaded terrorist strikes. This was because the terrorists usually launched surprise attacks on non-military locations and fled before the Suryavanshi soldiers could get there.

Raising his hand to quieten the crowd, Daksha continued, 'We beat them back because the time for truth to triumph has finally arrived! We beat them back because we were led by Father Manu's messenger! We beat them back because the time for justice has come!'

The murmurs grew louder. Had the Neelkanth finally arrived? Everyone had heard the rumours. But nobody believed them. There had been too many false declarations in the past.

Daksha raised his hand. He waited just enough for the anticipation to build up. And then jubilantly bellowed, 'Yes! The rumours are true. Our saviour has come! The Neelkanth has come!'

Shiva winced at being put up for display on the royal platform with his cravat removed. The Meluhan elite thronged around him, their statements buzzing in Shiva's ears.

'We had heard the rumours, my Lord. But we didn't believe them to be true.'

'We have nothing to fear anymore, my Lord. The days of evil are numbered!'

'Where are you from, my Lord?'

'Mount Kailash? Where is that, my Lord? Do you think I could go on a pilgrimage there?'

Answering these questions repeatedly and being confronted by the blind faith of these people disturbed Shiva. The moment he had a chance, he requested Daksha for permission to leave the court.

— ༀ☉ᠯ♀⊕ —

A few hours later, Shiva sat in the quiet comfort of his chamber, contemplating what had happened at the court. The cravat was back around his neck.

'By the Holy Lake, can I really deliver these people from their troubles?'

'What did you say, my Lord?' asked Nandi, who was sitting patiently at a distance.

'The faith your people place upon me makes me anxious,' said Shiva, loud enough for Nandi to hear. 'If there was a one-on-one battle, I could take on any enemy in order to protect your people. But I am no leader. And I am certainly not a "destroyer of evil".'

'I am sure that you can lead us to victory against anyone, my Lord. You beat them back on the road to Devagiri.'

'That wasn't a genuine victory,' said Shiva dismissively. 'They were a small platoon, aiming to kidnap and not to kill. If we face a well organised and large army, whose aim is to kill, the situation may be very different. To me it appears that Meluha is ranged against formidable and ruthless enemies. The solution cannot lie in reposing faith in an individual. Your people need to adapt to the changing times. Perhaps your innocent ways will find you helpless in the face of such a cold-blooded enemy. A new system is needed. I am hardly a God to perform miracles.'

'You are right, my Lord,' said Nandi, with all the conviction of a simple, lucky man not troubled by too many thoughts. 'A new system is required, and I obviously don't know what this new system should be. But I do understand one thing. More than a thousand years back, we faced a similar situation and Lord Ram came and taught us a better way. I am sure that, similarly, you will lead us to a superior path.'

'I am no Lord Ram, Nandi!'

How can this fool even compare me to Lord Ram, the Maryada Purushottam, the Ideal Follower of Laws?

'You are better than Lord Ram, my Lord,' said Nandi.

'Stop this nonsense, Nandi! What have I done to even

be compared with Lord Ram? Let alone be considered better?'

'But you *will* do deeds that will place you above him, my Lord.'

'Just shut up!'

— ⅄◍ᔕ♀⊛ —

The preparations for Shiva's tour of the empire were in full swing. Shiva, however, still found time for Sati's dance lessons every afternoon. They were developing a quiet friendship. But Shiva agonised over the fact that while she showed respect, there was no softening of emotions in her or expression of feelings.

In the meantime, Shiva's tribe had been brought over to Devagiri, where they were given comfortable accommodation and jobs. Bhadra, however, was not to stay with the Gunas. He had instead been assigned to accompany the Neelkanth on his voyage.

'*Veer*bhadra! When the hell did you get this name?' Shiva asked Bhadra, meeting him for the first time since his departure from Kashmir.

'Stupid reason actually,' smiled Bhadra, whose slight hump had disappeared completely, thanks to the magical Somras. 'On the journey here, I saved the caravan leader from a tiger attack. He gave me the title for a *brave man* before my name.'

'You fought a tiger single-handed?' asked Shiva, clearly impressed.

Bhadra nodded feeling awkward.

'Well, then you really deserve to be called Veerbhadra!'

'Yeah right!' smiled Bhadra, suddenly turning serious.

'The crazy label of "destroyer of evil"... Are you okay with this? You are not giving in to these pleas just because of your past, are you?'

'I am going with the flow right now, my friend. Something tells me that despite all my misgivings, I can actually help these people. These Meluhans are completely mad, no doubt. And I certainly can't do ALL that they expect of me. But I do feel that if I can make a difference, however small, I will be able to reconcile myself with my past.'

'If you are sure, then so am I. I will follow you anywhere.'

'Don't follow. Walk beside me!'

Veerbhadra laughed and embraced his friend. 'I've missed you Shiva.'

'I've missed you too.'

'Let's meet in the garden in the afternoon. I've got a great batch of marijuana.'

'It's a deal!'

Brahaspati too had sought permission to travel with Shiva. He explained that a Mesopotamian ship carrying some rare chemicals, essential for a critical experiment, was to dock at the port city of Karachapa soon. His team had to check and obtain those materials anyway. It would be a good idea to do this while travelling with Shiva. Daksha said that he had no problems with Brahaspati joining the tour if the Lord was okay with it. Shiva agreed enthusiastically with the suggestion.

Three weeks after the court announcement about the Neelkanth, the day finally dawned for the commencement of Shiva's tour of the empire. On the morning of the day itself, Daksha walked into Shiva's chambers.

'You could have summoned me, your Highness,' said Shiva with a Namaste. 'You did not need to come here.'

'It is my pleasure to come to your chambers, my Lord,' smiled Daksha, returning Shiva's greeting with a low bow. 'I thought I would introduce the physician who would be travelling with your entourage. She arrived from Kashmir last night.'

Daksha moved aside to let his escort show the doctor into the room.

'Ayurvati!' exclaimed Shiva, his face lit up in a brilliant smile. 'It's so good to see you again!'

'The pleasure is all mine, my Lord,' beamed Ayurvati, as she bent down to touch Shiva's feet.

Shiva immediately moved back to neatly side-step Ayurvati. 'I have told you before, Ayurvati,' said Shiva. 'You are a giver of life. Please don't embarrass me by touching my feet.'

'And you are the Neelkanth, my Lord. The destroyer of evil,' said Ayurvati with devotion. 'How can you deny me the privilege of being blessed by you?'

Shiva shook his head in despair and let Ayurvati touch his feet. He gently touched her head and blessed her.

A few hours later, Shiva, Sati, Parvateshwar, Brahaspati, Ayurvati, Krittika, Nandi and Veerbhadra set off. Accompanying them was a brigade of fifteen hundred soldiers, twenty-five handmaidens and fifty support staff for their security and comfort. They planned to travel by road till the city of Kotdwaar on the Beas river. From thereon, they would use boats to travel to the port city of Karachapa. Then they would move due east to the city of Lothal. Finally, they would move north by road to the inland delta of the Saraswati and then by boats back to Devagiri.

CHAPTER 12

Journey through Meluha

'Who was Manu?' asked Shiva. 'I have heard of him quite often being referred to as "the Father".'

The caravan had been travelling for a few days on the broad road from Devagiri to Kotdwaar. In the centre it consisted of a row of seven carriages identical to the ones used during the trip to Mandar. Five of them were empty. Shiva, Sati, Brahaspati and Krittika travelled in the second carriage. Parvateshwar was in the fifth, along with Ayurvati and his key brigadiers. The General's presence meant that every rule had to be adhered to strictly. Hence Nandi, whose rank did not allow him to travel in the carriage, was riding a horse with the rest of the cavalry. Veerbhadra had been inducted as a soldier in Nandi's platoon. Led by their respective captains, the brigade were in standard forward, rear and side defence formations around the caravan.

Both Brahaspati and Sati started answering Shiva simultaneously.

'Lord Manu was the...'

They both stopped talking.

'After you please, Brahaspati*ji*,' said Sati.

'No, no,' said Brahaspati with a warm smile. 'Why don't you tell him the story?'

He knew whose voice the Neelkanth would prefer.

'Of course not, Brahaspati*ji*. How can I supersede you? It would be completely improper.'

'Will somebody answer me or are you two going to keep up this elaborate protocol forever?' asked Shiva.

'Alright, alright,' laughed Brahaspati. 'Don't turn blue all over now.'

'That is hilarious Brahaspati,' smiled Shiva. 'Keep this up and you might actually get someone to laugh in a hundred years.'

As Brahaspati and Shiva chortled, Sati was astounded by the inappropriate manner in which the conversation was progressing. But if the revered chief scientist seemed comfortable, then she would desist from commenting. And in any case, how could she reprimand Shiva? Her code of honour forbade it. He had saved her life. Twice.

'Well, you are right about Lord Manu being the Father,' said Brahaspati. 'He is considered the progenitor of our civilisation by all the people of India.'

'Including Swadweepans?' asked Shiva incredulously.

'Yes, we believe so. In any case, Lord Manu lived more than eight and a half thousand years ago. He was apparently a prince from south India. A land way beyond the Narmada river, where the earth ends and the great ocean begins. That land is the Sangamtamil.'

'Sangamtamil?'

'Yes. Sangamtamil was the richest and most powerful country in the world at the time. Lord Manu's family, the Pandyas, had ruled that land for many generations. However, from the records left by Lord Manu, we know that by his time the kings had lost their old code of honour. Having degenerated into corrupt ways, they spent their days indulging in the pleasures of their fabulous wealth rather than being earnest about their duties and their spiritual life. Then a terrible calamity occurred. The seas rose and destroyed their entire civilisation.'

'My God!' exclaimed Shiva.

'Lord Manu had foreseen this day and had in fact prepared for it. He believed that it was the decadence his old country had fallen into that had incurred the wrath of the Gods. In order to escape the inevitable calamity, he led a band of his followers to the northern, higher lands in a fleet of ships. He established his first camp at a place called Mehragarh deep in the western mountains of present day Meluha. Deeply committed to establishing a moral and just society, he gave up his princely robes and became a priest. In fact the term for priests in India, pandit, is derived from Lord Manu's family name — Pandya.'

'Interesting. So how did Lord Manu's little band grow into the formidable India we see today?'

'The years immediately following their arrival at Mehragarh were harsh on them. With each year's monsoon, the flooding and sea tides would become stronger. But after many years and with the force of Lord Manu's prayers, the anger of the Gods abated and the waters stopped advancing. The sea, however, never receded to its original levels.'

'This means that somewhere in the deep south, the sea still covers the ancient Sangamtamil cities?'

'We believe so,' answered Brahaspati. 'Once the sea stopped advancing, Lord Manu and his men came down from the mountains. They were shocked to see that the minor stream that was the Indus had now become a massive river. Many other rivulets across northern India too had swollen and six great rivers had emerged — Indus, Saraswati, Yamuna, Ganga, Sarayu and Brahmaputra. Lord Manu said the rivers started flowing because the temperatures of our land rose with the wrath of the Gods. With the rise in temperatures, huge channels of ice or glaciers frozen high in the Himalayas began to melt, creating the rivers.'

'Hmm…'

'Villages, and later cities, grew on the banks of these rivers. Thus our land of the seven rivers, Sapt-Sindhu, was born out of the destruction of the Sangamtamil.'

'Seven? But you mentioned the creation of six rivers in North India.'

'Yes, that's true. The seventh river already existed. It is the Narmada and it became our southern border. Lord Manu strictly forbade his descendants to go south of the Narmada. And if they did so, they could never return. This is a law that we believe even the Chandravanshis adhere to.'

'So what are Lord Manu's other laws?'

'There are numerous laws actually. They are all listed in an extensive treatise called the Manusmriti. Would you be interested in listening to the entire text?'

'Tempting,' smiled Shiva. 'But I think I'll pass.'

'With your permission, my Lords, perhaps we can further discuss Lord Manu's guidance to our society over lunch,' suggested Krittika.

— 🕉 —

At a short distance from the road on which the Neelkanth's caravan travelled, a small band of about forty men trudged silently along the Beas. One in two men of the platoon carried a small coracle on his head. It was typical of this region. The locals made small and light boats made of bamboo, cane and rope, portable enough to be carried by a single man on his head. Each boat could ferry two people with relative safety and speed. At the head of the platoon was a young man with a proud battle scar adorning his face, his head crowned with a brown turban. A little ahead of him walked a hooded figure. With his head bowed, his eyes scrunched, he took slow methodical steps, his mind lost in unfathomable thoughts. His breathing was hard. He brought his hand up languidly to rub his masked forehead. There was a leather bracelet on his right wrist with the serpent Aum symbol embroidered on it.

'Vishwadyumna,' said the hooded figure. 'We will enter the river from here. Whenever we come close to populated areas, we will move away from the river to avoid detection. We have to reach Karachapa within two months.'

'Karachapa, my Lord?' asked a surprised Vishwadyumna. 'I was under the impression that we were to have a secret audience with the Queen outside Lothal.'

'No,' answered the hooded figure. 'We will meet her outside Karachapa.'

'Yes, my Lord,' answered Vishwadyumna, as he looked back in the direction of the road to Kotdwaar. He knew that his Lord would have dearly liked to make one more attempt to kidnap the princess. He also knew that it was foolhardy to endeavour to do so given the strength of the force accompanying the caravan. In any case, they were behind schedule for their main mission. They had to meet the Queen urgently.

Turning towards one of his soldiers, Vishwadyumna

ordered, 'Sriktaa, place your coracle in the river and give me your oar. I will row the Lord through this part of the journey.'

Sriktaa immediately did as instructed. Vishwadyumna and the hooded figure were the first of the platoon to enter the river. Vishwadyumna had already started rowing by the time his men started placing their boats into the waters. At a distance further down the river, the hooded figure saw two women lounging carelessly on a boat. One of the women was sloppily splashing water from the side of the boat on to her friend who was making a hopeless attempt at avoiding getting wet. Their childish game caused their boat to sway dangerously from side to side. The hooded figure saw that the women had not detected a crocodile that had entered the river from the opposite bank. Having spied what must have looked like an appetising meal, the crocodile was swimming swiftly towards the women's boat.

'Look behind you!' shouted the hooded figure, as he motioned to Vishwadyumna to row rapidly in their direction.

The women could not hear him from the distance. What they did see, however, was two men rowing towards them. They could see that one of them was almost a giant covered from head to toe in a strange robe, his face hidden behind a mask. This man was making frantic gestures. Behind the duo were a large number of soldiers swiftly pushing their boats on to the river. That was all the warning the women needed. Thinking that the men were coming towards them with evil intent, the women put all their effort into hastily rowing away from the hooded figure's boat. Into the path of the crocodile.

'No!' shouted the hooded figure.

He grabbed the oar from Vishwadyumna, using his powerful arms to row rapidly. He was shortening the distance between them by the minute. But not fast enough. As the crocodile closed in on the women's boat it dived underwater and charged at it, rocking it with its massive body. The tiny vessel tilted and capsized, throwing the women into the Beas.

Screams of terror rent the air as the women fought to stay afloat. The crocodile had moved too far ahead in its dash. Turning around, it swam towards the struggling women. The delay of those crucial seconds proved fateful for the women. The rescue boat moved in between the crocodile and them. Turning towards Vishwadyumna, the hooded figure ordered, 'Save the women.'

Before Vishwadyumna could react, he had flung his robe aside and dived into the river. With his knife held tight between his teeth, he swam towards the advancing crocodile. Vishwadyumna pulled one of the women into the boat. She had already lost consciousness. Turning to the other woman, he reassured, 'I am coming back soon.'

Vishwadyumna turned and paddled vigorously towards the bank. On the way he passed some of his soldiers. 'Row quickly. The Lord's life is in danger.'

The other soldiers paddled towards the area where the hooded figure had dived into the river. The water had turned red with blood from the battle raging under water. The soldiers said a silent prayer to Lord *Varun*, the *God of the water and the seas*, hoping that the blood did not belong to their Lord.

One of the soldiers was about to jump into the water with his sword when the hooded figure emerged onto the surface, soaked in blood. It was that of the crocodile. He swam forcefully towards the other woman who was on the verge of losing consciousness. Reaching her in the nick of time, he pulled her head out of the water. Meanwhile, two of the Chandravanshi soldiers dived off their coracle.

'My Lord, please get into the boat,' said one of them. 'We will swim ashore.'

'Help the woman first,' replied the hooded figure.

The soldiers pulled the unconscious woman on to the coracle. The hooded figure then carefully climbed aboard and rowed towards the shore. By the time he reached the river bank, the other woman had been revived by Vishwadyumna. She was obviously disoriented by the rapid chain of events.

'Are you alright?' Vishwadyumna asked the woman.

In answer, the woman looked beyond Vishwadyumna and screamed. Vishwadyumna turned around. On the river bank, the hooded figure was coming ashore carrying the other woman's limp body. His clothes were glued to his massive body. To the disoriented woman, the crocodile's blood all over his clothes, seemed like that of her friend.

'What have you done, you beast?' shrieked the woman.

The Naga looked up abruptly. His eyes showed mild surprise but he refrained from saying anything. He gently laid the unconscious woman on the ground. As he did so, the mask on his face came undone. The woman next to Vishwadyumna stared at him with horror.

'Naga!' she screeched.

Before Vishwadyumna could react, she leapt to her feet and fled screaming, 'Help! Help! A Naga is eating my friend!'

The Naga looked at the fleeing woman with melancholic eyes. He shut the windows to his tormented soul and shook his head slightly. Vishwadyumna meanwhile turned to see his Lord's face for the first time in years. He immediately lowered his gaze, but not before he had seen the rare emotion of intense pain and sorrow in his Lord's normally expressionless eyes. Seething with anger, Vishwadyumna drew his sword, swearing to slay the ungrateful wench he had just saved.

'No, Vishwadyumna,' ordered the Naga. Pulling his mask back on, he turned to his other soldiers. 'Revive her.'

'My Lord,' argued Vishwadyumna. 'Her friend will bring others here. Let's leave this woman to her fate and go.'

'No.'

'But my Lord, someone may come any time now. We must escape.'

'Not till we've saved her,' said the Naga, in his usual calm voice.

— ⋏⃝⫙⚲⊕ —

The royal party, including Nandi and Veerbhadra, were sitting together enjoying their lunch in the courtyard of the rest-house they had stopped at. Half the brigade had sat down for their meal. They needed all the energy they could muster in order to march in this scorching heat. Parvateshwar had come in to check on the food arrangements. He was especially concerned about Sati's comfort. However, he had refused to join them. He was going to eat later with his soldiers.

A loud commotion from the area of one of the perimeter guards disturbed Shiva. He got up to investigate, motioning to Brahaspati, Nandi and Veerbhadra to remain seated. Parvateshwar too had heard the racket and was moving towards the uproar.

'Please save her!' cried the woman. 'A Naga is eating her alive!'

'I am sorry,' answered the Captain. 'But we have strict orders. We are not to leave the vicinity of this rest-house under any circumstances.'

'What is the matter?' asked Parvateshwar.

The Captain spun around in surprise, saluted and bowed low. 'My Lord, this woman alleges that a Naga has attacked her friend. She's asking for help.'

Parvateshwar looked at the woman intensely. He would have liked nothing more than to chase the Naga party and destroy them. But his orders were crystal clear. He was not to leave the Neelkanth and Sati. Their protection was the only objective of the brigade. But he was a Kshatriya. What kind of Kshatriya would he be if he didn't fight to protect the weak? Seething at the restrictions forced upon him, Parvateshwar was about to say something when Shiva appeared.

'What's the matter?' asked Shiva.

'My Lord,' said the Captain in awe. He scarce believed that he was actually in the presence of the Neelkanth. 'This woman claims that her friend has been attacked by Nagas', he gasped. 'We are concerned that it may be a trap. We have heard about the Chandravanshi duplicity on the Mount Mandar road.'

Shiva heard his inner voice cry. *'Go back! Help her!'*

Drawing his sword in one smooth motion he told the woman, 'Take me to your friend.'

Parvateshwar looked at Shiva with respect. It was mild, but it was respect all the same. He immediately drew his own sword and turned to the Captain, 'Follow us with your platoon. Brigadier Vraka, command your men to be on alert for any surprise attack. The safety of our princess is paramount.'

Shiva and Parvateshwar ran behind the woman who seemed to lead them with ease. She was obviously a local. The Captain trailed them with his platoon of thirty soldiers. After sprinting for the larger part of half an hour, they finally reached the riverside to find a dazed woman sitting on the ground. Breathing heavily, she was staring in shock at an imaginary vision in the distance. There was blood all over her clothes, but strangely, no injury. There were many footsteps that appeared to be coming out of the river and going back in.

The Captain looked at the woman who had led them here with suspicious eyes. Turning to his soldiers, he ordered, 'Form a perimeter around the General and the Neelkanth. It could be a trap.'

'She was being eaten alive, I tell you,' screeched the woman, absolutely stunned to see her friend alive and unharmed.

'No she wasn't,' said Shiva calmly. He pointed at the corpse of the crocodile floating in the river. A large flock of crows had settled on the carcass, fighting viciously over its entrails. 'Somebody just saved her from that crocodile.'

'Whoever it was has rowed across the river, my Lord,' said the Captain, pointing towards the heavy footmarks close to the river.

'Why would a Naga risk his own life to save this woman?' asked Shiva.

Parvateshwar seemed equally surprised. This was completely unlike the usually blood thirsty Nagas they had dealt with until now.

'My Lords,' said the Captain, addressing both Shiva and

Parvateshwar. 'The women appear safe. Perhaps it is not wise for everybody to stay here. With your permission, I will escort these women back to their village and rejoin the caravan at Kotdwaar. You could retire to the rest-house.'

'All right,' said Parvateshwar. 'Take four soldiers along with you just in case.'

Both Shiva and Parvateshwar walked back, baffled by this inexplicable event.

— ⳤ◍ᴜⳡ⊕ —

It was late in the evening. Shiva, Brahaspati, Nandi and Veerbhadra sat quietly around the camp fire. Shiva turned to see Sati sitting on the rest-house veranda at a distance, along with Ayurvati and Krittika. They were absorbed in a serious conversation. Parvateshwar was moving among his soldiers, as usual, personally supervising the security arrangements of the camp and the comfort of his boys.

'It's ready, Shiva,' said Veerbhadra, handing over the chillum to the Neelkanth.

Shiva brought the pipe up to his lips and pulled hard. He relaxed visibly. Feeling the need for respite, he smoked some more before passing it back to his friend. Veerbhadra offered it to Brahaspati and Nandi, both of whom declined. Brahaspati stared at Shiva who kept stealing glances at Sati. He smiled and shook his head.

'What?' asked Shiva who had noticed Brahaspati's gesture.

'I understand your longing, my friend,' whispered Brahaspati. 'But what you are hoping for is quite difficult. Almost impossible.'

'It can't be easy when it's so valuable, can it?'

Brahaspati smiled and patted Shiva on his hand.

Veerbhadra knew what his friend needed. Dance and music. It always improved his mood. 'Don't people sing and dance in this wretched country?'

'Private Veerbhadra,' said Nandi, his tone different with a subordinate, 'firstly, this country is not wretched. It's the greatest land in the world.'

Veerbhadra playfully put his hands together in a mock apology.

'Secondly,' continued Nandi, 'we dance only when an occasion demands it, like the Holi festival or a public performance.'

'But the greatest joy derived from dancing is when you do it for no reason at all, Captain,' said Veerbhadra.

'I agree,' said Shiva.

Nandi immediately fell silent.

Without any warning, Veerbhadra suddenly burst forth into one of the folk songs of his region. Shiva smiled at his friend, for Veerbhadra was singing one of his favourites. Continuing to sing, Veerbhadra rose slowly and began dancing to the lilting tune, now accompanied by Shiva. The combination of marijuana and dance immediately changed his mood.

Brahaspati stared at Shiva, first in shock and then with pleasure. He noticed a pattern in their dancing, a smooth six-step combination that was repeated rhythmically. Shiva reached out and pulled Brahaspati and Nandi to their feet. They joined in, tentative at first. But it was only a matter of time before a reluctant Brahaspati was dancing with abandon. The group moved together in a circle around the fire, the singing louder and livelier.

Shiva suddenly darted out of the ring towards Sati. 'Dance with me.'

A flabbergasted Sati shook her head.

'Oh come on! If you can dance while your Guru*ji* and I watch, then why not here?'

'That was in pursuit of *knowledge*!' said Sati.

'So? Must all dance be solely towards that end?'

'I didn't say that.'

'Fine. Have it your way,' said Shiva with a frustrated gesture. 'Ayurvati, come!'

A startled Ayurvati didn't know how to react. Before she could decide on a course of action, Shiva held her hand and pulled her into the circle. Veerbhadra lured Krittika in as well. The group danced boisterously and sang loudly, making a racket in an otherwise quiet night. Sati got up agitatedly and glared at Shiva's back before running into the rest-house. Shiva's anger increased even more as he noticed her absence when he turned towards the veranda.

Damn!

He returned to his dance, his heart in a strange mixture of pain and joy. He turned once again towards the veranda. There was nobody.

Who's behind that curtain?

Shiva was dragged into the next move by Veerbhadra. It was some time later that he was in a position to look once again at the veranda. He could see Sati, outlined behind the curtain, staring at him. Only at him.

Wow!

A surprised and delighted Shiva swung back into his dance, moving in his prime form. He had to impress her!

CHAPTER 13

Blessings of the Impure

Kotdwaar was decked up in all its glory to receive the Neelkanth. Torches had been lit across the fort perimeter as if it was Diwali. Red and blue pennants, embellished with the Suryavanshi Sun, had been hung down the fort walls. In a rare breach of protocol, the governor had come outside the city to personally receive the Neelkanth. The following day, a public function had been organised after the Neelkanth had met the Kotdwaar elite at the local court. Sixty-five thousand people, practically the entire population of Kotdwaar, had converged for the event. Keeping in mind the vast number of attendees, the event had been organised outside the city platform to ensure that every person could be accommodated.

A speech delivered by Shiva convinced the Kotdwaarans that Meluha's days of trouble were soon to end. The remarkable effect Shiva seemed to have on the people was a revelation to him. Though he was careful with his words, telling them that he would do all he could to support the people of Meluha, the public made their own interpretations.

'The cursed Chandravanshis will finally be destroyed,' said one man.

'We don't have to worry about anything now. The Neelkanth will take care of everything,' said a woman.

Seated with Brahaspati and Sati on the speaker's platform, Parvateshwar was deeply unhappy with the public's reaction. Turning to the chief scientist, he said, 'Our entire society is based on the rule of law and we are not meant to blindly follow anyone. We are expected to solve our problems ourselves and not hope for miracles from a solitary man. What has this man done to deserve such blind faith?'

'Parvateshwar,' said Brahaspati politely, for he greatly respected him. 'I think Shiva is a good man. I think he cares enough to want to do something. And aren't good intentions the first step towards any good deed?'

Parvateshwar didn't completely agree. Never a believer in the legend of the Neelkanth, the General thought that every man or woman had to earn his station in life with training and preparation, and not just receive it on a silver platter because of a blue throat. 'Yes, that may be true. But intentions aren't enough. They have to be backed by ability as well. Here we are, putting an untrained man on a pedestal and acting as though he is our saviour. For all we know, he might lead us to complete disaster. We are acting on faith. Not reason or laws or even experience.'

'Sometimes one needs a little bit of faith when faced with a difficult situation. Reason doesn't always work. We may also need a miracle.'

'*You're* talking about miracles? A scientist?'

'You can have scientific miracles too, Parvateshwar,' smiled Brahaspati.

Parvateshwar was distracted by the sight of Shiva stepping off the platform. As he came down there was a surge of people wanting to touch his hand. The soldiers, led by Nandi and Veerbhadra, were holding them back. There was a blind man amongst them who looked like he might get injured in the melee.

'Nandi, let that man through,' said Shiva.

Nandi and Veerbhadra lowered the rope to let him in.

Another man shouted, 'I am his son. He needs me to guide him.'

'Let him in as well,' said Shiva.

The son rushed in and held his father's hand. The blind man, who seemed lost without his son's hand, smiled warmly as he recognised the familiar touch. He was led close to Shiva and the son said, 'Father, the Neelkanth is right in front of you. Can you sense his presence?'

Copious tears flowed from the blind man's eyes. Without thinking, he bent down to try and touch Shiva's feet. His son cried out in shock as he pulled the man back sharply.

'Father!' scolded the son.

Shiva was stunned by the harshness in the son's tone which was in sharp contrast with the loving manner in which he had spoken so far. 'What happened?'

'I am sorry, my Lord,' apologised the son. 'He didn't mean to. He just forgot himself in your presence.'

'I am sorry, my Lord,' said the blind man, his tears flowing stronger.

'What about?', asked Shiva.

'He is a vikarma, my Lord,' said his son, 'ever since disease blinded him twenty years ago. He should not have tried to touch you.'

Sati, who was now standing near Shiva, had heard the entire conversation. She felt sympathy for the blind man. She knew the torment of having even your touch considered impure. But what he had tried to do was illegal.

'I am sorry, my Lord,' continued the blind man. 'But please don't let your anger with me stop you from protecting our country. It is the greatest land that *Parmatma* created. Save it from the evil Chandravanshis. Save us, my Lord.'

The blind man continued to cry while folding his hands in a penitent Namaste. Shiva was shaken by the dignity of the blind man.

He still loves a country that treats him so unfairly.

Why? Even worse he doesn't even appear to think he's being treated unfairly.

Tears welled up in Shiva's eyes as he realised that he was looking at a man whom fate had been very unkind to.

I will stop this nonsense.

Shiva stepped forward and bent down. The flabbergasted son trembled in disbelief as he saw the Neelkanth touch the feet of his vikarma father. The blind man was at sea for a moment. When he did understand what the Neelkanth had done, his hand shot up to cover his mouth in shock.

Shiva rose and stood in front of the blind man. 'Bless me, sir, so that I find the strength to fight for a man as patriotic as you.'

The blind man stood dumb-struck. His tears dried up in his bewilderment. He was about to collapse when Shiva took a quick step forward to hold him, lest he fall to the ground. The blind man found the strength to say, '*Vijayibhav*'. *May you be victorious.*

The son caught hold of his father's limp body as Shiva released him. The entire crowd was stunned into silence by what the Neelkanth had done. Forget the gravity of touching a vikarma, the Neelkanth had just asked to be blessed by one. Shiva turned to see Parvateshwar's enraged face. Shiva had broken the law. Broken it brazenly and in public. Next to him stood Sati. Her face, her eyes, her entire demeanour expressionless.

What the hell is she thinking?

— ☥⦾᚛ᚄ⊕ —

Brahaspati and Sati entered Shiva's chambers as soon as he was alone. Shiva's smile at seeing two of his favourite people in the world disappeared on hearing Sati's voice, 'You must get a shudhikaran done.'

He looked at her and answered simply, 'No.'

'No? What do you mean no?'

'I mean No. Nahin. Nako,' said Shiva, adding the words for 'no' in the Kashmiri and the Kotdwaar dialect, for good measure.

'Shiva,' said Brahaspati, keeping his composure. 'This is no laughing matter. I agree with Sati. The governor too was worried about your safety and has arranged for a pandit. He waits outside as we speak. Get the ceremony done now. '

'But I just said I don't want to.'

'Shiva,' said Sati, reverting to her usual tone. 'I respect you immensely. Your valour. Your intelligence. Your talent. But you are not above the law. You have touched a vikarma. You have to get a shudhikaran. That is the law.'

'Well if the law says that my touching that poor blind man is illegal, then the law is wrong!'

Sati was stunned into silence by Shiva's attitude.

'Shiva, listen to me,' argued Brahaspati. 'Not doing a shudhikaran can be harmful to you. You are meant for bigger things. You are important to the future of India. Don't put your own person at risk out of obstinacy.'

'It's not obstinacy. You tell me, honestly, how can it harm me if I happened to touch a wronged man, who I might add, still loves his country despite the way he has been ostracised and ill-treated?'

'He may be a good man Shiva, but the sins of his previous birth will contaminate your fate,' said Brahaspati.

'Then let them! If the weight on that man's shoulders lessens, I will feel blessed.'

'What are you saying Shiva?' asked Sati. 'Why should you carry the punishment of someone else's sins?'

'Firstly, I don't believe in the nonsense that he was punished for the sins of his previous birth. He was just stricken by an illness, plain and simple. Secondly, if I choose to carry the weight of someone else's so called sins, why should it matter to anyone?'

'It matters because we care about you!' cried Brahaspati.

'Come on Sati,' said Shiva. 'Don't tell me you believe in this rubbish.'

'It is not rubbish.'

'Look, don't you want me to fight for you? Stop this unfairness that your society has subjected you to?'

'Is that what this is about? *Me?*' asked Sati, outraged.

'No,' retorted Shiva immediately, then added. 'Actually yes. This is also about you. It is about the vikarma and the unfairness that they have to face. I want to save them from leading the life of an outcast.'

'I DON'T NEED YOUR PROTECTION! I CANNOT BE SAVED!' shouted Sati, before storming out of the room.

Shiva glared at her retreating form with irritation. 'What the hell is it with this woman?!'

'She's right Shiva,' advised Brahaspati. 'Don't go there.'

'You agree with her on this vikarma business? Answer from your heart, Brahaspati. Don't you think it is unfair?'

'I wasn't talking about that. I was talking about Sati.'

Shiva continued to glare at Brahaspati defiantly. Everything in his mind, body and soul told him that he should pursue Sati. That his life would be meaningless without her. That his soul's existence would be incomplete without her.

'Don't go there, my friend,' reiterated Brahaspati.

— ᛉ◍ᚢᚐ⊕ —

The caravan left the river city of Kotdwaar on a royal barge led and followed by two large boats of equal size and grandeur as the royal vessel. Typical of the Meluhan security system, the additional boats were to confuse any attacker as to which boat the royal family may be on. The entire royal party was in the second boat. Each of the three large boats was manned by a brigade of soldiers. Additionally, five small and quick cutter boats kept pace on both sides of the royal convoy, protecting the sides in case of an ambush.

'The rivers are the best way to travel when the monsoon is not active, my Lord,' said Ayurvati. 'Though we have good roads connecting all major cities, they cannot match the rivers in terms of speed and safety.'

Shiva smiled at Ayurvati politely. He was not in the frame of mind for much conversation. Sati had not spoken to Shiva since that fateful day at Kotdwaar when he had refused to undergo a shudhikaran.

The royal barge stopped at many cities along the river. The routine seemed much the same. Extreme exuberance would manifest itself in each city on the arrival of the Neelkanth.

It was a kind of reaction that was quite unnatural in Meluha. But then, a Neelkanth didn't grace the land every day.

'Why?' asked Shiva of Brahaspati, after many days of keeping quiet about the disquiet in his troubled heart.

'Why what?'

'You know what I am talking about, Brahaspati,' said Shiva, narrowing his eyes in irritation.

'She genuinely believes that she deserves to be a vikarma,' answered Brahaspati with a sad smile.

'Why?'

'Perhaps because of the manner in which she became a vikarma.'

'How did it happen?'

'It happened during her earlier marriage.'

'What! Sati was married?!'

'Yes. That was around ninety years ago. It was a political marriage with one of the noble families of the empire. Her husband's name was Chandandhwaj. She got pregnant and went to Maika to deliver the child. It was the monsoon season. Unfortunately, the child was stillborn.'

'Oh my God!' said Shiva, empathising with the pain Sati must have felt.

'But it was worse. On the same day, her husband, who had gone to the Narmada to pray for the safe birth of their child, accidentally drowned. On that cursed day, her life was destroyed.'

Shiva stared at Brahaspati, too stunned to react.

'She became a widow and was declared a vikarma on the same day.'

'But how can the husband's death be considered her fault?' argued Shiva. 'That's completely ridiculous.'

'She wasn't declared a vikarma because of her husband's death. It was because she gave birth to a stillborn child.'

'But that could be due to any reason. The local doctors could have made a mistake.'

'That doesn't happen in Meluha, Shiva,' said Brahaspati calmly. 'Giving birth to a stillborn child is probably one of the worst ways in which a woman can become a vikarma. Only giving birth to a Naga child would be considered worse. Thank God that didn't happen. Because then she would have been completely ostracised from society.'

'This has to be changed. The concept of vikarma is unfair.'

Brahaspati looked at his friend intensely. 'You might save the vikarma, Shiva. But how do you save a woman who doesn't want to be saved? She genuinely believes that she deserves this punishment.'

'Why? I'm sure she is not the first Meluhan woman to give birth to a stillborn. There must have been others before her. And there will be many more after her.'

'She was the first *royal* woman to give birth to a stillborn. Her fate has been a source of embarrassment to the emperor. It raises questions about his ancestry.'

'How would it raise questions about his lineage? Sati is not his birth daughter. She would also have come from Maika, right?'

'No, my friend. That law was relaxed for families of nobility around two hundred and fifty years back. Apparently in the "national interest", noble families were allowed to keep their birth-children. Some laws can be amended, provided ninety per cent of the Brahmins,

Kshatriyas and Vaishyas above a particular chosen-tribe and job status vote for the change. There have been rare instances of such unanimity. This was one of them. Only one man opposed this change.'

'Who?'

'Lord Satyadhwaj, the grandfather of Parvateshwar. Their family vowed not to have any birth children after this law was passed. Parvateshwar honours that promise to this day.'

'But if the birth law could be changed,' said Shiva working things out, 'why couldn't the law of vikarma?'

'Because there aren't enough noble families affected by that law. That is the harsh truth.'

'But all this goes completely against Lord Ram's teachings!'

'Lord Ram's teachings also say that the concept of the vikarma is correct. Don't you want to question that?'

Shiva glanced at Brahaspati silently, before looking out at the river.

'There is nothing wrong with questioning Lord Ram's laws, my friend,' said Brahaspati. 'There were times when he himself acknowledged a higher rationale. The issue is your motive for wanting to change the law. Is it because you genuinely think that the law itself is unfair? Or is it because you are attracted to Sati and you want to remove an inconvenient law which stands in your path?'

'I genuinely think the vikarma law is unfair. I have felt it from the moment I found out about it. Even before I knew Sati was a vikarma.'

'But Sati doesn't think that the law is unfair.'

'She is a good woman. She doesn't deserve to be treated this way.'

'She is not just a good woman. She is one of the finest I have ever met. She is beautiful, honest, straight-forward, brave and intelligent — everything a man could possibly want in a woman. But you are not just another man. You are the Neelkanth.'

Shiva turned around and rested his hands on the craft's railing. He looked into the distance at the dense forest along the riverbanks as their boat glided over the water. The soothing evening breeze fanned Shiva's long locks.

'I've told you before, my friend,' said Brahaspati. 'Because of that unfortunate blue throat, every decision you take has many ramifications. You have to think many times before you act.'

— ⚹◎⛎♌⊕ —

It was late in the night. The royal fleet had just set sail from the city of Sutgengarh on the Indus. The emotions at Sutgengarh had erupted in the now predictable routine of exuberance at the sight of the Neelkanth. The saviour of their civilisation had finally arrived.

Their saviour, however, was in his own private hell. Sati had maintained her distance from Shiva for the last few weeks. His pain was deep, his loneliness constant.

The fleet's next port of call was the famous *Mohan Jo Daro* or the *Platform of Mohan*. The city, on the mighty Indus, was dedicated to a great philosopher-priest called Lord Mohan, who had lived in this region many thousands of years ago. Once he had met with the people of Mohan Jo Daro, Shiva expressed a desire to visit the temple of Lord Mohan. This temple stood further downstream outside the main city platform. The governor of Mohan

Jo Daro had offered to accompany the Lord Neelkanth there in a grand procession. Shiva however insisted on going alone. He felt drawn to the temple. He felt that it would offer some solutions to his troubled heart.

The temple itself was simple. Much like Lord Mohan himself. A small nondescript structure announced itself as the birthplace of the sage. The only sign of the temple's significance was the massive gates in the four cardinal directions of the compound. As instructed by Shiva, Nandi and Veerbhadra, along with their platoon, waited outside.

Shiva, with his comforting cravat back around his neck, walked up the steps feeling tranquil after a long time. He rang the bell at the entrance and sat down against a pillar with his eyes shut in quiet contemplation. Suddenly, an oddly familiar voice asked: 'How are you, my friend?'

CHAPTER 14

Pandit of Mohan Jo Daro

Shiva opened his eyes only to behold a man who seemed almost a replica of the pandit he had met at the Brahma temple, in what seemed like another life. He sported a similar long flowing white beard and a big white mane. He wore a saffron dhoti and angvastram. The wizened face wore a calm and welcoming smile. If it hadn't been for this pandit's much taller frame, Shiva could have easily mistaken him for the one he had met at the Brahma temple.

'How are you, my friend?' repeated the pandit as he sat down.

'I am alright, Pandit*ji*,' said Shiva, using the Indian term '*ji*' as a form of respect. He couldn't understand why, but the intrusion was welcome to him. It almost seemed as though he was drawn to this temple because he was destined to meet the pandit. 'Do all pandits in Meluha look alike?'

The man smiled warmly. 'Not all the pandits. Just us.'

'And who might *"us"* be, Pandit*ji*?'

'The next time you meet one of us, we will tell you,' said the Pandit cryptically. 'That is a promise.'

'Why not now?'

'At this point of time, our identity is not important,' smiled the Pandit. 'What is important is that you are disturbed about something. Do you want to talk about it?'

Shiva took a deep breath. Gut instinct told him that he could trust this man.

'There is this task that I supposedly have to do for Meluha.'

'I know. Though I wouldn't dismiss the Neelkanth's role as a "task". He does much more than that.' Pointing at Shiva's throat, the Pandit continued, 'A strip of cotton cloth cannot cover divine brilliance.'

Shiva looked up with a wry smile. 'Well, Meluha does seem like a wonderful society. And I want to do all I can to protect it from evil.'

'Then what is the problem?'

'It is that I find some grossly unfair practices in this nearly perfect society. And that this is inconsistent with the ideals that Meluha aspires to.'

'What practices are you referring to?' asked the Pandit.

'For example, the way the vikarma are treated.'

'Why is it unfair?'

'How can anyone be sure that these people committed sins in their previous birth? And that their present sufferings are a result of that? It might be sheer bad luck. Or a random act of nature.'

'You're right. It could be. But do you think that the fate of the vikarma is about them personally?'

'Isn't it?'

'No it isn't,' explained the Pandit. 'It is about the society as a whole. The vikarma acceptance of their fate is integral to the stability of Meluha.'

Shiva frowned.

'What any successful society needs, O Neelkanth, is flexibility with stability. Why would you need flexibility? Because every single person has different dreams and capabilities. The birth son of a warrior could have the talent to be a great businessman. Then society needs to be flexible enough to allow this son to change his vocation from his father's profession. Flexibility in a society allows change, so that all its members have the space to discover their true selves and grow to their potential. And if every person in a society achieves his true potential, society as a whole also achieves its true potential.'

'I agree.'

But what does this have to do with the vikarma?

'I'll come to the obvious question in a bit. Just bear with me,' said the Pandit. 'If we believe that flexibility is key to a successful society, then the Maika system is designed to achieve it in practice. No child knows what the professions of his birth-parents are. He is independent to pursue what his natural talent inspires him to do.'

'I agree. The Maika system is almost breathtakingly fair. A person can credit or blame *only himself* for what he does with his life. Nobody else. But this is about flexibility. What about stability?'

'Stability allows a person the freedom of choice, my friend. People can pursue their dreams only when they are living in a society where survival is not a daily threat. In a society without security and stability, there are no intellectuals or businessmen or artists or geniuses. Man is constantly in fight or flight mode. Nothing better than an animal. Where is the luxury then to allow ideas to be nurtured or dreams to be pursued? That is the way all humans were before we formed societies. Civilisation is very fragile. All it takes is a few decades of chaos for us to forget humanity and turn into animals. Our base natures can take over very fast. We can forget that we are sentient beings, with laws and codes and ethics.'

'I understand. The tribes in my homeland were no better than animals. They didn't even want to live a better life!'

'They didn't know a better life was possible, Neelkanth. That is the curse of constant strife. It makes us forget the most beautiful aspects of being human. That is why society must remain stable so that it is not pushed into a situation of having to fight for survival.'

'All right. But why would allowing people to achieve their potential cause instability? In fact, it should make people happier with their lives and thereby make society increasingly stable.'

'True, but only partially. People are happy when their life changes for the better. But there are two situations in which change can lead to chaos. First, when people face a change imposed by others, in situations that they cannot understand. This scares them almost as much as the fear of death. When change happens too fast, they resist it.'

'Yes, change forced by others is difficult to accept.'

'And too rapid a change causes instability. That is the bedrock of Lord Ram's way of life. There are laws which help a society change slowly and allow it to remain stable. At the same time, it allows its citizens the freedom to follow their dreams. He created an ideal balance between stability and flexibility.'

'You mentioned a second situation...'

'The second is when people *cannot* make the transition they want in order to improve their lives for reasons beyond their control. Say there is an exceptional warrior who loses his hand-eye coordination due to a disease. He is still a fighter, but not extraordinary any more. The odds are that he will be frustrated about what he perceives as injustice meted out to him. He is likely to blame his doctor, or even society at large. Many such discontented people can become a threat to society as a whole.'

Shiva frowned. He didn't like the logic. But he also knew that one of the main reasons why the Pakratis had rejected the peace offer made by his uncle years ago was because their diseased and old chief was desperate to live up to his earlier reputation of being an exceptional warrior who could have defeated the Gunas.

'Their combined rage can lead to unrest, even violence,' said the Pandit. 'Lord Ram sensed that. And that is why the concept of vikarma came into being. If you make a person believe that his misfortune in this birth is due to his sins in his previous birth, he will resign himself to his fate and not vent his fury on society at large.'

'But I disagree that ostracising the vikarma can work. It would only lead to a progressive increase in pent up anger.'

'But they are not ostracised. Their living expenses are subsidised by the government. They can still interact with family members. They are free to achieve personal excellence in their chosen fields, wherever possible. They can also fight to protect themselves. They cannot, however, be in a position to influence others. And this system has worked for one thousand years. Do you know how common rebellion was in India before Lord Ram created this empire? And most of the times, the rebellions were not led by farsighted men who thought they would create a better way of life for the common man. They were led by men discontented with their lot in life. People who were a lot like the vikarma. These rebellions usually caused chaos and decades were lost before order was restored.'

'So what you are saying is that anyone who is frustrated with life should simply resign himself to being a vikarma,' said Shiva. 'Why?'

'For the larger good of society.'

Shiva was aghast. He could not believe what he was hearing. He deeply disliked the arguments being presented to him. 'I am sorry, but I think this system is completely unfair. I have heard that almost one twentieth of the people in Meluha are vikarma. Are you going to keep so many people as outcast forever? This system needs to change.'

'You can change it. You are the Neelkanth. But remember, no system is absolutely perfect. In Lord Ram's time, a lady called Manthara triggered a series of events which led to the loss of millions of lives. She had suffered terribly due to her physical deformities. And then, fate put her in a position of influence over a powerful queen and thus over the entire kingdom. Therefore, the karma of one maladjusted victim of fate led to the mass destruction that followed. Would it not have been better for everybody if this person had been declared a vikarma? There are no easy answers. Having said that, maybe you are right. Maybe there are so many vikarma now that it can lead to a tipping point, tumble society into chaos. Do I have the solution to this problem? No. Maybe you could find it.'

Shiva turned his face away. He believed in his heart that the vikarma system was unfair.

'Are you concerned about *all* the vikarma, O Neelkanth?' asked the Pandit. 'Or just one in particular?'

— ⸸◉ᘮ⸸⊕ —

'What is the Lord doing in there?' asked Nandi. 'He is taking too long.'

'I don't know,' said Veerbhadra. 'All I know is that if Shiva says he needs to do something, I accept it.'

'Why do you call the Lord by his name?'

'Because that is his name!'

Nandi smiled at the simple answer and turned to look at the temple.

'Tell me Captain,' said Veerbhadra coming close to Nandi. 'Is Krittika spoken for?'

'Spoken for?'

'I mean,' continued Veerbhadra. 'Is she off limits?'

'Off limits?'

'You know what I mean,' said Veerbhadra turning beet red.

'She is a widow,' said Nandi. 'Her husband died fifteen years back.'

'Oh, that's terrible!'

'Yes, it is,' said Nandi, as he smiled at Veerbhadra. 'But to answer your question, she is "not spoken for" right now.'

— ⋏◎Ⴀ⅄⊕ —

'My Lady, may I say something?' asked Krittika.

Sati turned from the guest-room window to look at Krittika with a surprised frown. 'Have I ever stopped you from speaking your mind? A true Suryavanshi always speaks her mind.'

'Well,' said Krittika. 'Sometimes, it may not be so bad to lose control.'

Sati frowned even more.

Krittika spoke quickly, before her courage deserted her. 'Forget about him being the Neelkanth, my Lady. Just as a man, I think he is the finest I have seen. He is intelligent and brave, funny and kind, and worships the ground you walk on. Is that really so bad?'

Sati glared at Krittika; she didn't know if she was more upset with Krittika for what she was saying or with herself for experiencing feelings which were apparently so evident.

Krittika continued, 'Maybe, just maybe, breaking the rules can lead to happiness.'

'I am a Suryavanshi,' said Sati, her voice dropping. 'Rules are *all* that I live by. What have I got to do with happiness? Don't ever dare to speak to me about this again!'

— ⟨ symbols ⟩ —

'Yes, there is this particular vikarma,' admitted Shiva. 'But that is not why I think the vikarma law is unfair.'

'I know that,' said the Pandit. 'But I also know that what troubles you right now is your relationship with that one in particular. You don't want her to think that you would change the law, however justified you feel in doing so, just to get her. Because if Sati believes that, she will never come to you.'

'How do you know her name?' asked Shiva, flabbergasted.

'We know many things, my friend.'

'My entire life is meaningless without her.'

'I know,' smiled the Pandit. 'Perhaps I can help you.'

Shiva frowned. This was unexpected.

'You want her to reciprocate your love. But how can she when you don't even understand her?'

'I think I understand her. I love her.'

'Yes, you do love her. But you don't understand her. You don't know what she wants.'

Shiva kept quiet. He knew the Pandit was right. He was thoroughly confused about Sati.

'You can hazard a guess at what she wants,' continued the Pandit, 'with the help of the theory of transactions.'

'What?' asked a flummoxed Shiva.

'It makes up the fabric of society.'

'Excuse me, but what does this have to do with Sati?'

'Indulge me for a while, Neelkanth,' said the Pandit. 'You are aware that the cloth which has been spun into your clothes, is created when cotton threads are woven together, right?'

'Yes,' answered Shiva.

'Similarly, transactions are threads that when woven together make up a society, its culture. Or in the case of a person, they weave together his character.'

Shiva nodded.

'If you want to know the strength of a cloth, you inspect the quality of its weave. If you want to understand a person's character, look closely at his interpersonal behaviour or his transactions.'

'Alright,' said Shiva slowly, absorbing the Pandit's words. 'But transactions are...'

'I'll explain,' interrupted the Pandit. 'Transactions are interactions between two individuals. It could be trading goods, like a Shudra farmer offering grain for money from a Vaishya. But it could also be beyond material concerns, like a Kshatriya offering protection to a society in return for power.'

Shiva nodded in agreement. 'Transactions are about give and take.'

'Exactly. According to this logic, if you want something from someone, you have to give that person something he wants.'

'So what do you think she wants?' asked Shiva.

'Try and understand Sati's transactions. What do you think she wants?'

'I don't know. She is very confusing.'

'No, she isn't. There is a pattern. Think. She is probably the most eminent vikarma in history. She has the power to rebel if she wants to. She certainly has the spirit since she never backs off from a fight. But she does not rebel against the vikarma law. Neither does she fade into the background like most vikarmas and live her life in anonymity. She follows the commandments, and yet, she does not whine and complain. However unfairly life treats her, she conducts herself with dignity. Why?'

'Because she is a righteous person?'

'That she is, no doubt. But that is not the reason. Remember, in a transaction, you give something because you want something in return. She is accepting an unfair law without trying to make anyone feel guilty about it. And most importantly, she continues to use her talents to contribute to the good of society whenever she can. What do you think a person who is giving all this in her transactions with society wants in return?'

'Respect,' answered Shiva.

'Exactly!' beamed the Pandit. 'And what do you think you do when you try to *protect* such a person?'

'Disrespect her.'

'Absolutely! I know it comes naturally to you to want to protect any good person who appears to be in need. But control that feeling where Sati is concerned.

Respect her. And she will feel irresistibly drawn towards you. She gets many things from the people who love her. What she doesn't get is what she craves for the most — respect.'

Shiva looked at the Pandit with a grateful smile. He had found his answer.

Respect.

— ⋏◍Ⴎ⅄⊕ —

After two weeks, the Neelkanth's convoy reached the city of Karachapa at the confluence of the Indus and the Western Sea. It was a glittering city which had long grown beyond the one platform that it had been built on. The *Dwitiya* or *second* platform, had been erected fifty years ago on an even grander scale than the first one. The Dwitiya platform was where the Karachapa elite lived. The Governor, a diminutive Vaishya called Jhooleshwar, had heard of and followed the new tradition of receiving the Neelkanth outside the city.

Karachapa, with its hundred thousand citizens, was at its heart a frontier trading city. Therefore it was an act of foresight by Lord Brahmanayak, Emperor Daksha's father, to have appointed a Vaishya as its governor over a hundred years ago. Jhooleshwar had ruled the city extraordinarily well, gilding its fate in gold. He was considered its wisest and most efficient governor ever. Karachapa had long overtaken Lothal in the eastern part of the empire to become Meluha's premier city of commerce. While foreigners such as Mesopotamians and Egyptians were allowed into this liberal city, they couldn't travel further inland without express royal permission.

Jhooleshwar escorted the Neelkanth on an excursion to the Western Sea on his very first day in Karachapa. Shiva had never seen the sea and was fascinated by the near infinite expanse of water. He spent many hours at the port where Jhooleshwar proudly expounded upon the various types of ships and vessels that were manufactured at the shipyard attached to the Karachapa port. Brahaspati accompanied them to the port in order to check on the imports he was expecting from the Mesopotamian merchants.

At the state dinner organised for Shiva, Jhooleshwar proudly announced that a *yagna*, a *ceremonial fire sacrifice*, was being organised the next day in honour of the Neelkanth, under the auspices of Lord Varun and the legendary Ashwini Kumar twins. The Ashwini Kumar twins were celebrated ancient seafarers who had navigated ocean routes from Meluha to Mesopotamia and beyond. Their maps, guidance and stories were a source of inspiration and learning for this city of seamen.

After dinner, Shiva visited the chambers where Sati and Krittika were housed.

'I was wondering,' said Shiva, still careful with Sati since she had gone back to being formal with him, 'will you be coming to the yagna tomorrow?'

'I am very sorry, Lord Neelkanth,' said Sati courteously. 'But it may not be possible for me to attend the ceremony. I am not allowed to attend such yagnas.'

Shiva was about to say that nobody would question her since she would be attending with the Neelkanth. But he thought better of it. 'Perhaps we could practice some dance tomorrow? I cannot remember the last time we had a dance session.'

'That would be nice. I have not had the benefit of your instruction in a long time,' said Sati.

Shiva nodded unhappily at Sati — the freeze in their relationship tormented him. Bidding goodbye, he turned to leave.

Krittika glanced at Sati, shaking her head imperceptibly.

CHAPTER 15

Trial by Fire

The little boy hurried through a dusty goat trail, trying to avoid the sharp stones, bundling into his fur coat. The dense, wet forest encroached upon the path menacingly. It was difficult to see beyond the trees lining the narrow path. The boy was sure that there were terrible monsters lurking in the dense foliage, waiting to pounce on him if he slowed down. His village was but a few hours away. The sun was rapidly setting behind the mountains. Monsters love the darkness — he had heard his mother and grandmother say repeatedly when he was being difficult. He would have liked being accompanied by an elder, as monsters didn't trouble the elders.

His heart skipped a beat as he heard a strange heaving sound. He immediately drew out his short sword, suspecting an attack from behind. His friends had heard many stories about the monsters of the forests. The cowards never attacked from the front.

He stood still straining to determine the direction of the sound. It had a peculiar repetitive rhythm and seemed vaguely familiar. He felt as though he had heard it before. The heaving was now accompanied by a heavy grunting male voice. This was not a monster! The boy felt excitement course through his body. He had heard his friends whisper and giggle about it, but had never seen the act himself. This was his chance!

He crept slowly into the foliage, his sword dangling by his side. He did not have to go too far when he came upon the source of the sound. It came from a small clearing. He hid behind a tree trunk and peeped.

It was a couple. They seemed to be in a hurry. They had not even disrobed completely. The man was extraordinarily hairy — almost like a bear. The boy could only see his back from this angle. He had a frontal view of the woman though. She was astonishingly beautiful! Her wavy hair was long and lustrous. The partly torn blouse revealed a firm breast, with deep red welts upon them owing to the brutal intercourse. Her skirt had been ripped apart and revealed exquisite long legs. The boy was excited beyond imagination. Wait till his best friend Bhadra heard of this!

As he enjoyed the show, his disquiet grew. Something seemed amiss. The man was in the throes of passion while the woman lay passive — almost dead. Her hands lay lifeless by her side. Her mouth was tightly shut. She was not whispering encouragements to her lover. Were those tears of ecstasy rolling down her cheeks? Or was she being forced? But how could that be? The man's knife lay within the woman's reach. She could have picked up the blade and stabbed him if she wanted.

The boy shook his head. He tried to silence his conscience. 'Just shut up. Let me look.'

And then came the moment that would haunt him for the rest of his life. The woman's eyes suddenly fell upon him.

'HELP!' she cried out, 'Please help!'

The startled boy fell back, dropping his sword. The hairy monster turned to see who the woman was calling. The boy quickly picked up his sword and fled, ignoring the searing pain on his frost-bitten foot as he ran. He was terrified by the thought of the man chasing him. He could hear the man's heavy breathing.

The boy leapt onto the goat trail and sped towards his village.

He could still hear the heavy breathing. It was drawing closer every second. The boy suddenly swerved to his left, pivoted and slashed back with his sword.

There was nobody there. No sound of heavy breathing. The only sound was the haunting plea of a distraught woman.

'Help! Please help!'

The little boy looked back. That poor woman.

'Go back! Help her!' cried his inner voice.

He hesitated for a moment. Then turned and fled towards his village.

NO! GO BACK! HELP HER!

Shiva woke up sweating, his heart pounding madly. He instinctively turned around, wanting desperately to go back to that dreadful day. To redeem himself. But there would be no redemption. The woman's terrified face came flooding back. He shut his eyes. But how do you shut your eyes to an image that is branded on your mind?

He pulled his knees up and rested his head upon them. Then he did the only thing that helped. He cried.

— 𝍐◉ᠠ𝍐⊕ —

The yagna platform had been set up at the central square of the Dwitiya platform. For Karachapa, it was not the usual austere affair that was typical of Meluha. The frontier city had decorated the venue with bright colours that vied for attention. The platform itself had been painted in a bright golden hue. Colourfully decorated poles, festooned with flowers, held aloft a *shamiana*, a *cloth canopy*. Red and blue pennants, with the Suryavanshi symbol painted on them, hung proudly from many poles. The entire atmosphere was that of pomp and show.

Jhooleshwar received Shiva at the head of the platform

and guided him to his ritual seat at the yagna. At the governor's repeated requests, Shiva had removed his cravat for the duration of the ceremony. Parvateshwar and Brahaspati sat to the right of the Neelkanth while Jhooleshwar and Ayurvati sat to his left. Nandi and Veerbhadra had also been invited to sit behind Shiva. Though this was unorthodox, Jhooleshwar had acceded to the Neelkanth's request. Jhooleshwar governed a cosmopolitan border city and believed that many of the strict Meluhan laws could be bent slightly for the sake of expediency. His liberal attitude had made Karachapa a magnet for people from a wide variety of races and a hub for the exchange of goods, services and ideas.

Shiva looked towards Sati's balcony, which overlooked the central square in the distance. Though Sati was not allowed to step onto the platform while the yagna was being conducted, she could look on at the proceedings from the safe distance of her chambers. Shiva noticed her standing behind the balcony curtain, with Krittika by her side, observing the proceedings.

As was the custom before such a yagna, the pandit stood up and asked formally, 'If anybody here has any objection to this yagna, please speak now. Or forever hold your peace.'

This was just a traditional question, which wasn't actually supposed to be answered. Hence there was an audible, collective groan when a voice cried out loudly, 'I object.'

Nobody needed to look to recognise where the voice came from. It was Tarak, an immigrant from the ultra-conservative northwest regions of the empire. Ever since Tarak had come to Karachapa, he had taken it upon himself to be the 'moral police' of this 'decadent city of sin'.

Shiva strained his neck to see who had objections. He saw Tarak standing at the back, at the edge of the puja platform, very close to Sati's balcony. He was a giant of a man with an immense stomach, a miner's bulging muscular arms and a fair face that was cut up brutally due to a lifetime of strife. He cut an awesome figure. It was obvious, without even looking at his amulets, that Tarak was a Kshatriya who had made his living working in the lower rungs of the army.

Jhooleshwar glared at Tarak in exasperation. 'What is it now? This time we have ensured that we have not used the white Chandravanshi colours in our decorations. Or do you think the water being used for the ceremony is not at the correct temperature prescribed by the Vedas?'

The gathering sniggered. Parvateshwar looked at Jhooleshwar sharply. Before he could reprimand the Governor for his cavalier reference to the Vedas, Tarak spoke up. 'The law says no vikarma should be allowed on the yagna platform.'

'Yes,' said Jhooleshwar. 'And unless you have been declared a vikarma, I don't think that law is being broken.'

'Yes it is!'

There were shocked murmurs from the congregation. Jhooleshwar raised his hand.

'Nobody is a vikarma here, Tarak,' said Jhooleshwar. 'Now please sit down.'

'Princess Sati defiles the yagna with her presence.'

Shiva and Parvateshwar looked sharply at Tarak. Jhooleshwar was as stunned as the rest of the assembly by Tarak's statement. 'Tarak!' said Jhooleshwar. 'You go too far. Princess Sati is confined to the guest-house, abiding by the laws of the yagna. She is not present on the yagna platform. Now sit down before I have you whipped.'

'On what charge will you have me whipped, Governor?' yelled Tarak. 'Standing up for the law is not a crime in Meluha.'

'But the law has not been broken!'

'Yes it has. The exact words of the law is that no vikarma can be on the same platform while a yagna is being conducted. The yagna is being conducted on the Dwitiya platform of the city. By being on the same platform, the princess defiles the yagna.'

Tarak was technically correct. Most people interpreted that law to mean that a vikarma could not be on the *prayer ceremony platform*. However, since Karachapa, like most Meluhan cities, was built on a platform, a strict interpretation of the law would mean that Sati should not be anywhere on the *entire Dwitiya platform*. To keep the yagna legal, she would either have to move to the other platform of the city or outside the city walls.

Jhooleshwar was momentarily taken aback as Tarak's objection was accurate in principle. He tried a weak rally. 'Come, come Tarak. You are being too conscientious. I think that is too strict an interpretation. I think...'

'No, Shri Jhooleshwar*ji*,' reverberated a loud voice through the gathering.

Everybody turned to see where the sound came from. Sati, who had come out on her balcony, continued. 'Please accept my apologies for interrupting you, Governor,' said Sati with a formal Namaste. 'But Tarak's interpretation of the law is fair. I am terribly sorry to have disturbed the yagna. My entourage and I shall leave the city immediately. We will return by the beginning of the third prahar, by which time the ceremony should be over.'

Shiva clenched his fist. He frantically wanted to wring Tarak's neck but he controlled himself with superhuman effort. Within minutes Sati was out of the guest-house, along with Krittika and five personal bodyguards. Shiva turned to look at Nandi and Veerbhadra, both of whom rose to join Sati. They understood that Shiva wanted them to ensure her safety outside the city.

'It is disgusting that you did not realise this yourself,' Tarak said scornfully to Sati. 'What kind of a princess are you? Don't you respect the law?'

Sati looked at Tarak. Her face calm. She refused to be drawn into a debate and waited patiently for her guards to prepare the horses.

'I don't understand what a vikarma woman is doing travelling with the convoy of the Neelkanth. She is polluting the entire journey,' raged Tarak.

'Enough!' intervened Shiva. 'Princess Sati is leaving with dignity. Stop your diatribe right now.'

'I will not!' screeched Tarak. 'What kind of a leader are you? You are challenging Lord Ram's laws.'

'Tarak!' yelled Jhooleshwar. 'The Lord Neelkanth has the right to challenge the law. If you value your life, you will not defy his authority.'

'I am a Meluhan,' shrieked Tarak. 'It is my right to challenge anyone breaking the law. A *dhobi,* a mere *washerman,* challenged Lord Ram. It was his greatness that he acceded to the man's objection and renounced his wife. I would urge the Neelkanth to learn from Lord Ram's example and use his brain while making decisions.'

'ENOUGH TARAK!' erupted Sati.

The entire congregation was stunned into silence by Tarak's remark. But not Sati. Something inside her snapped. She had tolerated too many insults for too long. And she had endured them with quiet dignity. But this time, this man had insulted Shiva. *Her* Shiva, she finally acknowledged to herself.

'I invoke the right of *Agnipariksha*,' said Sati, back in control.

The stunned onlookers could not believe their ears. *A trial by fire!*

This was getting worse by the minute. Agnipariksha, a duel unto death, enabled a contestant to challenge an unjust tormentor. It was called Agnipariksha as combat would be conducted within a ring of fire. There was no escape from the ring. The duellists had to keep fighting till one person either surrendered or died. An Agnipariksha was extremely rare these days. And for a woman to invoke the right was almost unheard of.

'There is no reason for this, my lady,' pleaded Jhooleshwar. Just like his subjects, he was terrified that Princess Sati might be killed in his city. The gargantuan Tarak would certainly slay her. The Emperor's wrath would be terrible. Turning to Tarak, Jhooleshwar ordered, 'You will not accept this challenge.'

'And be called a coward?'

'You want to prove your bravery?' spoke Parvateshwar for the first time. 'Then fight me. I will act as Sati's second for the challenge.'

'Only I have the right to appoint a second, *pitratulya*,' said Sati, reverentially referring to Parvateshwar as being '*like a father*'. Turning to Tarak, she said, 'I am appointing no second. You will fight with me.'

'You will do no such thing Tarak,' Brahaspati objected this time.

'Tarak, the only reason you won't fight is if you are afraid of being killed,' said Shiva.

Every person turned towards the Neelkanth, shocked by his words. Turning to Sati, Shiva continued, 'Citizens of Karachapa, I have seen the Princess fight. She can defeat anyone. Even the Gods.'

Sati stared at Shiva, shocked.

'I accept the challenge,' growled Tarak.

Sati nodded at Tarak, climbed on her white steed and turned to leave. At the edge of the square, she pulled up her horse and turned to take one more look at Shiva. She smiled at him, turned and rode away.

— ⟰⟐⟓⚲⊕ —

It was the beginning of the third prahar when Shiva and Brahaspati stole quietly into the local *varjish graha*, the *exercise hall*, to observe Tarak exercising along with two partners. The day's yagna had been a disaster. With everyone petrified that the princess would die the next day, no one was inclined to participate in the ceremony. However, as the yagna had been called, it had to be conducted or the Gods would be offended. The congregation went through the motions and the yagna was called to a close.

Tarak's famed fearsome blows on his hapless partners filled Brahaspati's soul with dread and he came to an immediate decision. 'I'll assassinate him tonight. She will not die tomorrow.'

Shiva turned in stunned disbelief towards the chief scientist. 'Brahaspati? What are you saying?'

'Sati is too noble to meet a fate such as this. I am willing to sacrifice my life and reputation for her.'

'But you are a Brahmin. You are not supposed to kill.'

'I'll do it for you,' whispered Brahaspati, emotions clouding his judgement. 'You will not lose her, my friend.'

Shiva came close to Brahaspati and hugged him. 'Don't corrupt your soul, my friend. I am not worth such a big sacrifice.'

Brahaspati clung to Shiva.

Stepping back, Shiva whispered, 'In any case, your sacrifice is not required. For as sure as the sun rises in the east, Sati will defeat Tarak tomorrow.'

— ⵢⵧⵀⵣⵙ —

A few hours into the third prahar, Sati returned to the guest house. She did not go up to her room, but summoned Nandi and Veerbhadra to the central courtyard, drew her sword and began her practise with them.

A little later Parvateshwar walked in, looking broken. His expression clearly conveyed his fear that this might be the last time he would talk to Sati. She stopped practising, sheathed her sword and folded her hands into a respectful Namaste. 'Pitratulya,' she whispered.

Parvateshwar came close to Sati, his face distraught. She could not be sure but it seemed as though he had been crying. She had never seen even a hint of a tear in his confident eyes. 'My child,' mumbled Parvateshwar.

'I am doing what I think is right,' said Sati. 'I am happy.'

Parvateshwar couldn't find the strength to say anything. For a brief moment, he considered assassinating Tarak at night. But that would be illegal.

Just then, Shiva and Brahaspati walked in. Shiva noticed Parvateshwar's face. This was the first time he had seen any sign of weakness in the General. While he could understand Parvateshwar's predicament, he did not like the effect it was having on Sati.

'I am sorry I am late,' said Shiva cheerily.

Everyone turned to look at him.

'Actually, Brahaspati and I had gone to the Lord Varun temple to pray for Tarak,' said Shiva. 'We prayed that the journey his soul would take to the other world would be comfortable.'

Sati burst out laughing. So did the rest of the party in the courtyard.

'Bhadra, you are not the right opponent for the practise,' said Shiva. 'You move too fast. Nandi you duel with the princess. And control your agility.'

Turning to Sati, Shiva continued, 'I saw Tarak practise. His blows have tremendous power. But the force of the blows slows him down. Turn his strength into his weakness. Use your agility against his movements.'

Sati nodded, absorbing every word. She resumed her practise with Nandi. Moving rapidly compared to Nandi's slower movements, Sati was able to succeed in a strike that could kill.

Suddenly, an idea struck Shiva. Instructing Nandi to stop, he asked Sati, 'Are you allowed to choose the combat weapon?'

'Yes. It's my prerogative as I threw the challenge.'

'Then choose the knife. It will reduce the reach of his strikes while you would be able to move in and out much quicker.'

'That's brilliant!' concurred Parvateshwar, while Brahaspati nodded.

Sati signalled her agreement immediately. Almost at the

same instant, Veerbhadra emerged with two knives. Giving one to Nandi, he gave the other to Sati. 'Practise, my Lady.'

— 大◎ᘮᛉ⊕ —

Sati and Tarak stood at the centre of a circular stadium. This was not the main Rangbhoomi of Karachapa, which was huge in its proportions. This one had been constructed next to the main stadium, for music concerts that the Mesopotamian immigrants in Karachapa loved. The arena was of the exact dimensions required for an agnipariksha. Not so big that a person could simply steer clear of the other contestant and not too small so that the combat would end too soon. There were stands around the ground and a capacity crowd of over twenty thousand had come to watch the most important duel in Karachapa for the last five hundred years.

A silent prayer sprang to every lip. Work a miracle, O Father Manu, let Princess Sati win. Or at the very least, live. Both Tarak and Sati greeted each other with a Namaste, repeating an ancient pledge to fight with honour. Then, turning towards the statue of Lord Varun at the top of the main stand, they bowed and asked for blessings from the God of the Water and the Seas. Jhooleshwar had vacated his ceremonial seat right below the statue of Lord Varun for Shiva. The governor sat to Shiva's left with Ayurvati and Krittika to his left. Brahaspati and Parvateshwar sat to Shiva's right. Nandi and Veerbhadra were in their now familiar position, behind Shiva. A bird courier had been sent to Daksha the previous day, informing him of the duel. However, there wasn't enough time to expect a reply.

At long last, Jhooleshwar stood up. He was nervous

about the agnipariksha, but appeared composed. In keeping with the custom, he raised a balled fist to his heart and boomed: *'Satya! Dharma! Maan!'* An invocation to *Truth. Duty. Honour.*

The rest of the stadium rang in agreement. 'Satya! Dharma! Maan!'

Tarak and Sati echoed. 'Satya! Dharma! Maan!'

Jhooleshwar nodded to the stadium keeper who lit the ceremonial oil lamp with the holy fire. The lamp spilled its fire on to the oil channel; the periphery of the central ground was aflame. The ring for the pariksha had been set.

Jhooleshwar turned to Shiva. 'My Lord, your instructions to begin the duel.'

Shiva looked at Sati with a confident smile. Then turning to the stadium, he declared loudly, 'Truth will always triumph in the purifying fire of Lord Agni!'

Tarak and Sati immediately drew their knives. Tarak held his knife in front of him, like most traditional fighters. He had chosen a strategy that played to his strengths. Keeping his knife in front of him allowed him to strike the moment Sati came close. He did not stir too much, allowing Sati to make her moves in front of him.

Sati, breaking all known rules of combat, held her knife behind her. She shifted the knife continuously from one hand to the other, while keeping a safe distance from her opponent. The aim was to confuse Tarak about the direction of her attack. Tarak on the other hand was watching Sati's movements like a hawk. He saw her right arm flex. The knife was now in her right hand.

Suddenly Sati leapt to the left. Tarak remained stationary. He knew that with her right hand holding the knife, the leftward movement was a feint. She would have to move to the right to bring her knife into play. Sure enough, moving quickly to the right, Sati swung her stabbing arm in an arc at Tarak's torso. But Tarak was prepared. Shifting his knife quickly to his left hand, he slashed viciously, cutting Sati across her torso. It wasn't a deep cut, but it appeared to hurt. The audience let out a collective gasp.

Sati retreated and rallied. She moved the knife to her back again, transferring it from one hand to the other. Tarak kept a close eye on her arms. The knife was in her left hand. He expected her to move to the right, which she did. He remained immobile, waiting for her to swerve suddenly to her left. She did, swinging her left arm as she moved. Tarak acted before her arm could even come close enough to do any damage. He swung ferociously with his right arm and cut her deep in the left shoulder. Sati retreated rapidly as the congregation moaned in horror. Some shut their eyes. They could not bear to look anymore. Most were praying fervently. If it had to be done, let it be done swiftly and not in a slow painful manner.

'What is she doing?' whispered a panic-stricken Brahaspati to Shiva. 'Why is she charging in so recklessly?'

Shiva turned to look at Brahaspati, also noticing Parvateshwar's face. Parvateshwar had a surprised, yet admiring grin on his face. Unlike Brahaspati, he knew what was going on. Turning back to look at the duel, Shiva whispered, 'She's laying a trap.'

At the centre, Sati was still transferring the knife between her hands behind her back. She feigned a move from her right to the left, but this time did not transfer the knife. She flexed her left arm, keeping the right arm holding the knife loose and relaxed.

Tarak was watching Sati closely, confident that he

was going to slowly bleed her to death. He believed the knife was in her left hand. He waited for her to move to the right, and then to the left, which she did in a swift veer. Expecting her left arm to come in, he sliced with his right hand. Sati neatly pirouetted back. Before a surprised Tarak could react, Sati had leapt to her right and brought her right hand in brutally onto his chest. The knife pierced Tarak's lung. The shock of the blow immobilised him. Blood spurted from his mouth. He dropped his knife and staggered back. Sati ruthlessly maintained the pressure and dug the knife in deeper, right up to the hilt.

Tarak stumbled back and collapsed onto the ground, motionless. The entire stadium was stunned. Sati's face had the expression of the Mother Goddess in fury. Eighty-five years of repressed anger had surfaced in that instant. She pulled the knife out, slowly twisting it to inflict maximum damage. Blood spewed out from Tarak's mouth at an alarming rate. Gripping the knife in both hands she raised her arms, aiming at Tarak's heart for a quick kill. Unexpectedly though, her expression then transformed from rage to serenity. It was almost as if someone had sucked out all the negative energy from within her. She turned around. Shiva, the destroyer of evil, sat on his throne, staring at her with a slight smile.

Then she looked at Tarak, and whispered. 'I forgive you.'

The stadium erupted in joy. Even if Lord Varun himself had scripted the fight, it wouldn't have been so perfect. It had everything that the Suryavanshis held dear. Defiant when under pressure, yet magnanimous in victory.

Sati raised her knife and shouted, 'Jai Shri Ram!'

The entire stadium repeated, 'Jai Shri Ram!'

Sati turned towards Shiva and roared once again, 'Jai Shri Ram!'

'Jai...,' Shiva's words were clogged by the knot in his throat.

The Lord won't mind this time if I don't complete the cry.

Shiva glanced away from Sati, lest he show his tears to the woman he loved. Regaining control of himself, he looked back at her with a radiant smile. Sati continued to stare at Shiva. Emotions that had been dormant in her for too long rippled through her being as she saw Shiva's admiration. When she couldn't bear it any longer, she shut her eyes.

CHAPTER 16

The Sun and Earth

There was an impromptu celebration that night in Karachapa. Their princess was safe. The insufferable Tarak had been defeated. Many people in Karachapa believed that even his own mother must have loathed the surly preacher. He had few supporters in the liberal city. But there were rules for duels. Hence the moment Sati had forgiven Tarak, paramedics had rushed in to take him to the hospital. Surgeons had laboured for six hours to save his life. Much to the dismay of the town folk, they had succeeded.

'Have you heard about the poem of the sun and the earth?' Sati asked Shiva.

They were standing on the balcony of the governor's palace while a boisterous party raged inside.

'No,' said Shiva with a seductive grin, coming a little closer to her. 'But I'd love to hear it.'

'Apparently the earth sometimes thinks of the possibility of coming closer to the sun,' said Sati. 'But she can't do that. She is so base and his brilliance so searing, that she will cause destruction if she draws him closer.'

What now?

'I disagree,' said Shiva. 'I think the sun burns for only as long as the earth is close to him. If the earth wasn't there, there would be no reason for the sun to exist.'

'The sun doesn't exist merely for the earth. It exists for every single planet in the solar system.'

'Isn't it really upto the sun to determine whom he chooses to exist for?'

'No,' said a melancholic Sati, looking at Shiva. 'The moment he becomes the sun, he answers a higher calling. He does not exist for himself. He exists for the greater good. His luminosity is the lifeblood of the solar system. And if the earth has any sense of responsibility, she will not do anything to destroy this balance.'

'So what should the sun do?' asked Shiva, his hurt and anger showing on his face. 'Just waste his entire life burning away? Looking at the earth from a distance?'

'The earth isn't going anywhere. The sun and the earth can still share a warm friendship. But anything more is against the laws. It is against the interests of others.'

Shiva turned away from Sati in anger. He looked northward to seek solace from his holy lake. Feeling nothing, he looked up at the skies, towards the Gods he did not believe in.

Dammit!

His clenched fist struck the balcony railing powerfully, dislodging some bricks before he stormed off.

— 𝕏⦿⅄⚛⊕ —

Outside the city walls, in a forested area, a few soldiers lay in wait. At a slight distance, two hooded figures were seated on large rocks. The Captain of the platoon of soldiers stood rigid in attention next to the duo. He scarce believed that he was standing next to the Queen herself. The privilege overwhelmed him.

One of the hooded figures raised his hand to motion for the Captain to step closer. On the hooded figure's wrist was a leather bracelet with the serpent Aum. 'Vishwadyumna, are you sure this is where we are supposed to meet him? He is late by nearly an hour.'

'Yes, my Lord,' replied Vishwadyumna nervously. 'This is exactly where he had said he would come.'

The other hooded figure turned and spoke in a commanding voice — a feminine one. A voice used to being obeyed without question. 'That man makes the Queen of the Nagas wait!' Turning to the other hooded figure, she continued, 'I trust you have worked this out in detail. I hope I haven't entered this vile territory in vain.'

The other hooded figure moved his fleshy hands in a motion asking the Queen for patience. 'Have faith, your Highness. This man is our key to giving the Suryavanshis a blow that they will never recover from.'

'Apparently, there was an Agnipariksha fight between the princess and a man in the city yesterday,' said Vishwadyumna suddenly, trying to impress the Queen with his sharp ear for local knowledge. 'I do not have the exact details. I just hope that our man was not involved in it.'

The Queen turned swiftly to the other hooded figure. Then back to Vishwadyumna. 'Please wait with the other soldiers.'

Vishwadyumna sensed he had said something he shouldn't have and quickly retreated before his Lord's stern gaze could reprimand him. This is why he had been told in training school that a good soldier never speaks unless spoken to.

'*She's* here?' asked the Queen with barely suppressed anger.

The other hooded figure nodded.

'I thought I'd told you to forget about this,' said the Queen sternly. 'There is nothing to be gained by this quest. Do you realise that your stupid attack on Mount Mandar might have led them to suspect that we have a mole in their midst?'

The male figure looked up in apology.

'Did you come here for her?'

'No, your Highness,' said the hooded figure with a deeply respectful tone. 'This was the place where he asked us to meet him.'

The Queen reached her hand out and gently patted the man's shoulder. 'Stay focussed, my child,' said the Queen softly. 'If we pull this off, it will be our biggest victory ever. Like you just said, we will strike a blow that they will find very difficult to recover from.'

The man nodded.

'And yet,' continued the Queen, pulling her hand back into the shelter of her black robes, 'your preoccupation with her provokes you into making uncharacteristic decisions. Are you aware of his clear message that she cannot be touched? Otherwise, the deal is off.'

The hooded figure stared at the Queen in surprise. 'How did you...'

'I am the Queen of the Nagas, my child,' she interrupted. 'I have more than one piece on the chessboard.'

The hooded figure continued to look at the Queen, ashamed about his poor call at Mount Mandar. The

Queen's next words added to his shame. 'You are making surprising mistakes, my child. You have the potential to be the greatest Naga ever. Don't waste it.'

'Yes, your Highness.'

The Queen appeared to relax.

'I think when we are alone now,' said the Queen, 'maybe you can call me *Mausi*. After all I am *your mother's sister*.'

'Of course, you are,' said the hooded figure as a smile reached his eyes. 'Whatever you say, mausi.'

— ⵣⵙⵜⵓⵁⵔ —

It had been two weeks since the Agnipariksha. Sati had recovered sufficiently for the convoy to continue its journey to its next destination. Shiva, Parvateshwar and Brahaspati sat together in Shiva's chambers at the guest-house.

'It's agreed then,' said Parvateshwar. 'I will make the arrangements for us to commence our journey a week from today. By that time, Sati should have recovered completely.'

'Yes, I think that is a suitable plan,' agreed Shiva.

'Parvateshwar, I will not be accompanying you any further,' said Brahaspati.

'Why?' asked Parvateshwar.

'Well, the new chemicals that I had ordered have arrived. I was considering going back with the consignment to Mount Mandar so that the experiments can begin as soon as possible. If we can get this right then the consumption of water for making the Somras will reduce drastically.'

Shiva smiled sadly. 'I am going to miss you my friend.'

'And I you,' said Brahaspati. 'But I am not leaving

the country. When you finish your tour, come to Mount Mandar. I'll take you around the sylvan forests near our facility.'

'Yes,' said Shiva with a grin. 'Perhaps you will reveal some of your scientific skills and discover a plausible explanation for the blue throat!'

Both Shiva and Brahaspati burst out laughing. Parvateshwar, who did not understand the private joke, looked on politely.

'Just one point, Brahaspati,' said Parvateshwar. 'I will not be able to divert any soldiers from the royal entourage. I will speak with Governor Jhooleshwar about sending some soldiers along with you on your return journey.'

'Thank you, Parvateshwar. But I am sure I will be fine. Why should a terrorist be interested in me?'

'There was another terrorist attack yesterday in a village some fifty kilometres from Mohan Jo Daro,' said Parvateshwar. 'The entire temple was destroyed and all the Brahmins killed.'

'Another one,' said Shiva, angered. 'That is the third attack this month!'

'Yes,' said Parvateshwar. 'They are getting bolder. And as usual, they escaped before any back-up could arrive to give them a real fight.'

Shiva clenched his fists. He had no idea how to counter the terror attacks. There was no way in which one could prepare for them since nobody knew where they would strike next. Was attacking Swadweep, the Chandravanshi's own country, the only way to stop this? Brahaspati kept quiet, sensing Shiva's inner turmoil. He knew there were no easy answers.

Looking at Shiva, Parvateshwar continued, 'I will also

get my people to make preparations for our journey. I'll meet you in the evening for dinner. I think Sati can finally join us. I will send instructions for Nandi and Veerbhadra to also join us. I know you like their company.'

Shiva was startled by Parvateshwar's uncharacteristic thoughtfulness. 'Thank you Parvateshwar. This is very kind of you. But I believe Krittika, Nandi and Veerbhadra are going to a flute recital tonight. That crazy Veerbhadra has even bought some jewels so that he won't look like a country bumpkin next to Nandi!'

Parvateshwar smiled politely.

'But it will be a pleasure to dine with you,' said Shiva.

'Thank you,' said Parvateshwar as he got up. After a few steps, he stopped and turned around. Overcoming his hesitation, he mumbled. 'Shiva!'

'Yes?' Shiva got up.

'I don't think we've talked about this,' said Parvateshwar, uncomfortable. 'But I would like to thank you for helping Sati in her agnipariksha. It was your clear thinking which led to victory.'

'No, no,' said Shiva. 'It was her brilliance.'

'Of course it was,' said Parvateshwar. 'But you gave her the confidence and the strategy to show her brilliance. If there is any person in the world that I relate to with a feeling beyond a sense of duty, it is Sati. I thank you for helping her.'

'You are welcome,' smiled Shiva, with enough sense to not embarrass Parvateshwar further by lengthening this conversation.

Parvateshwar smiled and folded his hands into a Namaste. While he had still not fallen prey to the country-wide 'Neelkanth fever', he was beginning to respect Shiva.

Earning Parvateshwar's esteem was a long journey that Shiva had only just begun. The General turned around and walked out of the room.

'He is not a bad sort,' said Brahaspati, looking at Parvateshwar's retreating back. 'He may be a little surly. But he is one of the most honest Suryavanshis I have ever met. A true follower of Lord Ram. I hope you don't get too upset by the ill-tempered things he says to you.'

'I don't,' said Shiva. 'In fact, I think very highly of Parvateshwar. He is one man whose respect I would certainly like to earn.'

Brahaspati smiled seeing yet another instance of Shiva's large heart. He leaned closer and said, 'You are a good man.'

Shiva smiled back.

'I had not answered you the last time you had asked me, Shiva,' continued Brahaspati. 'Honestly, I have never believed in the legend of the Neelkanth. I still don't.'

Shiva's smile became a little broader.

'But I believe in you. If there is one person capable of sucking the negative energy out of this land, I think it will be you. And I will do all I can to help you. In whatever way I can.'

'You are the brother I never had Brahaspati. Your mere presence is all the help I need.'

Saying so Shiva embraced his friend. Brahaspati hugged Shiva back warmly, feeling a sense of renewed energy course through him. He swore once again that he would never back off from his mission. No matter what. It wasn't just for Meluha. It was also for Shiva. His friend.

— ᚦ◎℧⚷⊕ —

Over three weeks after Sati's agnipariksha the seven-carriage convoy set off from Karachapa. Moving in a column, six of them were dummies as compared to the usual five. In the third carriage Shiva sat with Sati along with Parvateshwar and Ayurvati. It was the first time that Parvateshwar was travelling in the same carriage as Shiva. Krittika had volunteered to ride, claiming that she was missing the scenic beauty of the countryside. Veerbhadra was more than pleased to ride along with her in Nandi's platoon.

They had journeyed just a few days away from Karachapa when the convoy was brought to a halt by a large caravan travelling hurriedly in the opposite direction. Parvateshwar stepped out of the carriage to inquire. Brigadier Vraka came up to Parvateshwar and executed a military salute.

'What is the matter?'

'My Lord, they are refugees from the village of Koonj,' said Vraka. 'They are escaping a terrorist attack.'

'Escaping!' asked a surprised Parvateshwar. 'You mean the attack is still on?'

'I think so, my Lord,' said Vraka, his face filled with rage.

'Goddamit!' swore Parvateshwar. Neither Meluha nor he had ever got an opportunity like this. To be present at the right time and right place with a thousand five hundred soldiers while a terrorist attack was in progress. And yet, Parvateshwar's hands were tied. He was not allowed to take on any mission except to protect the Neelkanth and the Princess.

'What nonsense,' he thought to himself. 'My orders forbid me from following my Kshatriya dharma!'

'What's the matter, Parvateshwar?'

Parvateshwar turned to find Shiva right behind him. Sati and Ayurvati were getting out of the carriage as well. Before Parvateshwar could answer, a horrible noise tore through the quiet forest road. It was a sound Shiva had come to recognise. It declared the evil intentions of the conch-shell bearer, loud and clear. It announced that an attack had begun. A Naga attack had begun!

CHAPTER 17

The Battle of Koonj

'Where are they?' asked Parvateshwar.

'They are in my village, my Lord,' said the scared village headman. 'It's a short distance from here. Some five hundred Chandravanshi soldiers, led by five Nagas. They gave us thirty minutes to leave. But the Brahmins at the temple were detained.'

Parvateshwar clenched his fists to regain his control despite his fury.

'Our Pandit*ji* is a good man, my Lord,' said the village headman. Tears streamed out of his eyes. Vraka put a comforting hand on the headman's shoulder. But the gesture only made the headman even more miserable. Not knowing the fate of the village priest added to his guilt.

'We wanted to stay and fight alongside our Pandit and the other Brahmins,' sobbed the headman. 'They are men of God. They don't even know how to raise a weapon. How can they fight against this horde?'

Vraka let go of the headman as anger got the better of him.

'But Pandit*ji* ordered us to leave. He told us to flee with our women and children. He said he would face whatever

Lord Brahma has written in his fate. But if anyone deserves to be saved, it is them.'

Parvateshwar's nails dug into his skin. He was livid at the cowardly Chandravanshis for yet again attacking defenceless Brahmins and not Kshatriyas who could retaliate. He was incensed with his fate for having put him in a position where he could not take action. A part of him wanted to ignore his orders. But he was bound not to break the law.

'THIS NONSENSE HAS TO STOP!'

Parvateshwar looked up to see which voice had echoed his thoughts. The expression on Shiva's face almost rocked him back on his feet for a moment. The intense fury visible in the Neelkanth would have brought even a Deva to a standstill.

'We are good people,' raged Shiva. 'We are not scared chicken who should turn and flee! Those terrorists should be on the run. They should be the ones feeling the wrath of the Suryavanshis!'

A villager standing behind the headman said, 'But they are terrorists! We cannot defeat them. The Pandit*ji* knew it. That is why he ordered us to run.'

'But we have a thousand five hundred soldiers,' said Shiva, irritated with the display of such cowardice. 'And there are another five hundred of you. We outnumber them four to one. We can crush them. Teach them a lesson they will remember.'

The headman argued. 'But they have Nagas! They are supernatural, blood-thirsty killers! What chance do we have against such evil?'

Shiva had the presence of mind to realise that superstition can only be countered by another stronger belief. He climbed the carriage pedestal to stand tall. The villagers stared at him. He ripped off his cravat and threw it away. He didn't need it anymore.

'I am the Neelkanth!'

All the soldiers looked up mesmerised at the destroyer of evil. They were overjoyed to see him truly accept his destiny. Those ignorant of the Neelkanth's arrival beheld the living legend in a daze.

'I am going to fight these terrorists,' roared Shiva. 'I am going to show them that we are not scared anymore. I am going to make them feel the pain we feel. I am going to let them know that Meluha is not going to roll over and let them do what they want.'

Pure energy coursed through the huddled mass that stood in front of Shiva, straightening their spines and inspiring their souls.

'Who's coming with me?'

'I am,' bellowed Parvateshwar, feeling the suffocating restraints imposed on him fall away by Shiva's pronouncement.

'I am,' echoed Sati, Nandi, Veerbhadra and Vraka.

'I am,' echoed every single soul standing there.

Suddenly the scared villagers and soldiers were transformed into a righteous army. The soldiers drew their swords. The villagers grabbed whatever weapons they could from the travelling armoury.

'To Koonj,' yelled Shiva, mounting a horse and galloping ahead.

Parvateshwar and Sati quickly unharnessed the horses from the cart and raced behind Shiva. The Suryavanshis charged behind them, letting out a cry louder than any Naga conch shell. As they stormed into Koonj, the horror of what had transpired hit them. The Chandravanshis had ignored the rest of the village and concentrated on the area that would distress the Meluhans the most — their venerated temple. Decapitated bodies of the Brahmins lay around the shrine. They had been gathered together and executed. The temple itself was ruthlessly destroyed and set aflame. The gruesome sight enraged the Suryavanshis. They charged like crazed bulls. The Chandravanshis stood no chance. They were completely outnumbered and overwhelmed. They lost ground quickly. Just as the Chandravanshis began to retreat the five Nagas rallied them around. Against crushing odds, the Nagas grimly fought the righteous Suryavanshis with unexpected grit.

Parvateshwar fought like a man possessed. Shiva, who had never seen the General battle, was impressed with his skill and valour. Like Shiva, Parvateshwar knew that the key to victory were the Nagas. As long as they were alive, the Suryavanshis would feel terrified and the Chandravanshis would draw inspiration from them. He attacked one of them with frenzied aggression.

The Naga skilfully parried Parvateshwar's attack with his shield. Bringing his sword down, he tried to strike Parvateshwar's exposed shoulder. What he didn't know was that Parvateshwar had deliberately left his flank exposed. Swinging to the side to avoid the blow, Parvateshwar let his shield clap to his back as he swiftly drew a knife held in a clip behind. He hurled it at the Naga's exposed right shoulder. His cry told Parvateshwar that the knife had penetrated deep.

The injured Naga roared in defiant fury. To Parvateshwar's utter amazement, he swung his sword arm – with the knife still buried in his shoulder - and brought it back into play with an agonising grunt. Parvateshwar brought his shield back up and blocked the slightly weaker strike from the Naga. He brought his sword up in a stab but the Naga was too quick and deflected it. Swerving left, Parvateshwar rammed his shield down hard on the knife still buried in the Naga's shoulder. The knife chipped through the shoulder bone. The Naga snarled in pain and stumbled. That was the opening that Parvateshwar needed. Bringing his sword up in a brutal upward stab, he pushed it ruthlessly through the Naga's heart. The Naga froze as Parvateshwar's sword ripped the life out of him. Parvateshwar pushed his sword in deeper, completing the kill. The Naga fell back motionless.

Parvateshwar was not above the Meluhan fascination with a Naga face. He knelt down and tore the Naga's mask off to reveal a horrifying countenance. The Naga's nose was pure bone and had grown to almost form a bird-like beak. His ears were ridiculously large while his mouth was grotesquely constricted. He looked like a vulture in human form. Parvateshwar quickly whispered what every Suryavanshi said when he brought down a worthy opponent, 'Have a safe journey to the other side, brave warrior.'

One down four to go, thought Parvateshwar rising. Correction, two down, three to go. He saw Shiva bring down a gigantic Naga in the distance. Both Shiva and Parvateshwar looked at each other and nodded. Shiva pointed towards Parvateshwar's back. Parvateshwar turned to see a ferocious Naga fighting five Suryavanshis singlehandedly. He turned back to look at Shiva and nodded. Shiva turned to charge at another Naga as Parvateshwar turned towards the one marked for him.

Shiva dashed through the pitched battle scene towards the Naga who had just killed a Suryavanshi soldier. He leapt high as he ran in close, with his shield in front to prevent a swinging strike. The Naga had brought his own shield up to prevent what he expected from Shiva — the orthodox up to down swinging strike from a good height. Shiva, however, surprised him by thrusting in his sword sideward, neatly circumventing the Naga's shield and gashing his arm. The Naga bellowed in pain and fell back. He straightened and held his shield high again, realising that Shiva was going to be a much more formidable enemy.

As Shiva grimly fought the fearless Naga, he did not notice another one at a distance. This Naga could see that their assault was being progressively pushed back. It was a matter of time before the Nagas and the Chandravanshis would have to retreat. This Naga would have to face the ignominy of having led the first failed attack. And he could see that it was Shiva who had led the counter-offensive. That man had to be destroyed for the future of the mission. The Naga drew his bow forward.

Shiva meanwhile, unaware of the danger, had wedged his sword a little into the Naga's stomach. The Naga grimly fought on, stepping back slowly while ramming Shiva with his shield. He tried in vain to swing his sword down to slice Shiva, who kept his own shield at the ready. Shiva kept fending the Naga's blows while pressing ahead, pushing the sword in deeper and deeper. In a few more seconds, the Naga's soul gave up. It slipped away as his body bled to death and collapsed. Shiva looked down at the fallen Naga in awe.

These people maybe evil, but they are fearless soldiers.

Shiva looked to the left to find that Parvateshwar too

had killed the Naga he had engaged. He continued to turn slowly, trying to find the last Naga. Then he heard a loud shout from the person he had come to love beyond reason.

'S – H – I – V – A.'

Shiva turned to his right to find Sati racing towards him. He looked behind her to see if anyone was chasing her. There was nobody. He frowned. Before he could react, Sati leapt forward. A jump timed to perfection.

The Naga at the distance had released the *agnibaan* or the *fire arrow*, one of the legendary poisoned arrows of their people. The venom on its tip burned its victim's body from the inside, causing a slow, painful death that would scar the soul for many births. The arrow had been aimed at Shiva's neck. It sped unerringly on its deadly mission. However, the Naga had not calculated the possibility of someone obstructing its path.

Sati twisted her body in mid-air as she leapt in front of Shiva. The arrow slammed into her chest with brutal force, propelling her airborne body backward. She fell to Shiva's left, limp and motionless. A stunned Shiva stared at Sati's prone body, his heart shattering.

The destroyer of evil roared in fury. He charged at the Naga like a wild elephant on the brink of insanity, his sword raised. The Naga was momentarily staggered by the fearsome sight of the charging Neelkanth. But to his credit, he rallied. He swiftly drew another arrow from his quiver, loaded it and let it fly. Shiva swung his sword to deflect the arrow, barely missing a step or decreasing his manic speed. The increasingly panic-stricken Naga loaded another arrow and shot again. Shiva swung his sword once more, deflecting the arrow easily, picking up more speed. The Naga reached back to draw another arrow. But it was too late. With a fierce yell, Shiva leapt high as he neared the Naga. He swung his sword viciously, decapitating the Naga with one swing of his sword. The Naga's lifeless body fell in a heap as his severed head flew with the mighty blow, while his still pumping heart spewed blood through the gaping neck.

The Neelkanth's vengeance was not quenched. Screaming, Shiva bent down and kept hacking at the Naga's inert body, ruthlessly slashing it to bits. No assertion of reason, no articulation of sanity could have penetrated Shiva's enraged mind. Except for a soft, muffled, injured voice that was barely audible in the din of battle. But he heard her.

'Shiva…'

He turned back to look at Sati lying in the distance, her head raised slightly.

'Sati!'

He sped towards her, bellowing, 'Parvateshwar! Get Ayurvati! Sati has fallen!'

Ayurvati had already seen Sati's injured body. The Chandravanshis were retreating in haste. Ayurvati ran towards Sati, as did Parvateshwar on hearing Shiva's call. Shiva reached her first. She was motionless, but alive. She was breathing heavily as the arrow had pierced her left lung, flooding her innards with her blood. She couldn't speak as the force of the blow had made the blood gush from her mouth. But she continued to stare at Shiva. Her face had a strange smile, almost serene. She kept opening her mouth as if trying to say something. Shiva desperately wanted to hold her, but he kept his hands locked together as he tried frantically to control his tears.

'O Lord Brahma!' cried Ayurvati as she reached Sati and

recognised the arrow. 'Mastrak! Dhruvini! Get a stretcher. Now!'

Parvateshwar, Ayurvati, Mastrak and Dhruvini carried Sati to one of the village houses with Shiva following closely. Ayurvati's other assistants had already begun cleaning the hut and setting the instruments for the surgery.

'Wait outside, my Lord,' said Ayurvati to Shiva, raising her hand.

Shiva wanted to follow Ayurvati into the hut, but Parvateshwar held him back by touching his shoulder. 'Ayurvati is one of the best doctors in the world, Shiva. Let her do her job.'

Shiva turned to look at Parvateshwar, who was doing an admirable job of controlling his emotions. But it took one look into his eyes for Shiva to know that Parvateshwar was as afraid for Sati as he was. Probably more than he had been before Sati's agnipariksha. Suddenly a thought struck Shiva. He turned and hurried to the closest Naga body. Bending quickly, he checked the right wrist. Finding nothing there, he turned and rushed to the other Naga dead body.

Meanwhile, Parvateshwar had rallied his disturbed mind enough to realise the important tasks that needed to be done. He beckoned Vraka and ordered, 'Place guards over the prisoners of war. Get doctors to attend to all the injured, including the Chandravanshis.'

'The injured Chandravanshis have already taken their poison, my Lord,' said Vraka. 'You know they will never want to be caught alive.'

Parvateshwar looked at Vraka with a withering look, clearly indicating that he wasn't interested in the details and Vraka should get to the task at hand.

'Yes, my Lord,' said Vraka, acknowledging Parvateshwar's silent order.

'Arrange a perimeter for any counter-attack,' continued Parvateshwar, his consciousness already drawn back to Sati's condition in the house behind him. 'And…'

Vraka looked up at Parvateshwar, surprised by his Lord's hesitation. He had never seen his Lord hesitate before. But Vraka had the good sense to not say anything. He waited for his Lord to complete his statement.

'And…' continued Parvateshwar. 'There should be some courier-pigeons still alive in the temple. Send a red coloured letter to Devagiri. To the Emperor. Tell him Princess Sati is seriously injured.'

Vraka looked up in disbelief. He had not heard about Sati. But wisely, he did not say anything.

'Tell the Emperor,' continued Parvateshwar, 'that she has been shot by an agnibaan.'

'O Lord Indra!' blurted Vraka unable to control his shocked dismay.

'Do it now, Brigadier!' snarled Parvateshwar.

'Yes, my Lord,' said Vraka with a weak salute.

Shiva meanwhile had already checked the wrists of four of the Nagas. None of them wore the leather bracelet with the serpent aum that Shiva had come to recognise. He reached the last one. The one who had shot Sati. The wretched one who Shiva had hacked. Shiva kicked the Naga's torso with intense hatred before trying to find his right arm. It took him some time to find the severed limb. Locating it, he raised the remnants of the robe to check the wrist. There was no leather bracelet. It wasn't him.

Shiva came back to the hut to find Parvateshwar seated on a stool outside. Krittika was standing beside the hut entrance, sobbing uncontrollably. Veerbhadra was holding her gently, comforting her. A distraught Nandi stood at Veerbhadra's side, his face stunned into a blank expression. Parvateshwar looked up at Shiva and pointed to the empty stool next to him with a weak smile. He was making brave attempts to appear under control. Shiva sat down slowly and looked into the distance, waiting for Ayurvati to come out.

— ᛏ◍ᚒ⼕⊕ —

'We have removed the arrow, my Lord,' said Ayurvati.

Shiva and Parvateshwar were standing in the hut, looking at an unconscious Sati. Nobody else was allowed in. Ayurvati had clearly stated that Sati did not need the risk of increased infection. And nobody dared argue with the formidable Ayurvati on medical matters. Mastrak and Dhruvini had already fanned out to support the other medical officers treating the injured Suryavanshi soldiers.

Shiva turned towards the right side of the bed and saw the bloodied tong that had been used to stretch Sati's innards so that the arrow could be pulled out. That tong would never be used again. It had been infected with the agnibaan poison. No amount of heat or chemicals would make the instrument sterile and safe again. Next to the tong lay the offending arrow, wrapped in neem leaves, where it would stay for one full day, before being buried deep in a dry grave to ensure that it would not cause any more harm.

Shiva looked at Ayurvati, his eyes moist, unable to find the strength to ask the question that raged in his heart.

'I will not lie to you, my Lord,' said Ayurvati, in the

detached manner that doctors will themselves into, to find the strength in traumatic circumstances. 'It doesn't look good. Nobody in history has survived an agnibaan which has penetrated one of the vital organs. The poison will start causing an intense fever in some time, which will result in the failing of one organ after another.'

Helplessly Shiva looked at Sati and then turned pleadingly towards Ayurvati, who fought hard to rein in her tears and retain her composure. She couldn't afford to lose control. She had many lives to save in the next few hours.

'I am sorry, my Lord,' said Ayurvati. 'But there really is no cure. We can only give some medicines to make her end easier.'

Shiva glared angrily at Ayurvati. 'We are not giving up! Is that clear?'

Ayurvati looked at the ground, unable to meet Shiva's eye.

'If the fever is kept under control, then her organs will not be damaged, right?' asked Shiva, as a glimmer of hope entered his being.

Ayurvati looked up and said, 'Yes, my Lord. But that is not a final solution. The fever caused by an agnibaan can only be delayed, not broken. If we try and control the fever, it will come back even stronger once the medicines are stopped.'

'Then we will control the fever forever!' cried Shiva. 'I will sit by her side all my life if needed. The fever will not rise.'

Ayurvati was about to say something to Shiva, but thought better of it and kept silent. She would come back to Shiva in a few hours. She knew that Sati could not be saved. It was impossible. Precious time was being wasted in this futile discussion. Time that could be used to save other lives.

'Alright, my Lord,' said Ayurvati, quickly administering the medicines to Sati that would keep her fever down. 'This should keep her fever down for a few hours.'

She looked up at Parvateshwar standing at the back for an instant. Parvateshwar knew that keeping the fever down would only lengthen Sati's agony. But he shared the glimmer of hope that Shiva felt.

Turning back towards Shiva, Ayurvati said, 'My Lord, you too are injured. Let me dress your wounds and I'll leave.'

'I am alright,' said Shiva, not taking his eyes off Sati for an instant.

'No, you are not, my Lord,' said Ayurvati firmly. 'Your wounds are deep. If they catch an infection, then it could be life threatening.'

Shiva did not answer. He just kept looking at Sati and waved his hand dismissively.

'Shiva!' shouted Ayurvati. Shiva looked up at her. 'You cannot help Sati if you yourself become unwell!'

The harsh tone had the desired effect. While Shiva did not move from his place, he let Ayurvati dress his wounds. Ayurvati then quickly tended to Parvateshwar's wounds and left the hut.

— ⋏⦿�⋔⊕ —

Shiva looked at the prahar lamp in the hut. It had been three hours since Ayurvati had removed the arrow. Parvateshwar had left the hut to look after the other injured and make the preparations for setting up camp, since the convoy was going to stay in Koonj for some time. That was Parvateshwar's way. If he was confronted with an ugly situation that he could do nothing about, he did not wallow in his misery. He would drown himself in his work so that he did not have to think about the crisis.

Shiva was different. Many years back, he had sworn that he would never run away from a difficult situation. Even if there was absolutely nothing he could do. He hadn't left Sati's side for a moment. He sat patiently by her bed, waiting for her to recover. Hoping for her to recover. Praying for her to recover.

'Shiva…' a barely audible whisper broke the silence.

Shiva looked at Sati's face. Her eyes were slightly open. Her hand had moved indiscernibly. He pulled his chair closer, careful not to touch her.

'I'm so sorry,' cried Shiva. 'I should never have got us into this fight.'

'No, no,' murmured Sati. 'You did the right thing. You have come to Meluha to lead us and to destroy evil. You did your duty.'

Shiva continued to stare at Sati, overcome by grief. Sati widened her eyes a bit, trying to take in as much of Shiva as she could, in what she knew were her last moments. Death brings to a final end a soul's aspirations. Ironically, however, it is sometimes the hovering imminence of the end itself which gives a soul the courage to challenge every constraint and express even a long-denied dream.

'It is my time to go, Shiva,' whispered Sati. 'But before I go, I want to tell you that the last few months have been the happiest in my life.'

Shiva continued to look at Sati with moist eyes. His hands developed a life of their own and moved towards Sati. He checked himself in time.

'I wish you had come into my life earlier,' said Sati, letting out a secret that she hadn't even acknowledged to herself. 'My life would have been so different.'

Shiva's eyes tried frantically to restrain themselves, struggling against the despair that needed an outlet.

'I wish I had told you earlier,' murmured Sati. 'Because the first time that I am telling you will also probably be the last.'

Shiva continued to look at her, his voice choked.

Sati looked deeply into Shiva's eyes, whispering softly, 'I love you.'

The dam broke and tears poured down Shiva's grief-stricken face.

'You are going to repeat these words for at least another hundred years,' sobbed Shiva. 'You are not going anywhere. I will fight the God of death himself, if I have to. You are not going anywhere.'

Sati smiled sadly and put her hand in Shiva's. Her hand was burning. The fever had begun its assault.

CHAPTER 18

Sati and the Fire Arrow

'Nothing can be done, my Lord,' said a visibly uncomfortable Ayurvati.

She and Shiva were standing in a corner of the hut, at what they thought was a safe distance beyond the range of Sati's ears. Parvateshwar was standing beside them, holding his tears back.

'Come on, Ayurvati,' urged Shiva. 'You are the best doctor in the land. All we have to do is wait for the fever to break.'

'This fever cannot be broken,' reasoned Ayurvati. 'There is no cure for the agnibaan poison. We are only lengthening Sati's agony by keeping the fever low. The moment the medicines are stopped, the fever will recur with a vengeance.'

'Let it go, Shiva,' mumbled a frail voice from the bed. Everyone turned to stare at Sati. Her face wore a smile that comes only with the acceptance of the inevitable. 'I have no regrets. I have told you what I needed to. I am content. My time has come.'

'Don't give up on me, Sati,' cried Shiva. 'You are not gone yet. We will find a way. I will find a way. Just bear with me.'

Sati gave up. She didn't have the strength. She also knew that Shiva had to find his own peace with her death. And he wouldn't find that unless he felt he had done everything possible to save her.

'I can feel my fever rising,' said Sati. 'Please give me the medicines.'

Ayurvati glanced at Sati uncomfortably. All her medical training told her that she shouldn't do this. She knew that she was just increasing Sati's suffering by giving her medicines. Sati stared hard at Ayurvati. She couldn't give up now. Not when Shiva had asked her to hang on.

'Give me the medicines, Ayurvati*ji*,' repeated Sati. 'I know what I am doing.'

Ayurvati gave Sati the medicines. She gazed into Sati's eyes, expecting to find some traces of fear or anguish. There were none. Ayurvati smiled gently and walked back to Shiva and Parvateshwar.

'I know!' exclaimed Shiva. 'Why don't we give her the Somras?'

'What effect will that have, my Lord?' asked a surprised Ayurvati. 'The Somras only works on the oxidants and increases a person's lifespan. It doesn't work on injuries.'

'Look Ayurvati, I don't think anyone truly understands everything about the Somras. I know you know that. What you don't know is that the Somras repaired a frostbitten toe that I had lived with all my life. It also repaired my dislocated shoulder.'

'What!' said a visibly surprised Parvateshwar. 'That's impossible. The Somras does not cure physical disabilities.'

'It did in my case.'

'But that could also be because you are special, my Lord,' said Ayurvati. 'You are the Neelkanth.'

'I didn't drop from the sky, Ayurvati. My body is as human as Sati's. As human as yours. Let's just try it!'

Parvateshwar did not need any more convincing. He dashed out to find Vraka sitting on a stool. Vraka immediately rose and saluted his commander.

'Vraka,' said Parvateshwar. 'The temple may still have some Somras powder. It was the main production centre of the area. I want that powder. Now.'

'You will have it in ten minutes, my Lord,' boomed Vraka as he rushed off with his guards.

— ⚚◉℧⅄⊛ —

'There is nothing else to do but wait,' said Ayurvati as Sati fell asleep. The Somras had been administered — a stronger dose than usual. 'Parvateshwar, you are tired. You need to recover from your wounds. Please go and sleep.'

'I don't need sleep,' said Parvateshwar stubbornly. 'I am staying on guard with my soldiers at the perimeter. You can't trust those Chandravanshis. They may launch a counter-attack at night.'

A frustrated Ayurvati glared at Parvateshwar, her belief reinforced that the machismo of the Kshatriyas made them impossible patients.

'Are you going to bed, my Lord?' asked Ayurvati, turning towards Shiva, hoping that at least he would listen. 'There is nothing you can do now. We just have to wait. And you need the rest.'

Shiva just shook his head. Wild horses could not drag him away from Sati.

'We could arrange a bed in this hut,' continued Ayurvati.

'You could sleep here if you wish so that you can also keep an eye on Sati.'

'Thank you, but I am not going to sleep,' said Shiva, briefly looking at Ayurvati before turning towards Sati. 'I am staying here. You go to sleep. I will call you if there is any change.'

Ayurvati glared at Shiva and then whispered, 'As you wish, my Lord.'

A tired Ayurvati walked towards her own hut. She needed to get some rest since the next day would be busy. She would have to check the wounds of all the injured to ensure that recovery was proceeding properly. The first twenty-four hours were crucial. Her medical corps had been divided into groups to keep a staggered, all-night vigil for any emergencies.

'I will be with the soldiers, Shiva,' said Parvateshwar. 'Nandi and Veerbhadra are on duty outside along with some of my personal guards.'

Shiva knew what Parvateshwar actually wanted to say.

'I will call you as soon as there is a change, Parvateshwar,' said Shiva, looking up at the General.

Parvateshwar smiled weakly and nodded to Shiva. He rushed out before his feelings could cause him any embarrassment.

— ⱷ◉℧⚷⊕ —

Parvateshwar sat alone and silent, while his soldiers maintained a distance, out of respect. They knew when their Lord wanted to be left alone. Parvateshwar was lost in thoughts of Sati. Why should a person like her be put through so much suffering by the Almighty? He remembered her childhood. The day when he decided that here was a girl he would be proud to have as his Goddaughter.

That fateful day, when for the first and only time, he regretted his vow to not have any progeny of his own. Which foolish father would not want a child like Sati?

It was a lazy afternoon more than a hundred years ago. Sati had just returned from the Gurukul at the tender age of sixteen. Full of verve and a passionate belief in Lord Ram's teachings. Lord Brahmanayak still reigned over the land of Meluha. His son, Prince Daksha, was content being a family man, spending his days with his wife and daughter. He showed absolutely no inclination to master the warrior ways of the Kshatriya. Neither did he show the slightest ambition to succeed his father.

On that day, Daksha had settled down for a family picnic on the banks of the river Saraswati, a short distance from Devagiri. Parvateshwar was then a bodyguard to Daksha and was conscientious about his duties. He sat near the Prince, close enough to protect him, but far enough to give some privacy to the prince and his wife. Sati had wandered off into the forest in the distance, while remaining close to the river so that she was visible.

Suddenly Sati's cry ripped through the silence. Daksha, Veerini and Parvateshwar looked up startled. They rushed to the edge of the bank to see Sati at the river bend, ferociously battling a pack of wild dogs. She was blocking them to protect a severely injured woman. It could be seen even from the distance that the caste-unmarked, fair woman was a recent immigrant, who did not know that one never approached the banks without a sword to protect oneself from wild animals. She must have been attacked by the pack, which was large enough to bring down even a charging lion.

'Sati!' shouted Daksha in alarm.

Drawing his sword, he charged down the river to protect his daughter. Parvateshwar followed Daksha, his sword drawn for battle. Within moments, they had jumped into the fray. Parvateshwar charged aggressively into the pack, easily hacking many with quick strikes. Sati, rejuvenated by the sudden support, fought back the four dogs charging towards her all at once. Daksha fought ferociously, despite an obvious lack of martial skills, with the passionately protective spirit that only a parent feels for his offspring. But the animals could sense that Daksha was the weakest amongst their human enemies. Six dogs charged at him at the same time.

Daksha drove his sword forward in a brutal jab at the dog in front of him. A mistake. Even though Daksha felled the dog, his sword was stuck in the dead animal. That was all the opening that the other dogs needed. One charged viciously from the side, seizing Daksha's right forearm in its jaws. He roared in pain, but held on to his sword as he tried to wrestle his arm free. Another dog bit Daksha's left leg, yanking some of his flesh out. Seeing his Lord in trouble, Parvateshwar yelled in fury as he swung his sword at the body of the dog clinging to Daksha's arm, cleanly cutting the beast in half. Parvateshwar pirouetted around in the same smooth motion and slashed another dog charging at Daksha from the front. Sati moved in to protect Daksha's left flank as he angrily stabbed the dog that was clinging to his leg. Seeing their numbers rapidly depleting, the remaining dogs retreated yelping.

'Daksha!' sobbed Veerini, as she rushed to hold up her

collapsing husband. He was losing blood at an alarming rate from his numerous wounds, especially from the thigh. The dog's sharp incisor must surely have pierced a major artery. Parvateshwar quickly blew his distress conch shell. A cry for help reached the scouts at the closest crossing-house. Soldiers and paramedics would be with them in a few minutes. Parvateshwar bound his angvastram tight around Daksha's thigh to stem the bleeding. Then he quickly helped the injured foreign woman move closer to the royal party.

'Father, are you alright?' whispered Sati as she held her father's hand.

'Dammit, Sati!' shouted Daksha. 'What do you think you were doing?'

Sati fell silent at the violent response from her doting father.

'Who asked you to be a hero?' harangued Daksha, fuming at his daughter. 'What if something had happened to you? What would I do? Where would I go? And for whom were you risking your life? What difference does the life of that woman make?'

Sati continued to look down, distraught at the scolding. She had been expecting praise. The crossing-house soldiers and paramedics rushed to the scene. With efficient movements, they quickly stemmed the flow of Daksha's blood. After dressing Parvateshwar's and Sati's minor wounds rapidly, they carried Daksha on a stretcher. His wounds needed attention from the royal physician.

As Sati saw her father being carried away, she stayed rooted, deeply guilty about the harm her actions had caused. She was only trying to save a woman in distress. Wasn't it one of Lord Ram's primary teachings that it is the duty of the strong to protect the weak? She felt a soft touch on her shoulder. She turned to face Captain Parvateshwar, her father's severe bodyguard. Strangely though, his face sported a rare smile.

'I am proud of you, my child,' whispered Parvateshwar. 'You are a true follower of Lord Ram.'

Tears suddenly burst forth in Sati's eyes. She looked away quickly. Taking time to control herself she looked up with a wan smile at the man she would in days to come grow up to call Pitratulya. She nodded softly.

Jolted back into the present by a bird call, Parvateshwar scanned the perimeter, his eyes moist with emotion. He clutched his hands in a prayer and whispered, 'She's your true follower, Lord Ram. Fight for her.'

— ⋔⊚Ս⥳⊕ —

Shiva had lost track of time. Obviously, nobody had been assigned to reset the prahar lamps when so many lives were still in danger. Looking out of the window, he could see early signs of dawn. Shiva's wounds burned, crying for relief. But he wasn't going to give in. He sat quietly on his chair, next to Sati's bed, restraining himself from making any noise that would disturb her. Sati held his hand tightly. Despite the searing heat of her feverish body, Shiva did not move his hands away. His palms were sweaty due to the intense heat.

He looked longingly at Sati and softly whispered, 'Either you stay here or I leave this world with you. The choice is yours.'

He felt a slight twitch. He looked down to see Sati's hand move ever so slightly, beads of perspiration gliding down between their entwined palms. Though whose perspiration it was he could not say.

Is it Sati's or mine?

Shiva immediately reached out with his other hand towards Sati's forehead. It was burning even more strongly. But there were soft beads of perspiration on the temple. A burst of elation shot through Shiva's being.

— 人◎Ʊ쇼⊕ —

'By the great Lord Brahma,' whispered Ayurvati in awe. 'I have never seen anything like this.'

She was standing besides Sati's bed. The still sleeping Sati was sweating profusely. Her bed and garments were soaked. Parvateshwar stood by her side, his face aglow with hope.

'The agnibaan fever never breaks,' continued a stunned Ayurvati. 'This is a miracle.'

Shiva looked up, his face shimmering with the ecstasy of a soul that had salvaged its reason for existence. 'May the Holy Lake bless the Somras.'

Parvateshwar noticed Sati's hand clutched tightly in Shiva's but he did not comment. The bliss of this moment had finally crowded out his instinctive drive to stop something unacceptable under the laws of the land.

'My Lord,' said Ayurvati softly. 'We must bathe her quickly. The sweat must be removed. However, considering that her wounds cannot get wet, my nurses will have to rub her down.'

Shiva looked up at Ayurvati and nodded, not understanding the implication.

'Umm, my Lord,' said Ayurvati. 'That means you will have to leave the room.'

'Of course,' said Shiva.

As he got up to leave, Ayurvati said, 'My Lord, your hands would need to be washed as well.'

Shiva looked down, noticing Sati's sweat. He looked up at Ayurvati and nodded, 'I will do so immediately.'

— ⋏⊙⊍⋔⋔⊕ —

'This is a miracle, Sati. Nobody has ever recovered from an agnibaan!' said Ayurvati, beaming from ear to ear. 'I'll be honest. I had given up hope. It was the Lord's faith that has kept you alive.'

Sati was lying on her bed wearing a smile and freshly washed clothes. A new bed had been brought in with freshly laundered and sterilised linen. All traces of the toxic sweat triggered by the Somras had been removed.

'Oh no,' said a self-conscious Shiva. 'I did nothing. It was Sati's fighting spirit that saved her.'

'No, Shiva. It was you. Not me,' said Sati, holding Shiva's hand without any hint of tentativeness. 'You have saved me at so many levels. I don't know how I can even begin to repay you.'

'By never saying again that you have to repay me.'

Sati smiled even more broadly and held Shiva's hand tighter. Parvateshwar looked on gloomily at both of them, now unhappy with the open display of their love.

'All right,' said Ayurvati, clapping her hands together as if to signal the end of an episode. 'Much as I would like to sit here and chitchat with all of you, I have work to do.'

'What work?' asked Shiva playfully. 'You are a brilliant doctor. You have an exceptional team. I know that every single injured person has been saved. There is nothing more for you to do.'

'Oh there is, my Lord,' said Ayurvati with a smile. 'I have to put on record how the Somras can cure an agnibaan wound. I will present this at the medical council as soon as I return to Devagiri. This is big news. We must research the curative properties of the Somras. There is a lot of work to do!'

Shiva smiled fondly at Ayurvati.

Sati whispered, 'Thank you Ayurvati*ji*. Like thousands of others, I too owe my life to you.'

'You owe me nothing, Sati. I only did my duty.'

Ayurvati bowed with a formal Namaste and left the room.

'Well, even I...,' mumbled Parvateshwar awkwardly, as he walked out.

Parvateshwar was surprised to find Ayurvati waiting for him outside. She was standing at a safe distance from the guards. Whatever it was that she wanted to talk about, she did not want the others to hear.

'What is it, Ayurvati?' asked Parvateshwar.

'I know what's bothering you Parvateshwar,' said Ayurvati.

'Then how can you just stand by and watch? I don't think it is right. I know that this is not the correct time to say anything. But I will raise the issue when appropriate.'

'No, you shouldn't.'

'How can you say that?' asked a shocked Parvateshwar. 'You come from a rare family which did not have even one renegade Brahmin during the rebellion. Lord Ram insisted that the laws had to be followed strictly. He demonstrated repeatedly that even he wasn't above the law. Shiva is a good man. I won't deny that. But he cannot be above the law. Nobody can be above the law. Otherwise our society will collapse. You above all should know this.'

'I know only one thing,' said Ayurvati, determined. 'If the Neelkanth feels it is right, then it *is* right.'

Parvateshwar looked at Ayurvati as if he didn't recognise her. This could not be the woman he knew and admired, the woman who followed the law without exception. Parvateshwar had begun to respect Shiva. But the respect had not turned into unquestioning faith. He did not believe that Shiva was the one who would complete Lord Ram's work. In Parvateshwar's eyes, only Lord Ram deserved absolute obedience. Nobody else.

'In any case,' said Ayurvati, 'I have to leave. I have a theory to think about.'

— ⵊⵍⵓⵖⵟ —

'Really?' asked Shiva. 'You mean it is not necessary in Meluha that the Emperor's first-born son succeed him?'

'Yes,' replied Sati smiling.

Shiva and Sati had spent many hours over the previous week talking about matters important and mundane. Sati, while recovering quickly, was still bedridden. The convoy had set up camp at Koonj till such time as the injured were ready to travel. The journey to Lothal had been called off. Shiva and Parvateshwar had decided that it was better to return to Devagiri as soon as the wounded were able to.

Sati shifted slightly to relieve a bit of the soreness in her back. But she did not let go of Shiva's hand while doing so. Shiva leaned forward and pushed back a strand of hair that had slipped onto Sati's face. She smiled lovingly at him and continued, 'You see, till around two hundred and fifty years ago, the children of the kings were not his birth-children. They were drawn from the Maika system. So there was no question of knowing who the first-born was. We could only know his first-adopted.'

'Fair point.'

'But in addition, it was not necessary that the first-adopted child would succeed. This was another one of the laws that Lord Ram instituted for stability and peace. You see, in the olden days there were many royal families, each with their own small kingdoms.'

'All right,' said Shiva, paying as much attention to Sati's words as to the hypnotising dimples that formed on her cheeks when she spoke. 'These kings would probably be at war all the time, so that one of them could be overlord for however short a period.'

'Obviously,' smiled Sati, shaking her head at the foolishness of the kings before Lord Ram's time.

'Well, it is the same everywhere,' said Shiva, remembering the constant warfare in his part of the world.

'Battles for supremacy amongst the kings led to many unnecessary and futile wars, where the only ones who suffered were the common people,' continued Sati. 'Lord Ram felt it was ridiculous for the people to suffer so that the egos of their kings were fed. He instituted a system where a *Rajya Sabha*, the *ruling council*, consisting of all Brahmins and Kshatriyas of a specific rank, was created. Whenever the Emperor died or took sanyas, the council would meet and elect a new Emperor from amongst Kshatriyas of the rank of brigadier or above. The decision could not be contested and was inviolate.'

'I have said it before and I'll say it again,' said Shiva with a broad smile. 'Lord Ram was a genius.'

'Yes, he was,' said Sati, enthusiastically. 'Jai Shri Ram.'

'Jai Shri Ram,' repeated Shiva. 'But tell me, how come your father became the Emperor after Lord Brahmanayak? After all, his Highness is the first born of the previous Emperor, correct?'

'He was elected, just like every other Emperor of Meluha. Actually it was the first time in Meluhan history that a ruling emperor's son was elected Emperor,' said Sati proudly.

'Hmm. But your grandfather helped your father get elected?'

'I've never been sure about that. I know my grandfather would have liked it if my father had become Emperor. But I also know that he was a great man who followed the rules of Meluha and would not openly help his son. Lord Bhrigu, a great sage respected across the land, helped my father a great deal in his election.'

Shiva smiled at her as he tenderly ran his hand across the side of her face. Sati closed her eyes, exulting in the sensation. His hand glided along the side of her body to rest on her hand again. He squeezed it softly.

Shiva was about to ask more about the relationship between Daksha and Lord Bhrigu when the door suddenly swung open. Daksha, looking deeply exhausted, stormed in. Following him were Veerini and Kanakhala. Shiva immediately withdrew his hand before Daksha could see where it was. But Daksha had noticed the movement.

'Father!' cried a surprised Sati.

'Sati, my child,' sighed Daksha, kneeling next to Sati's bed. Veerini knelt next to Daksha and ran her hand lovingly over her daughter's face. She was crying. Kanakhala remained at a distance and greeted Shiva with a formal Namaste. Shiva returned Kanakhala's Namaste with a beaming smile. Parvateshwar and Ayurvati waited next to Kanakhala, politely leaving the royal family alone in their private moment. Nandi, Veerbhadra and Krittika stood behind them. A discreet aide silently brought in two chairs for the royal couple, placed them next to the bed and left just as quietly.

Daksha, Veerini and Kanakhala, accompanied by two thousand soldiers, had immediately left Devagiri on hearing the news of Sati's injury. They had sailed down the Saraswati to the inland delta of the river and then had ridden night and day to reach Koonj.

'I am alright, father,' said Sati, holding her mother's hand gently. Turning towards her mother, she continued, 'Seriously, mother. I am feeling better than ever. Give me one more week and I'll dance for you!'

Shiva couldn't suppress a grin even as both Daksha and Veerini smiled indulgently at Sati.

Looking at her father, Sati continued, 'I am sorry to have caused so much trouble. I know there are many more important tasks at hand and you had to unnecessarily rush here.'

'Trouble?' asked Daksha. 'My child, you are my life. You are nothing but a source of joy for me. And at this point of time, you can't imagine how proud I am of you.'

Veerini bent over and kissed Sati's forehead tenderly.

'I am proud of all of you,' continued Daksha looking back at Parvateshwar and Ayurvati. 'Proud that you supported the Lord in what had to be done. We actually fought back a terrorist attack! You can't imagine how much this has electrified the nation!'

Daksha soothingly continued to pat Sati's hand, as he turned to Shiva and said, 'Thank you, my Lord. Thank you for fighting for us. We know now that we have put our faith in the right man.'

Shiva could not find anything to say. He smiled awkwardly and acknowledged Daksha's faith with a slight nod and a courteous Namaste.

Turning to Ayurvati, Daksha asked, 'How is she now? I was told she is on her way to a total recovery.'

'Yes, your Highness,' said Ayurvati. 'She should be able to move in another week. And in three weeks, the only memory of the wound would be a scar.'

'You are not just the best doctor of this generation, Ayurvati,' said Daksha proudly. 'You are in fact the best doctor of all time.'

'Oh no, your Highness,' cried a flabbergasted Ayurvati, gently pinching her ear lobes to ward off any evil spirit that might take umbrage at the undeserved compliment. 'There are many far greater than me. But in this case, the miracle was Lord Neelkanth's and not mine.'

Looking briefly towards a visibly embarrassed Shiva before turning back to Daksha, Ayurvati continued, 'I thought we had lost her. She got the terrible fever after we pulled the agnibaan out. You know that there are no medicines to cure the agnibaan fever, your Highness. But the Lord refused to lose hope. It was his idea to give her the Somras.'

Daksha turned to Shiva with a grateful smile and said, 'I have one more thing to thank you for, my Lord. My daughter is part of my soul. I wouldn't have been able to survive without her.'

'Oh no, I did nothing,' said Shiva, self-conscious. 'It was Ayurvati who treated her.'

'Therein lies your humility, my Lord,' said Daksha. 'You truly are a worthy Neelkanth. In fact, you are a worthy Mahadev!'

An astounded Shiva stared at Daksha, his expression serious. He knew who the previous *Mahadev*, the *God of Gods*, was. He did not believe he deserved to be compared to Lord Rudra. His deeds did not qualify him for that honour.

'No, your Highness. You speak too highly of me. I am no Mahadev.'

'Oh yes you are, my Lord,' said Kanakhala and Ayurvati almost simultaneously. Parvateshwar looked on, silent.

Not wanting to press the issue as Shiva disliked being called Mahadev, Daksha turned towards Sati, 'What I don't understand is why you jumped in front of the Lord to take the arrow. You have never believed in the legend. You have never had faith in the Neelkanth like I have. Why then did you risk your own life for the Lord?'

Sati did not say anything. She looked down with an uncomfortable smile, embarrassed and ill-at-ease. Daksha turned to Shiva to see him wearing the same sheepish expression as Sati's. Veerini looked at her husband intently. She waited for him to rise and speak to Shiva. Suddenly Daksha stood up and walked around the bed towards Shiva, his hands folded in a formal Namaste. A surprised Shiva rose and returned Daksha's Namaste, with a slight bow of his head.

'My Lord, perhaps for the first time in her life, my daughter is tongue-tied in my presence,' said Daksha. 'And I have also come to understand that you will willingly give unto others but never ask for anything for yourself. Hence I must make the first move.'

Shiva continued to stare at Daksha, frowning.

'I will not lie to you, my Lord,' continued Daksha. 'The laws classify my daughter as a vikarma, because she had given birth to a still-born decades back. It is not a very serious crime. It could have been due to the past life karma of the child's father. But the law of the land holds that both the father and the mother be blamed for the tragedy. My darling daughter was put in the category of a vikarma, because of this incident.'

Shiva's expression made it clear that he thought the vikarma law was unfair.

'It is believed that vikarma people are carriers of bad fate,' continued Daksha. 'Hence if she marries again, she will pass on her bad fate to her husband and possibly her future children.'

Veerini looked at her husband with inscrutable eyes.

'I know my daughter, my Lord,' continued Daksha. 'I have never seen her do anything even remotely wrong. She is a good woman. In my opinion, the law that condemns her is unfair. But I am only the Emperor. I cannot change the law.'

Parvateshwar glared angrily at Daksha, upset that he served an Emperor who held the law in such low esteem.

'It breaks my heart that I cannot give my daughter the happy life that she deserves,' sobbed Daksha. 'That I cannot save her from the humiliation that a good soul like her suffers daily. What I can do, though, is ask you for help.'

Sati looked at her father with loving eyes.

'You are the Neelkanth,' continued Daksha. 'In fact you are more than that. I genuinely believe that you are a Mahadev, even though I know you don't like to be called one. You are above the law. You can change the law if you wish. You can override it if you want.'

An aghast Parvateshwar glowered at Daksha. How could the Emperor be so dismissive of the law? Then his eyes fell on Shiva. His heart sank further.

Shiva was staring at Daksha with undisguised delight. He had thought that he would have to convince the Emperor about Sati. But here he was, quite sure that the Emperor was about to offer his daughter's hand to him.

'If you decide to take my daughter's hand, my Lord, no power on earth can stop you,' contended Daksha. 'The question is: do you want to?'

All the emotions in the universe surged through Shiva's being. His face wore an ecstatic smile. He tried to speak but his voice was choked. He bent down, picked up Sati's hand gently, brought it to his lips and kissed it lovingly. He looked up at Daksha and whispered, 'I will never let go of her. Never.'

A stunned Sati stared at Shiva. She had dared to love over the last week, but had not dared to hope. And now her wildest dream was coming true. She was going to be his wife.

An overjoyed Daksha hugged Shiva tightly and said softly, 'My Lord!'

Veerini was sobbing uncontrollably. The spectre of a lifetime's injustice had been lifted off Sati. She looked up at Daksha, almost willing to forgive him. Ayurvati and Kanakhala stepped up and congratulated the Emperor, the Queen, Shiva and Sati. Nandi, Krittika and Veerbhadra, who had heard the entire conversation, expressed their joy. Parvateshwar stood rooted near the door, furious with such disregard for Lord Ram's way.

Shiva, at long last, regained control of himself. Firmly gripping Sati's hand, he looked at Daksha, 'But your Highness, I have a condition.'

'Yes, my Lord.'

'The vikarma law…'

'It doesn't need to be changed, my Lord,' said Daksha. 'If you decide to marry my daughter, then the law cannot stop you.'

'All the same,' said Shiva. 'That law must be changed.'

'Of course, it will be my Lord,' said a beaming Daksha. Turning towards Kanakhala, he continued, 'Make a proclamation to be signed by the Neelkanth, saying that from now on any noble woman who gives birth to a still-born child will not be classified as vikarma.'

'No, your Highness,' interrupted Shiva. 'That is not what I meant. I want the entire vikarma law scrapped. Nobody will be a vikarma from now on. Bad fate can strike anyone. It is ridiculous to blame their past lives for it.'

Parvateshwar looked at Shiva in surprise. Though he did not like even a comma being changed in any of Lord Ram's laws, he appreciated that Shiva was remaining true to a fundamental canon of Lord Ram's principles — the same law applies to everybody, equally and fairly, without exceptions.

Daksha however looked at Shiva in shock. This was unexpected. Like all Meluhans, he too was superstitious about the vikarma. His displeasure was not with the vikarma law itself but with his daughter being classified as one. But he quickly recovered and said, 'Of course, my Lord. The proclamation will state that the entire vikarma law has been scrapped. Once you sign it, it will become law.'

'Thank you, your Highness,' smiled Shiva.

'My daughter's happy days are back,' exulted Daksha, turning to Kanakhala. 'I want a grand ceremony at Devagiri when we return. A wedding the likes of which the world has not seen before. The most magnificent wedding ever. Call in the best organisers in the land. I want no expense spared.'

Daksha turned to look at Shiva for affirmation. Shiva looked at Sati to admire her joyous smile and glorious dimples. Turning towards Daksha, he said, 'All I want, your Highness, is to get married to Sati. I wouldn't mind the simplest ceremony in the world or the most magnificent. So long as all of you, Brahaspati and the Gunas are present, I will be happy.'

'Excellent!' rejoiced Daksha.

CHAPTER 19

Love Realised

There was an air of celebration in Devagiri when the royal caravan arrived three weeks later. Kanakhala, who had arrived in Devagiri earlier, ensured that all the preparations for the most eagerly-awaited wedding in a millennium had been accomplished. Her arrangements, as always, had been impeccable.

The various wedding ceremonies and celebrations had been spread over seven days, each day filled with an exuberant variety of events. By the usually sober Suryavanshi standards, the city had been decorated extravagantly. Colourful banners hung proudly from the city walls, splashing festive beauty on the sober grey exteriors. The roads had been freshly tiled in the sacred blue colour. All the restaurants and shops served their customers free of charge for the seven days of revelry, subsidised at state expense. The buildings had been freshly painted at government cost to make Devagiri appear like a city that had been established the previous day.

A massive channel had been rapidly dug along the far side of the Saraswati where a part of the river had been diverted. The channel was in the open in some parts and went underground in others. Filters injected a red dye into the water as soon as it entered the channel and removed it just as efficiently when the water flowed back into the river. The channel formed a giant *Swastika*, an ancient symbol which literally translates into *'that which is associated with well-being'* or very simply, a lucky charm. From any of the three city platforms, a Meluhan could look in reverence at the enormous impression of the revered Swastika in the royal red Suryavanshi colour formed by the flow of the holy Saraswati. Some of the protective giant spikes around the entry drawbridges of the three platforms had been cleared. In their stead, giant rangolis, visible from miles away, had been drawn to welcome all into the capital. Kanakhala had wanted to clear all the spikes surrounding Devagiri, but Parvateshwar had vetoed it, citing security reasons.

Elite families from across the empire had been invited to attend the festivities. People of distinction ranging from governors to scientists, generals to artists and even sanyasis had trooped into Devagiri to celebrate the momentous occasion. Ambassadors of eminent countries, such as Mesopotamia and Egypt, had been given permits for a rare visit to the capital of Meluha. Jhooleshwar had cannily used the distinctive honour granted to ambassadors to wrangle some additional trade quotas. Brahaspati had come down from Mount Mandar with his retinue. Only a skeletal security staff of Arishtanemi soldiers had been left behind at the mountain. It was the first time in history that seven days would elapse at Mount Mandar without any experiments!

The first day had two pujas organised in the name of Lord Indra and Lord Agni. They were the main Gods of the people of India and their blessings were sought before any significant event. And an event as momentous as the wedding of the millennium could only begin with their sanction. This particular puja, however, celebrated their warrior form. Daksha eloquently explained the reason. The Meluhans were not just celebrating the marriage between the Neelkanth and their princess. They were also celebrating the massive defeat of the despised terrorists at Koonj. According to him, the echoes of Koonj would reverberate deep in the heart of Swadweep. The Suryavanshi vengeance had begun!

This puja was followed by the formal marriage ceremonies of Shiva and Sati. After which, though some of the celebrations were still on, Shiva excused himself and tugged Sati along with him.

'By the Holy Lake!' exclaimed Shiva, shutting the door to their private chamber behind him. 'This is only the first day! Is every day going to be as long?'

'It doesn't seem to make a difference to you! You walked out when you pretty well pleased!' teased Sati.

'I don't care about those damned ceremonies!' growled Shiva, ripping his ceremonial turban off and flinging it aside. He stared at Sati fervently, slowly moving towards her, his breathing heavy.

'Oh yes of course,' mocked Sati, with a playfully theatrical expression. 'The Neelkanth gets to decide what is important and what is not. The Neelkanth can do anything he wants.'

'Oh yes he can!'

Sati laughed mischievously and ran to the other side of the bed. Shiva dashed towards her from the opposite side as he hurled his angvastram off in one smooth motion.

'Oh yes he can...'

— ⵀⵔⵙⵟⵘⵁ —

'Remember what I've told you to say,' whispered Nandi to Veerbhadra. 'Don't worry. The Lord will give his permission.'

'What...' whispered a groggy Shiva as he was woken up gently by Sati.

'Wake up, Shiva,' whispered Sati tenderly, her hair falling over his face, teasing his cheeks. 'Careful now,' murmured Sati softly, as Shiva looked at her longingly. 'Nandi, Krittika and Veerbhadra are waiting at the door. They have something important to say to you.'

'Hmmm?' growled Shiva, as he walked towards the door and glared at the trio. 'What is it Nandi? Isn't there someone beautiful in your life that you would like to bother at this hour instead of troubling me?'

'There's nobody like you, my Lord,' said Nandi, with a low bow and a chaste Namaste.

'Nandi, you better stop this nonsense or you are going to remain a bachelor all your life!' joked Shiva.

As everybody laughed loudly, Krittika remained anxious about the task at hand.

'Well, what did you want to talk about?' asked Shiva.

Nandi nudged Veerbhadra roughly. Shiva turned to Veerbhadra with a quizzical look.

'Bhadra, since when do you need the support of so many people to speak to me?' asked Shiva.

'Shiva...' murmured Veerbhadra nervously.

'Yes?'

'It's like this...'

'It's like what?'

'Well, you see...'

'I am seeing Bhadra.'

'Shiva, please stop making him more nervous than he

already is,' said Sati. Looking towards Veerbhadra, she continued, 'Veerbhadra, speak fearlessly. You haven't done anything wrong.'

'Shiva,' whispered Veerbhadra timidly, his cheeks the colour of beetroot. 'I need your permission.'

'Permission granted,' said Shiva, amused by now. 'Whatever it is that you want it for.'

'Actually, I am considering getting married.'

'A capital idea!' said Shiva. 'Now all you have to do is convince some blind woman to marry you!'

'Shiva!' reprimanded Sati gently.

'Well, I've already found a woman,' said Veerbhadra, before his courage could desert him. 'And she's not blind...'

'Not blind?!' exclaimed Shiva, his eyebrows humorously arched in wide disbelief. 'Then she is stupid enough to tie herself for the next seven births to a man who wants someone else to determine his marriage!'

Veerbhadra gazed at Shiva with an odd mixture of embarrassment, contrition and incomprehension.

'I've said this to you earlier, Bhadra,' said Shiva, 'There are many customs of our tribe that I don't like. And one of the primary ones amongst them is that the leader has to approve the bride of any tribesman. Don't you remember how we made fun of this ridiculous tradition as children?'

Veerbhadra glanced at Shiva and immediately down again, still unsure.

'For God's sake man, if you are happy with her, then I am happy for you,' said an exasperated Shiva. 'You have my permission.'

Veerbhadra looked up in surprised ecstasy as Nandi nudged him again. Krittika looked at Veerbhadra, as a long held breath escaped with massive relief. She turned to Sati and silently mouthed the words, 'Thank you.'

Shiva walked towards Krittika and hugged her warmly. A startled Krittika held back for an instant, before the warmth of the Neelkanth conquered her Suryavanshi reserve. She returned the embrace.

'Welcome to the tribe,' whispered Shiva. 'We are quite mad, but at heart we are good people!'

'But how did you know?' said Veerbhadra. 'I never told you that I loved her.'

'I am not blind, Bhadra,' smiled Shiva.

'Thank you,' said Krittika to Shiva. 'Thank you for accepting me.'

Shiva stepped back and said, 'No. Thank *you*. I was always concerned about Bhadra. He is a good, dependable man, but too simple-minded about women. I was worried about how married life would treat him. But there is no reason to worry anymore.'

'Well, I too want to tell you something,' said Krittika. 'I had never believed in the legend of the Neelkanth. But if you can transform Meluha like you have transformed my lady, then you are worthy of even being called the Mahadev!'

'I don't want to be called the Mahadev, Krittika. You know I love Meluha as much as I love Sati. I will do all that I possibly can.' Turning towards Veerbhadra, Shiva ordered, 'Come here, you stupid oaf!'

Veerbhadra came forward, embraced Shiva affectionately and whispered, 'Thank you.'

'Don't be stupid. There's no need for a "thank you"!' said Shiva with a grin.

Veerbhadra smiled broadly.

'And listen!' snarled Shiva in mock anger. 'You are going to answer to your best friend over the next chillum we share on how you dared to love a woman for so long without even speaking to me about it!'

Everybody laughed out loud.

'Will a good batch of marijuana make up for it?' asked Veerbhadra, smiling.

'Well, I'll think about it!'

— ⚹🌀ᘮᛉ⊕ —

'Doesn't she look tired?' asked a concerned Ayurvati, looking at Sati.

Sati had just gotten up from the prayer platform as she and her mother had been excused for this particular ceremony. This was only for the bridegroom and the father of the bride. The pandits were preparing for the puja, which would take a few moments.

'Well, it has been six days of almost continuous celebrations and pujas,' said Kanakhala. 'Though it is the custom that all this be done for a royal wedding, I can understand her being tired.'

'Oh, I wouldn't say it has anything to do with the six *days* of pujas,' said Brahaspati.

'No?' asked Kanakhala.

'No,' answered Brahaspati, mischievously. 'I think it has to do with the five *nights*.'

'What?' exclaimed Ayurvati, then blushed a deep red as the meaning of Brahaspati's words dawned on her.

Parvateshwar, who was sitting next to Kanakhala, glared at Brahaspati for the highly improper remark. Brahaspati guffawed as the ladies giggled quietly. An assistant pandit turned around in irritation. But on seeing the seniority of the Brahmins sitting behind him, he immediately swallowed his annoyance and returned to his preparations.

Parvateshwar however had no such compunctions. 'I can't believe the kind of conversation I am being forced to endure!' He rose to walk to the back of the congregation.

This made even Kanakhala and Ayurvati chortle. One of the senior pandits turned to signal that the ceremony was about to begin, making them fall silent immediately.

The pandits resumed the invocations of the shlokas. Both Shiva and Daksha continued to pour the ceremonial ghee into the sacred fire at regular intervals while saying, 'Swaha'.

In between two successive swahas, there was enough time for Shiva and Daksha to talk softly to each other. They spoke of Sati. And only Sati. To any neutral observer, it would have been difficult to decide who loved the princess more. The pandit took a momentary break in his recitation of the shlokas, the cue for Shiva and Daksha to pour some more ghee into the sacred fire with a 'Swaha.' A little ghee spilled onto Daksha's hands. As Shiva immediately pulled the napkin on his side to wipe it off, he noticed the chosen-tribe amulet on Daksha's arm. He was stunned on seeing the animal there, but had the good sense to not comment. Daksha meanwhile had also turned and noticed Shiva's gaze.

'It wasn't my choice. My father chose it for me,' said Daksha, with a warm smile, while wiping the ghee off his hands. There was not a hint of embarrassment in his voice. If one looked closely though, one could see just a hint of defiance in his eyes.

'Oh no, your Highness,' mumbled Shiva, a little mortified. 'I didn't mean to look. Please accept my apologies.'

'Why should you apologise, my Lord?' asked Daksha. 'It is my chosen-tribe. It is worn on the arm so that everyone can see it and classify me.'

'But you are far beyond your chosen-tribe, your Highness,' said Shiva politely. 'You are a much greater man than what that amulet symbolises.'

'Yes,' smiled Daksha. 'I really showed the old man, didn't I? The Neelkanth did not choose to appear in his reign. He came in mine. The terrorists were not defeated in his reign. They were defeated in mine. And the Chandravanshis were not reformed in his reign. They will be reformed in mine.'

Shiva smiled cautiously. Something about the conversation niggled at him. He stole one more glance at the amulet on Daksha's arm. It represented a humble goat, one of the lowest chosen-tribes amongst the Kshatriyas. In fact, some people considered the goat chosen-tribe to be so low that its wearer could not even be called a full Kshatriya. Shiva turned back towards the sacred fire on receiving the verbal cue from the pandit. Scooping some more ghee, he poured it into the fire with a 'Swaha'.

— ⚛☉∪⚶⊕ —

At nightfall, in the privacy of their chambers, Shiva had considered asking Sati about the relationship between Emperor Brahmanayak and his son, Daksha. But for some reason, his instincts told him that he would have to be careful in how he asks the questions.

'How was the relationship between Lord Brahmanayak and your father?'

Sati stopped playing with Shiva's flowing locks. She took

a deep breath and whispered, 'It was strained at times. They were very different characters. But Lord Bhrigu...'

The conversation was interrupted by a knock on the door.

'What is it?' growled Shiva.

'My Lord,' Taman, the doorkeeper, announced nervously. 'The Chief Scientist Brahaspati*ji* has requested an audience with you. He insists that he must meet with you tonight.'

Shiva was always happy to meet Brahaspati. But before answering the doorkeeper, he looked at Sati with a raised eyebrow. Sati smiled and nodded. She was aware that Shiva placed great value upon his relationship with Brihaspati.

'Let Brahaspati*ji* in, Taman.'

'Yes, my Lord.'

'My friend,' said Brahaspati. 'My apologies for disturbing you so late.'

'You never need to apologise to me, my friend,' answered Shiva.

'Namaste, Brahaspati*ji*,' said Sati, bending to touch the Chief Scientist's feet.

'*Akhand saubhagyavati bhav*,' said Brahaspati, blessing Sati with the traditional invocation that may *her husband always be alive and by her side*.

'Well,' said Shiva to Brahaspati, 'what is so important that you had to pull yourself out of bed so late in the night?'

'Actually, I didn't get the chance to speak to you earlier.'

'I know,' said Shiva, smiling towards Sati. 'Our days have been full with one ceremony after another.'

'I know,' said Brahaspati nodding. 'We Suryavanshis love ceremonies! In any case, I wanted to come and speak with you personally, since I have to leave for Mount Mandar tomorrow morning.'

'What?' asked a surprised Shiva. 'You have survived all this for the last six days. Surely you can survive one more?'

'I know,' said Brahaspati, crinkling his eyes apologetically. 'I would have loved to stay but there is an experiment that had already been scheduled. The preparations have been going on for months. The Mesopotamian material required for it has already been prepared. We are going to test the stability of the Somras with lesser quantities of water. I have to go early and ensure that the experiment begins correctly. My fellow scientists will remain here to keep you company!'

'Right,' said Shiva sarcastically. 'I really do love their constant theorising about everything under the sun.'

Brahaspati laughed. 'I really do have to go, Shiva. I am sorry.'

'No need to apologise, my friend,' said Shiva smiling. 'Life is long. And the road to Mount Mandar short. You are not going to get rid of me that easily.'

Brahaspati smiled, his eyes full of love for a man he had begun to consider his brother. He stepped forward and hugged Shiva tightly. Shiva was a little surprised. It was usually Shiva who would move to embrace Brahaspati first, and Brahaspati would normally respond later, a little tentatively.

'My brother,' whispered Brahaspati.

'Ditto,' mumbled Shiva.

Stepping slightly back but still holding Shiva's arms, Brahaspati said, 'I would go anywhere for you. Even into Patallok if it would help you.'

'I would never take you there, my friend,' answered Shiva with a grin, thinking that he himself wasn't about to venture into *Patallok*, the *land of the demons.*

Brahaspati smiled warmly at Shiva. 'I hope to see you soon, Shiva.'

'You can count on it!'

Turning to Sati, Brahaspati said, 'Take care, my child. It is so good to see you finally get the life you deserve.'

'Thank you, Brahaspati*ji*.'

CHAPTER 20

Attack on Mandar

'How are you, my friend?'

'What the hell am I doing here?' asked a startled Shiva.

He found himself sitting in the Brahma temple in Meru. Sitting in front of him was the Pandit whom he had met during his first visit to Meru, many months back.

'You called me here,' said the Pandit smiling.

'But how and when did I get here?' asked Shiva, astounded.

'As soon as you went to sleep,' replied the Pandit. 'This is a dream.'

'I'll be damned!'

'Why do you swear so much?' asked the Pandit frowning.

'I only swear when the occasion demands,' grinned Shiva. 'And what's wrong with swearing?'

'Well, I think it reflects poor manners. It shows, perhaps, a slight deficiency in character.'

'On the contrary, I think it shows tremendous character. It shows that you have the strength and passion to speak your mind.'

The Pandit guffawed, shaking his head slightly.

'In any case,' continued Shiva. 'Now that you are here,

why don't you tell me what you people are called? I was promised I would be told the next time I met one of you.'

'But you haven't met one of us again. This is a dream. I can only tell you what you already know,' said the Pandit, smiling mysteriously. 'Or something that already exists in your consciousness that you haven't chosen to listen to as yet.'

'So that's what this is all about! You are here to help me discover something I already know!'

'Yes,' said the Pandit, his smile growing more enigmatic.

'Well, what is it that we are supposed to talk about?'

'The colour of that leaf,' beamed the Pandit, pointing towards the many trees that could be seen from the temple, through its ostentatiously carved pillars.

'The colour of that leaf?!'

'Yes.'

Frowning strongly, Shiva sighed, 'Why, in the name of the Holy Lake, is the colour of that leaf important?'

'Many times a good conversational journey to find knowledge makes attaining it that much more satisfying,' said the Pandit. 'And more importantly, it helps you understand the context of the knowledge much more easily.'

'Context of the knowledge?'

'Yes. All knowledge has its context. Unless you know the context, you may not understand the point.'

'And I'll know all that by talking about the colour of that leaf?'

'Yes.'

'By the Holy Lake, man!' groaned Shiva. 'Let's talk about the leaf then.'

'All right,' laughed the Pandit. 'Tell me. What is the colour of that leaf?'

'The colour? It's green.'

'Is it?'

'Isn't it?

'Why do you think it appears green to you?'

'Because,' said Shiva, amused, 'it *is* green.'

'No. That wasn't what I was trying to ask. You had a conversation with one of Brahaspati's scientists about how the eyes see. Didn't you?'

'Oh that, right,' said Shiva slapping his forehead. 'Light falls on an object. And when it reflects back from that object to your eyes, you see that object.'

'Exactly! And you had another conversation with another scientist about what normal white sunlight is made of.'

'Yes, I did. White light is nothing but the confluence of seven different colours. That is why the rainbow is made up of seven colours since it is formed when raindrops disperse sunlight.'

'Correct! Now put these two theories together and answer my question. Why does that leaf appear green to you?

Shiva frowned as his mind worked the problem out. 'White sunlight falls on that leaf. The leaf's physical properties are such that it *absorbs* the colours violet, indigo, blue, yellow, orange and red. It doesn't absorb the colour green, which is then reflected back to my eyes. Hence I see the leaf as green.'

'Exactly!' beamed the Pandit. 'So think about the colour of that leaf from the perspective of the leaf itself. What colour it absorbs and what it rejects. Is its colour green? Or is it every single colour in the world, *except* green?'

Shiva was stunned into silence by the simplicity of the argument being presented to him.

'There are many realities. There are many versions of what may appear obvious,' continued the Pandit. 'Whatever appears as the unshakeable truth, its exact opposite may also be true in another context. After all, one's reality is but perception, viewed through various prisms of context.'

Shiva turned slowly towards the leaf again. Its lustrous green colour shone through in the glorious sunlight.

'Are your eyes capable of seeing another reality?' asked the Pandit.

Shiva continued to stare at the leaf as it gradually altered its appearance. The colour seemed to be dissolving out of the leaf as its bright green hue gradually grew lighter and lighter. It slowly reduced itself to a shade of grey. As a stunned Shiva continued to stare, even the grey seemed to dissolve slowly, till the leaf was almost transparent. Only its outline could be discerned. It appeared as though numerous curved lines of two colours, black and white, were moving in and out of the outline of the leaf. It almost seemed as if the leaf was nothing but a carrier, which the black and white curved lines used as a temporary stop on their eternal journey.

It took some time for Shiva to realise that the surrounding leaves had also been transformed into their outlines. As his eyes panned, he noticed that the entire tree had magically transformed into an outline, with the black and white curved lines flowing in and out, easily and smoothly. He turned his head to soak in the panorama. Every object, from the squirrels on the trees to the pillars of the temple had all been transformed into outlines of their apparent selves. The same black and white curved lines streamed in and out of them.

Turning to the Pandit for an explanation, he was stunned

to see that the priest himself was also transformed into an outline of his former self. White curved lines were flooding out of him with frightening intensity. Strangely though, there were no black lines around him.

'What the...'

Shiva's words were stopped by the outline of the Pandit pointing back at him. 'Look at yourself, my Karmasaathi,' advised the Pandit.

Shiva looked down. 'I'll be damned!'

His body too had been transformed into an outline, completely transparent inside. Torrents of black curved lines were gushing furiously into him. On close examination he could see that they were not lines at all. They were, in fact, tiny waves which were jet black in colour. The waves were so tiny that from even a slight distance, they appeared like lines. There wasn't even a hint of the white waves close to Shiva's outlined body. 'What the hell is going on?'

'The white waves are positive energy and the black are negative,' said the Pandit's outline. 'They are both important. Their balance crucial. It will be cataclysmic if they fall out of sync.'

Shiva looked up at the Pandit, puzzled. 'So why is there no positive energy around me? And no negative energy around you?'

'Because we balance each other. The Vishnu's role is to transmit positive energy,' said the Pandit. The white lines pouring feverishly out of the Pandit seemed to flutter a bit whenever he spoke. 'And the Mahadev's role is to absorb the negative. Search for it. Search for negative energy and you will fulfil your destiny as a Mahadev.'

'But I am no Mahadev. My deeds till now are not deserving of that title.'

'It doesn't work that way, my friend. The title isn't at all the result of one's deeds. Deeds, however noble, will follow the rightful belief in you that you are the Mahadev. It matters little what others think. Believe you are the Mahadev, and you will become one.'

Shiva frowned.

'Believe!' repeated the Pandit.

BOOM! A distant reverberation echoed through the ambience. Shiva turned his eyes towards the horizon.

'It sounds like an explosion,' whispered the Pandit's outline.

The distant, insistent voice of Sati came riding in. 'S-H-I-V-A...'

BOOM! Another explosion.

'S-H-I-V-A...'

'It looks like your wife needs you, my friend.'

Shiva looked with astonishment at the outline of the Pandit, unable to decipher where the sound came from.

'Maybe you should wake up,' advised the Pandit's disembodied voice.

'S-H-I-V-A'

A groggy Shiva woke up to find Sati staring at him with concern. He was still a little bleary from the outlandishly strange dream state that he had just been yanked out of.

'Shiva!'

BOOM!

'What the hell was that?' cried Shiva, alert now.

'Someone is using *daivi astras*!'

'What? What are *daivi astras*?'

A clearly stunned Sati spoke agitatedly, '*Divine weapons!* But Lord Rudra had destroyed all the *daivi astras*! Nobody has access to them anymore!'

Shiva was completely alert by now, his battle instincts primed. 'Sati, get ready. Wear your armour. Bind your weapons.'

Sati responded swiftly. Shiva slipped on his armour, coupled his shield to it and tied his sword to his waist. He slipped on his quiver smoothly and picked up his bow. Noting that Sati was ready, he kicked the door open. Taman and eight other guards had their swords drawn, ready to defend their Neelkanth against any attack.

'My Lord, you should wait inside,' said Taman. 'We will hold the attackers here.'

Shiva stared hard at Taman, frowning at his well-intentioned words. Taman immediately stepped aside. 'I am sorry, my Lord. We will follow you.'

Before Shiva could react, they heard footsteps rushing in towards them in the hallway. Shiva immediately drew his sword. He strained his ears to assess the threat.

Four footsteps. Just two men to attack a royal hallway! This didn't make sense.

One pair of footsteps dragged slightly. The terrorist was clearly a large man using considerable willpower to make his feet move faster than his girth allowed.

'Stand down, soldiers,' ordered Shiva suddenly. 'They are friends.'

Nandi and Veerbhadra emerged around the corner, running hard, with their swords at the ready.

'Are you alright, my Lord?' asked Nandi, admirably not out of breath.

'Yes. We are all safe. Did the two of you face any attacks?'

'No,' answered Veerbhadra, frowning. 'What the hell is going on?'

'I don't know,' said Shiva. 'But we're going to find out.'

'Where's Krittika?' asked Sati.

'Safe in her room,' answered Veerbhadra. 'There are five soldiers with her. The room is barred from the inside.'

Sati nodded, before turning to Shiva. 'What now?'

'I want to check on the Emperor first. Everybody, files of two. Keep your shields up for cover. Sati at my side. Nandi in the middle. Taman, Veerbhadra, at the rear. Don't light any torches. We know the way. Our enemies don't.'

The platoon moved with considerable speed and stealth, mindful of possible surprise attacks from the terrorists. Shiva was troubled by what he had heard. Or rather, what he hadn't. Apart from the repeated explosions, there was absolutely no other sound from the palace. No screams of terror. No sound of panicked footsteps. No clash of steel. Nothing. Either the terrorists had not begun their real attack as yet, or Shiva was late and the attack was already over. Shiva frowned as a third alternative occurred to him. Maybe there were no terrorists in the palace itself. Maybe the attack was being mounted from a distance, with the *daivi astras* that Sati spoke of.

Shiva's platoon reached Daksha's chambers to find his guards at the door tense and ready for battle.

'Where is the Emperor?' asked Shiva.

'He is inside, my Lord,' said the royal guard Captain, recognising the Neelkanth's silhouette immediately. 'Where are they, my Lord? We've been waiting for an attack ever since we heard the first explosion.'

'I don't know, Captain,' replied Shiva. 'Stay here and block the doorway. Taman, support the Captain here with your men. And remain alert.'

Shiva opened the Emperor's door. 'Your Highness?'

'My Lord? Is Sati all right?' asked Daksha.

'Yes, she is, your Highness,' said Shiva, as Sati, Nandi and Veerbhadra followed him into the chamber. 'And the Queen?'

'Shaken. But not too scared.'

'What was that?'

'I don't know,' answered Daksha. 'I would suggest that you and Sati stay here for now till we know what's going on.'

'Perhaps it maybe advisable for you to stay here, your Highness. We cannot risk any harm coming your way. I am going out to help Parvateshwar. If this is a terrorist attack, we need all the strength we have.'

'You don't have to go, my Lord. This is Devagiri. Our soldiers will slay all the terrorists dim-witted enough to attack our capital.'

Before Shiva could respond, there was a loud insistent knocking on the door.

'Your Highness? Request permission to enter.'

'*Parvateshwar!*' thought Daksha. '*Observing protocol even at a time like this!*'

'Come in!' growled Daksha. As Parvateshwar entered, Daksha let fly. 'How in Lord Indra's name can this happen, General? An attack on Devagiri? How dare they?'

'Your Highness,' intercepted Shiva. Sati, Nandi and Veerbhadra were in the chambers. He could not allow Parvateshwar to be insulted in their presence, least of all in Sati's. 'Let us first find out what is going on.'

'The attack is not on Devagiri, your Highness,' glared Parvateshwar, his impatience with his Emperor having put him on edge. 'My scouts saw massive plumes of smoke coming from the direction of Mount Mandar. I believe it is under attack. I have already given orders for my troops and the station Arishtanemi to be ready. We leave in an hour. I need your permission to depart.'

'The explosions were in Mandar, Pitratulya?' asked Sati incredulously. 'How powerful must they have been to be heard in Devagiri!'

Parvateshwar looked gloomily at Sati, his silence conveying his deepest fears. He turned towards Daksha. 'Your Highness?'

Daksha seemed stunned into silence. Or was that a frown on his forehead? Parvateshwar could not be sure in the dim light.

'Guards, light the torches!' ordered Parvateshwar. 'There is no attack on Devagiri!'

As the torches spread their radiance, Parvateshwar repeated, 'Do I have your permission, my Lord?'

Daksha nodded softly.

Parvateshwar turned to see Shiva looking shocked. 'What happened, Shiva?'

'Brahaspati left for Mount Mandar yesterday.'

'What?' asked a startled Parvateshwar, who had not noticed the chief scientist's absence in the celebrations of the previous day. 'O Lord Agni!'

Shiva turned slowly towards Sati, drawing strength from her presence.

'I will find him, Shiva,' consoled Parvateshwar. 'I am sure he is alive. I will find him.'

'I'm coming with you,' said Shiva.

'And so am I,' said Sati.

'What?' asked Daksha, the light making his agonised expression clear. 'You both don't need to go.'

Shiva turned to Daksha, frowning. 'My apologies, your Highness. But I must go. Brahaspati needs me.'

As Parvateshwar and Shiva turned to leave the royal chambers, Sati bent down to touch her father's feet. Daksha seemed too dazed to bless her and Sati did not want to remain too far behind her husband. She quickly turned to touch her mother's feet.

'*Ayushman bhav*,' said Veerini.

Sati frowned at the odd blessing — '*May you live long'*. She was going into a battle. She wanted victory, not a long life! But there was little time to argue. Sati turned and raced behind Shiva as Nandi and Veerbhadra followed closely.

CHAPTER 21

Preparation for War

The noise of the explosions stopped within an hour of the first. It wasn't much later that Shiva, Parvateshwar, Sati, Nandi and Veerbhadra, accompanied by a brigade of one thousand five hundred cavalry, were on their way to Mount Mandar. Brahaspati's scientists rode with the brigade, sick with worry about their leader's fate. They rode hard and hoped to cover the day-long distance to the mountain in fewer than eight hours. It was almost at the end of the second prahar, with the sun directly overhead that the brigade turned the last corner of the road where the forest cover cleared to give them their first glimpse of the mountain.

An angry roar rent the air as the soldiers sighted what admittedly had been the heart of their empire. Mandar had been ruthlessly destroyed. The mountain had a colossal crater at its centre. It was almost as if a giant Asura had struck his massive hands right through the core of the mountain and scooped it out. The enormous buildings of science were in ruins, their remnants scattered across the plains below. The giant churners at the bottom of the mountain were still functioning, their eerie sound making the gruesome picture even more macabre.

'Brahaspati!' roared Shiva, as he rode hard, right into the heart of the mountain, where miraculously the pathway still stood strong.

'Wait Shiva,' called out Parvateshwar. 'It could be a trap.'

Shiva, unmindful of any danger, continued to gallop up the pathway through the devastated heart of the mountain. The brigade, with Parvateshwar and Sati in the lead, rode fast, trying to keep up with their Neelkanth. They reached the top to be horrified by what they saw. Parts of the buildings hung limply on broken foundations, some structures still smouldering. Scorched and unrecognisable body parts, ripped apart by the repeated explosions, were strewn all over. It was impossible to even identify the dead.

Shiva tumbled off his horse, his face devoid of even a ray of hope. Nobody could have survived such a lethal attack. 'Brahaspati…'

— ⋏⊚⛢⊹⊕ —

'How did the terrorists get their hands on the *daivi astras*?' asked an agitated Parvateshwar, the fire of vengeance blazing within him.

The soldiers had been ordered to collect all the body parts and cremate them in separate pyres, to help the departed on their onward journey. A manifest was being drawn up of the names of those believed dead. The first name on the list was that of Brahaspati, Chief Scientist of Meluha, Sarayupaari Brahmin, Swan chosen-tribe. The others were mostly Arishtanemi, assigned to the task of protecting Mandar. It was a small consolation that the casualties were minimal since most of the mountain's residents were in Devagiri for the Neelkanth's marriage. The list was going to be sent to the great sanyasis in Kashmir, whose powers over the spiritual force were considered second to none. If the sanyasis could be cajoled into reciting prayers for these departed souls, then it could be hoped that their grisly death in this birth would not mar their subsequent births.

'It could have also been the Somras, General,' said Panini, one of Brahaspati's assistant chief scientists, offering another plausible explanation.

Shiva looked up suddenly on hearing Panini's words.

'The Somras did this! How?' asked a disbelieving Sati.

'The Somras is very unstable during its manufacturing process,' continued Panini. 'It is kept stable by using copious quantities of the Saraswati waters. One of our main projects was to determine whether we could stabilise the Somras while using less water. Much lesser than at present.'

Shiva remembered Brahaspati talking about this. He leaned over to listen intently to Panini.

'It was one of the dream projects of...' Panini found it hard to complete the statement. The thought that Brahaspati, the greatest scientist of his generation, the father-figure to all the learned men at Mount Mandar, was gone, was too much for Panini to bear. He was choked by the intense pain he felt inside. He stopped talking, shut his eyes and hoped the terrible moment would pass. Regaining a semblance of control over himself, he continued, 'It was one of Brahaspati*ji*'s dream projects. He had come back to organise the experiment that was to begin today. He didn't want us to miss the last day of the celebrations. So he came alone.'

Parvateshwar was numb. 'You mean this could have been an accident?'

'Yes,' replied Panini. 'We were all aware that the experiment was risky. Maybe that is why Brahaspati*ji* decided to begin without us.'

The entire room was stunned into silence by this unexpected information. Panini retreated into his private hell. Parvateshwar continued to gaze into the distance, shocked by the turn of events. Sati stared at Shiva, holding his hand, deeply worried about how her husband was taking the death of his friend. And that it may all have been just a senseless mishap!

— ✳◉Ʊ⬧⊕ —

It was late into the first hour of the fourth prahar. It had been decided that the brigade would set up camp at the base of the ruined mountain. They would leave the following day, after all the ceremonies for the departed had been completed. Two riders had been dispatched to Devagiri with the news about Mandar. Parvateshwar and Sati sat at the edge of the mountain peak, whispering to each other. The drone of Brahmin scientists reciting Sanskrit shlokas at the base of the mountain floated up to create an ethereal atmosphere of pathos. Nandi and Veerbhadra stood at attention, a polite distance from Parvateshwar and Sati, looking at their Lord.

Shiva was walking around the ruins of the Mandar buildings, lost in thought. It was tearing him apart that he hadn't seen any recognisable part of Brahaspati. Everybody in Mandar had been mutilated beyond recognition. He desperately searched for some sign of his friend. Something he could keep with himself. Something he could cling on to, which would soothe his tortured soul in the years of mourning that he would go through. He walked at a snail's pace; his eyes combing the ground. They suddenly fell upon an object he recognised only too well.

He slowly bent down to pick it up. It was a bracelet made of leather, burnt at the edges, its back-hold destroyed. The heat of the fiery explosions had scorched its brown colour to black at most places. The centre however, with an embroidered design, was astonishingly unblemished. Shiva brought it close to his eyes.

The crimson hue of the setting sun caused the Aum symbol to glow. At the amalgam of the top and bottom curve of the Aum were two serpent heads. The third curve, surging out to the east, ended in a sharp serpent head, with its forked tongue striking out threateningly.

It was him! He killed Brahaspati!

Shiva swung around, eyes desperately scanning the limbs scattered about, hoping to find the owner of the bracelet or some part of him. But there was nothing. Shiva screamed silently. A scream audible only to him and Brahaspati's wounded soul. He clutched the bracelet in his fist till its still burning embers burnt into his palms. Clasping it even more firmly, he swore a terrible vengeance. He vowed to bring upon the Naga a death that would scar him for his next seven births. That Naga, and his entire army of vice, would be annihilated. Piece by bloody piece.

'Shiva! Shiva!' The insistent call yanked him back to reality.

Sati was standing in front of him, gently touching his hand. Parvateshwar stood next to her, disturbed. Nandi and Veerbhadra stood to the other side.

'Let it go, Shiva,' said Sati.

Shiva continued to stare at her, blank.

'Let it go, Shiva,' repeated Sati softly. 'It's singeing your hand.'

Shiva opened his palm. Nandi immediately lunged forward to pull the bracelet out. Screaming in surprised agony, Nandi dropped the bracelet as it scalded his hand. How did the Lord hold it for so long?

Shiva immediately bent down and picked up the bracelet. This time carefully. His fingers were holding the less charred edge, the part with the Aum symbol. He turned to Parvateshwar. 'It was not an accident.'

'What?' cried a startled Parvateshwar.

'Are you sure?' asked Sati.

Shiva looked towards Sati and raised the bracelet, the serpent Aum clearly coming into view. Sati let out a gasp of shock. Parvateshwar, Nandi and Veerbhadra immediately closed in to stare intently at the bracelet.

'Naga...,' whispered Nandi.

'The same bastard who attacked Sati in Meru,' growled Shiva. 'The same Naga who attacked us on our return from Mandar. The very, bloody, same, son of a bitch.'

'He will pay for this Shiva,' said Veerbhadra.

Turning towards Parvateshwar, Shiva said, 'We ride to Devagiri tonight. We declare war.'

Parvateshwar nodded.

— 𝍐⊚Ⴑ𐌙⊛ —

The Meluhan war council sat quietly, observing five minutes of silence in honour of the martyrs of Mandar. General Parvateshwar and his twenty-five brigadiers sat to the right of Emperor Daksha. To Daksha's left sat the Neelkanth, the administrative Brahmins led by Prime Minister Kanakhala and the governors of the fifteen provinces.

'The decision of the council is a given,' said Daksha, beginning the proceedings. 'The question is when do we attack?'

'It will take us at the most a month to be ready to march, your Highness,' said Parvateshwar. 'You know that there are no roads between Meluha and Swadweep. Our army would have to travel through dense, impenetrable forests. So even if we begin the march in a month, we will not be in Swadweep before three months from today. So time is of the essence.'

'Then let the preparations begin.'

'Your Highness,' said Kanakhala, adding a Brahmin voice of reason to the battle cry of the Kshatriyas. 'May I suggest an alternative?'

'An alternative?' asked a surprised Daksha.

'Please don't misunderstand me,' said Kanakhala. 'I understand the rage of the entire nation about what happened at Mandar. But we want vengeance against the perpetrators of the crime, not all of Swadweep. Could we try and see whether a scalpel might work before we bring out the mighty war sword?'

'The path you suggest is one of cowardice, Kanakhala,' said Parvateshwar.

'No Parvateshwar, my aim is to seek our vengeance at minimum cost to Meluhan lives,' said Kanakhala politely. 'After all, discretion is the better part of valour.'

'My soldiers are resolute and will defend Meluha to the death, Madam Prime Minister.'

'I know they will,' said Kanakhala, maintaining her composure. 'And I know that you too are willing to shed your blood for Meluha. My suggestion is that we send an emissary to Emperor Dilipa and request him to surrender the terrorists who perpetrated this attack. We can threaten that if he doesn't co-operate, we will attack with all the might at our disposal.'

His eyes scowling with impatience, Parvateshwar said, '*Request* him? And why would he listen? For decades, the Swadweepans have got away with their nefarious activities because they think we don't have the stomach for a fight. And if we talk about this "scalpel approach" after an outrage like Mount Mandar, they will be convinced that they can mount any attack at will and we will not respond.'

'I disagree, Parvateshwar,' said Kanakhala. 'They have mounted terrorist attacks because they are scared that they cannot take us on in a direct fight. They are afraid that they cannot withstand our superior technology and war-machines. I am only thinking about what Lord Shiva had said when he had first come here. Can we try talking to them before we fight? This may be an opportunity to get them to admit that there are sections in their society who are terrorists. If they hand them over, we may even find ways of coexisting.'

'I don't think Shiva thinks like that anymore,' said Parvateshwar, pointing towards the Neelkanth. 'He too wants vengeance.'

Shiva sat silently, his face expressionless. Only his eyes glowered with the terrible anger seething within.

'My Lord,' said Kanakhala looking towards Shiva, her hands folded in a Namaste. 'I hope that at least you understand what I am trying to say. Even Brahaspati would have wanted us to avoid violence, if possible.'

The last sentence had an effect on Shiva similar to a torrential downpour on a raging fire. He turned towards Kanakhala and gazed into her eyes, before turning towards Daksha. 'Your Highness, what Kanakhala says is right. Perhaps we can send an emissary to Swadweep to give them an opportunity to atone for their sins. Striving for a peaceful resolution will help in avoiding the deaths of innocents. However, I would still suggest that we begin war preparations. We should be prepared for the possibility that the Chandravanshis may reject our offer.'

'The Mahadev has spoken,' said Daksha. 'I propose that this be the decision of the war council. All in favour, raise your hands.'

Every hand in the room was raised. The die had been cast. There would be an attempt at peace. If that didn't work, the Meluhans would attack.

— ⵣ◉ᚒ♀⊕ —

'I have failed again, Bhadra,' cried Shiva. 'I can't protect anyone in need.'

Shiva was sitting next to Veerbhadra, in a private section of his palace courtyard. A deeply worried Sati had invited Veerbhadra to try and pull Shiva out of his mourning. Shiva had retreated into a shell, not speaking, not crying. She hoped her husband's childhood friend would succeed where she had failed.

'How can you blame yourself, Shiva?' asked Veerbhadra,

handing over the chillum to his friend. 'How can this be your fault?'

Shiva picked up the chillum and took a deep drag. The marijuana coursed through his body, but did not help. The pain was too intense. Shiva snorted in disgust and threw the chillum away. As tears flooded his eyes, he looked up at the sky and swore, 'I will avenge you, my brother. Even if it is the last thing I do. Even if I have to spend every moment of the rest of my life doing so. Even if I have to come back to this world again and again. I will avenge you!'

Veerbhadra turned towards Sati sitting in the distance, a worried look on his face. Sati got up and walked towards them. She came up to Shiva and held him tight, resting his tired head against her bosom, hoping to soothe Shiva's tortured soul. To Sati's surprise, Shiva did not raise his arms to wrap them around her. He just sat motionless. Breathing intermittently.

— 𑀓𑀝𑀉𑀔𑀷 —

'My Lord,' cried a surprised Vraka, as he stood to attention. Respectfully, so did the twenty-four other brigadiers for the Neelkanth had just been announced into the war room.

Parvateshwar rose slowly. He spoke kindly as he knew the pain Shiva still carried about Brahaspati's grisly death. 'How are you, Shiva?'

'I am alright, thank you.'

'We were discussing battle plans.'

'I know,' said Shiva. 'I was wondering if I could join in.'

'Of course,' said Parvateshwar, as he moved his chair to the side.

'The essential problem for us,' said Parvateshwar, trying to quickly bring Shiva up to speed, 'is the transport links between Meluha and Swadweep.'

'There aren't any, right?'

'Right,' answered Parvateshwar. 'After their last defeat at our hands a hundred years ago, the Chandravanshis destroyed the entire infrastructure that then existed between Meluha and Swadweep. They depopulated their border cities and moved them deeper into their empire. Forests grew where cities and roads once were. There is no river that flows from our territory into theirs. Basically, there is no way our huge, technologically superior war-machines can be transported to the borders of Swadweep.'

'That was their intention, obviously,' said Shiva. 'Your superiority is technology. Their superiority is their numbers. They have negated your strength.'

'Exactly. And if our war-machines are taken out of the equation, our one hundred thousand strong army may get inundated by their million soldiers.'

'They have a million strong army?' asked Shiva, incredulous.

'Yes, my Lord,' said Vraka. 'We can't be absolutely sure, but that is our estimate. However, we also estimate that the regulars in their army would not be more than a hundred thousand. The rest would be part-timers. Essentially, people such as small traders, artisans, farmers and any one without influence. They would be forcibly conscripted and used as cannon fodder.'

'Disgusting,' said Parvateshwar. 'Risking the lives of Shudras and Vaishyas for a job that should be done by Kshatriyas. Their Kshatriyas have no honour.'

Shiva looked towards Parvateshwar and nodded. 'Can't

we dismantle our war-machines, carry them to Swadweep and reassemble them?'

'Yes we can,' said Parvateshwar. 'But that is technically possible only for a few. Our most devastating machines which would give us the edge, like the long-range catapult, cannot be assembled outside a factory.'

'The long-range catapult?'

'Yes,' answered Parvateshwar. 'It can hurl huge boulders and smouldering barrels over distances of more than a kilometre. If used effectively they can soften, even devastate, the enemy lines before our cavalry and infantry begin their charge. Basically, the role that elephants used to play earlier.'

'Then why not use elephants?'

'They are unpredictable. No matter how effectively you train them, an army often loses control over them in the heat of the battle. In fact, in the previous war with the Swadweepans, it was their own elephants who brought about their downfall.'

'Really?' asked Shiva.

'Yes,' answered Parvateshwar. 'Our ploy of firing at the mahouts and generating tremendous noise with our war drums worked. The Chandravanshi elephants panicked and ran into their own army, shattering their lines, especially the ones composed of irregulars. All we had to do then was charge in and finish the job.'

'No elephants then.'

'Absolutely,' said Parvateshwar.

'So we need something that we can carry along with us and which can be used to soften their irregulars in order to negate their numerical superiority.'

Parvateshwar nodded. Shiva looked towards the window,

where a stiff morning breeze was making the leaves flutter. The leaves were green. Shiva stared harder. They remained green.

'I know,' said Shiva, looking at Parvateshwar suddenly, his face luminescent. 'Why don't we use arrows?'

'Arrows?' asked a surprised Parvateshwar.

Archery was the battle art of the most elite Kshatriyas, used for one-on-one duels. However, since one-on-one duels could only be fought between warriors of equal chosen-tribes, this skill was reduced to being a demonstration art for the crème de la crème. Archers earned huge respect for their rare skill, but they were not decisive in battles. There had been a time when bows and arrows were crucial in war strategies as weapons of mass destruction. That was the time of the *daivi astras*. Many of these astras were usually released through arrows. However, with the ban on *daivi astras* many thousands of years ago by Lord Rudra, the effectiveness of archery units in large-scale battles had reduced drastically.

'How can that reduce their numerical superiority, my Lord?' asked Vraka. 'Even the most skilled among the archers will take at least five seconds to aim, fire and execute a kill. He will not be able to kill more than twelve a minute. We have only one hundred Kshatriyas who are of the gold order of archers. The rest can shoot, but their aim cannot be relied upon. So we will not be able to kill more than one thousand two hundred of our enemies per minute. Certainly not enough against the Chandravanshis.'

'I am not talking about using arrows for one-on-one shooting,' said Shiva. 'I am talking about using them for softening the enemy, as weapons of mass destruction.'

Disregarding the confused expressions of his audience,

Shiva continued, 'Let me explain. Suppose we create a corps of archers of the lower Kshatriya chosen-tribes.'

'But their aim wouldn't be good,' said Vraka.

'That doesn't matter. Let us say we have at least five thousand such archers. Suppose we train them to just get the range right. Forget about the aim. Suppose their job is to just keep firing arrows in the general direction of the Chandravanshi army. If they don't have to aim, they can fire a lot more quickly. Maybe one arrow every two or three seconds.'

Parvateshwar narrowed his eyes as the brilliance of the idea struck him. The rest of his brigadiers were still trying to gather their thoughts.

'Think about it,' said Shiva. 'We would have five thousand arrows raining down on the Chandravanshis every two seconds. Suppose we can keep this up for ten minutes. An almost continuous shower of arrows. Their irregulars would break. The arrows would have the same effect as that of the elephants in the last war!'

'Brilliant!' cried Vraka.

'Perhaps,' mused Parvateshwar, 'our archers could be trained to release the arrows lying on their backs while holding up the bow with their feet. No doubt, accuracy would be somewhat compromised. But the effect would be far more deadly.'

'Excellent!' exclaimed Shiva. 'Because then the bows can be bigger. And the range longer.'

'And the arrows bigger and thicker, almost like small spears,' continued Parvateshwar. 'Strong enough to even penetrate leather and thick wooden shields. Only the soldiers with metal shields, like the regulars, would be safe from this.'

'Do we have our answer?' asked Shiva.

'Yes, we do,' answered Parvateshwar with a smile. He turned towards Vraka. 'Create this corps. I want five thousand men ready within two weeks.'

'It will be done, my Lord,' said Vraka.

— 𖠋◎🜃𐌀⊕ —

'What do you want to talk about, Shiva?' asked Parvateshwar, as he entered the metallurgy factory. He was accompanied by Vraka and Prasanjit, just as Shiva had requested. Vraka had reluctantly left the archery corps he had been training over the past week. However, he had been motivated to attend in expectation of another brilliant idea from the Neelkanth. He was not disappointed.

'I was thinking,' said Shiva, 'we would still need an equivalent of your stabbing ram to break their centre. The centre is where I assume their General would place their regulars. As long as they hold, our victory cannot be guaranteed.'

'Right,' said Parvateshwar. 'And we have to assume that these soldiers would be disciplined enough to stay in formation despite the barrage of arrows.'

'Exactly,' said Shiva. 'We can't transport the ram, right?'

'No we can't, my Lord' said Vraka.

'How about if we try to create a human ram?'

'Go ahead,' said Parvateshwar slowly, listening intently.

'Say we align the soldiers into a square of twenty men by twenty men,' said Shiva. 'We can have each one of them use his shield to cover the left half of his own body and the right half of the soldier to the left of him.'

'That will allow them to push their spear through, from in between the shields,' said Parvateshwar.

'Exactly,' said Shiva. 'And the soldiers behind can use their shields as a lid to cover themselves as well as the soldier in front. This formation would be like a tortoise. With the shields holding against any attack, much like a tortoise's shell, the enemy will not be able to break through, but our spears will cut into them.'

'We could have the strongest and most experienced soldiers in the front to make sure that the tortoise is well led,' said Prasanjit.

'No,' said Parvateshwar. 'Position the most experienced at the back and at the sides. To make sure that the square doesn't break in case the younger soldiers panic. This entire formation works only if the team stays together.'

'Right,' said Shiva, smiling at Parvateshwar's quick insight. 'And what if, instead of the usual spears, they carried this?'

Shiva raised a weapon that he had designed and the army metallurgy team had quickly assembled. Parvateshwar marvelled at the simple brilliance of it. It had the body of a spear. But its head had been broadened. On to the broadened head, two more spikes had been added, to the left and right of the main spear spike. Assaulting an enemy with this weapon would be like striking him with three spears at the same time.

'Absolutely brilliant Shiva,' marvelled Parvateshwar. 'What do you call it?'

'I call it a trishul.'

'Prasanjit,' said Parvateshwar. 'You are in charge of creating this corps. I want at least five tortoise formations ready by the time we march. I will assign two thousand men to you for this.'

'It will be done, my Lord,' said Prasanjit with a military salute.

Parvateshwar gazed at Shiva with respect. He knew that Shiva's ideas were brilliant. And the fact that he had come up with these tactics despite his profound personal grief was worthy of admiration. Maybe what the others say about Shiva could be true. Maybe he is the man who will finish Lord Ram's task. Parvateshwar hoped that Shiva would not prove him wrong.

— 入◎ᵾ�$⊕ —

Shiva sat in the royal meeting room, with Daksha and Parvateshwar at his side. Two legendary Arishtanemi brigadiers, Vidyunmali and Mayashrenik, sat at a distance. A muscular and once proud man stood in front of Shiva, pleading with folded hands.

'Give me a chance, my Lord,' said Drapaku. 'If the law has been changed, then why can't we fight?'

Drapaku was the man whose blind father had blessed Shiva in Kotdwaar. He had been a brigadier in the Meluhan army before the disease which blinded his father had also killed his wife and unborn child. He had been declared a vikarma along with his father.

But Shiva refused to be rushed. 'Tell me Drapaku, how is your father?'

'He is well, my Lord. And he will disown me if I don't support you in this dharmayudh.'

Shiva smiled softly. He too believed this was a *dharmayudh*, a *holy war*. 'But Drapaku, who will take care of him if something were to happen to you?'

'Meluha will take care of him, my Lord. But he would die a thousand deaths if I didn't go to battle with you. What kind of a son would I be if I didn't fight for my father's honour? For my country's honour?'

Shiva still seemed a little unsure. He could sense the discomfort of the others in the room. It had not escaped his notice that despite the repeal of the vikarma law, nobody had touched Drapaku when he had entered.

'My Lord, we are outnumbered heavily by the Chandravanshis,' continued Drapaku. 'We need every trained warrior we have. There are at least five thousand soldiers who can't battle since they have been declared vikarma. I can bring them together. We are willing, and eager, to die for our country.'

'I don't want you to die for Meluha, brave Drapaku,' said Shiva.

Drapaku's face fell instantly. He thought he would be returning home to Kotdwaar.

'However,' continued Shiva. 'I would like it if you killed for Meluha.'

Drapaku looked up.

'Raise your brigade, Drapaku,' ordered Shiva. Turning towards Daksha, he continued, 'We will call it the Vikarma Brigade.'

— 𝙓⊙𝕌𝟰⊕ —

'How can we have vikarmas in our army? This is ridiculous!' glared Vidyunmali.

Vidyunmali and Mayashrenik were in their private gym, preparing for their regular sword training.

'Vidyu…,' cajoled Mayashrenik.

'Don't "*Vidyu*" me, Maya. You know this is wrong.'

The usually calm Mayashrenik just nodded and let his impetuous friend vent his frustration.

'How will I face my ancestors if I die in this battle?' asked Vidyunmali. 'What will I answer if they ask me how I let a non-Kshatriya fight a battle that only we Kshatriyas should have fought? It is *our* duty to protect the weak. We are not supposed to use the weak to fight for us.'

'Vidyu, I don't think Drapaku is weak. Have you forgotten his valour in the previous Chandravanshi war?'

'He is a vikarma! That makes him weak!'

'Lord Shiva has decreed that there are no vikarmas anymore.'

'I don't think the Neelkanth truly knows right from wrong!'

'VIDYU!' shouted Mayashrenik.

Vidyunmali was surprised by the outburst.

'If the Neelkanth says it is right,' continued Mayashrenik, 'then it *is* right!'

CHAPTER 22

Empire of Evil

'This is the military formation that I think is ideal for the battle,' said Parvateshwar.

Vraka and Parvateshwar were sitting in the General's private office. The formation was that of a bow. The soldiers would be arranged in a wide semi-circular pattern. The slower corps, like the tortoises, would be placed at the centre. The flanks would comprise quicker units such as the light infantry. The cavalry would be at both ends of the bow, ready to be deployed anywhere on the battlefield or to ride along the sides of the bow for protection. The bow formation was ideal for a smaller army. It provided flexibility without sacrificing strength.

'It is ideal, my Lord,' said Vraka. 'What does the Mahadev have to say?'

'Shiva thinks it suits our requirements perfectly.'

Vraka did not like it when Parvateshwar referred to the Neelkanth by his name. But who was he to correct his General? 'I agree, my Lord.'

'I will lead the left flank,' said Parvateshwar. 'And you lead the right. Which is why I need your opinion on some tactics.'

'Me, my Lord?' asked an astonished Vraka. 'I thought the Mahadev would lead the other flank.'

'Shiva? No, I don't think he would be fighting this war, Vraka.'

Vraka looked up in surprise. But he remained silent.

Parvateshwar probably felt the need to explain, for he continued speaking. 'He is a good and capable man, no doubt. But the uppermost desire in his mind is retribution, not justice for Meluha. We will help him wreak vengeance when we throw the guilty Naga at his feet. He won't be putting his own life at risk in a war only to find one Naga.'

Vraka kept his eyes low, lest they betray the fact that he disagreed with his chief.

'To be fair,' said Parvateshwar. 'We cannot impose on him just because he has a blue throat. I respect him a lot. But I don't expect him to fight. What reason would there be for him to do that?'

Vraka looked up at Parvateshwar for a brief instant. Why was his General refusing to accept what was so obvious to everyone? Was he so attached to Lord Ram that he couldn't believe that another saviour had arrived on earth? Did he actually believe that Lord Ram could be the *only one*? Hadn't Lord Ram himself said that he is replaceable, only Dharma is irreplaceable?

'Furthermore,' continued Parvateshwar, 'he is married now. He is obviously in love. He is not going to risk Sati being bereaved again. Why should he? It's unfair of us to demand this of him.'

Vraka thought to himself, while not daring to voice his opinion. *The Mahadev will fight for all of us, General. He will battle to protect us. Why? Because that is what Mahadevs do.'*

Vraka was not aware that Parvateshwar was hoping for

something similar in his mind. He too wished that Shiva would rise to be a Mahadev and lead them to victory against the Chandravanshis. However, Parvateshwar had learned through long years of experience that while many men tried to rise up to Lord Ram's stature, none had ever succeeded. Parvateshwar had laid hopes on a few such men in his youth. And he had always been disillusioned at the end. He was simply preparing himself for another such expected disappointment from Shiva. He didn't plan to be left without a backup if Shiva refused to fight the battle against the Chandravanshis.

— ⋏◍ᚋ⇡⊛ —

The war council sat silently as Daksha read the letter that had come back from Swadweep — from the court of Emperor Dilipa. Daksha's reaction upon reading the letter left no doubt as to the message it contained. He shut his eyes, his face contorted in rage, his fist clenched tight. He handed the letter over to Kanakhala and sneered, 'Read it. Read it out loud so that the whole world may be sickened by the repugnance of the Chandravanshis.'

Kanakhala frowned slightly before taking the letter and reading it out loud. 'Emperor Daksha, Suryavanshi liege, protector of Meluha. Please accept my deep condolences for the dastardly attack on Mount Mandar. Such a senseless assault on peaceful Brahmins cannot but be condemned in the strongest of terms. We are shocked that any denizen of India would stoop to such levels. It is, therefore, with surprise and sadness that I read your letter. I assure you that neither me nor anyone in my command has anything to do with this devious attack. Hence I have to inform you, with regret, that there is nobody I can hand over to you. I hope that you understand the sincerity of this letter and will not make a hasty decision, which may have regrettable consequences for you. I assure you of my empire's full support in the investigation of this outrage. Please do inform us as to how we can be of assistance to you in bringing the criminals to justice.'

Kanakhala took a deep breath to compose herself. The anger over the typically Chandravanshi-like doubletalk was washing all over her, making her regret her earlier stand.

'It's personally signed by the Emperor Dilipa,' said Kanakhala, completing her reading of the letter.

'Not *Emperor* Dilipa,' growled a fuming Daksha. '*Terrorist* Dilipa of the Empire of Evil!'

'War!' arose a cry from the council, unanimous in its rage.

Daksha looked over at a scowling Shiva who nodded imperceptibly.

'War it is!' bellowed Daksha. 'We march in two weeks!'

— ⚕ ◯◯ ⛎ ⚢ ⊕ —

The bracelet seemed to develop a life of its own. It had swelled to enormous proportions, dwarfing Shiva. Its edges were engulfed in gigantic flames. The three colossal serpents, which formed the Aum, separated from each other and slithered towards Shiva. The one in the centre, while nodding towards the snake on its left, hissed, 'He got your brother. And the other one will soon get your wife.'

The serpents to the left and right scowled eerily.

Shiva pointed his finger menacingly at the serpent in the centre. 'You dare touch even a hair on her and I will rip your soul out of...'

'But I...' continued the serpent, not even acknowledging Shiva's

threat. 'I'm saving myself. I'm saving myself for you.'

Shiva stared at the serpent with impotent rage.

'I will get you,' said the serpent as its mouth opened wide, ready to swallow him whole.

Shiva's eyes suddenly opened wide. He was perspiring profusely. He looked around, but couldn't see a thing. It was extraordinarily dark. He reached out for Sati, to check if she was safe. She wasn't there. He was up in a flash, feeling a chill in his heart, almost expecting that the serpents had escaped his dreams and transformed into reality.

'Shiva,' said Sati, looking at him.

She was sitting at the edge of the bed. The tiny military tent they slept in could not afford the luxury of chairs. This tent had been their travelling home for the last one month as the Meluhan army marched towards Swadweep.

'What is it, Sati?' asked Shiva, his eyes adjusting to the dim light. He slipped the offending bracelet that he was tightly holding, back into his pouch.

When had I taken it out?

'Shiva,' continued Sati. She had tried to talk about this for the last two weeks. Ever since she had been sure of the news, she had not found an opportune moment. She had always managed to convince herself that this was minor news and it would not be right for her to trouble her husband with this, especially when he was going through one of the worst phases of his life. But it was too late now. He had to learn from her and not someone else. News like this did not remain secret in an army camp for long. 'I have something to tell you.'

'Yes,' said Shiva, though his dream still rankled. 'What is it?'

'I don't think I will be able to fight in the war.'

'What? Why?' asked a startled Shiva. He knew that cowardice was a word that did not exist in Sati's dictionary. Then why was she saying this? And why now, when the army had already marched for nearly a month through the dense forests that separated Meluha from Swadweep? They were already in enemy territory. There was no turning back. 'Sati, this is not like you.'

'Umm, Shiva,' said an embarrassed Sati. Such discussions were always difficult for the somewhat prudish Suryavanshis. 'I have my reasons.'

'Reasons?' asked Shiva. 'What…'

Suddenly the reason smacked Shiva like a silent thunderbolt. 'My God! Are you sure?'

'Yes,' said Sati, bashfully.

'By the Holy Lake! Am I going to be a father?'

Seeing the ecstasy on Shiva's face, Sati felt a pang of guilt that she hadn't informed him earlier.

'Wow!' whooped a thrilled Shiva as he swirled around with her in his arms. 'This is the best news I have heard in a long time!'

Sati smiled warmly and rested her head on his tired but strong shoulders.

'We will name our daughter after the one who has been the greatest comfort to you in the last two months, while I have been of no help,' said Shiva. 'We will name her Krittika!'

Sati looked up in surprise. She didn't believe that it was possible to love him even more. But it was. She smiled. 'It could be a son, you know.'

'Nah,' grinned Shiva. 'It will be a daughter. And I'll spoil her to high heavens!'

Sati laughed heartily. Shiva joined in. His first spirited laugh in over two months. He embraced Sati, feeling the negative energy dissipate from his being. 'I love you, Sati.'

'I love you too,' she whispered.

— 人◎Ͳ수⊕ —

Shiva raised the curtain to come out of the tent that Sati was ensconced in. Krittika and Ayurvati were with her. A retinue of nurses attended to her every need. Shiva had been obsessive about the health of his unborn child, questioning Ayurvati incessantly about every aspect of Sati's well-being.

The Suryavanshis had moved valiantly for nearly three months. The path had been more challenging than expected. The forest had reclaimed its original habitat with alarming ferocity. The army was attacked by wild animals and disease at every turn. They had lost two thousand men. And not one to the enemy. After weeks of hacking and marching, the scouts had finally managed to lead the Suryavanshi army to the Chandravanshis.

The Chandravanshis were camped on a sweeping plain called Dharmakhet. Their choice was clever. It was an expansive field that had enough room to allow the Chandravanshis to manoeuvre their million strong army. The full weight of their numerical superiority would come into play. The Suryavanshi army had tried to wait out the Chandravanshis, to test if they would lose patience and attack in a less advantageous area. But the Chandravanshis had held firm. Finally, the Suryavanshis moved camp to an easily defendable valley close to Dharmakhet.

Shiva looked up at the clear sky. A lone eagle flew

overhead, circling the royal camp, while five pigeons flew lower, unafraid of the eagle. A strange sign. His Guna shaman would have probably said that it's a bad time for battle, as the pigeons clearly have a hidden advantage.

Don't think about it. It is all nonsense in any case.

Breathing in the fresh morning air deeply, he turned right, towards Emperor Daksha's tent. Nandi was walking towards him.

'What is it Nandi?'

'I was just coming towards your tent, my Lord. The Emperor requests your presence. There's been a troubling development.'

Shiva and Nandi hurried towards Daksha's tastefully appointed royal tent. They entered to find Daksha and Parvateshwar engrossed in a discussion. Vraka, Mayashrenik and Drapaku sat at a distance. Drapaku was a little further away from the rest.

'This is a disaster,' groaned Daksha.

'Your Highness?' asked Shiva.

'My Lord! I'm glad you're here. We face complete disaster.'

'Let's not use words like that, your Highness,' said Shiva. Turning towards Parvateshwar, he asked, 'So your suspicions were correct?'

'Yes,' said Parvateshwar. 'The scouts just returned a few minutes back. There was a reason why the Chandravanshis were refusing to mobilise. They have despatched a hundred thousand soldiers in a great arc around our position. They will enter our valley by tomorrow morning. We will be sandwiched between their main force ahead of us and another hundred thousand behind us.'

'We can't fight on two fronts, my Lord,' cried Daksha. 'What do we do?'

'Was it Veerbhadra's scouts who returned with the news?' asked Shiva.

Parvateshwar nodded. Shiva turned towards Nandi, who rushed out immediately. Moments later, Veerbhadra stood before them.

'What route is the Chandravanshi detachment taking, Bhadra?' asked Shiva.

'To the east, along the steep mountains on our side. I think they intend to enter our valley some fifty kilometres up north.'

'Did you take a cartographer with you as Parvateshwar had instructed?'

Veerbhadra nodded, moved to the centre table and laid out the map on it. Shiva and Parvateshwar leaned across. Pointing to the route with his fingers, Veerbhadra said, 'This way.'

Shiva suddenly started as he noticed the ideal defensive position on the map, deep north of the Suryavanshi camp. He looked up at Parvateshwar. The same thought had occurred to the General.

'How many men do you think, Parvateshwar?'

'Difficult to say. It will be tough. But the pass looks defendable. It will need a sizeable contingent though. At least thirty thousand.'

'But we can't spare too many men. I am sure the battle with the main Chandravanshi army to the south will also happen tomorrow. It would be the best time for them to take up positions.'

Parvateshwar nodded grimly. The Meluhans might just have to retreat and manoeuvre for a battle from another, more advantageous position, he thought unhappily.

'I think five thousand men ought to do it, my Lords.'

Shiva and Parvateshwar had not noticed Drapaku move to the table. He was examining the pass that Shiva had just pointed out.

'Look here,' continued Drapaku, as Shiva and Parvateshwar peered.

'The mountains ahead constrict rapidly towards this pass, which is not more than fifty metres across. It doesn't matter how big their army is, each charge by the enemy into the pass cannot comprise more than a few hundred men.'

'But Drapaku, with a hundred thousand men, they can launch one charge after another, almost continuously,' said Mayashrenik. 'And with the mountains being so steep on the sides, you can't use any of our missiles. Victory is almost impossible.'

'It's not about victory,' said Drapaku. 'It's about holding them for a day so that our main army can fight.'

'I will do it,' said Parvateshwar.

'No, my Lord,' said Vraka. 'You are required for the main charge.'

Shiva looked up at Parvateshwar.

I need to be here as well.

'I can't do it either,' said Shiva, shaking his head.

Parvateshwar looked up at Shiva, disillusionment writ large on his face. While he had prepared his heart for disappointment, he had hoped that Shiva would prove him wrong. But it appeared clear to Parvateshwar that Shiva too would be simply watching the battle from the viewing platform being constructed for Daksha.

'Give me the honour, my Lord,' said Drapaku.

'Drapaku...,' whispered Mayashrenik, not putting into words what everyone else knew.

With only five thousand soldiers, the battle at the

northern pass against the Chandravanshi detachment was a suicide mission.

'Drapaku,' said Shiva. 'I don't know if...'

'I know, my Lord,' interrupted Drapaku. 'It is my destiny. I will hold them for one day. If Lord Indra supports me, I'll even try for two. Get us victory by then.'

Daksha suddenly interjected. 'Wonderful. Drapaku, make preparations to leave immediately.'

Drapaku saluted smartly and rushed out before any second thoughts were voiced.

— 𝖝⊙ᛏ𝟺⊕ —

In less than an hour the vikarma brigade was seen marching out of the camp. The sun was high up in the sky and practically the entire camp was awake, watching the soldiers set out on their mission. Everyone knew the terrible odds the vikarmas were going to face. They knew that it was unlikely that any of these soldiers would be seen alive again. The soldiers, though, did not exhibit the slightest hesitation or hint of fear, as they marched on. The camp stood in silent awe. One thought reverberated throughout.

How could the vikarmas be so magnificent? They are supposed to be weak.

Drapaku was at the lead, his handsome face smeared with war paint. On top of his armour, he wore a saffron angvastram. The colour of the Parmatma. The colour worn for the final journey. He didn't expect to return.

He stopped suddenly as Vidyunmali darted in front of him. Drapaku frowned. Before he could react, Vidyunmali had drawn his knife. Drapaku reached for his side arm. But Vidyunmali was quicker. He sliced his own thumb across the blade, and brought it up to Drapaku's forehead. In the tradition of the great brother-warriors of yore, Vidyunmali smeared his blood across Drapaku's brow, signifying that his blood will protect him.

'You're a better man than I am, Drapaku,' whispered Vidyunmali.

Drapaku stood silent, astonished by Vidyunmali's uncharacteristic behaviour.

Raising his balled fist high, Vidyunmali roared, 'Give them hell, vikarma!'

'Give them hell, vikarma!' bellowed the Suryavanshis, repeating it again and again.

Drapaku and his soldiers looked around the camp, absorbing the respect that they had been denied for so long. Way too long.

'Give them hell, vikarma!'

Drapaku nodded, turned and marched on before his emotions spoiled the moment. His soldiers followed.

'Give them hell, vikarma!'

— ⸸⊚Ủ⼇⊕ —

It was an uncharacteristically warm morning for that time of the year.

The Chandravanshi detachment had been surprised to find Meluhan soldiers at the northern pass the previous night. They had immediately attacked. The vikarmas had valiantly held the pass through the night, buying precious time for the main Suryavanshi army. This *had to be* the day of the main battle. Shiva was prepared.

Sati stood resplendent as she looped the aarti thali in small circles around Shiva's face. She stopped after seven turns, took some vermilion on her thumb and smeared it up Shiva's forehead in a long tilak. 'Come back victorious or don't come back at all.'

Shiva raised one eyebrow and grimaced. 'What kind of a send off is that?!'

'What? No, it's just...' stammered Sati.

'I know, I know,' smiled Shiva as he embraced Sati. 'It's the traditional Suryavanshi send off before a war, right?'

Sati looked up with moist eyes. Her love for Shiva was overcoming decades of Suryavanshi training. 'Just come back safe and sound.'

'I will, my love,' whispered Shiva. 'You won't get rid of me so easily.'

Sati smiled weakly. 'I'll be waiting.'

She stood up on her toes and kissed Shiva lightly. Shiva kissed her back and turned quickly, before his heart could fill his head with second thoughts. Lifting the tent curtain, he walked out. His eyes scanned the skies, keenly looking for omens. There were none.

Bloody good!

The distant drone of Sanskrit shlokas, accompanied by the beating of war drums in a smooth rhythmic pulse, wafted in over the dry winter breeze. This particular Suryavanshi custom had appeared odd to Shiva. But maybe there was something to the Brahmin 'Call for Indra and Agni', as this puja was called. The effect of the beats and the incantations were akin to a clarion call rousing a fierce spirit amongst the warriors. The beats would quicken once the battle began. Shiva was eager to throw himself into the battle. He turned and strode towards Daksha's tent.

'Greetings, your Highness,' said Shiva as he raised the curtain to enter the royal tent, where Parvateshwar was explaining the plans to the Emperor. 'Namaste, Parvateshwar.'

Parvateshwar smiled and folded his hands.

'What news of Drapaku, Parvateshwar?' asked Shiva. 'The last despatch I heard is at least three hours old.'

'The vikarma battle is on. Drapaku still leads them. He has bought us invaluable time. May Lord Ram bless him.'

'Yes,' agreed Shiva. 'May Lord Ram bless him. He just has to hold on till the end of this day.'

'My Lord,' said Daksha, hands folded in a formal Namaste, head bowed. 'It is an auspicious beginning. We will have a good day. Wouldn't you agree?'

'Yes it does seem so,' smiled Shiva. 'The news of Drapaku is very welcome. But perhaps this question may be better suited for the fourth prahar, your Highness.'

'I am sure the answer would be the same, my Lord. By the fourth prahar today, Emperor Dilipa will be standing in front of us, in chains, waiting for justice to be delivered.'

'Careful, your Highness,' said Shiva with a smile. 'Let us not tempt fate. We still have to win the war!'

'We will face no problems. We have the Neelkanth with us. We just need to attack. Victory is guaranteed.'

'I think a little more than a blue throat will be required to beat the Chandravanshis, your Highness,' said Shiva, his smile even broader. 'We shouldn't underestimate our enemy.'

'I don't underestimate them, my Lord. But I will not make the mistake of underestimating you either.'

Shiva gave up. He had learned that it was impossible to win a debate when pitched against Daksha's unquestioning conviction.

'Perhaps I should leave, your Highness,' said

Parvateshwar. 'The time has come. With your permission.'

'Of course, Parvateshwar. *Vijayibhav*,' said Daksha. Turning towards Shiva, Daksha continued, 'My Lord, they have built a viewing platform for us on the hill at the back.'

'Viewing platform?' asked Shiva, perplexed.

'Yes. Why don't we watch the battle from there? You would also be in a better position to direct it.'

Shiva narrowed his eyes in surprise. 'Your Highness, my position is with the soldiers. On the battlefield.'

Parvateshwar stopped in his tracks. Startled and delighted with having been proved wrong.

'My Lord, this is a job for butchers, not the Neelkanth,' said a concerned Daksha. 'You don't need to sully your hands with Chandravanshi blood. Parvateshwar will arrest that Naga and throw him at your feet. You can extract such a terrible retribution from him that his entire tribe would dread your justice for aeons.'

'This is not about *my* revenge, your Highness. It is about the vengeance of Meluha. It would be petty of me to think that an entire war is being fought just for me. This is a war between good and evil. A battle in which one has to choose a side. And fight. There are no bystanders in a *dharmayudh* — it is *a holy war.*'

Parvateshwar watched Shiva intently, his eyes blazing with admiration. These were Lord Ram's words. *There are no bystanders in a dharmayudh.*

'My Lord, we can't afford to risk your life,' pleaded Daksha. 'You are too important. I am sure that we can win this war without taking that gamble. Your presence has inspired us. There are many who are willing to shed their blood for you.'

'If they are willing to shed their blood for me, then I

must be willing to shed my blood for them.'

Parvateshwar's heart was swamped by the greatest joy an accomplished Suryavanshi could feel. The joy of finally finding a man worth following. The joy of finding a man worth being inspired by. The joy of finding a man, deserving of being spoken of in the same breath, as Lord Ram himself.

A worried Daksha came close to Shiva. He realised that if he had to stop the Neelkanth from this foolhardiness, he would have to speak his mind. He whispered softly, 'My Lord, you are my daughter's husband. If something were to happen to you, she would be bereaved twice in one life. I can't let that happen to her.'

'Nothing will happen,' whispered Shiva. 'And Sati would die a thousand deaths if her husband stayed away from a *dharmayudh*. She would lose respect for me. If she weren't pregnant, she would have been fighting alongside me, shoulder to shoulder. You know that.'

Daksha stared at Shiva, troubled and apprehensive.

Shiva smiled warmly. 'Nothing will happen, your Highness.'

'And what if it does?'

'Then it should be remembered that it happened for a good cause. Sati would be proud of me.'

Daksha continued to stare at Shiva, his face a portrait of agonised distress.

'Forgive me, your Highness, but I must go,' said Shiva with a formal Namaste, turning to leave.

Parvateshwar followed distracted, as if commanded by a higher force. As Shiva walked briskly out of the tent towards his horse, he heard Parvateshwar's booming voice. 'My Lord!'

Shiva continued walking.

'My Lord,' bellowed Parvateshwar again, more insistent.

Shiva stopped abruptly. He turned, a surprised frown on his face. 'I am sorry Parvateshwar. I thought you were calling out to his Highness.'

'No, my Lord,' said Parvateshwar. 'It was you I called.'

His frown deepened as Shiva asked, 'What is the matter, brave General?'

Parvateshwar came to a halt in rigid military attention. He kept a polite distance from Shiva. He could not stand on the hallowed ground that cradled the Mahadev. As if in a daze, Parvateshwar slowly curled his fist and brought it up to his chest. And then, completing the formal Meluhan salute, he bowed low. Lower than he had ever bowed before a living man. As low as he bowed before Lord Ram's idol during his regular morning pujas. Shiva continued to stare at Parvateshwar, his face an odd mixture of surprise and embarrassment. Shiva's respect for Parvateshwar made him uncomfortable with such idolatry.

Rising, but with his head still bent, Parvateshwar whispered, 'I will be honoured to shed my blood with you, my Lord.' Raising his head, he repeated, 'Honoured.'

Shiva smiled and touched Parvateshwar's arm. 'Well, if our plans are good my friend, hopefully we won't have to shed too much of it!'

CHAPTER 23

Dharmayudh, the Holy War

The Suryavanshis were arranged like a bow. Strong, yet flexible. The recently raised tortoise regiments had been placed at the centre. The light infantry formed the flanks, while the cavalry, in turn, bordered them. The chariots had been abandoned due to the unseasonal rain the previous night. They couldn't risk the wheels getting stuck in the slush. The newly reared archer regiments remained stationed at the back. Skilfully designed back rests had been fabricated for them, which allowed the archers to lie on their backs and guide their feet with an ingenious system of gears. The bows could be stretched across their feet and the strings drawn back up to their chins, releasing powerfully built arrows, almost the size of small spears. As they were behind the Suryavanshi infantry, their presence was hidden from the Chandravanshis.

The superior numerical strength of the Chandravanshis was apparent in the standard offensive formation in which their army was deployed. Their massive infantry was arranged in squads of five thousand. There were fifty such squads, comprising a full legion in a straight line. They stretched as far as the eye could see. There were three additional legions behind the first one, ready to finish off the job. This formation allowed a direct assault onto a numerically inferior enemy, giving the offence tremendous strength and solidity, but also making it rigid. The squads left spaces in between for the cavalry to charge if required. A study of the Suryavanshi formation had made the Chandravanshis move their cavalry from the rear to the flanks. This would enable a quicker charge at the flanks of the Suryavanshi formation and disrupt enemy lines. The Chandravanshi General had clearly read the ancient war manuals and was following them religiously, page by page. It would have been a perfect move against an enemy who also followed standard tactics. Unfortunately, he was up against a Tibetan tribal chief whose innovations had transformed the Suryavanshi attack.

As Shiva rode towards the hillock at the edge of the main battlefield, the Brahmins increased the tempo of their shlokas while the war drums pumped the energy to a higher level. Despite being outnumbered on a vast scale, the Suryavanshis did not exhibit even the slightest hint of nervousness. They had buried their fear deep.

The war cries of the clan-Gods of the various brigades rent the air.

'Indra dev ki jai!'

'Agni dev ki jai!'

'Jai Shakti devi ki!'

'Varun dev ki jai!'

'Jai Pawan dev ki!'

But these cries were forgotten in an instant as the soldiers saw a magnificent white steed canter in over the hillock carrying a handsome, muscular figure. A thunderous roar pierced the sky, loud enough to force the Gods out of their cloud palaces to peer at the events unfolding below. The Neelkanth raised his hand in acknowledgment. Following him was General Parvateshwar, accompanied by Nandi and Veerbhadra.

Vraka was off his horse in a flash as Shiva approached him. Parvateshwar dismounted equally rapidly and was next to Vraka before Shiva could reach him.

'The Lord will lead the right flank, Brigadier,' said Parvateshwar. 'I hope that is alright.'

'It will be my honour to fight under his command, my Lord,' said a beaming Vraka. He immediately pulled out his Field Commander baton from the grip on his side, went down on one knee and raised his hand high, to handover the charge to Shiva.

'You people have to stop doing this,' said Shiva laughing. 'You embarrass me!'

Pulling Vraka up on his feet, Shiva embraced him tightly. 'I am your friend, not your Lord.'

A startled Vraka stepped back, his soul unable to handle the gush of positive energy flowing in. He mumbled, 'Yes, my Lord.'

Shaking his head softly, Shiva smiled. He gently took the baton from Vraka's extended hand and raised it high, for the entire Suryavanshi army to see. An ear-splitting cry ripped through the ranks.

'Mahadev! Mahadev! Mahadev!'

Shiva vaulted onto his horse in one smooth arc. Holding the baton high, he rode up and down the line. The Suryavanshi roar got louder and louder.

'Mahadev!'

'Mahadev!'

'Mahadev!'

'Suryavanshis!' bellowed Shiva, raising his hand. 'Meluhans! Hear me!'

The army quietened down to hear their living God.

'Who is a Mahadev?' roared Shiva.

They listened in rapt attention, hanging on to every word.

'Does he sit on a pitiable height and look on idly while ordinary men do what should be *his* job? No!'

Some soldiers were praying inaudibly.

'Does he lazily bestow his blessings while others fight for the good? Does he stand by nonchalantly and count the dead while the living sacrifice themselves to destroy evil? No!'

There was pin-drop silence as the Suryavanshis absorbed their Neelkanth's message.

'A man *becomes* a Mahadev when he fights for good. A Mahadev is not born as one from his mother's womb. He is forged in the heat of battle, when he wages a war to destroy evil!'

The army stood hushed, feeling a flood of positive energy.

'I am a Mahadev!' bellowed Shiva.

A resounding roar arose from the Suryavanshis. They were led by the *Mahadev*. The *God of Gods*. The Chandravanshis did not stand a chance.

'But I am not the only one!'

A shocked silence descended on the Suryavanshis. What did the Mahadev mean? He is not the only one? Do the Chandravanshis also have a God?

'I am not the only one! For I see a hundred thousand Mahadevs in front of me! I see a hundred thousand men willing to fight on the side of good! I see a hundred thousand men willing to battle evil! I see a hundred thousand men capable of destroying evil!'

The stunned Suryavanshis gaped at their Neelkanth as the import of his words permeated their minds. They dared not ask the question: Are we Gods?

Shiva had the answer: '*Har Ek Hai Mahadev!*'

The Meluhans stood astounded. *Every single one a Mahadev?*

'*Har Har Mahadev!*' bellowed Shiva.

The Meluhans roared. *All of us are Mahadevs!*

Pure primal energy coursed through the veins of each Suryavanshi. They were Gods! It didn't matter that the Chandravanshis outnumbered them ten to one. They were Gods! Even if the evil Chandravanshis outnumbered them a hundred to one, victory was assured. They were Gods!

'Har Har Mahadev!' cried the Suryavanshi army.

'Har Har Mahadev!' yelled Shiva. 'All of us are Gods! Gods on a mission!'

Drawing his sword, he pulled the reins of his horse. Rising on its hind legs with a ferocious neigh, the horse pirouetted smartly to face the Chandravanshis. Shiva pointed his sword at his enemies. 'On a mission to destroy evil!'

The Suryavanshis bellowed after their Lord. Har Har Mahadev!

The cry rent the air. Har Har Mahadev!

Victory would not be denied. Har Har Mahadev!

The long spell of evil would end today. Har Har Mahadev!

As the army roared like the Gods that they were, Shiva rode on towards a beaming Parvateshwar who was flanked by Nandi, Veerbhadra and Vraka.

'Nice speech,' grinned Veerbhadra.

Shiva winked at him. He then turned his horse towards Parvateshwar. 'General, I think it's time we start our own rainfall.'

'Yes, my Lord,' nodded Parvateshwar. Turning his horse around, he gave the orders to his flag bearer. 'The archers.'

The flag bearer raised the coded flag. It was red with a vicious black lightening darned on it. The message was repeated by flag bearers across the lines. The Suryavanshi infantry immediately hunched down on its knees. Shiva, Parvateshwar, Vraka, Nandi and Veerbhadra dismounted rapidly, pulling their horses down to their knees. And the arrows flew in a deadly shower.

The archers had been placed in a semi-circular formation, to cover as wide a range of the Chandravanshi army as possible. Five thousand archers rained death on the Chandravanshis as the sky turned black with a curtain of arrows. The hapless Swadweepans were easy prey in their tight formations. The arrows, nearly as powerful as short spears, easily penetrated the leather and wooden shields of the irregular Chandravanshi soldiers. Only the regulars held metal shields. Within minutes, the first legion of irregulars had begun to break their line and yield precious ground. They were taking too many casualties to hold on to their position. The irregulars started running back, causing chaos. Confusion reigned in the legions behind.

Parvateshwar turned towards Shiva. 'I think we should lengthen the range, my Lord.'

Shiva nodded in reply. Parvateshwar nodded to his flag bearer who relayed the message. The archers stopped shooting for just a few moments. Turning their wheels right, they rapidly raised the height of their foot rests.

With the longer range quickly set, they drew their arrows. And let fly. The arrows hit the second legion of the Chandravanshis now. The pincer attack of the retreating first Chandravanshi legion and the concurrent hail of arrows created bedlam in the second legion.

Shiva noticed the Chandravanshi cavalry moving into position to attack. He turned to Parvateshwar. 'General, their cavalry is moving out. They would aim to flank us and attack the archers. Our cavalry needs to meet them midfield.'

'Yes, my Lord,' said Parvateshwar. 'I'd anticipated this move from the Chandravanshis. That's why I had positioned two cavalries, led by Mayashrenik and Vidyunmali, on the flanks.'

'Perfect! But General, our cavalry must not move too far ahead or our arrows will injure our own men. Nor must they retreat. They have to hold their position. At least for another five minutes.'

'I agree. Our archers need more time to finish their job.'

Parvateshwar turned to his flag bearer with detailed instructions. Two couriers set off rapidly to the left and right. Within moments, the eastern and western Arishtanemi, led by Mayashrenik and Vidyunmali respectively, thundered out to meet the Chandravanshi counter-attack.

Meanwhile, the disarray in the second legion of the Chandravanshi army increased as the unrelentingly ruthless wall of arrows pounded down upon them. The Suryavanshi archers, unmindful of their tiring limbs or bleeding hands, bravely continued their unremitting assault. The second legion line started breaking as the Chandravanshis tried desperately to escape the ruthless carnage.

'Higher range, my Lord?' asked Parvateshwar, pre-empting Shiva's words. Shiva nodded in reply.

Meanwhile the Suryavanshi and Chandravanshi cavalries were engaged in fierce combat on the eastern and western ends of the battlefield. The Chandravanshis knew that they had to break through. A few more minutes of the Suryavanshi archers' assault and the battle would be all but lost. They fought desperately, like wounded tigers. Swords cut through flesh and bone. Spears pierced body armour. Soldiers, with limbs hanging half-severed, continued to battle away. Horses, with missing riders, attacked as if their own lives depended on it. The Chandravanshis were throwing all their might into breaking through the line that protected the archers. But to their misfortune, they had run into the fiercest brigadiers amongst the Suryavanshis. Mayashrenik and Vidyunmali fought ferociously, holding the mammoth Chandravanshi force at bay.

The archers meanwhile had begun their onslaught on the third legion of the Chandravanshis. Their legions were either bleeding to death or deserting in great numbers. Some of them, however, held on grimly and courageously. When their shields were not strong enough to block the arrows, they used the bodies of their dead comrades. But they held the line.

'Do we stop now and charge, my Lord?' asked Parvateshwar.

'No. I want the third legion devastated as well. Let it go on for a few more minutes.'

'Yes, my Lord. We should get half the archers to raise their range farther, so that we can target the forward sections of the fourth legion as well. Confusion would rein right into the heart of their troops if their lines are also broken.'

'You are right, Parvateshwar. Let's do that.'

Meanwhile, the Chandravanshi cavalry on the western flank, sensing the hopelessness of their charge, began to retreat. Some Arishtanemi riders moved to give chase but Vidyunmali stopped them. As the Chandravanshis retreated, Vidyunmali ordered his troops to hold their positions, lest the Chandravanshis launch a counter-attack. Seeing their enemy ride rapidly back to their lines, Vidyunmali ordered a withdrawal to their initial position on the flank of the bow formation.

The Chandravanshis facing Mayashrenik, however, were made of sterner stuff. Despite suffering severe casualties, they fought grimly, refusing to retreat. Locked in battle, Mayashrenik and his men fiercely held their ground. Suddenly, the hail of arrows stopped. The archers had been ordered to stand down. Now that their mission was accomplished without their intervention, the Chandravanshi brigadier ordered a retreat of his cavalry. Mayashrenik, in turn, withdrew his troops quickly to his earlier position in preparation for the main charge, which he knew was just a few moments away.

'General, shall we?' asked Shiva, nodding towards the left flank.

'Yes, my Lord,' replied Parvateshwar.

As Parvateshwar turned to mount his horse, Shiva called out, 'Parvateshwar?'

'Yes, my Lord.'

'Race you to the last line of the Chandravanshis!'

Parvateshwar raised his eyebrows in surprise, smiling broadly. 'I will win, my Lord.'

'We'll see,' grinned Shiva, his eyes narrowed in a playful challenge.

Parvateshwar rapidly mounted his horse and rode to his command on the left. Shiva, followed by Vraka, Nandi and Veerbhadra rode to the right. Prasanjit geared his tortoise corps in the centre for the attack.

'Meluhans!' roared Shiva, dismounting smoothly. 'They lie in front of you! Waiting to be slaughtered! It ends today! Evil ends today!'

'Har Har Mahadev!' bellowed the soldiers as the Meluhan conch shell, announcing the Suryavanshi attack, was blown.

With an ear-shattering yell, the infantry charged towards the Chandravanshis. The tortoise corps moved in their slow, inexorable pace towards the Chandravanshi centre. The sides of the bow formation moved quicker than the centre. The cavalry cantered along the flanks, protecting the infantry from an enemy charge. Courageous remnants of the third and fourth legions of the Chandravanshis meanwhile were rapidly forming their lines once again to face the Suryavanshi onslaught. But the mass of dead bodies of their fallen comrades did not allow them the space to form their traditional Chaturanga formation, which could have allowed some lateral movement. They were huddled together in a tight but thin line when the Suryavanshis fell upon them.

The Suryavanshi battle plan was being executed immaculately. The tightly curved line of highly trained and vicious soldiers had the tortoise corps at the centre with the flanking line of light infantry slightly behind. The unstoppable tortoise corps tore ruthlessly into the Chandravanshi centre. The shields provided protection for the corps against the best Chandravanshi swordsmen, while their trishuls ripped through the Swadweepans.

The Chandravanshis had but two choices. Either fall to the trishul, or be pushed towards the sides where the Suryavanshis were now bearing down hard on them. Even as the centre of the Chandravanshi army broke under the unrelenting assault, the Suryavanshi flanks tore through their sides.

Shiva was leading his flank ferociously into the Chandravanshis, decimating all in front of him. To his surprise, he found the enemy lines thinning. Letting his fellow soldiers charge ahead of him, he rose to his full height to observe the movements. A part of the Chandravanshi line that had been opposing him had withdrawn only to regroup at the centre of the battlefield. They were attacking the only exposed flank of the tortoise corps, their right side, which could not be protected by shields. Someone in the Chandravanshi army was using his brain. If any of the tortoises broke, the Chandravanshis would swarm through the centre in a tight line, devastating the Suryavanshis.

'Meluhans!' roared Shiva. 'Follow me!'

Shiva's flag bearer raised his pennant. The soldiers followed. The Neelkanth charged into the sides of the Chandravanshi lines that were bearing down on the tortoises. Caught in a pincer attack between the trishuls and the charge from Shiva's flank, the spirit of the Chandravanshis finally broke.

What was once a mighty Chandravanshi army was now reduced to independent stragglers fighting valiantly for a losing cause. Shiva and Parvateshwar steered their men into completing the job. Victory was absolute. The Chandravanshi army had been comprehensively routed.

CHAPTER 24

A Stunning Revelation

Sati rushed out of her tent, followed by Krittika and Ayurvati.

'A little slowly, Sati,' cried Ayurvati, running to keep up. 'In your condition…'

Sati turned and grinned at Ayurvati, but did not reduce her pace. She hastened towards the royal tent where Shiva and Parvateshwar would no doubt be after the declaration of victory. Nandi and Veerbhadra stood guard at the entrance. They moved aside to let Sati in, but barred Ayurvati and Krittika.

'I am sorry, Lady Ayurvati,' said Nandi apologetically, his head bowed. 'I have strict instructions to not let anybody in.'

'Why?' asked a surprised Ayurvati.

'I don't know, my Lady. I am very sorry.'

'That's alright,' said Ayurvati. 'You're only doing your job.'

Veerbhadra looked at Krittika. 'I'm sorry darling.'

'Please don't call me that in public,' whispered Krittika, embarrassed.

Sati pulled the curtain aside and entered the tent.

'I don't know, my Lord,' said Parvateshwar. 'It doesn't make sense.'

Sati was surprised that Parvateshwar had called Shiva 'My Lord'. But her joy at seeing Shiva safe brushed these thoughts aside. 'Shiva!'

'Sati?' mumbled Shiva, turning towards her.

Sati froze. He didn't smile when he saw her. He didn't have the flush of victory on his face. He hadn't even got his wounds dressed.

'What's wrong?' asked Sati.

Shiva stared at her. His expression worried her deeply. She turned towards Parvateshwar. He looked at her for an instant with an obviously forced smile. One that was measured, obviously concealing bad tidings. 'What is it, Pitratulya?'

Parvateshwar looked at Shiva, who spoke at last. 'Something about this war troubles us.'

'What could be troubling you?' asked a surprised Sati. 'You have delivered the greatest victory ever to the Suryavanshis. This defeat of the Chandravanshis is even more comprehensive than what my grandfather had achieved. You should be proud!'

'I didn't see any Nagas with the Chandravanshis,' said Shiva.

'The Nagas weren't there?' asked Sati. 'That doesn't make sense.'

'Yes,' said Shiva, his eyes carrying a hint of foreboding. 'If they were so thick with the Chandravanshis, then they would have been present on the battlefield. If they were being used by the Chandravanshis against us, then their skills would have been even more useful in the battle. But where were they?'

'Maybe they've fallen out with each other,' suggested Sati.

'I don't think so,' said Parvateshwar. 'This war was triggered by their joint attack on Mandar! Why would they not be here?'

'Shiva, I am sure you'll figure it out,' said Sati. 'Don't trouble yourself.'

'Dammit Sati!' yelled Shiva. 'I can't figure it out! That's why I am worried!'

A startled Sati stepped back. His uncharacteristic vehemence stunned her. This was most unlike him. Shiva immediately realised what he had done and reached out his bloodied hand. 'I'm sorry Sati. It's just that I...'

The conversation was interrupted as Daksha, accompanied by an aide, raised the curtain and swaggered into the room.

'My Lord!' cried Daksha as he hugged Shiva tight.

Shiva flinched. His wounds hurt. Daksha immediately stepped back.

'I'm so sorry, my Lord,' said Daksha. Turning to his aide he continued, 'Why is Ayurvati outside? Bring her in. Let her tend to the Lord's wounds.'

'No wait,' said Shiva to the aide. 'I had said that I didn't want to be disturbed. There is always time to address the wounds later.' Shiva turned towards Daksha. 'Your Highness, I need to speak about something...'

'My Lord, if you will allow me first,' said Daksha, as enthusiastic as a little boy who had just been given a long denied sweet. 'I wanted to thank you for what you have done for me. For Meluha. We have done what even my father could not do! This is an absolute victory!'

Shiva and Parvateshwar looked briefly at each other before Daksha garnered their attention again.

'Emperor Dilipa is being brought here even as we speak,' said Daksha.

'What?' Parvateshwar's surprise was evident. 'But we have just dispatched soldiers to their camp. They couldn't possibly have arrested him so soon.'

'No Parvateshwar,' said Daksha. 'I had sent my personal guards much earlier. We could see from the viewing platform that the Chandravanshis had already lost by the time the Lord and you had begun the third charge. That is the benefit of the perspective you get from a distance. I was worried that Dilipa might escape like the coward he is. So I sent off my personal guards to arrest him.'

'But, your Highness,' said Parvateshwar, 'shouldn't we discuss the terms of surrender before we bring him in? What are we going to offer?'

'Offer?' asked Daksha, his eyes twinkling with the euphoria of triumph. 'Frankly, we don't really need to offer anything considering that he was routed. He is being brought here as a common criminal. However, we will show him how kind Meluha can be. We will make him such an offer that his next seven generations will be singing our praises!'

Before a surprised Shiva could ask what exactly Daksha had in mind, the crier of the Royal Guard announced the presence of Dilipa outside the tent. Accompanying him was his son, Crown Prince Bhagirath.

'Just a minute, Kaustav,' said Daksha, as he went into a tizzy, organising the room exactly as he would have liked it to be. He sat down on a chair placed in the centre of the room. Daksha requested Shiva to sit to his right. As Shiva sat, Sati turned to leave the tent. Shiva reached out to hold her hand. She turned, felt his silent plea and walked behind his seat to sit down on a chair. Parvateshwar sat to the Emperor's left.

Daksha then called out loudly, 'Let him in.'

Shiva was anxious to see the face of evil. Despite his misgivings about the absence of the Nagas, he genuinely believed that he had fought a righteous war on the right side. Seeing the defeated face of the evil king of the Chandravanshis would complete the victory.

Dilipa walked in. Shiva straightened up in surprise. Dilipa was nothing like what he had expected. He had the appearance of an old man, a sight that was rare in Meluha due to the Somras. Despite his age, Dilipa had a rakishly handsome bearing. He was of medium height, had dark skin and a slightly muscular build. His clothes were radically different from the sober Meluhan fare. A bright pink dhoti, gleaming violet angvastram and a profusion of gold jewellery adorning most parts of his body, combined to give him the look of a dandy. The laughter lines around his lips spoke of his humourous disposition. A trimmed salt and pepper beard, accompanied by thick white hair under his extravagantly coloured crown, completed the effete look while adding an intellectual air.

'Where's the Crown Prince Bhagirath?' asked Daksha.

'I have asked him to wait outside since he can be a little hotheaded,' said Dilipa. He looked only at Daksha, refusing to acknowledge the presence of the others in the room. 'Don't you Meluhans have any custom of offering a seat to your guests?'

'You are not a guest, Emperor Dilipa,' said Daksha. 'You are a prisoner.'

'Yes. Yes. I know. Can't you get a joke?' asked Dilipa

superciliously. 'So what is it that you people want this time?'

Daksha stared at Dilipa quizzically.

'You have already stolen the Yamuna waters a hundred years back,' continued Dilipa. 'What else do you want?'

Shiva turned in surprise towards Daksha.

'We did not steal the Yamuna waters,' yelled Daksha angrily. 'They were ours and we took them back!'

'Yes whatever,' dismissed Dilipa with a wave of his hand. 'What are your demands this time?'

Shiva was astonished at how the conversation was progressing. They had just defeated this evil man. He should have been penitent. But here he was, being condescending and self-righteous.

Daksha looked at Dilipa with wide eyes and a kindly smile. 'I don't want to take anything. Instead, I want to give you something.'

Dilipa raised his eyebrows warily. '*Give* us something?'

'Yes, I intend to give you the benefit of our way of life.'

Dilipa continued to stare at Daksha with suspicion.

'We are going to bring to you our superior way of life,' continued Daksha, his eyes marvelling at his own generosity. 'We are going to reform you.'

Dilipa said with half a snigger, '*Reform* us?'

'Yes. My General, Parvateshwar, will govern your empire as Viceroy of Swadweep. You will continue to be the titular head. Parvateshwar will ensure that your corrupt people are brought in line with the Meluhan way of life. We will live together as brothers now.'

Parvateshwar turned towards Daksha, stunned. He had not expected to be despatched to Swadweep.

Dilipa appeared to have difficulty in controlling his

laughter. 'You actually think your straight-laced men can run Swadweep? My people are mercurial. They are not going to listen to your moralising!'

'Oh, they will,' sneered Daksha. 'They will listen to everything we say. Because you don't know where the actual voice comes from.'

'Really? Where does it come from? Do enlighten me.'

Daksha motioned towards Shiva and said, 'Look who sits with us.'

Dilipa turned to Daksha's right and asked incredulously, 'Who's he? What in Lord Indra's name is so special about him?'

Shiva squirmed, feeling increasingly uncomfortable.

Daksha spoke a little louder. 'Look at his throat, oh king of the Chandravanshis.'

Dilipa looked again with the same arrogance towards Shiva. Despite the dried smattering of blood and gore, the blue throat blazed. Suddenly, Dilipa's haughty smile disappeared. He looked shocked. He tried to say something, but he was at a loss for words.

'Yes, oh corrupt Chandravanshi,' scoffed Daksha, moving his hands for dramatic effect. 'We have the Neelkanth.'

Dilipa's eyes reflected the surprised agony of a child who'd just been stabbed from behind by his own father. An increasing dread gripped Shiva's heart. This was far from what he had expected.

Daksha continued his hectoring. 'The Neelkanth has sworn to destroy the evil Chandravanshi way of life. You HAVE to listen.'

A bewildered Dilipa stared at Shiva for what seemed like an eternity. At long last, he recovered enough to softly whisper, 'Whatever you say.'

Before Daksha could bluster further, Dilipa turned and staggered towards the tent curtain. At the exit, he turned around to look at Shiva once again. Shiva swore that he could see a few tears in those proud, haughty eyes.

As soon as Dilipa left the tent, Daksha got up and hugged Shiva, lightly, so as to not hurt the Neelkanth. 'My Lord, did you see the look on his face. It was precious!'

Turning towards Parvateshwar, he continued, 'Parvateshwar, Dilipa is broken. You will have no trouble controlling the Swadweepans and bringing them around to our way of life. We will go down in history as the men who found a permanent solution to this problem!'

Shiva wasn't paying attention. His troubled heart desperately searched for answers. How could a struggle that appeared so righteous, just a few hours back, now suddenly appear so wrong? He turned towards Sati, forlorn. She gently touched his shoulder.

'What are you thinking, my Lord?' asked Daksha, intruding into Shiva's troubled thoughts.

Shiva just shook his head.

'I just asked if you would like to travel in Dilipa's carriage to Ayodhya?' asked Daksha. 'You deserve the honour, my Lord. You have led us to this glorious victory.'

This conversation did not appear important to Shiva at this point. He did not have the energy to think of an answer. He just nodded in an absentminded manner.

'Wonderful. I'll make all the arrangements,' said Daksha. Turning towards his aide, he continued, 'Send Ayurvati in to immediately dress the Lord's wounds. We need to leave by tomorrow morning to make sure that we have control over Ayodhya, before chaos reigns in the aftermath of Dilipa's defeat.'

With a Namaste towards Shiva, Daksha turned to leave. 'Parvateshwar, aren't you coming?'

Parvateshwar gazed at Shiva, his face creased with concern.

'Parvateshwar?' repeated Daksha.

Taking a quick look at Sati, Parvateshwar turned to leave. Sati moved forward, holding Shiva's face gently. Shiva's eyes seemed to droop with the heavy weight of tiredness. Ayurvati lifted the curtain carefully. 'How are you, my Lord?'

Shiva looked up, his eyes half shut. He was descending into a strange sleep. He yelled suddenly, 'Nandi!'

Nandi came rushing in.

'Nandi, can you find me a cravat?'

'Cravat, my Lord?' asked Nandi.

'Yes.'

'Umm. But why, my Lord?'

'BECAUSE I NEED IT!' shouted Shiva.

Shocked at the violence of his Lord's reply, Nandi hurriedly left the chamber. Sati and Ayurvati looked at Shiva in surprise. Before they could say anything, however, he suddenly collapsed. Unconscious.

— ⵣⵚⵝⵞⴲ —

He was running hard, the menacing forest closing in on him. He was desperate to get beyond the reach of the trees before they laid their ravenous claws upon him. Suddenly, a loud insistent cry pierced through the silence.

'Help! Please help!'

He stopped. No. He wouldn't run away this time. He would fight that monster. He was the Mahadev. It was his duty. Shiva turned around slowly, his sword drawn, his shield held high.

'Jai Shri Ram!' he yelled, as he raced back towards the clearing. The bushy thorns slashed his legs. Bleeding and terrified, he ran hard.

I will reach her in time.

I will not fail her again.

My blood will wash away my sin.

He sprang through the thicket, disregarding the thorns that cut deep into his flesh. Landing into the clearing, his shield was held defensively, his sword gripped low to retaliate. But nobody attacked. A strange laughter finally broke through his concentration. He lowered his shield. Slowly.

'Oh Lord!' he shrieked in agony.

The woman lay stricken on the ground, a short sword buried deep into her heart. The little boy stood on her side. Stunned. His hand was bloodied with the struggle of his kill. The hairy monster sat on the rocky ledge, pointing at the little boy. Laughing.

'NO!' screamed Shiva, as he awoke with a start.

'What happened, Shiva?' asked a worried Sati, darting to hold his hand.

Shiva looked around the room, startled. A worried Parvateshwar and Ayurvati got up too. 'My Lord?'

'Shiva, it's alright. It's alright,' whispered Sati, gently running her hand along Shiva's face.

'You were poisoned, my Lord,' said Ayurvati. 'We think that some of the Chandravanshi soldiers may have had poisoned weapons. It has affected many others as well.'

Shiva slowly regained his composure. He got off his bed. Sati tried to help him up, but he insisted on doing it himself. His throat felt excruciatingly parched. He stumbled over to the ewer, followed closely by Sati. He reached over and gulped down some water.

'It seems like I have been asleep for many hours,' said Shiva, finally noticing the lamps and the dark sky beyond.

'Yes,' said a worried Ayurvati. 'Close to thirty-six hours.'

'Thirty-six hours!' cried a surprised Shiva, before collapsing on to a comfortable chair. He noticed a forbidding figure sitting at the back, his right eye covered in a bandage, his amputated left hand in a sling. 'Drapaku?'

'Yes, my Lord,' said Drapaku, as he tried to get up and salute.

'My God, Drapaku! It's so good to see you. Please sit down!'

'It is heavenly to see you, my Lord,'

'How was your end of the battle?'

'I lost too many men, my Lord. Almost half of them. And this arm and eye,' whispered Drapaku. 'But by your grace, we held them till the main battle was won.'

'It wasn't my grace, my friend. It was your bravery,' said Shiva. 'I am proud of you.'

'Thank you, my Lord.'

Sati stood next to her husband, gently caressing his hair. 'Are you sure you want to sit, Shiva? You can lie down for a while.'

'I have slouched around for long enough, Sati,' said Shiva with a weak smile.

Ayurvati smiled. 'Well, the poison certainly didn't affect your sense of humour, my Lord.'

'Really? Is it still that bad?' grinned Shiva.

Parvateshwar, Drapaku and Ayurvati laughed weakly. Sati didn't. She was watching Shiva intently. He was trying too hard. He was trying to forget, trying to get others to focus on something other than himself. Was this dream much worse than the others?

'Where is his Highness?' asked Shiva.

'Father left for Ayodhya this morning,' said Sati.

'My Lord,' said Parvateshwar, 'His Highness felt that it would not be right to keep Swadweep without a sovereign for so long, under the circumstances. He felt it was important that the Suryavanshi army marched across the empire immediately, with Emperor Dilipa as prisoner, so that the Swadweepans know and accept the new dispensation.'

'So we're not going to Ayodhya?'

'We will, my Lord,' said Ayurvati. 'But in a few days when you are strong enough.'

'Some twelve thousand of our soldiers remain with us,' said Parvateshwar. 'We will march to Ayodhya when you are ready. His Highness insisted that Emperor Dilipa leave behind one of his family members with our unit as hostage to ensure that no Swadweepan attacks our much smaller force.'

'So we have one of Emperor Dilipa's family members in our camp?'

'Yes, my Lord,' said Parvateshwar. 'His daughter, Princess Anandmayi.'

Ayurvati smiled, shaking her head slightly.

'What?' asked Shiva.

Ayurvati looked sheepishly at Parvateshwar and then grinned at Sati. Parvateshwar glared back at Ayurvati.

'What happened?' asked Shiva again.

'Nothing important, my Lord,' clarified Parvateshwar, looking strangely embarrassed. 'It's just that she is quite a handful.'

'Well, I'll ensure that I remain out of her way then,' said Shiva, smiling.

— ⱵꙨꚃⱵ⊕ —

'So this route seems to be the best,' said Parvateshwar, pointing at the map.

Shiva, along with the other poisoned soldiers, had recovered completely over the last five days. The march to Ayodhya was scheduled for the next day.

'I think you are right,' said Shiva, his mind going back to the meeting with the Emperor of Swadweep.

It's pointless feeling sorrowful for Dilipa. I'm quite sure he was posturing during our meeting. The Chandravanshis are evil. They are capable of any deception. Our war was righteous.

'We plan to leave in the morning, my Lord,' said Parvateshwar. Turning towards Sati, he continued, 'You can finally see the birthplace of Lord Ram, my child.'

'Yes Pitratulya,' smiled Sati. 'But I don't know if these people would have kept his temple unharmed. They may have destroyed it in their hatred.'

Their conversation was interrupted by a loud commotion.

Parvateshwar turned around with a frown. 'What is going on out there, Nandi?'

'My Lord,' said Nandi from the other side of the curtain. 'The Princess Anandmayi is here. She has some demands. But we can't fulfil them. She insists on meeting you.'

'Please tell her Highness to wait in her tent,' growled Parvateshwar. 'I will be over in a few minutes.'

'I cannot wait General!' screamed a strong feminine voice from across the curtain.

Shiva signalled to Parvateshwar to let her in. Parvateshwar

turned towards the curtain. 'Nandi, Veerbhadra, bring her in. But check her person for any weapons.'

In a few moments, Anandmayi, flanked by Nandi and Veerbhadra, entered Shiva's tent. Shiva raised his eyebrow at her appearance. She was taller than her father. And distractingly beautiful. A deep walnut coloured complexion complemented a body that was voluptuous, yet muscular. Her doe-eyes cast a seductive look while her lips were in a perpetual pout, sensual yet intimidating. She was provocatively clothed, with a dhoti that had been tied dangerously low at the waist and ended many inches above her knees, while being agonizingly tight at her curvaceous hips. It was just a little longer than the loincloth that the Meluhan men wore during their ceremonial baths. Her blouse was similar to the cloth piece that Meluhan women tied, except that it had been cut raunchily at the top to the shape of her ample breasts, affording a full view of her generous cleavage. She stood with her hips tilted to the side, exuding raw passion.

'You really think I can hide some weapons in this?' charged Anandmayi, pointing at her clothes.

A startled Nandi and Sati glared at her, while Shiva and Veerbhadra sported a surprised smile. Parvateshwar shook his head slightly.

'How are you doing, Parvateshwar?' asked Anandmayi, flashing a smile while scanning him from top to bottom, her eyebrows raised lasciviously.

Shiva couldn't help smiling as he saw Parvateshwar blush slightly.

'What is it you desire, Princess?' barked Parvateshwar. 'We are in the middle of an important meeting.'

'Will you really give me what I desire, General?' sighed Anandmayi.

Parvateshwar blushed even deeper. 'Princess, we have no time for nonsensical talk!'

'Yes,' groaned Anandmayi. 'Most unfortunate. Then perhaps you can help me get some milk and rose petals in this sorry little camp you are running.'

Parvateshwar turned towards Nandi in surprise. Nandi blabbered, 'My Lord, she doesn't want just a glass, but fifty litres of milk. We can't allow that with our rations.'

'You are going to drink fifty litres of milk?' cried Parvateshwar, his eyes wide in astonishment.

'I need it for my beauty bath, General!' glowered Anandmayi. 'You are going to take us on a long march from tomorrow. I cannot go unprepared.'

'I will try and see what I can do,' said Parvateshwar.

'Don't *try,* General. *Do it,*' admonished Anandmayi.

Shiva couldn't control himself any longer. He burst out laughing.

'What the hell do you think you are laughing at?' glared Anandmayi, turning towards Shiva.

'You will speak to the Lord with respect, Princess,' yelled Parvateshwar.

'The *Lord*?' grinned Anandmayi. 'So he is the one in charge? The one Daksha was allegedly showing off?'

She turned back towards Shiva. 'What did you say to trouble my father so much that he isn't even talking anymore? You don't look all that threatening to me.'

'Be careful about what you say, Princess,' advised Parvateshwar fiercely. 'You don't know whom you are speaking with.'

Shiva raised his hand at Parvateshwar, signalling him to calm down. But Anandmayi was the one who required soothing.

'Whoever you are, you will all be finished when our Lord comes. When he descends to Swadweep and destroys the evil of your kind.'

What?!

'Take her out of here, Nandi,' yelled Parvateshwar.

'No wait,' said Shiva. Turning towards Anandmayi, he asked, 'What did you mean by saying "*when your Lord will descend to Swadweep and destroy the evil of our kind*"?'

'Why should I answer you, *Parvateshwar's Lord?*'

Parvateshwar moved rapidly, drawing his sword and pointing it towards Anandmayi's neck. 'When the Lord asks something, you will answer!'

'Do you always move that fast?' asked Anandmayi, her eyebrows raised saucily. 'Or can you take it slow sometimes?'

Bringing his sword menacingly close, Parvateshwar repeated, 'Answer the Lord, Princess.'

Shaking her head, Anandmayi turned towards Shiva. 'We wait for our Lord who will come to Swadweep and destroy the evil Suryavanshis.'

Strong lines of worry began creasing Shiva's handsome face. 'Who is your Lord?'

'I don't know. He hasn't shown himself as yet.'

An unfathomable foreboding sunk deep into Shiva's heart. He was profoundly afraid of his next question. But he knew that he had to ask it. 'How will you know that he is your Lord?'

'Why are you so interested in this?'

'I need to know!' snarled Shiva.

Anandmayi frowned at Shiva as if he was mad. 'He will not be from the Sapt-Sindhu. Neither a Suryavanshi nor a Chandravanshi. But when he comes, he will come on our side.'

Shiva's inner voice whispered miserably that there was more. Clutching the armrest of his chair, he asked, 'And?'

'And,' continued Anandmayi, 'his throat will turn blue when he drinks the Somras.'

An audible gasp escaped Shiva as his body stiffened. The world seemed to spin. Anandmayi frowned, even more confused about the strange conversation.

Parvateshwar glowered fiercely at Anandmayi. 'You are lying, woman! Admit it! You are lying!'

'Why would I...'

Anandmayi stopped in mid-sentence as she noticed Shiva's cravat covered throat. The arrogance suddenly vanished from her face. She found her knees buckling under her. Pointing weakly with her hands, she asked, 'Why is your throat covered?'

'Take her out, Nandi!' ordered Parvateshwar.

'Who are you?' shouted Anandmayi.

Nandi and Veerbhadra tried to pull Anandmayi out. With surprising strength, she struggled against them. 'Show me your throat!'

They held on to her arms and dragged her backwards. She kicked Veerbhadra in the groin, causing him to double up in pain as she turned towards Shiva once again. 'Who the hell are you?'

Shiva stared down at the table unable to find the strength to even glance at Anandmayi. He held his armrest tightly. It seemed to be the only stable thing in a world spinning desperately out of control.

Tottering towards her, Veerbhadra pinned Anandmayi's hands from behind as Nandi threw an arm around her neck. Anandmayi bit Nandi's arm brutally. As a howling

Nandi pulled his arm back, she screamed again, 'Answer me, dammit! Who are you?'

Shiva looked up for one brief instant into Anandmayi's tormented eyes. The pain they conveyed lashed his soul. The flames of agony burned his conscience.

A shocked Anandmayi suddenly became immobile. The misery in her eyes would have stunned the bravest of Meluhan soldiers. In a broken voice, she whispered, 'You are supposed to be on our side...'

She allowed herself to be hauled out by Nandi and Veerbhadra. Parvateshwar kept his eyes down. He dared not look at Shiva. He was a good Suryavanshi. He would not humiliate his Lord by looking at him when he was at his weakest. Sati, on the other hand, would not leave her husband to suffer alone. She came to his side and touched his face.

Shiva looked up, his eyes devastated and filled with the tears of sorrow. 'What have I done?'

Sati held Shiva tightly, holding his throbbing head against her bosom. There was nothing she could say that would alleviate his pain. All she could do was hold him.

An agonized whisper suffused the tent with its resonant grief. 'What have I done?'

CHAPTER 25

Island of the Individual

It was another three weeks before Shiva's entourage reached Ayodhya, the capital of the Swadweepans. They had travelled along a decrepit, long-winding road to the Ganga, and then sailed eastward to the point where the mighty river welcomed the waters of the Sarayu. Then they had cruised north, up the Sarayu, to the city of Lord Ram's birth. It was a long and circuitous route, but the quickest possible keeping in mind the terrible road conditions in *Swadweep*, the *island of the individual*.

The excitement in the hearts of the Meluhan soldiers was beyond belief. They had heard legends about Lord Ram's city. But not one had ever seen it. *Ayodhya*, literally *the impregnable city*, was the land first blessed by Lord Ram's sacred feet. They expected a gleaming city beyond compare, even if it had been defiled by Chandravanshi presence. They expected the city to be an oasis of order and harmony even if all the surrounding land had been rendered chaotic by the Chandravanshis. They were disappointed.

Ayodhya was nothing like Devagiri. At first glance, it promised much. The outer walls were thick and looked astonishingly powerful. Unlike the sober grey Meluhan walls, the exterior of Ayodhya had been extravagantly painted with every possible colour in God's universe. Each alternate brick, however, was painted in pristine white, the royal colour of the Chandravanshis. Numerous pink and blue banners festooned the city towers. These banners had not been put up for any special occasion, but were permanent fixtures adorning the city.

The road curved suddenly along the fort wall to the main entrance, so as to prevent elephants and battering rams from getting a straight run to the mighty doors. At the top of the main gates, a wonderfully ornate, horizontal crescent moon had been sculpted into the walls. Below it was the Chandravanshi motto. *'Shringar. Saundarya. Swatantrata.' Passion. Beauty. Freedom.*

It was only when they entered the city that a blow was delivered to the precision and order loving Meluhans. Krittika described it as a 'functioning pandemonium'. Unlike all Meluhan cities, Ayodhya was not built on a platform — so it was obvious that if the Sarayu river ever flooded in the manner that the temperamental Indus did, the city would be inundated. The numerous city walls, built in seven concentric circles, were surprisingly thick and strong. However, it didn't need a general's strategic eye to notice that the concentric walls had not been planned by a military mastermind. They were in fact added in a haphazard manner, one after the other, when the city had extended beyond the previous perimeter. This explained why there were many weak points along each wall, which an enemy laying siege could easily exploit. Perhaps that was why the Chandravanshis preferred to battle outside in a far away battleground rather than defend their city.

The infrastructure was a sorry indictment of the Chandravanshi penchant for debate as an excuse for inaction. The roads were nothing better than dirt tracks. There was, however, one notable exception — the neatly paved and strikingly smooth *Rajpath*, the *royal road*, which led straight from the outer walls through to the opulent royal palace. The Swadweepans joked that instead of finding potholes on their road, they actually had to search for some stretch of road amongst the potholes! This was a far cry from the exceptionally well-planned, sign-posted, paved and tediously standard roads of Meluhan cities.

There were, what can only be called 'encroachments', all over the city. Some open grounds had been converted into giant slums as illegal immigrants simply pitched their tents on public areas. The already narrow roads had been made even narrower by the intrusion of the cloth tents of the homeless. There was constant tension between the rich home-owning class and the poor landless who lived in slums. The emperor had legalised all encroachments established before 1910 BC. Which meant that slum dwellers could not be removed unless the government created alternative accommodation for them. The minor problem was that the Chandravanshi government was so hideously inefficient that they hadn't managed to build even one new house for slum dwellers in the last twelve years. Now there was talk of extending the deadline further. The encroachments, the bad roads, the poor construction combined to give an impression of a city in a state of terminal decline.

The Meluhans were outraged. What had these people done to Lord Ram's great city? Or was it always like this?

Is that why Lord Ram had crossed the Sarayu river to establish his capital at far-away Devagiri on the Saraswati?

And yet, as the initial shock at the ugliness and frenzied disorder wore away, the Meluhans began to find strange and unexpected charm in this city of constant chaos. None of the Ayodhyan houses were similar, unlike the Meluhan cities where even the royal palace was built to a standard design. Here each house had its own individual allure. The Swadweepans, unencumbered by strict rules and building codes, created houses that were expressions of passion and elegance. Some structures were so grand that the Meluhans were amazed with the divine engineering talent that must have created it. The Swadweepans had none of the restraint of the Meluhans. Everything was painted bright — from orange buildings to parrot green ceilings to shocking pink windows! Civic-minded rich Swadweepans had created grand public gardens, temples, theatres and libraries, naming them after their family members, since they had received no help from the government. The Meluhans, despite finding it strange that a public building should be named after a private family, were impressed with the grandeur of these structures. It was a vibrant city that had exquisite beauty existing alongside hideous ugliness. Ayodhya both disgusted as well as fascinated the Meluhans.

The people were living embodiments of the Chandravanshi way of life. The women wore skimpy clothes, brazen and confident about their sexuality. The men were equally fashion and beauty conscious — what Meluhans would call dandies. The relationship between the men and women could only be characterised as one teetering on extremes. Extreme love coexisting with extreme hate, expressed with extreme loudness, all built on the foundations of extreme passion. Nothing was done in small measure in Ayodhya. Moderation was a word that did not exist in their dictionary.

Therefore, it was no surprise that the mercurial people of Ayodhya scoffed at Daksha's proclaimed intention to 'reform' them. Daksha entered a sullen city, whose populace lined silently along the sides of the Rajpath, refusing to welcome the conquering force. Daksha, who had expected the Ayodhya residents to welcome him with showers of petals since they had finally been freed from their evil rulers, was surprised with the cold reception he got. His mind attributed it to a dictat by the Chandravanshi royalty.

Shiva, who arrived a week later, was under no such illusions. He had expected far worse than just a quiet greeting. He had expected to be attacked. He had expected to be vilified for not standing up for the Swadweepans, who also believed in the legend of the Neelkanth. He had expected to be hated for choosing the so-called wrong side. But while he had begun to suspect that the Chandravanshis were not quite evil, he was not prepared to classify the Suryavanshis as the 'wrong side' either. He still felt that the Meluhans were almost without exception honest, decent, law-abiding people who could be unhesitatingly trusted. Shiva was deeply confused about his karma and his future course of action. He missed Brahaspati's keen wit and advice.

His thoughts weighing heavily upon him, Shiva quickly disembarked from the curtained cart and turned towards the Chandravanshi palace. For a moment, he was startled by the grandeur of Dilipa's abode. But he quickly pulled himself together, reached out for Sati's hand, and began climbing the hundred steps towards the main palace platform. Parvateshwar trudged slowly behind. Shiva glanced briefly beyond Sati, to find Anandmayi ascending the steps quietly. She had not spoken to Shiva since that terrible encounter when she had realised who he was. She climbed with an impassive face, her eyes set on her father.

'Who the hell is that man?' asked an incredulous Swadweepan carpenter, held back at the edge of the palace courtyard by Chandravanshi soldiers.

'Why are our Emperor and the sincere madman waiting for him on the royal platform, and that too in full imperial regalia?'

'Sincere madman?' asked his friend.

'Oh, haven't you heard? That is the new nickname for that fool Daksha!'

The friends burst out laughing.

'Shush!' hissed an old man, standing next to them. 'Don't you young people have any shame? Ayodhya is being humiliated and you think it's a joke.'

Meanwhile, Shiva had reached the royal platform. Daksha bent low with a Namaste as Shiva smiled weakly and returned the greeting.

Dilipa, with moist eyes, bent low towards Shiva. He cried in a soft whisper, 'I am not evil, my Lord. We are not evil.'

'What was that?' asked Daksha, his ears straining to hear Dilipa's whispered words.

Shiva's choked throat refused to utter a sound. Not hearing anything from Dilipa either, Daksha shook his head and whispered, 'My Lord, perhaps this is an opportune moment to introduce you to the people of Ayodhya. I am sure it will galvanize them into action once they know that the Neelkanth has come to their rescue.'

Before an anguished Shiva could answer, his caring wife spoke, 'Father, Shiva is very tired. It has been a long journey. May he rest for some time?'

'Yes, of course,' mumbled Daksha apologetically. Turning towards Shiva, he said, 'I am sorry, my Lord. Sometimes my enthusiasm gets the better of me. Why don't you rest today? We can always introduce you at the court tomorrow.'

Shiva looked up at Dilipa's angst-ridden eyes. Unable to bear the tormented gaze any longer, Shiva looked beyond the Chandravanshi emperor, towards his courtiers standing at the back. Only one pair of eyes did not have a look of incomprehension. It was at that moment that Shiva realised that except for Anandmayi, nobody else in Dilipa's court knew of his identity. Not even Dilipa's son, Bhagirath. Dilipa had not spoken to a soul. Clearly, neither had Daksha. Possibly in the hope of a grand unveiling of the secret, in the presence of Shiva himself.

'My Lord.'

Shiva turned towards Parvateshwar. 'Yes,' he said in a barely audible whisper.

'I will lead the army out since the ceremonial march is over,' said Parvateshwar. 'They will be stationed outside the city in the camp set up for the earlier contingent. I will be back at your service within two hours.'

Shiva nodded faintly.

— 人◎Ｕ♀⊗ —

It had been a few hours since their arrival in Ayodhya. Shiva had not spoken a word. He stood quietly at the window of his chamber, staring out as the afternoon sun washed the city in its dazzling glory. Sati sat silently by his side, holding his hand, drawing on all the energy that she possessed and then passing it on to him. He continued to stare out, towards a grand structure right in the heart of the city. It appeared to be built of white marble from this distance. For an unfathomable reason, looking at it seemed to soothe Shiva's soul. It was built upon the highest point in the city, on a gently sloping hill, clearly visible from every part of Ayodhya. Shiva mused as to why that building was so important that it occupied the highest point in the city, instead of the royal palace.

A loud insistent knocking intruded upon his thoughts.

'Who is it?' growled Parvateshwar, rising from his chair at the back of the chamber.

'My Lord,' answered Nandi. 'It is the Princess Anandmayi.'

Parvateshwar groaned softly before turning towards Shiva. The Neelkanth nodded.

'Let her in, Nandi,' ordered Parvateshwar.

Anandmayi entered, her smiling demeanour startling Parvateshwar who frowned in surprise. 'How may I help you, your Highness?'

'I have told you so many times how you can help me, Parvateshwar,' teased Anandmayi. 'Perhaps if you listened to the answer rather than repeating the question again and again, we may actually get somewhere.'

Parvateshwar's reaction was a combination of embarrassment and anger. Shiva smiled weakly, for the first time in three weeks. Somehow the fact that Anandmayi seemed to have returned to her usual self made Shiva happy.

Anandmayi turned towards Shiva with a low bow. 'The truth has just come to me, my Lord. I am sorry about my sullenness earlier. But I was deeply troubled at the time. Your being on the side of the Suryavanshis can have only one of two explanations. Either we are evil. Or you are not who we think you are and the legend is false. Accepting either of these explanations would destroy my soul.'

Shiva looked at Anandmayi attentively.

'But I have finally realised,' continued Anandmayi. 'The legend is not false. And we are obviously not evil. It is just that you are too naive. You have been misled by the evil Suryavanshis. I will set it right. I will show you the goodness of our path.'

'We are not evil,' glowered Parvateshwar.

'Parvateshwar,' sighed Anandmayi. 'I have told you earlier. That lovely mouth of yours can be put to much better uses than mere talking. You shouldn't waste your breath unnecessarily.'

'Stop your impudence, woman!' cried Parvateshwar. 'You think we are evil? Have you seen the way you treat your own people? Hungry eyes have stared at me all through our journey. Children lie abandoned on the side of potholed highways. Old desperate women beg for alms throughout your "impregnable city", while the Swadweepan rich lead lives better than a Meluhan emperor. We have a perfect society in Meluha. I may agree with the Lord and accept that maybe you are not evil. But you certainly don't know how to take care of your people. Come to Meluha to see how citizens should be treated. Your lives will improve with our method of governance.'

'Improve?' argued an agitated Anandmayi. 'We are not perfect, I agree. There are many things that our empire could do better, I agree. But at least we give our people freedom. They are not forced to follow some stupid laws mandated by an out of touch elite.'

'Give them freedom? Freedom to do what? Loot, steal, beg, kill?'

'I don't need to argue with you about our culture. Your puny mind will not be able to understand the advantages of our ways.'

'I don't want to! It disgusts me to see the way this empire has been managed. You have no norms. No control. No laws. It is no wonder that despite not being evil, you have contaminated yourselves by allying with the Nagas. By fighting like cowardly terrorists and not brave Kshatriyas. You may not be evil, but your deeds certainly are!'

'Nagas? What the bloody hell are you talking about? Do you think we are mad that we will ally with the Nagas? You think we don't know how that will pollute our souls for the next seven lives? And terrorism? We have never resorted to terrorism. We have strained against our natural instincts to avoid a war with your cursed people for the last hundred years. Hence we have retreated from the border provinces. We have cut all ties with you. We have even learned to live with the reduced flow of the Ganga ever since you stole the Yamuna from us. My father told you that we had nothing to do with the attack on Mount Mandar! But you did not believe us. And why should you? You needed an excuse to attack us again!'

'Don't lie to me. At least not in front of the Mahadev! Chandravanshi terrorists have been found with the Nagas.'

'My father told you that nobody under our control

had anything to do with the attack on Mandar. We have nothing to do with the Nagas. It's possible that some Chandravanshis, just like some Suryavanshis, could have helped the terrorists. Had you cooperated with us, we may have even found the criminals!'

'What rubbish! No Suryavanshi would ally with those monsters. As for some Chandravanshis assisting the terrorists, you'll have to answer for that. Swadweep is under your control!'

'Had you not snapped diplomatic ties with Swadweep it would not be lost on you that we are a confederacy far removed from your authoritarian structure. Ayodhya is only the overlord. Other kings within Swadweep pay us tribute for protection during war. Otherwise, they have the freedom to administer their kingdoms any which way they choose.'

'How is that possible? Are you saying that the Emperor of Swadweep doesn't administer his own empire?'

'Please,' begged Shiva, stopping the argument which reflected the debate raging in his mind. He did not want to be troubled by questions for which he had no answers. At least not just as yet.

Parvateshwar and Anandmayi immediately fell silent.

Turning slowly towards the window again, he asked, 'What is that building, Anandmayi?'

'That, my Lord,' said Anandmayi, smiling happily at being spoken to first, 'is the *Ramjanmabhoomi* temple, built at the site of *Lord Ram's birthplace*.'

'You have built a temple to Lord Ram?' asked a startled Parvateshwar. 'But he was a Suryavanshi. Your sworn enemy.'

'We did not build the temple,' said Anandmayi, raising

her eyes in exasperation. 'But we have refurbished and maintained it lovingly. And furthermore, what makes you think Lord Ram was our sworn enemy? He may have been misled into following a different path, but he did a lot of good for the Chandravanshis as well. He is revered as a God in Ayodhya.'

Parvateshwar's eyes widened in shock. 'But he had sworn to destroy the Chandravanshis.'

'If he had vowed to destroy us, we wouldn't exist today, would we? He left us unharmed because he believed that we were good. That our way of life deserved to survive.'

Parvateshwar's mind searched for answers, disturbed by the strength of her arguments.

'You know what Lord Ram's full ceremonial name is?' asked Anandmayi, pressing home her advantage.

'Of course I do,' scoffed Parvateshwar. 'Lord Ram, Suryavanshi Kshatriya of the Ikshvaku clan. Son of Dashrath and Kaushalya. Husband of Sita. Honoured and respected with the title of the seventh Vishnu.'

'Perfect,' beamed Anandmayi. 'Except for one minor mistake. You have missed one small word, General. You have missed the word *Chandra*. His full name was Lord *Ram Chandra*.'

Parvateshwar frowned.

'Yes, General,' continued Anandmayi. 'His name meant "*the face of the moon*". He was more Chandravanshi than you seem to imagine.'

'This is typical Chandravanshi double-talk,' argued Parvateshwar, gathering his wits. 'You are lost in words rather than focussing on deeds. Lord Ram had said that only a person's karma determines his identity. The fact that his name had the word moon in it means nothing.

His deeds were worthy of the sun. He was a Suryavanshi to the core.'

'Why couldn't he have been both Suryavanshi and Chandravanshi?'

'What nonsense is that? It's not possible. It's contradictory.'

'It appears impossible to you only because your puny mind cannot understand it. Contradictions are a part of nature.'

'No, they aren't. It is impossible that one thing be true and the opposite not be false. The universe cannot accept that. One scabbard can house just one sword!'

'That is so only if the scabbard is small. Is it your case that Lord Ram was not so sublime as to have two identities?'

'You are just playing with words!' glared Parvateshwar.

Shiva had stopped listening. He turned towards the window and faced the temple. He could feel it in every pore of his body. He could feel it in his soul. He could hear the soft whisper of his inner voice.

Lord Ram will help you. He will guide you. He will soothe you. Go to him.

— 人◎Ư4⊛ —

It was the third hour of the third prahar when Shiva stole into the chaotic Ayodhya streets all by himself. He was on his way to meet Lord Ram. Sati had not offered to come along. She understood that he needed to be alone. Wearing a cravat and a loose shawl for protection, with a sword and shield as a measure of abundant precaution, Shiva ambled along, taking in the strange sights and smells of the Chandravanshi capital. Nobody recognised him. He liked it that way.

The Ayodhyans seemed to live their life without even the slightest hint of self-control. Loud emotional voices assaulted Shiva's ears as if a hideous orchestra was trying to overpower the senses. The common people either laughed like they had just gulped an entire bottle of wine or fought as if their lives depended on it. Shiva was pushed and shoved on several occasions by people rushing around, hurling obscenities and calling him blind. There were manic shoppers bargaining with agitated shopkeepers at the bazaar and it almost seemed like they would come to blows over ridiculously small amounts of money. For both the shoppers as well as the shopkeepers, the harried negotiation wasn't about the cash involved. It was about their pride in having struck a good bargain in itself.

Shiva noticed that a large number of couples had crowded into a small garden on the side of the road doing unspeakable things to each other. They seemed to brazenly disregard the presence of voyeuristic eyes on the street or in the park itself. He noticed with surprise that the prying eyes were not judgemental, but excited. Shiva noted the glaring contrast with the Meluhans who would not even embrace each other in public.

Shiva suddenly started in surprise as he felt a feminine hand brush lightly against his backside. He turned sharply to find a young woman grin back at him and wink. Before Shiva could react, he spotted a much older woman walking right behind. Thinking that she was the younger woman's mother, Shiva decided to let the indiscretion pass for fear of causing any embarrassment. As he turned, he felt a hand on his backside once again, this time more insistent and aggressive. He turned around and was shocked to find the mother smiling sensuously at him. A flabbergasted Shiva hurried down the road, escaping the bazaar before any more passes could disturb his composure.

He continued walking in the direction of the towering Ramjanmabhoomi temple. As he approached it, the unassailable jangle of Ayodhya dimmed significantly. This was a quiet residential area of the city. Probably for the rich, judging by the exquisite mansions that lined the avenues. Turning to the right, he came upon the road which led to his destination. It curved gently up the hill, caressing its sides in a smooth arc. This was probably the only road in Ayodhya, besides the Rajpath, which was not pitted with potholes. Magnificent gulmohur trees rose brilliantly along the flanks of the road, their dazzling orange leaves lighting the path for the weary and the lost. The path that led to Lord Ram.

Shiva closed his eyes and took a deep breath as anxiety gnawed at his heart. What would he find? Would he find peace? Would he find answers? Would he, as he hoped, find that he had done some good? Good that wasn't visible to him right now. Or would he be told that he had made a terrible mistake and thousands had died a senseless death? Shiva opened his eyes slowly, steeled himself and began walking, softly repeating the name of the Lord.

Ram. Ram. Ram. Ram.

A little farther up, Shiva's chant was disturbed. At a bend in the road, he saw an old, shrivelled man, who appeared like he hadn't eaten in weeks. He had a wound on his ankle which had festered because of the humidity and neglect. He was dressed in a torn jute sack, which was tied precariously at his waist and hung from his shoulders with a hemp rope. Sitting on the sidewalk, his thin right hand scratched his head vigorously, disturbing the lice going about their job diligently. With his weak left hand, he precariously balanced a banana leaf which held a piece of bread and some gruel. It looked like the kind of food distributed at cheap restaurants on the donations of a few kindly or guilty souls. The kind of food that would not even be fed to animals in Meluha.

Intense anger surged through Shiva. This old man was begging, nay suffering, at the doors of Lord Ram's abode and nobody seemed to care. What kind of government would treat its people like this? In Meluha, the government assiduously nurtured all its citizens. There was enough food for everyone. Nobody was homeless. The government actually worked. The old man would not have had to endure this humiliation had he lived in Devagiri!

The anger in Shiva gave way to a flood of positive energy, as he realised that he had found his answer. He knew now that Parvateshwar was right. Maybe the Chandravanshis were not evil, but they led a wretched existence. The Suryavanshi system would improve their lives dramatically. There would be abundance and prosperity all around when Parvateshwar took charge of the moribund Chandravanshi administration. There *will* be some good that will come out of this war. Maybe he had not made such a terrible mistake after all. He thanked Lord Ram. He thought that he had found his answer.

Fate, however, conspired to deny Shiva this small consolation. The old beggar noticed Shiva's stare and met it equally. The warm empathy in Shiva's eyes and the compassion of his smile prompted the ancient man to smile in return. However, it wasn't the smile of a broken man begging for alms. It was the warm welcoming smile of a man at peace with himself. Shiva was taken aback.

The old man smiled even more warmly while raising his weak hand with great effort. 'Would you like some food, my son?'

Shiva was stunned. He felt humbled by the selfless gesture of the man he had thought was deserving of only pity.

Observing Shiva staring fixedly, the old man repeated, 'Would you like to eat with me, son? There is enough for both of us.'

An overwhelmed Shiva could not find the strength to speak. There wasn't enough food for even one man in fact. Why was this man offering to share what little food he had? It didn't make sense.

Thinking Shiva was hard of hearing, the old man spoke a little louder. 'My son, sit with me. Eat.'

Shiva struggled to find the strength to shake his head slightly. 'No thank you, sir.'

The old man's face fell immediately. 'This is good food,' he said, his eyes reflecting his hurt. 'I would not have offered it to you otherwise.'

Shiva realised that he had insulted the old man's pride. He had just treated him like a beggar. 'No, no, that's not what I meant. I know it's good food. It's just that I...'

The old man softly interrupted Shiva's words. 'Then sit with me, my son.'

Shiva nodded quietly. He sat down on the pavement. The old man turned towards Shiva and placed the banana leaf on the ground, in between the two of them. Shiva looked at the bread and watery gruel, which until a few moments back had appeared unfit for humans. The old man looked up at Shiva, his half blind eyes beaming. 'Eat.'

Shiva picked up a small morsel of the bread, dipped it in the gruel and swallowed. It slipped into his body easily, but weighed heavy upon his soul. He could feel his righteousness being squeezed out of him as the poor, old man beamed generously.

'Come on, my son. If you are going to eat so little, how will you maintain your big muscular body?'

A startled Shiva glanced up at the old man; the circumference of those shrunken arms would have been smaller than Shiva's wrist. The old man was taking ridiculously small bites, moving larger portions of the bread towards Shiva. Shiva could not find the courage to look up any more. As his heart sank deeper and his tears rose, he continued to eat the portion the old man had given him. The food was over in no time.

Freedom. Freedom for the wretched to also have dignity. Something impossible in Meluha's system of governance.

'Are you full now, my son?'

Shiva nodded slowly, still not daring to look into the old man's eyes.

'Good. Go. It's a long walk up to the temple.'

Shiva looked up, bewildered by the astounding generosity being shown to him. The old man's sunken cheeks were spread wide as he smiled affectionately. He was on the verge of starvation, and yet he had given practically all his food to a stranger. Shiva cursed his own heart for the blasphemy he had committed. The blasphemy of believing that he could actually 'save' such a man. Shiva found himself bending forward, as if in the volition of a greater power. He extended his arms and touched the feet of the old man.

The old man raised his hand and touched Shiva's head tenderly, blessing him. 'May you find what you are looking for, my son.'

Leaden with guilt and remorse, Shiva rose heavily, his self-rightousness crushed by the old man's munificence. He had his answer. What he had done was wrong. He had made a terrible mistake. These people were not evil.

CHAPTER 26

The Question of Questions

The road to the Ramjanmabhoomi temple clung to the sides of a gently sloping hill and ended its journey at Lord Ram's abode. It afforded a breathtaking view of the city below. But Shiva did not see it. Neither did he see the magnificent opulence of the gigantic temple nor the gorgeously landscaped gardens around it. The temple was sheer poetry, written in white marble, composed by the architect of the Gods. The architect had designed a grand staircase leading up to the main temple platform, which was awe-inspiring and yet inviting. Colossal ornate marble statues in sober blue and grey had been engraved on the platform. Elaborately carved pillars supported an ostentatious yet tasteful ceiling of blue marble. The architect obviously knew that Lord Ram's favourite time of the day was the morning. On the ceiling, the morning sky, as it would have been seen in the absence of the temple roof, had been lovingly painted. On top of the ceiling, the temple spire shot upwards to a height of almost one hundred metres, like a giant Namaste to the Gods. The Swadweepans, to their credit, had not imposed their garish sensibilities on the temple. Its restrained beauty was in keeping with the way the sober Lord Ram would have liked it.

Shiva did not notice any of this. Nor did he look at the intricately carved statues in the inner sanctum. Lord Ram's idol at the centre was surrounded by his beloveds. To the right was his loving wife, Sita, and to the left was his devoted brother, Lakshman. At their feet, on his knees, was Lord Ram's most fervent and favourite disciple, Hanuman, of the *Vayuputra* tribe, *the sons of the Wind God.*

Shiva could not find the strength to look Lord Ram in the eyes. He feared the verdict he would receive. He crouched behind a pillar, resting against it, grieving. When he couldn't control his intense feelings of guilt anymore, his eyes released the tears they had been holding back. Shiva made desperate attempts to control his tears, but they kept flowing as though a dam had burst. He bit into his balled fist, overcome by remorse. He curled his legs up against his chest and rested his head on his knees.

Drowning in his sorrow, Shiva did not feel the compassionate hand on his shoulder. On getting no reaction, the hand squeezed his shoulder lightly. Shiva recognised the touch but kept his head bowed. He did not want to appear weak, be seen with tears in his eyes. The gentle hand, old and worn with age, withdrew quietly, while its owner waited patiently until Shiva had composed himself. When the time was right, he came forward and sat down in front of him. A sombre Shiva did a formal Namaste to the Pandit, who looked almost exactly like the Pandits that Shiva had met at the Brahma temple at Meru and the Mohan temple at Mohan Jo Daro. He sported the same flowing white beard and a white mane. He wore a saffron dhoti and angvastram, just like the other pandits did. The wizened face had the same calm, welcoming smile. Shiva couldn't help noticing though that this one's girth was far more generous.

'Is it really so bad?' asked the Pandit, his eyes narrowed and head tilted slightly, in the typically Indian empathetic manner.

Shiva shut his eyes and lowered his head again. The Pandit waited patiently for Shiva's reply. 'You don't know what I have done!'

'I do know.'

Shiva looked up at the Pandit, his eyes full of surprise and shame.

'I know what you have done, Oh Neelkanth,' said the Pandit. 'And I ask again, is it really so bad?'

'Don't call me the Neelkanth,' glared Shiva. 'I don't deserve the title. I have the blood of thousands of innocents on my hands.'

'Many more than thousands have died,' said the Pandit. 'Probably hundreds of thousands. But do you really think they wouldn't have died had you not been around? Is their blood really on your hands?'

'Of course it is! It was my stupidity that led to this war. I had no idea what I was doing. A responsibility was thrust upon me and I wasn't worthy of it! Hundreds of thousands have perished as a result!'

Shiva curled up his fist and pounded his forehead, desperately trying to soothe the throbbing heat on his brow. The Pandit stared in mild surprise at the deep red blotch on Shiva's forehead, right between his eyes. It was not the colour of a blood clot. It was a much deeper hue, almost black. The Pandit chose silence though his surprise was barely controlled. The time was not yet ripe. The moment of revelation had not yet come.

'And it's all because of me,' moaned Shiva, his eyes moistening again. 'It's all my fault.'

'Soldiers are Kshatriyas, my friend,' said the Pandit, a picture of calm. 'Nobody forces them to die. They choose their path, knowing full well the risk it entails. *And also* the possible glory that comes with it. The Neelkanth is not the kind of person on whom responsibility can be thrust against his will. You *chose* this. You were *born* for it.'

Shiva looked at the Pandit startled. His eyes seemed to ask, 'Born for it?'

The Pandit ignored the question posed by Shiva's eyes. 'Everything happens for a reason. If you are going through this turmoil, there is a divine plan in it.'

'What bloody divine reason can there be for so many deaths?'

'The destruction of evil? Wouldn't you consider that a very important reason?'

'But I did not destroy evil!' yelled Shiva. 'These people aren't evil. *They're just different*. Being different isn't evil.'

The Pandit's face broke into his typically enigmatic smile. 'Exactly. They are not evil. They are just different. You have realised it very quickly, my friend, a lot earlier than the previous Mahadev.'

Shiva was perplexed by the Pandit's words. 'Lord Rudra?'

'Yes! Lord Rudra.'

'But he did destroy evil. He destroyed the Asuras.'

'And, who said the Asuras were evil?'

'I read it...' Shiva stopped mid-sentence. He finally understood.

'Yes,' smiled the Pandit. 'You have guessed correctly.

Just like the Suryavanshis and the Chandravanshis see each other as evil, so did the Devas and the Asuras. So if you are going to read a book written by the Devas, what do you think the Asuras are going to be portrayed as?'

'You mean they were just like today's Suryavanshis and Chandravanshis?'

'More so than you can imagine. The Devas and the Asuras, just like the Chandravanshis and the Suryavanshis, represent two balancing life forces — a duality.'

'Duality?'

'Yes, a duality that is one of the many perspectives of the universe — the masculine and the feminine. The Asuras and the Suryavanshis represent the masculine. The Devas and the Chandravanshis speak for the feminine. The names change, but the life forces they embody remain the same. They will always exist. Neither can ever be destroyed. Otherwise the universe will implode.'

'And they see their fight with the other as the eternal struggle between good and evil.'

'Exactly,' beamed the Pandit, marvelling at Shiva's keen mind even in his time of distress. 'But they haven't been fighting all the time. Sometimes, there have been long periods of cooperation as well. In times of strife, which usually happens when there is evil, it is easy to blame each other. The difference between two dissimilar ways of life gets portrayed as a fight between good and evil. Just because the Chandravanshis are different from the Suryavanshis doesn't mean that they are evil. Why do you think the Neelkanth had to be an outsider?'

'So that he would not be biased towards any one way of life,' said Shiva, as a veil lifted before his eyes.

'Exactly! The Neelkanth has to be above all this. He has to be devoid of any bias.'

'But I was not free of biases. I was convinced that the Chandravanshis are evil. Maybe what Anandmayi says is right. Maybe I am naive, easily misled.'

'Don't be so hard on yourself, my friend. You cannot drop from the sky knowing everything, can you? You would have to enter the equation from one side or the other. And whichever side you entered from, you would obviously be coloured by their ways, while viewing the other side as evil. You have realized your error early. Lord Rudra did not recognise it till it was almost too late. He had nearly destroyed the Asuras before he grasped the simple fact that they were not evil, just different.'

'*Nearly* destroyed them? You mean some Asuras still exist?'

The Pandit smiled mysteriously. 'That conversation is for another time my friend. What you need to understand is that you are not the first Mahadev who was misled. And you will not be the last. Imagine, if you will, what Lord Rudra's feelings of guilt must have been.'

Shiva kept quiet, his eyes downcast. The knowledge of Lord Rudra's guilt did not reduce the shame that racked his soul. Reading his thoughts, the Pandit continued. 'You made the best decision you could under the circumstances. I know that this will be cold comfort, but being the Neelkanth isn't easy. You will have to bear the burden of this guilt. I know the kind of person you are. It *will* be a heavy burden. Your challenge is not to suppress the guilt or the pain. You have too good a heart to be able to do that. Your challenge is to stay true to your karma, to your duty, *in spite* of the pain. That is the fate and the duty of a Mahadev.'

'But what kind of a Mahadev am I? Why am I required? How am I to destroy evil if I don't know what evil is?'

'Who has said that your job is to destroy evil?'

A startled Shiva stared hard at the Pandit. He disliked the irritating word games that these pandits seemed to love to indulge in.

Glimpsing the anger in Shiva's eyes, the Pandit clarified immediately. 'The strength that evil has is overestimated, my friend. It is not so difficult to annihilate. All it takes is for a few good men to decide that they will fight it. At practically all the times that evil has raised its head, it has met the same fate. It has been destroyed.'

'Then why am I required?'

'You are required for the most crucial task: To answer that most important question.'

'What?'

'*What* is evil?'

'*What is evil?*'

'Yes. Many wars have been fought amongst men,' said the Pandit. 'And many more will be fought in the future. That is the way of the world. But it is only a Mahadev who can convert one of these wars into a battle between good and evil. It is only the Mahadev who can recognise evil and then lead men against it. Before evil raises its ugly head and extinguishes all life.'

'But how do I recognise evil?'

'I can't help you there my friend. I am not the Mahadev. This is a question you must find the answer to. But you have the heart. You have the mind. Keep them open and evil will appear before you.'

'*Appear?*'

'Yes,' explained the Pandit. 'Evil has a relationship with

you. It will come to you. All you have to do is recognise it when it appears. I have only one suggestion. Don't be hasty in trying to recognise evil. Wait for it. It *will* come to you.'

Shiva frowned. He looked down, trying to absorb the strange conversation. He turned towards Lord Ram's idol, seeking some direction. He did not find the judgement-filled eyes he had expected to see. Instead, he saw a warm, encouraging smile.

'Your journey is not over, my friend. Not by a long shot. It has just begun. You have to go on. Otherwise evil will triumph.'

Shiva's eyes cleared up a bit. His burden didn't feel any lighter, but he felt strong enough to carry it. He had to keep walking to the very end.

Shiva looked up at the Pandit and smiled weakly. 'Who are you?'

The Pandit smiled. 'I know the answer had been promised to you. And a promise made by any of us is binding on all of us. I will not break it.'

Shiva gazed at the Pandit, waiting for the answer.

'We are the Vasudevs.'

'The Vasudevs?'

'Yes. Each Vishnu leaves behind a tribe which is entrusted with two missions.'

Shiva continued to watch the Pandit intently.

'The first mission is to help the next Mahadev, if and when he appears.'

'And the second?'

'The second is that one of us will become the next Vishnu, whenever we are required to do so. The seventh Vishnu, Lord Ram, entrusted this task to his trusted lieutenant, Lord Vasudev. We are his followers. We are the tribe of Vasudev.'

Shiva stared at the Pandit, absorbing the implications of this information. He frowned as one inference suddenly occurred to him. 'Did the Mahadevs also leave some tribes behind? Did Lord Rudra?'

The Pandit smiled, deeply impressed by Shiva's intellect. The Mohan Jo Daro Secretary was correct. *This man is capable of being a Mahadev.*

'Yes. Lord Rudra did leave behind a tribe. The tribe of Vayuputra.'

'Vayuputra?' asked Shiva. The name sounded oddly familiar.

The Pandit placed his hand on Shiva's shoulder. 'Leave this for another time, my friend. I think we have spoken enough for today. Go home. You need your good wife's comforting embrace. Tomorrow is another day. And your mission can wait till then. For now, go home.'

Shiva smiled. An enigmatic smile. Out of character with his simple Tibetan ways. But he had become an Indian now. He leaned forward to touch the Pandit's feet. The Pandit placed his hand on Shiva's head to bless him, speaking gently, 'Vijayibhav. Jai Guru Vishwamitra. Jai Guru Vashishtha.'

Shiva nodded, accepting the blessings with grace. He got up, turned and walked towards the temple steps. At the edge of the platform, he turned around to look at the Pandit once again. The Pandit was sitting on his haunches, touching his head reverentially to the ground that Shiva had just vacated. Shiva smiled and shook his head slightly. Looking beyond the Pandit, he gazed intently at the idol of Lord Ram. He put his hands together in a Namaste and paid his respects to the Lord.

His burden didn't feel any lighter. But he felt strong enough to carry it.

He turned and began descending the steps. To his surprise, Sati was right in the middle of the compound leaning against a statuesque Apsara cast in stone. He smiled. There was nobody in the world whom he would much rather see at this time.

Walking towards her, he teased, 'Are you always going to follow me around?'

'I know when you need to be alone,' smiled Sati. 'And when you need me.'

Shiva froze suddenly. He could see a robe flapping behind the trees, a short distance from Sati. The light evening breeze gave away the position of the skulking man. Sati followed Shiva's gaze and turned around. A robed figure, wearing a Holi mask, emerged from behind the trees.

It is him!

Shiva's heart started beating faster. He was still a considerable distance away from Sati. The Naga was too close for comfort. The three stood rooted to their spots, assessing the situation, evaluating the others next move. It was Sati who moved first. Shifting quickly, she pulled a knife from her side-hold and flung it at the Naga. The Naga barely stirred. The knife missed him narrowly, slamming hard into the tree behind him, burying deep into the wood.

Shiva moved his hand slowly towards his sword.

The Naga reached behind, pulled the knife out of the tree and in a strange act, tied it tightly to his right wrist with a cloth band. Then he moved, quickly.

'Sati!' screamed Shiva, as he drew his sword and started sprinting towards his wife, pulling his shield forward as he ran.

...to be continued

www.authoramish.com

Glossary

Agni:	God of fire
Agnipariksha:	A trial by fire
Angaharas:	Movement of limbs or steps in a dance
Ankush:	Hook-shaped prods used to control elephants
Annapurna:	The Hindu Goddess of food, nourishment and plenty; also believed to be a form of Goddess Parvati
Anshan:	Hunger. It also denotes voluntary fasting. In this book, Anshan is the capital of the kingdom of Elam
Apsara:	Celestial maidens from the court of the Lord of the Heavens – Indra; akin to Zeus/Jupiter
Arya:	Sir
Ashwamedh yagna:	Literally, the Horse sacrifice. In ancient times, an ambitious ruler, who wished to expand his territories and display his military prowess, would release a sacrificial horse to roam freely through the length and breadth of any kingdom in India. If any king stopped/captured the horse, the ruler's army would declare war against the challenger, defeat the king and annexe that territory. If an opposing king did not stop the horse, the kingdom would become a vassal of the former
Asura:	Demon

Ayuralay:	Hospital
Ayurvedic:	Derived from Ayurved, an ancient Indian form of medicine
Ayushman bhav:	May you have a long life
Baba:	Father
Bhang:	Traditional intoxicant in India; milk mixed with marijuana
Bhiksha:	Alms or donations
Bhojan graham:	Dining room
Brahmacharya:	The vow of celibacy
Brahmastra:	Literally, the weapon of Brahma; spoken of in ancient Hindu scriptures. Many experts claim that the description of a Brahmastra and its effects are eerily similar to that of a nuclear weapon. I have assumed this to be true in the context of my book
Branga:	The ancient name for modern West Bengal, Assam and Bangladesh. Term coined from the conjoint of the two rivers of this land: *Brahmaputra* and *Ganga*
Brangaridai:	Literally, the heart of Branga. The capital of the kingdom of Branga
Chandravanshi:	Descendants of the moon
Chaturanga:	Ancient Indian game that evolved into the modern game of chess
Chillum:	Clay pipe, usually used to smoke marijuana
Choti:	Braid
Construction of Devagiri royal court platform:	The description in the book of the court platform is a possible explanation for the mysterious multiple-column buildings made of baked brick discovered at Indus Valley sites, usually next to the public baths, which many historians suppose could have been granaries
Dada:	Elder brother

Daivi Astra:	Daivi = Divine; Astra = Weapon. A term used in ancient Hindu epics to describe weapons of mass destruction
Dandakaranya:	Aranya = forest. Dandak is the ancient name for modern Maharashtra and parts of Andhra Pradesh, Karnataka, Chhattisgarh and Madhya Pradesh. So Dandakaranya means the forests of Dandak
Deva:	God
Dharma:	Dharma literally translates as religion. But in traditional Hindu belief, it means far more than that. The word encompasses holy, right knowledge, right living, tradition, natural order of the universe and duty. Essentially, dharma refers to everything that can be classified as 'good' in the universe. It is the Law of Life
Dharmayudh:	The holy war
Dhobi:	Washerman
Divyadrishti:	Divine sight
Dumru:	A small, hand-held, hour-glass shaped percussion instrument
Egyptian women:	Historians believe that ancient Egyptians, just like ancient Indians, treated their women with respect. The anti-women attitude attributed to Swuth and the assassins of Aten is fictional. Having said that, like most societies, ancient Egyptians also had some patriarchal segments in their society, which did, regrettably, have an appalling attitude towards women
Fire song:	This is a song sung by Guna warriors to agni (fire). They also had songs dedicated to the other elements viz: *bhūmi* (earth), jal (water), *pavan* (air or wind), *vyom* or *shunya* or *akash* (ether or void or sky)

Fravashi:

Is the guardian spirit mentioned in the *Avesta*, the sacred writings of the Zoroastrian religion. Although, according to most researchers, there is no physical description of Fravashi, the language grammar of *Avesta* clearly shows it to be feminine. Considering the importance given to fire in ancient Hinduism and Zoroastrianism, I've assumed the Fravashi to be represented by fire. This is, of course, a fictional representation

Ganesh-Kartik relationship:

In northern India, traditional myths hold Lord Kartik as older than Lord Ganesh; in large parts of southern India, Lord Ganesh is considered elder. In my story, Ganesh is older than Kartik. What is the truth? Only Lord Shiva knows

Guruji:

Teacher; ji is a term of respect, added to a name or title

Gurukul:

The family of the guru or the family of the teacher. In ancient times, also used to denote a school

Har Har Mahadev:

This is the rallying cry of Lord Shiva's devotees. I believe it means 'All of us are Mahadevs'

Hariyupa:

This city is currently known as Harappa. A note on the cities of Meluha (or as we call it in modern times, the Indus Valley Civilisation): historians and researchers have consistently marvelled at the fixation that the Indus Valley Civilisation seemed to have for water and hygiene. In fact historian M Jansen used the term 'wasserluxus' (obsession with water) to describe their magnificent obsession with the physical and symbolic aspects of water, a term Gregory Possehl builds upon in his brilliant book, *The Indus Civilisation — A Contemporary Perspective*. In the book, *The Immortals of Meluha*, the obsession with water is shown to arise due to its cleansing of the toxic sweat and urine triggered by consuming the Somras. Historians have also marvelled at the level of sophisticated standardisation in the Indus Valley Civilisation. One of the examples of this was the bricks, which across the entire civilisation, had similar proportions and specifications

Holi:	Festival of colours
Howdah:	Carriage placed on top of elephants
Indra:	The God of the sky; believed to be the King of the Gods
Jai Guru Vishwamitra:	Glory to the teacher Vishwamitra
Jai Guru Vashishtha:	Glory to the teacher Vashishtha. Only two Suryavanshis were privileged to have had both Guru Vashishtha and Guru Vishwamitra as their gurus (teachers) viz. Lord Ram and Lord Lakshman
Jai Shri Brahma:	Glory to Lord Brahma
Jai Shri Ram:	Glory to Lord Ram
Janau:	A ceremonial thread tied from the shoulders, across the torso. It was one of the symbols of knowledge in ancient India. Later, it was corrupted to become a caste symbol to denote those born as Brahmins and not those who'd acquired knowledge through their effort and deeds
Ji:	A suffix added to a name or title as a form of respect
Kajal:	Kohl, or eye liner
Karma:	Duty and deeds; also the sum of a person's actions in this and previous births,

	considered to limit the options of future action and affect future fate
Karmasaathi:	Fellow traveller in karma or duty
Kashi:	The ancient name for modern Varanasi. Kashi means the city where the supreme light shines
Kathak:	A form of traditional Indian dance
Kriyas:	Actions
Kulhads:	Mud cups
Maa:	Mother
Mandal:	Literally, Sanskrit word meaning circle. Mandals are created, as per ancient Hindu and Buddhist tradition, to make a sacred space and help focus the attention of the devotees
Mahadev:	Maha = Great and Dev = God. Hence Mahadev means the greatest God or the God of Gods. I believe that there were many 'destroyers of evil' but a few of them were so great that they would be called 'Mahadev'. Amongst the Mahadevs were Lord Rudra and Lord Shiva
Mahasagar:	Great Ocean; Hind Mahasagar is the Indian Ocean
Mahendra:	Ancient Indian name meaning conqueror of the world
Mahout:	Human handler of elephants
Manu's story:	Those interested in finding out more about the historical validity of the South India origin theory of Manu should read Graham Hancock's pathbreaking book, *Underworld*
Mausi:	Mother's sister, literally translating as *maa si* i.e. like a mother
Maya:	Illusion
Mehragarh:	Modern archaeologists believe that Mehragarh is the progenitor of the Indus

Valley civilisation. Mehragarh represents a sudden burst of civilised living, without any archaeological evidence of a gradual progression to that level. Hence, those who established Mehragarh were either immigrants or refugees **Meluha:** The land of pure life. This is the land ruled by the Suryavanshi kings. It is the area that we in the modern world call the Indus Valley Civilisation

Meluhans:	People of Meluha
Mudras:	Gestures
Naga:	Serpent people
Namaste:	An ancient Indian greeting. Spoken along with the hand gesture of open palms of both the hands joined together. Conjoin of three words. 'Namah', 'Astu' and 'Te' — meaning 'I bow to the Godhood in you'. Namaste can be used as both 'hello' and 'goodbye'
Nirvana:	Enlightenment; freedom from the cycle of rebirths
Oxygen/ anti-oxidants theory:	Modern research backs this theory. Interested readers can read the article 'Radical Proposal' by Kathryn Brown in the *Scientific American*
Panchavati:	The land of the five banyan trees
Pandit:	Priest
Paradaeza:	An ancient Persian word which means 'the walled place of harmony'; the root of the English word, Paradise
Pariha:	The land of fairies. Refers to modern Persia/Iran. I believe Lord Rudra came from this land
Parmatma:	The ultimate soul or the sum of all souls

Parsee immigration to India:	Groups of Zoroastrian refugees immigrated to India perhaps between the 8th and 10th century AD to escape religious persecution. They landed in Gujarat, and the local ruler Jadav Rana gave them refuge
Pashupatiastra:	Literally, the weapon of the Lord of the Animals. The descriptions of the effects of the Pashupatiastra in Hindu scriptures are quite similar to that of nuclear weapons. In modern nuclear technology, weapons have been built primarily on the concept of nuclear fission. While fusion-boosted fission weapons have been invented, pure fusion weapons have not been invented as yet. Scientists hold that a pure nuclear fusion weapon has far less radioactive fallout and can theoretically serve as a more targeted weapon. In this trilogy, I have assumed that the Pashupatiastra is one such weapon
Patallok:	The underworld
Pawan Dev:	God of the winds
Pitratulya:	The term for a man who is 'like a father'
Prahar:	Four slots of six hours each into which the day was divided by the ancient Hindus; the first prahar began at twelve midnight
Prithvi:	Earth
Prakrati:	Nature
Puja:	Prayer
Puja thali:	Prayer tray
Raj dharma:	Literally, the royal duties of a king or ruler. In ancient India, this term embodied pious and just administration of the king's royal duties
Raj guru:	Royal sage

Rajat:	Silver
Rajya Sabha:	The royal council
Rakshabandhan:	Raksha = Protection; Bandhan = thread/ tie. An ancient Indian festival in which a sister ties a sacred thread on her brother's wrist, seeking his protection
Ram Chandra:	Ram = Face; Chandra = Moon. Hence Ram Chandra is 'the face of the moon'
Ram Rajya:	The rule of Ram
Rangbhoomi:	Literally, the ground of colour. Stadia in ancient times where sports, performances and public functions would be staged
Rangoli:	Traditional colourful and geometric designs made with coloured powders or flowers as a sign of welcome
Rishi:	Man of knowledge
Sankat Mochan:	Literally, reliever from troubles. One of the names of Lord Hanuman
Sangam:	A confluence of two rivers
Sanyasi:	A person who renounces all his worldly possessions and desires to retreat to remote locations and devote his time to the pursuit of God and spirituality. In ancient India, it was common for people to take sanyas at an old age, once they had completed all their life's duties
Sapt Sindhu:	Land of the seven rivers – Indus, Saraswati, Yamuna, Ganga, Sarayu, Brahmaputra and Narmada. This was the ancient name of North India
Saptrishi:	One of the 'Group of seven Rishis'
Saptrishi Uttradhikari:	Successors of the Saptrishis
Shakti Devi:	Mother Goddess; also Goddess of power and energy
Shamiana:	Canopy
Shloka:	Couplet
Shudhikaran:	The purification ceremony

Sindhu:	The first river
Somras:	Drink of the Gods
Sundarban:	Sundar = beautiful; ban = forest. Hence, Sundarban means beautiful forest
Svarna:	Gold
Swadweep:	The Island of the individual. This is the land ruled by the Chandravanshi kings
Swadweepans:	People of Swadweep
Swaha:	Legend has it that Lord Agni's wife is named Swaha. Hence it pleases Lord Agni, the God of Fire, if a disciple takes his wife's name while worshipping the sacred fire. Another interpretation of Swaha is that it means offering of self
Tamra:	Bronze
Thali:	Plate
Varjish graha:	The exercise hall
Varun:	God of the water and the seas
Vijayibhav:	May you be victorious
Vikarma:	Carrier of bad fate
Vishnu:	The protector of the world and propagator of good. I believe that it is an ancient Hindu title for the greatest of leaders who would be remembered as the mightiest of Gods
Vishwanath:	Literally, the Lord of the World. Usually refers to Lord Shiva, also known as Lord Rudra in his angry avatar. I believe Lord Rudra was a different individual from Lord Shiva. In this trilogy, I have used the term Vishwanath to refer to Lord Rudra
Yagna:	Sacrificial fire ceremony

Episode from *The Secret of the Nagas*

The Gates of Branga

'Why are you back so soon? You have enough medicines for a year.'

Divodas was shocked at the manner in which Major Uma was speaking. She was always strict, but never rude. He had been delighted that she had been posted at the gates. Though he hadn't met her in years, they had been friends a long time back. He had thought he could use his friendship with her to gain easy passage into Branga.

'What is the matter, Uma?' asked Divodas.

'It is Major Uma. I am on duty.'

'I'm sorry Major. I meant no disrespect.'

'I can't let you go back unless you give me a good reason.'

'Why would I need a reason to enter my own country?'

'This is not your country anymore. You chose to abandon it. Kashi is your land. Go back there.'

'Major Uma, you know I had no choice. You know the risks to the life of my child in Branga.'

'You think those who live in Branga don't? You think we don't love our children? Yet we choose to live in our own land. You suffer the consequences of your choice.'

Divodas realised this was getting nowhere. 'I have to meet the King on a matter of national importance.'

Uma narrowed her eyes. 'Really? I guess the King has some important business dealings with Kashi, right?'

Divodas breathed in deeply. 'Major Uma, it is very important that I meet the King. You must trust me.'

'Unless you are carrying the Queen of the Nagas herself on one of your ships, I can't see anything important enough to let you through!'

'I'm carrying someone far more important than the Queen of the Nagas.'

'Kashi has really improved your sense of humour, Divodas,' sneered Uma. 'I suggest you turn back and shine your supreme light somewhere else.'

The snide pun on Kashi's name convinced Divodas that he was facing a changed Uma. An angry and bitter Uma, incapable of listening to reason. He had no choice. He had to get the Neelkanth. He knew Uma used to believe in the legend.

'I'll come back with the person who is more important than the Queen of the Nagas herself,' said Divodas, turning to leave.

— ⋏◍�⊕ —

The small cutter had just docked at the Branga office. Divodas alit first. Followed by Shiva, Parvateshwar, Bhagirath, Drapaku and Purvaka.

Uma, standing outside her office, sighed. 'You really don't give up, do you?'

'This is very important, Major Uma,' said Divodas.

Uma recognised Bhagirath. 'Is this the person? You think I should break the rules for the Prince of Ayodhya?'

'He is the Prince of Swadweep, Major Uma. Don't forget that. We send tribute to Ayodhya.'

'So you are more loyal to Ayodhya as well now? How many times will you abandon Branga?'

'Major, in the name of Ayodhya, I respectfully ask you to let us pass,' said Bhagirath, trying hard not to lose his temper. He knew the Neelkanth did not want any bloodshed.

'Our terms of the Ashwamedh treaty were very clear, Prince. We send you a tribute annually. And Ayodhya never enters Branga. We have maintained our part of the agreement. The orders to me are to help you maintain your part of the bargain.'

Shiva stepped forward. 'If I may...'

Uma was at the end of her patience. She stepped forward and pushed Shiva. 'Get out of here.'

'UMA!' Divodas pulled out his sword.

Bhagirath, Parvateshwar, Drapaku and Purvaka too drew out their swords instantly.

'I will kill your entire family for this blasphemy,' swore Drapaku.

'Wait!' said Shiva, his arms spread wide, stopping his men.

Shiva turned towards Uma. She was staring at him, shocked. The angvastram that he had wrapped around his body for warmth had come undone, revealing his *neel kanth,* the prophesied blue throat. The Branga soldiers around Uma immediately went down on their knees, heads bowed in respect, tears flooding their eyes. Uma continued to stare, her mouth half open.

Shiva cleared his throat. 'I really need to pass through, Major Uma. May I request your cooperation?'

Uma's face turned mottled red. 'Where the hell have you been?'

Shiva frowned.

Uma bent forward, tears in her eyes, banging her small fists on Shiva's well-honed chest. 'Where the hell have you been? We have been waiting! We have been suffering! Where the hell have you been?'

Shiva tried to hold Uma, to comfort her. But she sank down holding Shiva's leg, wailing. 'Where the hell have you been?'

A concerned Divodas turned to another Branga friend also posted at the border. His friend whispered, 'Last month, Major Uma lost her only child to the plague. Her husband and she had conceived after years of trying. She was devastated.'

Divodas looked at Uma with empathy, understanding her angst. He couldn't even begin to imagine what would happen to him if he lost his baby.

Shiva, who had heard the entire conversation, squatted. He cradled Uma in the shelter of his arms, as though trying to give her his strength.

'Why didn't you come earlier?' Uma kept crying, inconsolable.

— 𑀰𑀖𑀉𑀤𑀖 —

The entire crew on all five ships was crowded on the

port and starboard side, watching the operation in awe and wonder. Shiva's men were totally astounded by the Branga gates. They had seen the platform close in on their ship with frightening force. Then the hooks were secured to the chains. The Brangas, after the go-ahead from respective ship captains, began towing the fleet.

Shiva was standing aft. Looking at the office at the gate entrance.

Every Branga not working on the gate machinery was on his knees, paying obeisance to the Neelkanth. But Shiva was staring at a broken woman curled up against the wall in foetal position. She was still crying.

Shiva had tears in his eyes. He knew Uma believed that fate had cheated her daughter. She believed that if the Neelkanth had arrived a month earlier, her child would still be alive. But the Neelkanth himself was not so sure.

What could I have done?

He continued to stare at Uma.

Holy Lake, give me strength. I will fight this plague.

The ground staff got the signal. They released the accumulator machines and the pulleys began turning, moving the ship rapidly forward.

Seeing the vision of Uma retreating swiftly, Shiva whispered, 'I'm sorry.'

Other Titles by Amish

The Shiva Trilogy

The fastest-selling book series in the history of Indian publishing

THE SECRET OF THE NAGAS
(Book 2 of the Trilogy)

The sinister Naga warrior has killed his friend Brahaspati and now stalks his wife Sati. Shiva, who is the prophesied destroyer of evil, will not rest till he finds his demonic adversary. His thirst for revenge will lead him to the door of the Nagas, the serpent people. Fierce battles will be fought and unbelievable secrets revealed in the second part of the Shiva trilogy.

THE OATH OF THE VAYUPUTRAS
(Book 3 of the Trilogy)

Shiva reaches the Naga capital, Panchavati, and prepares for a holy war against his true enemy. The Neelkanth must not fail, no matter what the cost. In his desperation, he reaches out to the Vayuputras. Will he succeed? And what will be the real cost of battling Evil? Read the concluding part of this bestselling series to find out.

Indic Chronicles

LEGEND OF SUHELDEV

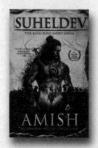

Repeated attacks by Mahmud of Ghazni have weakened India's northern regions. Then the Turks raid and destroy one of the holiest temples in the land: the magnificent Lord Shiva temple at Somnath. At this most desperate of times, a warrior rises to defend the nation. King Suheldev —fierce rebel, charismatic leader, inclusive patriot. Read this epic adventure of courage and heroism that recounts the story of that lionhearted warrior and the magnificent Battle of Bahraich.

www.authoramish.com

The Ram Chandra Series

The second fastest-selling book series in the history of Indian publishing

RAM – SCION OF IKSHVAKU
(Book 1 of the Series)

He loves his country and he stands alone for the law. His band of brothers, his wife, Sita, and the fight against the darkness of chaos. He is Prince Ram. Will he rise above the taint that others heap on him? Will his love for Sita sustain him through his struggle? Will he defeat the demon Raavan who destroyed his childhood? Will he fulfil the destiny of the Vishnu? Begin an epic journey with Amish's latest: the Ram Chandra Series.

SITA – WARRIOR OF MITHILA
(Book 2 of the Series)

An abandoned baby is found in a field. She is adopted by the ruler of Mithila, a powerless kingdom ignored by all. Nobody believes this child will amount to much. But they are wrong. For she is no ordinary girl. She is Sita. Through an innovative multi-linear narrative, Amish takes you deeper into the epic world of the Ram Chandra Series.

RAAVAN – ENEMY OF ARYAVARTA
(Book 3 of the Series)

Raavan is determined to be a giant among men, to conquer, plunder, and seize the greatness that he thinks is his right. He is a man of contrasts, of brutal violence and scholarly knowledge. A man who will love without reward and kill without remorse. In this, the third book in the Ram Chandra Series, Amish sheds light on Raavan, the king of Lanka. Is he the greatest villain in history or just a man in a dark place, all the time?

Non-fiction

IMMORTAL INDIA

Explore India with the country's storyteller, Amish, who helps you understand it like never before, through a series of sharp articles, nuanced speeches and intelligent debates. In *Immortal India*, Amish lays out the vast landscape of an ancient culture with a fascinatingly modern outlook.

DHARMA – DECODING THE EPICS FOR A MEANINGFUL LIFE

In this genre-bending book, the first of a series, Amish and Bhavna dive into the priceless treasure trove of the ancient Indian epics, as well as the vast and complex universe of Amish's Meluha, to explore some of the key concepts of Indian philosophy. Within this book are answers to our many philosophical questions, offered through simple and wise interpretations of our favourite stories.